ANCIENT ILLUSIONS

ANCIENT ILLUSIONS

JOANNE PENCE

QUAIL HILL PUBLISHING

Quail Hill Publishing

PO Box 64

Eagle, ID 83616

Visit our website at www.quailhillpublishing.net

Quail Hill Publishing Print Book: October 2018

First Quail Hill E-book: October 2018

Excerpts from *The Wandering Ghost, the Odyssey of Lafcadio Hearn* by Jonathan Cott, © 1990 Alfred A.. Knopf, Inc.

Excerpts from *A Fantastic Journey: The Life and Literature of Lafcadio Hearn* by Paul Murray, © 1993, Japan Library.

Cover image: © turk_stock_photographer

ISBN: 978-1-949566-33-8

ANCIENT ILLUSIONS

CHAPTER 1

Nightmare, the most awful form of dream ... You feel afraid without knowing why. Then you have the impression that something is acting upon you ... you wish to escape, to get away from the influence that is making you afraid. Then you find it not easy to escape...

—Lafcadio Hearn

Cape Cod, Massachusetts

Michael Rempart parked his rental car along the road on the ocean side of Cape Cod. The sky over the Atlantic was dark with clouds as a storm rolled in.

From this location he could see Wintersgate on a bleak rise near the water's edge. A few stands of firs stood nearby, their limbs bent and stretching away from the ocean. The massive house was gray and forbidding with a high stone turret on one corner, as if the long-ago builder couldn't decide between a grand manor or a castle, and ended up with a structure that was neither. Instead, it was monstrous and unsettling.

Sixteen years had passed since Michael last walked the floors of his family home. Sixteen years, during which he gained renown as an archaeologist, and traveled over much of the world, but had never ventured back to Cape Cod. "You aren't welcome here," were his father's last words to him. There was nothing welcoming here; the place itself was threatening.

Now, he stood with shoulders hunched against the biting wind. Forty-two years old, he was tall, with a rangy build and a tan from time spent working remote dig sites. Solitary, with few friends, his coworkers felt he actively discouraged camaraderie. Even on digs where people often grew close, they stayed away as if an unseen barrier lay between them.

He had been that way most of his life, and he attributed it to his upbringing behind the morose walls of Wintersgate. That was why this sudden compulsion to return there made no sense to him. He had no idea why he would want to face the father he had spent his earliest years fearing, and his later years loathing. But he did. He struggled to ignore the feeling. And then his nightmares began.

In every one, he was back at Wintersgate facing his father, his all too present personal demons, and trying to find answers to the questions that had haunted him throughout his life.

In the end, he gave in. And now he was here.

The wind grew fierce as he got into the rental. He ran his hands through wavy, jet-black hair. No sense putting off the inevitable, he told himself. Still, as he started the car for the drive to Wintersgate, he felt a tightness in his chest and a quickening of his pulse over what he was about to face.

William Claude Rempart was at work, as usual, in his laboratory on the second floor of Wintersgate. Shelves with flasks and bottles of minerals, chemicals, reference books, and botched experiments, each carefully labeled, covered the room.

He moved slowly. His hands quivered with age as he gathered the chemicals he needed and placed them on one side of the lab table. Last of all, he picked up a philosopher's stone, the prime agent of alchemy, and rubbed the stone with his thumb, feeling its warmth, its power. Those ignorant fools who knew nothing about alchemy would think he was caressing a chunk of reddish pink rock. Poor sots, he thought. In his hand, he held the key to life.

William Claude was an alchemist, a position past ages called a sorcerer or a wizard. He knew to be an alchemist meant doing more than mixing chemicals together. Any idiot could do that. It required the ability to imbue one's creation with a life-force, an ability few people possessed. He believed it was a powerful family trait transmitted from one generation to the next.

Not that William Claude cared one whit about family. He cared about himself, and the aging wearing down his body. He looked at the sunken flesh of his hands, the sagging skin and brown age marks. His face's wrinkled skin felt soft and thin, while his shoulders had become stooped. Each day he found it increasingly difficult to stand as straight and tall as he once had. He was eighty-eight years old, which made it imperative he learn to perfect the alchemy he had worked on all his life.

Most people thought the goal of alchemy was to create gold. They were wrong.

Alchemists not only wanted to create gold, the perfect metal that would not rot, but to develop the perfect *man,* one that would not age. In other words, one who would be immortal.

His thoughts were interrupted by the sound of rain hitting the windows as a streak of lightning flashed across the sky. Thunder soon followed.

He placed the philosopher's stone on a solid gold plate on the worktable. He had already prepared beakers of chemicals, and they were in varying stages of development. He picked up the latest vial he had been working on when a stabbing headache struck. He gripped the edge of the table with one hand, his eyes squeezed shut until the pain began to recede. But then another bolt hit like a knife slashing into his temple, and he fell to his knees.

He dropped the vial and a pool of blue liquid puddled before him. In it, he saw his son, Michael. His only living child. He gasped for breath against the pain.

"Michael," he whispered, touching the liquid with his fingertips. He pulled himself to his feet and tried to reach Michael's thoughts with his mind. As always, he failed. But strangely, although he couldn't penetrate Michael's mind, William Claude knew his son was near.

"Finally, it must be working." He was so pleased he almost smiled.

William Claude's mind raced as he unlocked the cabinet door and removed a gold-filled elixir. He poured out a tablespoon of potion and drank it. Then he sat as it slowly warmed, enriched, and rejuvenated him. He had waited sixteen years for Michael to come home.

Now, he could put his plan in place.

CHAPTER 2

OXFORD, England

Thunder shook the bedroom window.

Ceinwen Davies opened her eyes as lightning flashed, illuminating the dormitory room with its two beds, two bureaus, two desks, and one tiny closet. The room was yellow, with a sheer white curtain covering the lone window. Beyond that, everything was tasteless and utilitarian.

Her roommate, Rachel Gooding, tossed more vigorously with each peal of thunder. It wouldn't be long now, Ceinwen thought.

"No!" Rachel awoke and sat bolt upright in her bed.

Ceinwen let out the breath she'd been holding. *Right on time.* "Are you okay, Rachel?" She asked as she switched on a bedside lamp.

Rachel had clamped both hands over her mouth as if she hoped to belatedly silence her cries. Her eyes were wide, frightened. "I'm sorry," she murmured, lowering her hands. "It was a nightmare. Another stupid nightmare."

"It's okay. Everything will be all right. The storm will abate soon. It may have already."

Rachel drank some water, then lay back in the bed. "I hope so." Her voice was tiny. She rolled over to face the wall, but Ceinwen knew it would be at least an hour before the girl settled down enough to go back to sleep.

Ceinwen looked around the spartan space before shutting the light and lying down again, wondering for the umpteenth time what she should do, if anything, about this situation.

She was from Wales, something she never grew tired of pointing out to people who tried to pronounce her name "Sign-win" or some other such oddity. "Kane-when" was as close as most people could get to the Welsh pronunciation. Tall and attractive, with lush dark auburn hair and large eyes the color of jade, she had grown up in Cardiff where her father owned a pub, and her two older brothers were trying to make a living by running one of the few remaining textile mills in Wales. They nearly went bankrupt a few years back, but an uptick in the economy that brought a public willing to spend big bucks on quality, handmade Welsh woolens saved them. Ceinwen had no idea why her brothers found such a life fulfilling.

She didn't. After attending the University of Cardiff, one of the top schools for journalism in the UK, she left home with her degree and never returned except for holidays, funerals, and weddings. That was eleven years ago.

Her dream was to see the world. She first went to Copenhagen where she found a job with the UK's *Daily Mail*. To her surprise, her editor discovered she had an extraordinary ability to ferret out unexplained, potentially paranormal happenings. As a result, he sent her to cover stories about the supernatural throughout Europe. She could often provide her readers with plausible explanations to debunk claims being made. The most common explanation had to do with an overabundance of liquor, and once, with a secret test being conducted by a government entity.

She soon began scouting the globe for other strange phenomena. One of the most interesting, unfortunately too far from her territory for the newspaper to send her to investigate, was a bizarre occurrence that took place in the United States – hardly an area known for paranormal happenings.

Two years earlier, eight students and teachers from Boise State University in Idaho, led by a well-respected visiting professor of anthropology named Dr. Lionel Rempart, traveled to the interior of the state and disappeared. While conducting a massive search, an elite search party also vanished. Not until several months later did the few survivors, three members of the university group and three of the searchers, make their way back to civilization.

That so many individuals could vanish caused rampant speculation among paranormal experts. Their curiosity worsened when none of the survivors would talk about what had happened while they were missing.

Ceinwen wanted to know their story and periodically checked to see if any new information was available. She even set up news alerts on her phone. She knew that the sheriff who led the search had returned to his job, but the others had dropped from the public's radar.

Then, while at her desk in Copenhagen some eight months ago, an alert sounded directing Ceinwen to a small article in an Idaho newspaper mentioning that Rachel Gooding, one of the survivors, had been awarded a full scholarship to Oxford University's graduate program in archeology ... or archaeology, as the British spelled it.

Ceinwen could hardly believe her luck. One of the people she most wanted to speak to would be in her own backyard.

She requested permission to audit some of Oxford's archeology classes. When the request was denied, she pulled every string she could think of, and was finally given approval to sit in on some lectures. The newspaper granted her request for a year's leave of absence to conduct and develop this undercover research. As an unrepentant workaholic, she had managed to save up enough money over the years to give up a salary for that period.

Once at Oxford, she tracked down Rachel Gooding. The girl was shy and awkward, but frighteningly brilliant. It was no mystery why the school awarded her a full scholarship. Also, it was the first time she'd traveled outside the US. She appreciated Ceinwen's friendly attention since most of the other students found her somewhat odd.

To Ceinwen, Rachel's background was almost as fascinating as her lost-in-the-wilderness experience. She had grown up on a farm in Eastern Idaho, near Utah, and was a member of The Church of Jesus Christ of Latter-Day Saints. Ceinwen once saw *Book of Mormon* in a London theater, but other than that, the religious group was a complete mystery to her.

Rachel willingly talked to Ceinwen about her home and religion, but whenever the topic of her disappearance came up, she said she couldn't discuss it. Ceinwen explained to Rachel that she had been a journalist whose work mainly involved paranormal phenomena, and because of that she knew of Rachel's experience in Idaho. Rachel had been amazed that anyone in England would have heard of it. Ceinwen then added a "white lie" to the story. She told Rachel she was tired of being a reporter, and since archeology interested her, she had returned to study it.

Ceinwen soon grew fond of the reserved young woman, and when she learned how little money Rachel had, she offered to room with her to cut expenses. It wasn't complete altruism, of course. Rooming together gave more chance for Rachel to let something slip about her Idaho experience. Ceinwen was still waiting.

Ironically, Ceinwen believed she, more than Rachel, had been the one most affected by their friendship. Most people Ceinwen had dealt with over her years as a reporter had a devious streak a mile wide. Rachel helped her remember how likable and innocent people could be. She made Ceinwen feel like a cynic and a fraud, and had Ceinwen thinking journalism might not be the right field for her to be in.

But then, about three weeks ago, Rachel began having terrible night-mares. At first, just a few, but now they hit every night. Although Rachel wouldn't say what she was dreaming about, it was clear to Ceinwen that the dreams were growing increasingly violent. It now had reached the point that Rachel was afraid to go to sleep, and once awakened by a night-mare, often remained awake the rest of the night. Even her professors noticed her exhaustion and increasingly unhealthy pallor.

The last few days, Rachel began taking sleeping pills. They did nothing to stop the nightmares. Ceinwen feared it wouldn't be long before Rachel increased the dose and started on the path to dependency.

CHAPTER 3

As Michael approached the main doors of Wintersgate, he looked up at its frieze of winged griffins lurking over the entry and found their expressions to be as malevolent as he remembered.

Stedman, his father's valet, opened the door. "Master Michael, welcome home."

Michael shook hands with the man who had worked for the family over thirty years. His hair was thinner now, but he still had a cartoonish undertaker look about him, skinny and dour in an impeccable black suit, white shirt, and black bowtie.

"Good to see you, Stedman." He realized he had never known the man's first name. "Is my father home?"

"He is in his laboratory. Come in and make yourself comfortable. I'll let him know you're here." Stedman picked up Michael's suitcase.

As Michael stepped into the house, his head began to ache. The air felt stale, and he noticed a sour taste in his mouth.

He paused in the foyer. Once, he had believed Wintersgate's massive entry hall was beautiful with white marble floors, crimson wallpaper, and a white ceiling bordered by gold. But as he looked it over now, he saw that the wallpaper had darkened and turned blotchy with age, the white ceiling had yellowed, and the chandelier no longer sparkled.

To the right was an elegantly curved staircase, and to the left hung a grotesque tapestry of St. George bloodily killing a dragon. The tapestry had given Michael nightmares as a little boy. Near it, double doors led to a large, drafty drawing room.

He crossed the foyer to what his parents called the breakfast room, although they used it for much more than breakfast. Semi-circular, floor-to-ceiling bow windows at the far end provided a magnificent view of the Atlantic. A comfortable sitting area was set up in front of them while the center of the room held the table and chairs where the family ate all but the most formal meals. That is, when there had been a family.

It was the only "downstairs" room that Michael's mother had decorated, and the only room Michael had ever liked besides his own and his mother's tower room. The others were too big, dark, stultifying, and intimidating.

As Michael anxiously waited for his father, he stood by the windows looking out at the storm. As he'd driven onto Wintersgate's property, it had hit with fury. Now, the rain fell in sheets.

His headache grew worse as he waited over twenty minutes before he heard footsteps behind him.

William Claude Rempart seemed smaller than Michael remembered. His hair was snow white now, and framed his face in a halo-like cloud. But he appeared healthy, even robust, for a man of eighty-eight.

Michael squared his shoulders, standing erect as scowling black eyes took in every detail about him, and seemed to find him wanting.

"This is a surprise," William Claude's words were curt, his voice as deep and reverberating as always.

Michael wasn't sure how to greet his father, opting for a simple, "Hello, father."

William Claude's lips tightened. "It's been a long time." He walked to an armchair covered in a yellow fabric decorated with bluebirds and sat. Michael remembered that his mother had loved the pattern, calling it a French toile. Seeing the upholstery now faded and worn saddened him, yet another sign of loss and the passing of time.

Michael took a seat facing his father as Stedman brought in a tray with coffee, brandy, and an array of appetizers. He poured their drinks and left the room.

William Claude reached for his brandy. "Archeology has been good to you, I understand. Finding that Spanish galleon some years back and getting a TV show."

Michael found the whole episode an embarrassment. At the time it happened, he was young, bitter, and wanted to prove to the world that he could be important, that he was worth something. He had taken a ridiculous risk going after a treasure dismissed and mocked by better men than he. It had paid off. Hollywood had decided he had star-quality good looks and had dubbed him a "real-life Indiana Jones." For a while he even headlined a National Geographic series on archeology.

That attention led to opportunities for fascinating digs and more discoveries. Yet the attention he most sought never came.

Eventually, he stopped hoping for it.

"I'm glad that part of my life is over," he admitted.

"I should think so. Someone in town gave Stedman a copy of some tawdry magazine. *People*, I believe it was called." William Claude sniffed. "Pictures of you with beautiful women. Starlets. I half expected to hear you would star in some outlandish adventure film. Quite beneath you, Michael."

Michael felt irritation stir. He worked to tamp down his reaction. "I'm here so we can talk."

"Good." William Claude finished the brandy and put the snifter back on the table. "Have you attempted alchemy yet?"

"You say that as if you expect I will."

"I do."

"And I do my best to keep away from the occult."

"Not successfully, from what I've heard." William Claude's eyes narrowed. "For example, your strange adventure in China last year, and an ancient, highly valued pearl."

The words surprised Michael. He had done all he could to keep the episode quiet. "I can't imagine where you would have heard such a thing."

"Who knows?" William Claude shrugged, then his lips curved sardonically. "Was it worthwhile, or just another publicity stunt?"

Michael sucked in his breath. Coming here, facing this man, hadn't been easy. "Neither. The stories about the pearl were all false. It's worth nothing."

William Claude's lips pursed. "I assumed the pearl was, in fact, a philosopher's stone."

"Only to someone who sees alchemy wherever he looks," Michael said with a mocking tone.

"And rightly so!" William Claude bristled. "So tell me, what did you do with the pearl?"

"Nothing worth discussing."

His father smirked. "Afraid I might steal it, are you?"

"Of course not." Michael stared hard at the man now, at dark eyes similar to his own. "But I'm not here to talk about the pearl. I'm here for answers to my own questions."

The smirk broadened.

Michael glared. "I want to know what happened sixteen years ago. It's well beyond time for me to learn the truth."

A low chuckling began deep in William Claude's throat and erupted into a bark of laughter. "Of course you do. You're so predictable, Michael."

Michael remembered other times his father had laughed at and mocked him. The memory, the laughter, made the pounding in his head grow worse.

Abruptly, William Claude's laughter ended, and he coldly eyed his son. "You haven't gone back to archeology, have you? Not after what happened to Lionel."

The headache became a migraine, and streaks of color flashed before Michael's eyes as he thought of his older brother, Lionel, who had been William Claude's favorite. "I'm not quite back yet," he murmured, "but archeology is my passion."

"As alchemy should be."

"But never was." Michael's voice grew hard and determined even as he rubbed his brow. "You know, don't you, that alchemy is the reason Lionel is dead?"

"If Lionel had used it properly, he would still be alive." William Claude's eyes were harsh, but his expression gradually eased. "You shouldn't mock it, not with your abilities. As much as I hate to admit it, you are one of the fortunate Rempart men blessed by the alchemical world."

"If so, it's hardly a blessing."

"But there, you're wrong." William Claude leaned forward in the chair. "I see your head hurts. Let me help." He pressed his hand across Michael's forehead.

The hand felt icy, but the pulsating throbs immediately ceased, and the flashes of light hurting his eyes vanished. Despite that, Michael jerked back in his chair. He was shocked; his father never touched him. And he couldn't ignore the sense that something was wrong, perhaps evil, about it.

William Claude dropped his hand. His lips spread wide and thin in a grin. "You should rest, Michael," he said as he stood. "Dinner is at eight."

CHAPTER 4

RACHEL'S EYELIDS FLUTTERED, but then opened wide as they moved from all-white walls to the tube taped to her arm. She gasped, scared.

Ceinwen placed a hand on Rachel's shoulder to steady her. "It's okay. You passed out. You're in Oxford's infirmary and they're giving you fluids. Dehydration, they said. You should be fine soon."

Rachel took a deep breath. "I remember walking across campus to get lunch, and then ... nothing."

"You did scare a few folks," Ceinwen said wryly.

"How did I get here?" Rachel asked. "And why are you here?"

"I was sitting in a coffee shop and saw what happened," Ceinwen said. "When the medics arrived, I told them you're a student and that I'm your roommate. They asked me to come along. You were out of it. Not making a whit of sense."

Rachel looked stricken.

"Do you remember anything at all?" Ceinwen asked.

"Only a killer headache. I remember thinking how beautiful Oxford looked that morning, the spires and towers against a bright blue sky, but ..."

"But?"

"It was weird. All of a sudden, I smelled sage and dust, as if I were home, back in the high desert. Maybe I was hungry, and somehow, that triggered me to feel homesick." Rachel dropped her gaze, her expression troubled.

"Maybe," Ceinwen murmured. "Anything else?"

Rachel swallowed hard. It was a look of fright, one Ceinwen had seen often enough when Rachel awoke from one of her many nightmares.

"What was it?" she asked.

"Nothing. Nothing at all." Rachel rubbed her eyes, her temple. "It might have simply been another nightmare."

"But you were awake," Ceinwen said. "You seemed to be in a trance."

"I don't know what's happening anymore." Rachel bowed her head.

"A counselor will talk to you soon. I've heard your teachers say you're working yourself too hard, that you need time away, and since you've already turned in your papers and have no finals, you could leave school now. Start summer vacation a week or two early and rest."

Rachel shook her head. "My schoolwork has nothing to do with this. I enjoy the classes. In fact, I don't find them hard at all. If anything, they're too easy."

"But this was a warning about something. You need to listen to it."

Rachel looked away.

"Listen." Ceinwen waited until Rachel's gaze met hers. "Could all that's happening to you now--the nightmares, the trance or whatever it was-- be connected with the strange occurrence in Idaho?"

"No." Her lips pressed together. "It can't be."

"What is it, then?"

"It must be what I said. I'm homesick. Maybe I do need to go home for a short while," she murmured.

"Home to Idaho?"

"Yes."

Ceinwen hadn't expected that. The thought of joining Rachel and visiting the area where so many strange things supposedly happened was beyond exciting. Of course, the possibility was strong that the whole disappearance story was nothing more than a murderous rampage, or even a hoax—but finally, she'd learn the truth. Maybe there was even a book in it. She didn't doubt her ability, once there, to find out what really happened to all those people. "Look, if you don't mind, I'd like to go with you. I love to travel and I enjoy your company. What if you pass out while you're traveling? No one will understand. It'd be good to have a friend with you."

Rachel shook her head. "I'm sure I was dehydrated like the doctors said. Nothing more than that. Besides, it's expensive and I don't have the money to pay you back."

"I wouldn't let you. I can afford it, and I love new places, new experiences. Besides, I've never been to Idaho, or any place remotely like the American West. I'd like to come along."

"There's not much to see," Rachel said, her mouth downturned.

Ceinwen gave her an indulgent smile. "Let me be the judge of that."

CHAPTER 5

THE EVENING BEFORE, despite being at the dinner table at eight on the dot, Michael had eaten alone. The housekeeper, Patience, had told him his father was tired, and had requested a light supper in his room. The quality of the dinner surprised Michael—filet mignon, braised asparagus, French onion soup, and a bottle of Chateau Lafite Rothschild to wash it down. He half expected his father to have given orders that Michael be served only bread and water.

But trying to sleep that night had been another story. He dreamed about his childhood, one filled with memories of his mother and brother.

In the dream, his mother had been just as he remembered her; the way he would always remember her. Lionel had faded in and out. He had few memories of his older brother. Ten years' difference in age was a lifetime to a young boy, and both boys had spent most of those years at different boarding schools. As adults, they were never close. But as the dream continued, it changed. He watched his mother and Lionel die and decay into horrible, malformed creatures that reached out to him, wanting him to join them.

He had forced himself awake, but once awake, felt he wasn't alone in the room. Ghosts walked the halls of this house. He had believed that as a boy and continued to do so now. Ghosts, or something worse.

He switched on the lamp. He was in his old bedroom. It should have been a typical teenage boy's room filled with posters and books, stereo equipment, and sports paraphernalia, but it had none of that. Instead, it had a single bed with a high wooden headboard, a dark wooden desk with an ancient computer and printer, and three bookcases filled with scholarly tomes as well as several science fiction and historical fiction novels. More than any person, those books had been his friends as he grew up.

Perhaps being in the room he had used as a child had caused the strange dream. Despite his rationalizations, a couple of hours passed before he could sleep again.

That morning, more than ever, he wanted the answers that he had come here to obtain. Then, he planned to leave Wintersgate and never return.

In the breakfast room, a sideboard held a choice of breads, eggs, sausage, and fresh fruit, along with coffee, tea, and orange juice. After the meal, he took the stairs two at a time up to the laboratory where, in the past, his father could always be found.

He knocked, but received no answer. To his surprise, the door was locked.

His father's bedroom and study were also empty, as was the patio. Finally he went into the kitchen to talk to the cook. Patience told him Stedman had driven William Claude to town in the Bentley. She had no idea when they would return.

Michael walked down to the beach, and after a brief hike, headed back to the house. As William Claude had not yet returned, he went into the library. The room had been out of bounds for Michael until he was of college age and William Claude no longer feared his "grimy, sticky, little boy hands" touching the books. Of course, once in college, Michael had no time or interest to go through his father's library.

The light in the room was poor, and the shelves high. He had just begun to pour over a section with a number of very old tomes about the Reformation when he heard a book fall to the hardwood floor with a distinctive "thwack."

A thin book lay on the floor across the room. He went over and picked it up to find it had the strange name, *Kwaidan*, written by an author with an equally strange name, Lafcadio Hearn.

Something about them, however, resonated with Michael. Not until he flipped through the book to see it was a collection of Japanese ghost stories did he remember what it was. Several of the stories had been made into an art-house movie years earlier. In college, Michael had watched it on video with a few of his fellow students and discussed it deep into the night over beer – probably the best way to talk about ghost stories. Michael smiled from the memory as he flipped through the book's pages.

Near the end of the book was a piece of linen paper. Michael took it out. The ink had faded, but the old-fashioned script was neatly written and still legible:

In the world of sleep, all the dead people we loved meet us again; the father recovers his long-buried child, the husband his lost wife, separated lovers find the union that was impossible in this world, those whom we lost sight of in early years—dead sisters, brothers, friends—all come back to us as loving, and as young, and perhaps even more beautiful than they could really have been. In the world of sleep, there is no growing old; there is immortality, there is everlasting youth.

The passage was startling, almost as if whoever wrote it had known about his dream—or about the part of it he had enjoyed before it turned into a nightmare.

No one had signed the passage, and there was no other indication as to who had written it. Michael noticed several books by Lafcadio Hearn on the shelf, including an empty space were *Kwaidan* must have sat. He wondered why it fell, but this was an old house that probably creaked and shifted and settled over the years. His footsteps alone might have caused it to topple over. He was about to put it back on the shelf when he noticed a small bundle of papers there written by the same hand as the note he'd just read. Included were letters that had been signed, "Lafcadio."

Down the hall, he heard the front door open and shut. William Claude had returned. Michael left the papers but took *Kwaidan* with him to the breakfast room. William Claude sat near the windows.

"Did you have an interesting time out?" Michael asked.

"A doctor's visit. I'm not ready to push up the grass yet, boy, so don't get your hopes up."

Michael held his tongue, then glanced down at the book in his hands. "I saw your collection of Lafcadio Hearn writings. I didn't think Japan interested you."

"It doesn't. All those books were here when I inherited the house. I'm surprised you've heard of him."

"I've heard little except that he's one of the first Westerners with real literary skill to write about life in Japan."

"Sit down, Michael. I'm getting a crick in my neck trying to talk to you." William Claude rang for Stedman to bring them some whiskey and soda, then eased back in his chair, legs crossed, as he put tobacco in his pipe. "Actually, Hearn might interest you, him being a devotee of the Japanese occult and alchemy."

"Alchemy? That's hard to believe." Michael sat as William Claude took two more puffs on the pipe.

"He was an interesting man, son of an Army surgeon for the British, and a saucy Greek woman. Apparently, when his father was reassigned away from Greece, his mother moved to Dublin to live with her in-laws." He took another puff. "The Hearns were elevated in Ireland's Protestant society, and when the colorful Greek Orthodox woman showed up with three unruly children, to say she was unwelcome was putting it mildly." William Claude chuckled at the image.

"I can imagine," Michael said.

"She soon returned to Greece alone. Lafcadio never saw her again."

"She abandoned him?" Michael asked, surprised a mother would do that.

"She did. And after his father married a woman more socially acceptable, he also paid no more attention to his half-Greek offspring. Relatives doled out the children, and the aunt who was 'stuck' with Lafcadio soon shipped him off to boarding school. He was always small and shy, and after losing an eye playing sports he was sure he looked ugly, and that people were hell-bent for an excuse to abandon him as his mother, father, and aunt had done."

His father stopped speaking as Stedman brought in their drinks, giving Michael a moment to reflect on Hearn's childhood. He understood it. He had rarely spent time with other children when he lived at Wintersgate, so when he was sent to boarding school he had no idea how to fit in. After his mother died, he felt rudderless, and his sense of loneliness grew worse. A couple of times he had "acted out" in school. The first time William Claude went to the school to handle it. The second time, it was Stedman.

Michael hated thinking about those days.

Stedman soon left the room.

"Is that why he went to Japan? To get as far away from that family as possible?" Michael asked.

"He wanted to get away, but his first stop was the U.S.," William Claude said. "In Cincinnati, Ohio, he got a job on the city's newspaper, and then married a woman whose mother had been a slave and her father an Irish plantation owner. To him, the two shared having been abandoned by their Irish fathers. Lafcadio had no idea that in the U.S. such an inter-racial marriage was illegal. He was immediately fired, and soon after, he and the woman had a falling out."

Michael shook his head. "And since they weren't really married ..."

William Claude nodded. "Exactly. So off he went to New Orleans where he became fascinated with voodoo. That brought him to the West Indies where he met Victor Rempart."

The name surprised Michael. "Victor? The man who built Wintersgate?"

"That's right. Victor left France and moved to Martinique when he was twenty-five. There, he and Lafcadio talked about voodoo and such, as well as about alchemy. They realized that the Hearn family was from the same part of Ireland as John Kelley, our famous alchemist ancestor. They discovered they had other ancestors in common and so must be cousins."

"Cousins? Lafcadio Hearn is a relative?"

"So it seems," William Claude said with a shrug. "Anyway, Victor grew tired of the heat in Martinique and headed north, ending up buying these twenty acres and building Wintersgate. When his talented cousin's wanderlust caused him to want to go to Japan, Victor helped him out."

"And that's why so many of Lafcadio's unpublished letters and such are in this house?" Michael asked.

"Yes, although I don't know why he sent them to Victor."

"Interesting," Michael said.

"But unimportant." William Claude finished his drink. "What's impor-tant is that Victor's money, obtained through alchemy, allowed him to help the poor man, cousin or not."

"With you, it always goes back to alchemy, doesn't it?"

"Why else would I want you here?"

The words thundered in Michael's head. "What are you talking about?"

"It's time for you to help. Your power is great. I have a need for it."

Michael stood. "I didn't come here to help you! I came here for the truth!"

"The truth? What truth?" William Claude stopped, then rolled his eyes. "My God. Are you still blathering about that woman? She's not important."

Michael stiffened. *That woman* was Irina Petrescu. She was the daughter of William Claude's housekeeper. "She was important to me," he shouted.

"Was! Was! She's nothing now. What's important is alchemy and all we can do with it."

Michael froze. "What do you mean, she's nothing now?"

"She's dead."

Michael stared. "No. I don't believe you."

"I heard it from her mother this past winter."

Michael felt himself crumbling inside.

Irina ... dead. Of all possibilities that had crossed his mind about how he would reconcile himself to the past, he had never thought she might die before he could see her once more. "What happened to her?" His voice was barely above a whisper.

"Auto accident. Single car. That's all I know."

Michael's flesh turned ice cold.

"I'm sorry, Michael," his father said. "Sorry that you never understood everything I did was for you, for what I believed would be best for you." His lips curled into a bitter sneer. "I would never have allowed that woman into this family. Her family was the cause of your mother's death, the cause of so much trouble and sorrow."

The words were like so much noise spinning around and around in Michael's head. "What are you talking about?"

William Claude's gaze turned cold and hard. "Do you think I would have allowed her to be rewarded with any part of the Rempart heritage? And if the two of you had children, do you imagine I would have allowed what my ancestors built to go to them? Never!"

Michael stood, furious. "Instead, this heritage you're so proud of may well end with me. I hardly see love, marriage, and a family in my future."

The look William Claude cast on his son was one of pure contempt. "That may be for the best. You don't deserve to be a Rempart!"

Michael walked away, in no mood to hear any more of his father's rant, his mind filled with Irina's death.

In his room, he sat on the bed trying not to think, trying not to acknowledge the shock he felt. But he had no tears. As a young man, he had shed too many because of her. Then, one day, they stopped.

Since then, he had learned to control such feelings and to hold every-thing—*everything*—inside. Only a couple of times in his life had he allowed his emotions, his "alchemist nature," loose. That was when he had learned just how strong and potentially terrible his power could be. At times, knowing he was William Claude's son actually scared him.

CHAPTER 6

Salmon, Idaho

A feeling of dread hung over the coffee shop next door to the sheriff's office in Salmon, Idaho. It was early morning, and the local ranchers and townspeople gathered there were scared, including a stringer for the *Idaho Statesman*. All of them remembered the strange things that had happened two years earlier, and they were all wondering if this might be round two. The Lemhi County sheriff, Jake Sullivan, had gone into the River of No Return Wilderness Area two days earlier to investigate some strange livestock mutilations, and hadn't returned.

A search party had been gathered, and they awaited their assignments. In charge was a deputy sheriff from Idaho Falls. Deputy Sheriff Brunswick had more experience dealing with difficult situations than Salmon's Deputy Bill Mallick. Mallick remembered the heat that had rained down on Jake Sullivan earlier when eight students and teachers from Boise State vanished in the wilderness area. Mallick was glad to let Brunswick handle it.

Just then, the door opened, and in walked the focal point of their angst, Sheriff Jake Sullivan. Jake was barrel-chested and broad-shouldered, with close-cropped brown hair mottled with gray, and a craggy, weather-beaten face. Born in Salmon, he had left it for Los Angeles where he joined the police force and worked his way to a detective in Robbery-Homicide. When things didn't turn out as planned in California, he had returned to Idaho where life was supposed to be a lot quieter.

"I heard you guys might be looking for me," he said with a grin.

"Jake!" Charlotte Reed stood up. She and Jake had lived together almost two years, ever since they met during the search for the missing university group in the back country north of the Salmon River. A widow, she had worked as a forgery investigator for the Immigration and Customs Enforcement agency. Her expertise was in Ancient Egyptian and Mesopotamian art and antiquities.

Jake opened his arms and, as soon as he did, she ran to him. "You had us worried, you old coot! Where were you?"

The two kissed and hugged, and then Jake faced the room. "Thank you, everyone. I never imagined you'd mobilize so quickly, but it's good to know you have my back." He turned to Deputy Sheriff Brunswick and extended his hand. "Thanks for coming."

"I'm glad you're okay," Brunswick said, shaking Jake's hand.

"So am I," Mallick said, as the deputy gave the sheriff a quick, awkward hug.

"What happened?" Brunswick asked.

Putting an arm around Charlotte's shoulders, Jake again spoke to the group. "Someone jumped me out there—knocked me off my horse. When I came to, my horse, satellite phone, and gun were gone. I walked toward the river and the next day reached Corn Creek Landing. But then I didn't see a soul until sundown when a couple came by in a boat. Their communications equipment had stopped working, and they didn't know why. We didn't travel when it was dark, so it took a while to make it back here. Soon as we got back—about ten minutes ago—I heard about this meeting and rushed over. So, please excuse my appearance."

"You're safe," Charlotte said. "Who cares."

"Listen, Jake," Brunswick said, "I'd like you to fill me in on what's going on out there. It sounds plenty strange, and maybe I can offer help. But for now, I'll keep an eye on things while you get some sleep."

Jake nodded. He was exhausted.

The coffee shop owner, Emily Parker, a woman Charlotte had grown uncharacteristically jealous of, handed Jake a cup of coffee. "I thought you could use this," she said with a dimpled smile. "And, if you're hungry, I made you some eggs, sausage, and biscuits. I know how much you love them." She put the plate on a nearby table.

"Perfect! Thanks. I'm starving," he said as he walked to the food. "Want some, too?" he asked Charlotte.

"I'm fine."

They sat as he ate. She was being unusually quiet.

"Are you okay?" he asked after a while.

"Other than being scared to death, you mean?"

"I'm sorry," Jake said.

She gave him a long, worried look. "You always are. But that doesn't make it easier."

"I don't know what you're getting at."

"I know you don't." Her tone was quiet and sad. "That's the problem. There's something drawing you away from me, from Salmon, from every-thing important to us. It's changed you. Whenever you go out the Salmon River Road to Telichpah Flats or beyond, you come back even worse. And this time, you almost didn't come back at all."

He put down the biscuit, his brows crossed. "I don't know why you feel this way. That's not how I see it."

"Right. It's all my imagination," she said. "But it isn't. Something is wrong."

"You've got that right, at least!" He was angry now. "Someone crazy is mutilating sheep and cattle, and my job is to find the son of a bitch."

"It's more than that."

"I agree." He picked up the biscuit and took another bite, his demeanor calmer as he said, "The amount of livestock killed has been unusual."

"I'm saying the *manner* of the deaths is the problem."

"And you think something surreal is going on?" Jake asked.

"Not surreal. Supernatural."

"You're wrong—and you'll see that when I catch the very human bastards behind this mess." He finished his breakfast and stood. "Let's go home."

CHAPTER 7

MICHAEL SPENT the afternoon on the patio reading *Kwaidan*, which he found quite enjoyable. The ghost stories of Lafcadio Hearn were poignant —and of course more exotic—than those by Edgar Allan Poe or H. P. Lovecraft. And they were tinged more with human sadness than with fear.

Being here also caused him to remember how much he always loved Wintersgate's setting: the beach, the cliffs edging it, the choppy blue waves of the Atlantic. He understood why his father wanted to protect it, but it made no sense that his father wanted to keep it away from Irina Petrescu, or what her family might have had to do with his mother's death.

When Michael returned to the house, Patience told him William Claude had retired for the night. Once again, Michael dined alone.

After dinner, a call from Charlotte Reed surprised him.

"Michael, I'm sorry to bother you, but something is going on here in Salmon." She told him about the animal mutilations and the nervousness all around her.

"How's Jake handling it?" Michael asked.

"He tries to ignore it, or deny it's anything weird. Instead, he bellows at people—including me—who try to talk about it."

"Why do you think that is?"

There was a pause. "He thinks people are still nervous."

"Which is not unreasonable," Michael said. "What happened out there two years ago was unique and frightening. So now, anything weird would naturally have people up in arms."

"Maybe." Her voice was tiny.

"You think I should go out there and talk to Jake? Check things out for myself?"

"I don't know. I hate to say it, but there could be something else going on."

"Like what?"

"Something mundane ... something I don't want to admit."

"You'll need to explain, Charlotte," he said.

"God, I don't know if I can bring myself to say it."

"Hey, you can talk to me, you know," he said gently. "Out with it. Okay?"

She hesitated, but once she began, the words tumbled from her like a dam bursting. "I think he may be seeing another woman. He denies it, but I've seen him with her several times. And he looked happy! He told me I was seeing things. But I wasn't. Maybe it's as simple as that. He's met someone else."

"Do you really think that's what's going on?" Michael asked.

"I don't know, Michael. A part of me says 'no,' and yet.... The other woman—what a clichéd life I'm living—is probably ten years younger than me, with long, shiny blond hair, and a body that looks like the best money can buy. Why wouldn't Jake be interested?"

"Because he has you at home waiting for him."

"Thank you, Michael. I knew there was a reason I like you so much."

"How long has this been going on?"

"Two, three weeks I'd say."

"I just can't imagine Jake caring about anyone else. Maybe the live-stock deaths have him rattled. It can't be anything serious with Miss Salmon, Idaho there."

Charlotte tried to laugh at his lame joke. "I hope you're right. I'm sorry I troubled you. But I think our conversation helped me put things in perspective."

"I'll come out there if it might help," he said.

"No. Not yet, at least. I'll try talking to Jake. But thank you for offering, and for listening."

The conversation over, Michael couldn't help but reflect on it. He had the feeling this wasn't the last he would hear about it.

After a while, he returned to the library to look at more of the Lafcadio Hearn material.

One book of stories and essays with the awkward title of *Kotto, Being Japanese Curios, with Sundry Cobwebs,* had a bookmark jutting out of the top. He flipped to the page and found a lightly penciled arrow directing his eye to a passage that began, *"Transmutations there may be.... But nothing essential can be lost. We shall inevitably bequeath our part to the making of the future cosmos—to the substance out of which another intelligence will slowly be evolved."*

As Michael continued the passage, he discovered that Hearn followed the philosophy of the alchemist—that nothing ever died, but transmuted into some future form of life. The belief was that the atoms that made up everything in the world never ceased to be, but continued to exist in different forms. They become part of the inevitable chain of life, and all of us are a part of that chain.

Michael turned his attention back to the books. He selected three of them and took them to his bedroom where he stayed up half the night reading and then fell asleep, too tired for dreams.

Vancouver, British Columbia

Every day, Li Jianjun said a little prayer that Michael Rempart would decide to do an archeological dig in some remote corner of the world. The remoter, the better.

Jianjun was Michael's assistant and technical expert. Age thirty-seven, born in China, now a Canadian citizen and a computer genius, he handled the logistics for the digs, including getting all necessary governmental okays. It was a job that could take weeks, but Jianjun never minded fighting with government bureaucrats. He had never yet failed to receive a go-ahead. Maybe he didn't always act in the most up-and-up way, but he did nothing that would harm anyone. Just a few hacks into government systems and databases, and things turned in his favor.

Right now, he'd hack into the Pentagon if it would get him a job away from home. Working with Michael, traveling the world, looking into strange pieces of antiquity was more fascinating than he had ever imagined it could be. Not because of the archeology—that was Michael's area—

but because of the people he met and the places he saw. His job provided the best, and the worst, parts of his life.

The best because he never felt as alive or as needed as when he worked with Michael. And because the last time they had worked together, he met a woman named Kira Holt. She made him realize how wonderful life could be.

But he couldn't think about Kira now. Not when he was home with Linda, his wife, who hated him. And that reminded him of the worst part of his job—encountering people and other creatures that seem to want him dead.

Living with his wife, he should have been used to it.

The last time he spoke with Michael, the archeologist was in New Mexico and had needed no assistance. That meant Jianjun remained stuck at home.

Jianjun was so ready to travel he would be willing to return to Mongolia, as desolate a place as he had ever seen in his life. He would even be willing to drink more of that awful yak milk if it would help. If not, there were a lot of islands around Indonesia he wouldn't mind seeing. Right now, the jungles of Papua-New Guinea sounded good, cannibals notwithstanding, a clear sign of how desperate he was. Anything was better than staying home one more week. He couldn't remember ever having been so bored or, frankly, so unhappy.

He was going through internet news sites trying to find some exciting place in the world to pique Michael's interest when his phone rang. It was an international call.

"Li Jianjun?" asked an accented voice.

"Yes."

"I am Yamato Toru, calling from Japan. I have been trying for several days to reach Doctor Michael Rempart, but he does not answer my call or messages. I am hoping you can help."

"I'll try, but if he doesn't want to talk to you, there's little I can do," Jianjun said dismissively. Michael received a lot of weird requests from people.

"Let me explain," Yamato said. "I work for a family, the Nakamura family, whose ancestor was a daimyo, an important position if you know Japanese history."

Jianjun had watched plenty of "samurai" films, and he knew daimyo as regional feudal lords. Samurai were their soldiers. "I know what daimyo are."

"The Nakamura family has owned their land for many centuries. They have found many possessions buried on the land—items that would interest an archeologist. We would like to offer Doctor Rempart the opportunity to come here to the Nakamura estate to study the daimyo's treasures."

"How old are these items?"

"Some are from very early dynasties, 700 A.D., perhaps. We are in Western Honshu."

Jianjun recognized Honshu as being the largest Japanese island. Tokyo was in the east, the important historical cities of Kyoto and Nara in the center, but he couldn't think of anything much in the west.

"I doubt he'll be interested," Jianjun said. "I mean, the guy practically lives in museums all over the world. He's seen a lot of stuff from all kinds of dynasties—and far older than fourteen hundred years."

"But the family would like an honest, outside opinion on what their items are worth. They are hoping Doctor Rempart will be interested in helping them."

"I see." Jianjun did see: if the family called in a Japanese archeologist, and the items were truly old, the government might confiscate them as antiquities belonging to the state. But evaluating items wasn't Michael's area of interest. "Doctor Rempart prefers discovering antiquities, not pricing what's already been found."

"But many of the items have symbols from alchemy etched on them," Yamato said hurriedly. "And we've heard that subject interests Doctor Rempart. And, possibly, some symbols are ... may I say, demonic."

Jianjun sighed. Demons scared him, but unfortunately, they intrigued Michael. Jianjun had encountered enough demons last year in China to last a lifetime. He used to think that alchemy and the demonic had no relationship at all, but then he learned that alchemy was a lot more than some sorcerer trying to turn cheap metals into gold. Something far more sinister existed in one arm of the ancient practice: the desire for immortality, a desire that had opened some alchemists to evil and the demonic.

Jianjun also heard the fear in Yamato's voice. Clearly, more was going on than Yamato would say. "I'll talk to Dr. Rempart about this. I'll get back to you."

"I studied your boss before calling you because I had grave doubts of the stories I heard about him," Yamato said. "I thought he might be a con artist or thief posing as an archeologist. But the more I learned, the more convinced I became that he is an honest man. I have also read that he prefers to be left alone, but may get involved if something interests him on a personal level. I hope you can convince him that this is an area he would find personally interesting. Very interesting, in fact."

"Personally? Why is that?"

"If he looks at what we have here, I believe he will find it so."

"I have no idea what you mean, and I doubt Michael will understand it either," Jianjun said. "But I'll talk to him."

CHAPTER 8

THE NEXT MORNING William Claude joined Michael for breakfast.

"I've been thinking," William Claude said. "The Chinese pearl that attracts demons must be a very dangerous thing to own."

"If such a thing existed."

"I'm sure there are forces that want the pearl," William Claude continued. "Perhaps demonic forces. I've already lost one son to this madness. I don't want to lose another."

"I'm sure you don't." Michael's voice was flat as he leaned back in the chair and folded his arms.

"I do care about you, boy! I suggest you bring the pearl to Wintersgate. It will be safe here. I have top-of-the-line security."

Michael understood exactly what William Claude most cared about. "The pearl isn't what you think it is."

William Claude's jowls worked as he tried to control his irritation. "What if something were to happen to you? Someone else should know how to locate it."

"No one else needs to know."

"Don't you have an assistant, some Chinese whiz kid, who's supposed to know everything? He must know how to find it."

"He doesn't," Michael said firmly.

His father studied him to see if he was lying. Michael did all he could to keep steady eye contact and not give away anything that might endanger Jianjun. William Claude, he knew, could be a dangerous man.

William Claude decided to try reason. "From my research, I've heard it said that the pearl is one of the strongest philosopher's stones the world has ever known. With it, I might develop a means to immortality. I don't want to die. And you won't either when you reach my age. Together, with my knowledge of alchemical formulas and your innate oneness, your gift and affinity for all things alchemical, we'll be able to do it."

"Your quest for immortality is unnatural and wrong," Michael said. "You know it is, and so do I."

William Claude reached out and placed his hand on Michael's forearm. This time, instead of feeling cold, the hand emitted heat and raw power.

"Think well, boy." William Claude said. His hand grew hot on Michael's arm as his fingers tightened. "Think about how much you don't want to disappoint me. You've never really wanted to disappoint me. You've always wanted to please, to have me look on you with favor, to have me care about you as much as I did Lionel. This, Michael, this will give you what you've always wanted from me."

Michael yanked his arm free.

———

William Claude stormed into his laboratory. He was sick and tired of the obstinacy of his son. Did Michael really think he was that stupid?

He made a phone call. "It's me. Tell them they've got to step up the action. It's not working yet. Time to push – a lot. It's got to be bad. Something no one can ignore."

The excuses he was hearing only made him angrier. "If they can't do it, I'll find someone who can! They have one more week."

He hung up, fuming.

After he calmed down a bit, he thought of a way he might help his own cause.

Time to step up his own side of things.

He smiled. After all, God wasn't the only one who helped those who help themselves...

CHAPTER 9

MICHAEL FOUND himself in the library seated on a wingback chair and holding the letters of Lafcadio Hearn. He didn't remember choosing to come here, or even walking through the downstairs hallway to the library.

Nevertheless, he began to read the material in his hands, and soon realized he had discovered a kindred spirit.

I ought never to have been born in this century, I think sometimes, because I live forever in dreams of other centuries and other faiths and other ethics.

Michael often felt that way. Maybe they really were cousins.

He had other feelings of connection with the shy, peculiar, peripatetic man who had lived more than a century earlier, including one that echoed a common complaint of his when Hearn wrote: *The so-called improvements in civilization have apparently resulted in making it impossible to see, hear, or find anything out. You're improving yourselves out of the natural world.*

Michael laughed aloud at that. Such feelings had led to Michael's passion for archeology, for learning about the past and its people.

He also felt compassion for the lonely man who best expressed himself when hidden behind the nib of his pen. Since Hearn had always expected people would find fault with him, and thereby abandon him and the friendship he offered, he went on the attack at the slightest provocation. With his vicious tongue, he often insulted his friends and acquaintances so badly they would cut off their friendships to avoid further confrontation or humiliation.

Ironically, Hearn's longest relationship resulted from his arranged marriage. Koizumi Setsuko was age twenty-two, from an impoverished samurai family, when the forty-year-old Lafcadio arrived in Matsue, Japan. He had been given a job as an English teacher, but it quickly became obvious to those around him that he needed help cooking, shopping, traveling, and so on. A colleague set up a meeting between him and Setsuko. They decided that, in exchange for her taking care of his household to give him time to write for U.S. publications as well as to teach in local schools, he would assume financial responsibility for his in-laws. Despite its irregular beginnings, and the fact that he spoke little Japanese, and she even less English, he and Setsuko seemed content together, and remained so until Lafcadio's death from a heart attack at age fifty-four in 1904. They had three sons and one daughter. Lafcadio even became a Japanese citizen in order to assure that his wife and children would inherit from him after his death. He took his wife's family's name as his Japanese name, and to this day the people of Japan refer to him as Koizumi Yakumo.

Michael was thinking about the strange and melancholy man when his cell phone vibrated.

It was his assistant, Li Jianjun.

"I got a weird call from Japan, from a guy who works for what was once a big daimyo family."

"A daimyo? How feudal. Why was he calling?"

"This guy, Yamato Toru, wants to find you, but I'm not sure why. He gave a couple of different stories. First, he said you might want to help the family, their name is Nakamura, evaluate old stuff they have."

"Sounds boring." Michael got a lot of these calls. Most times, he directed people to contact the *Antiques Roadshow*, not him.

"Yeah, I told him that wasn't your thing," Jianjun added. "But then he said you might find a personal interest in it."

"Personal? I can't imagine. Did he say why?"

"A lot of the items have symbols from alchemy. He knew your interest in the subject."

"Alchemy. The hell with that," Michael said. After tangling with his father, Michael didn't want to hear about it.

"You never know, boss. The alchemy angle might be worth checking out. I never ... I mean, *you've* never spent much time in Japan. I wouldn't mind going there first if you'd like. I could look over the area, check out the family. Make sure they aren't going to palm off some Made in China junk on you."

Michael couldn't help but smile. He was well aware of Jianjun's miserable home life. "Look, if nothing comes of this trip I'm on, we just might go there."

"You're still at that dig in New Mexico, right?" Jianjun asked.

"Actually, I'm in Cape Cod visiting my father."

"Holy cow!" Jianjun exclaimed. "After that, you'll definitely want to go to Japan. It's pretty much on the other side of the world—about as far from the old man as you can get."

A good point, Michael thought. "I'll keep that in mind."

CHAPTER 10

A DOZEN RANCH owners filled the Telichpah Flat general store for a meeting with the county sheriff. Their ranches centered around the Salmon River which flowed through a canyon about five thousand feet deep and nearly two hundred miles long. When Lewis and Clark encountered the dangerous gorge in 1805, they turned away and headed north, following their guide, Sacajawea. Early fur trappers also avoided the Salmon River canyon, as did the nearby Tukudeka, Shoshone, and Nez Perce tribes. Not until the 1860s when the gravel bars of the river were found to contain small quantities of gold dust did prospectors move in to explore the area. Miners worked sluice boxes along the high-water line through the depression years of the 1930s until all the gold was mined out.

A few of those explorers and prospectors filed for homesteads and were given deeds to create small ranches. Ownership was grandfathered to them and their heirs when the area became protected from further development under the Wilderness Act of the US Congress.

Life was harsh for homesteaders in the remote, solitary land, and continues to be. Some say the Tukudeka or Shoshone-Bannock tribes were the first to use the name "River of No Return" since canoes that went down the Salmon almost never came back. Early Army Corps of Engineers guides who tried to find a path along it for a railroad, ended up declaring it to be the most difficult terrain they had ever attempted to cross in the US.

To this day, not only is there no railroad along the Salmon River, but no roads at all transverse the entire east to west journey of the river. Access to most of the ranches is only by small planes or horseback, and their power comes from small hydro plants, solar panels, and propane flown in by air. Satellite phones provide the main means of communication, and bush planes handle most of the US and private mail services such as FedEx.

But despite the difficult conditions and isolation of their lives, the residents found out about strange mutilations and deaths happening around them, and called for a meeting.

"You've got to do something, or we take this into our own hands," Larry Pollack said. He was a big man with a florid face, bald head, clenched fists, and a Smith and Wesson .44 magnum in his shoulder holster.

"And it ain't gonna be pretty," Wade Cox added, then crossed his arms and spread his feet wide as he sat in a teetering chair. He glared at the others in the room, and they all kept their distance.

"Calm down, guys." Sheriff Jake Sullivan stretched out his hands, palms facing downward, trying to ease the tension. The Telichpah Flats location brought back memories of a couple of years ago when the general store was the eye of a media storm after the Boise State University group vanished.

"We know about all the deaths that took place out here a couple years ago," Wade added, "much as those of you involved tried to keep it secret. And I swear, something weird is going on again. Something I don't like one damn bit."

"And we sure as hell ain't gonna sit around and watch our neighbors get picked off one by one," Larry Pollack added.

"Nobody is sitting around doing nothing." Jake had to shout to be heard over the grumbling around him. "And none of your neighbors has gotten killed."

"Yet!" A voice in the back spat out the word.

Jake spoke louder. "The county wants to find out what's happening out there as much as you do."

"Yeah, but it's not 'out there' to us," Wade said. "It's 'here.' It's home. You can't deny things got bad two years ago because you were one of the ones lost."

"I can't deny things happened," Jake said, struggling to keep his voice calm. "But a lot of what you heard was rumor and nonsense. You know how the press likes to sensationalize every little thing."

"Like college kids and teachers on a field trip being killed?" Wade suggested with a disgust-filled smirk. Others nodded in agreement.

Jake knew this was a no-win situation, mainly because the ranchers were right to be worried. So was he. "Let's talk about what's happening *now*. How many of you have lost sheep or cattle, or have seen any of these strange mutilations?"

"Something killed two of my calves," Penny Schmidt bellowed. She was a big woman, nearly two-hundred pounds of pure muscle. "And I know a wolf or mountain lion didn't do it. I've lost sheep and lambs to them, and this attack was different. Ugly and different." Schmidt was as tough as they came out here in a land filled with strong, rugged people. She had taken over the ranch when her father died, married one of the ranch hands, and together they kept it going along with their three sons. That day, her husband stayed at the ranch while she piloted their single-engine plane to the meeting.

Jake eyed her as she spoke and noticed she kept rubbing her hands hard against her jeans, almost as if she were trying to rub something off them.

"I also found a female hog torn up in ways that aren't natural," Don Grover said, then swallowed hard.

"A sheep, mutilated, on my land," Wade Cox said.

Mitch Ivansen called out, "Two on mine."

Johnny Adesso waved his hand and when Jake looked his way, he stood. "My cattle dog, Sadie, never came home. It's not like her." He became choked up and quickly sat back down.

About half the ranchers answered Jake's question, but all of them were spooked. Jake did his best to calm them.

Ironically, most of the people there were upset because they feared Jake and the authorities wouldn't believe that anything bad was happening, and wouldn't help. But Jake believed them.

People throughout the area were growing increasingly agitated and upset. Not only were there strange mutilations of livestock, but fistfights were breaking out in town, and a couple guys tried to slice each other up with knives. Even he and Charlotte seemed to constantly bicker and argue with each other.

He didn't know what was causing all the commotion, but his biggest worry was that the deaths and mutilations would move from livestock and pets to humans.

CHAPTER 11

Two days passed, days that Michael spent reading about Lafcadio Hearn's life in Matsue and other parts of Japan, and how he ended up in Tokyo, which Hearn had called "detestable" because of its size and modernization. Michael could well imagine what Hearn would say if he saw it today.

While Michael enjoyed learning about Hearn, his reasons for coming to Wintersgate had made no progress. Michael and his father had reached an impasse.

His father refused to talk about anything but the pearl and alchemy. And Michael refused to talk about them. He would have liked to know more about the connection between his mother's death and Irina Petrescu, but William Claude refused to discuss it further.

It was time, Michael knew, to leave Wintersgate for good, and to accept there were some things he would never know. At best, returning here had helped him put some of the past to rest, and to realize his father had become pathetic with his unquenchable thirst for immortality. In the quest for the unnatural, even greater evil had descended on Wintersgate.

He headed for his bedroom to pack. But as he walked down the hall, he stopped and listened to the soft strains of a familiar sound from his boyhood. His mother had a music box that played the opening melody of Für Elise while a ballerina twirled, first in one direction, then in the other.

How could he be hearing it now?

He turned away from his bedroom to follow the sound. It led him to the opposite end of the hall and then up the stairs to the third floor. The music grew louder, but when he open the door to the tower room, his mother's private retreat, it abruptly stopped.

He walked into the room slowly. As he did, memories assailed him. His mother had kept her books, her needlework, and everything she loved there. William Claude never entered it. But Michael had often joined her. After her death, the door was kept shut, and he rarely entered it again.

The room was as he remembered it, filled with her belongings in chaotic disarray just the way it had been when she was alive. Somehow, she always knew where everything was.

He could feel her presence all around him. Someone had kept the room dusted, Patience, most likely. But nothing else had been done to it.

He should leave, he told himself. The past was over. Finished. It was time to move on.

But he couldn't. Not yet. He walked over to her bookshelf and glanced at the titles, a curious mixture of classics, romances, and murder mysteries. She seemed to have complete collections of Mary Stewart and Daphne DuMaurier. He remembered how, when he was very young, she would read children's books to him there. In later years, he would sit with her while reading his own books as she read hers or worked on her needlepoint or quilts.

On the bottom shelf he saw a book with a green leather binding. With no title on the spine, the book looked like a journal. He didn't remember ever seeing it before.

A glance at the flyleaf showed a young woman's script, and "Property of …" gave her maiden name, Jane Addams. It was his mother's diary. His fingers brushed over the cover, a cover that showed years of handling.

Michael knew little of her early life other than learning her father had struggled financially running a shop that sold dress material and sewing supplies, and that her parents had died in an accident. But he'd never been given any details about her. Now, with her diary, he could learn more.

He took the book, went over to the chair his mother had always sat in, and switched on the lamp. He hesitated. It was, after all, filled with her private thoughts.

Still, he had come here seeking answers. Given William Claude's recalcitrance about the past, the diary might be Michael's only means for any answers.

He couldn't help but look around the room, and wonder what had caused him to spot this little diary now when he had never noticed it in all the years he had looked at that bookshelf as a boy.

He opened the book and read. It began simply enough, talking about a young woman, fresh out of high school and looking forward to college but needing to earn money by working at the local library.

But quickly the tenor of the diary changed.

June 5th—

I met the most fascinating man today, William Claude Rempart. He is quite a scholar of history and is often in the library doing research. As we talked, to my amazement, he seemed interested in me. He's a few years older than me, but that couldn't matter less. I keep telling myself he was just being polite, but in my heart, I think there was something more. I can't wait to see him again.

Michael skimmed through two months' worth of such pages, feeling like some awful voyeur as he read of his mother's growing fascination with William Claude—even their first kiss. She was only eighteen, and William Claude twenty-five.

Michael was beyond stunned to read that "Claude" as she called him, soon took her on a whirlwind of travel, and gave her many gifts, including clothes. A while passed before Jane confessed to the diary how angry her parents were at what they considered wanton behavior.

Through this period, Jane noticed a dark side to Claude. There were times he troubled her, and a few times, he scared her. But she always found a reason to excuse him, or to decide she had acted too "silly" or too "girlish" and that it was no surprise for a man of the world to grow peevish with her. She always did all she could to make amends for aggravating him.

August 15—

Today, I became Mrs. William Claude Rempart. We were married by a Justice of the Peace without any family present. It would have been a perfect day, except that my parents refused to give us their blessing. But I've made my choice. They are nothing to me now, just as I am nothing to them. Claude is my life, and I will make him the best wife ever. As we left the Justice of the Peace, I saw many women looking at me with envy.

August 20—

My parents died yesterday when their car careened off a cliff. No one seems to know why it happened. Brake failure? Speed? I know Dad was a cautious man. It remains a mystery. But now sadness fills my heart, particularly since, this side of Heaven, we will never be able to repair the rift that came between us due to my marriage.

Over the course of several days, Jane continued to write of her grief over the death of her parents. She went to Claude more than once seeking consolation, but he gave her only the slightest indulgence.

Michael skimmed many of the ensuing pages as Jane learned to become a lady of the manor. The size of Wintersgate and all that went into maintaining it were new to her, and Claude often chided her for things she didn't know how to do, as well as those she had no idea she should be doing. Her greatest joy came when she learned she was pregnant. She was sure Claude was as thrilled as she was but simply didn't know how to show it.

Seven months later, she wrote of giving birth. Michael's eyes filled with tears as he read her anguish at learning the baby wasn't healthy. He couldn't bear to read about the baby girl's sickness and eventual death. He remembered his mother far too well, and as he read, her pain became his.

Her relationship with William Claude took a dangerous turn after baby Catherine's death. Claude stayed away for long periods of time, and when he was home, he locked himself away in his laboratory. Jane believed he had become obsessed with alchemy. He told her about his family history, that he came from a long line of alchemists, but she refused to believe in anything supernatural. She found his belief in alchemy incomprehensible.

Five years passed with few but the most trivial annotations in the diary, almost as if life had become meaningless, until Jane wrote that she was once again expecting a child. She was frightened throughout this pregnancy that she would again deliver a sickly child. But a healthy baby boy was born, and they named him Lionel.

Claude was ecstatic over Lionel, and hired a nurse to take care of the baby full-time, saying he didn't believe Jane knew anything about child-care. She told him she could learn, just as women from the dawn of time had learned to raise their children, but that wasn't good enough for Claude.

A few pages noted Lionel's first, second, and third birthdays, which were happy occasions that saw Claude in a good mood and willing to take part in the festivities with his wife. Jane scarcely mentioned Lionel's fourth and fifth birthdays, and she did nothing but annotate the day for later ones.

It was clear to Michael that by the time they sent Lionel to boarding school, he preferred Claude's company and his nurse's to that of his own mother. It sounded as if Claude had done all he could to turn Lionel against her. Also, Jane's unhappiness grew as Claude's dark side struck more often. There were times she couldn't break through his acrimony at all, and as the years went by, his dark periods became more prevalent until she concluded that he wasn't completely sane.

Ten years after Lionel's birth, Jane learned she was again expecting. This child, she determined Claude would not take from her.

April 8th—

I have given birth to a fine boy. When Claude came in to see him, I told him that the doctor hadn't been truthful with him, as he had been fearful of Claude's reaction. I said the boy was sickly, far too small to have been born yet. He probably wouldn't survive more than a year, if that. I said I would take care of him. No sense hiring a nurse—that would throw good money after bad. Claude turned away in disgust and said to do with the child as I pleased. I pleased to name him Michael.

Michael learned that he was, in fact, a smaller, more delicate infant than Lionel had been. Claude was surprised when the baby continued to live, but Jane assured him the damage had been done, and the boy would never see the inside of a schoolroom. By the time Michael was five, and it was clear he was robust and healthy, Claude found that his second son scarcely knew him, and seemed to fear him. Claude berated Jane for this, and said her constant pampering of the boy had "ruined" him, and had "spoiled" him beyond repair.

When Michael saw how harsh and mean Claude was to his beloved mother, he grew even more frightened of his father, which disgusted Claude all the more.

For Jane, Michael was her only joy.

August 30—

I'm not sure what to think. I expected to celebrate Claude's forty-fifth birthday, but he informed me he was actually fifty years old, that he had believed I would find him too old when we met, and had lied all these years about his age. I assured him his age made no difference.

But then he said age was very important to him. He had developed an elixir made with a quantity of gold dust that would slow the aging process and prolong his life. He then told me I, too, must take it. After all, I was thirty-eight years old, and soon would look aged.

I'm sure the man has gone quite insane.

She wrote nothing in the diary for some time before returning to it to express her unhappiness with William Claude over sending Michael away to boarding school. She didn't want to do it, and fought with William Claude about his decision.

There, the diary ended. Michael didn't need a diary entry to know what happened. He went away to school and spent some of the most miserable years of his life there.

Michael left the tower room to step out onto its private deck, then walked to the stone railing and stared out at the ocean. He remembered his mother well and thought he had never seen anyone as lovely or as loving. Her words about William Claude's dark side and his increasing descent into madness confirmed Michael's own feelings.

"What happened to you, Mom?" he whispered.

He doubted he would ever know. He was too young when she died to understand what was going on in her life. After her death, as he grew up in this house, he spent years searching Wintersgate, but found nothing to explain her death—if there even was a "reason" to be found. It was odd that during those searches he had overlooked this diary.

What he would do with this new knowledge was unclear, his thoughts troubled and contradictory. He had a sense that a reckoning was meant to happen. But what, and when?

He kept the diary with him as he left the turret, his heart heavy. There were ghosts here, and he could all but feel their tears.

CHAPTER 12

CEINWEN WISHED she could confess to Rachel that she wanted to write a magazine article or possibly a book about all that happened when the university group vanished in Idaho's wilderness. But she knew that would cause Rachel to put up a barrier she couldn't overcome. So, she had lied, and continued to do so.

And now this liar was on her way to meet Rachel's big Mormon family. Ceinwen felt guilty—although not guilty enough to stop her investigation.

Ceinwen found them red-eye tickets at a decent price, and Rachel had handled the flights well except for a brief trance at Heathrow Airport. Just before boarding the Newark to Salt Lake City final leg of the flight, Rachel called her parents to let them know she was coming home, and that her college roommate was with her.

Her father, Stan, was waiting for them when they arrived in Salt Lake City. He was a large man with a bulbous nose, heavy jowls, and small blue eyes.

He caught Rachel up in a bear hug and then greeted Ceinwen warmly. Soon, they got into his monstrous Dodge Ram and headed into Idaho. The land quickly became flat and empty, and the dry ground looked like gravel broken up by an occasional sage or other spindly brush.

Not until they reached Idaho Falls did the countryside turn green. They were in a farming community. Before long, Stan turned onto a driveway that led to a large wood-framed farmhouse. He honked the horn, and people poured from the house to greet them.

Rachel introduced Ceinwen to her mother, five brothers, four sisters, their spouses, and children. Ceinwen had read that Latter-day Saints, as Mormons call themselves, believe large families are a blessing. If so, the Gooding family was truly blessed.

Everyone was interested in hearing about life in Oxford and had questions about everything from steak-and-kidney pie to driving on the "wrong" side of the road. The younger Gooding grandchildren liked listening to Ceinwen's accent, and found it hilarious that she was from Wales, which they thought had something to do with fish.

Rachel kept apologizing for all the questions, but Ceinwen loved them. Also, she could tell that Rachel was glad she was there to draw away attention from her sudden reappearance. It wasn't until Ceinwen saw Stan corner his daughter away from the others that she heard his worry that she might have flunked out. Rachel assured him the school year was over, her studies were fine, and she had come home because she missed him and her mother.

He seemed touched to hear it. Rachel gave the family no hint of her nightmares or that anything was troubling her, and Ceinwen had to wonder if any of them knew the extent of what had happened to her two years earlier.

After dinner, Ceinwen joined the women in the kitchen to help clean up.

Rachel's mother had only one interest: did Rachel have a boyfriend, and if so, was he LDS, or at least someone open to conversion? Her biggest fear was that Rachel would marry an Englishman and live far from home. Rachel did her best to put her mother's mind at rest about that.

Before long, her mother and sisters started plotting how they could find both Rachel and Ceinwen nice men in the area to marry so they could forget about going back to Oxford. From the way they talked, they believed—as Brigham Young had proclaimed some hundred-seventy years earlier—that he had led his people to the Promised Land, and if so, why would any sane person want to live anywhere else?

CHAPTER 13

HIS MOTHER'S diary confirmed Michael's resolve not to spend any more time in that house. He packed his bag and went in search of his father, only to learn from Patience that William Claude and Stedman were gone for the day. "Do you think they'll return tonight?"

"I'm afraid I don't know, sir."

Michael knew it would be pointless to wait. It wasn't as if he and William Claude would have a heartfelt farewell. "Tell him goodbye for me. I'm leaving now."

"And where will you be headed, sir?" Patience asked

Good question. But then an idea came to him. "If my father asks, tell him I'm going to Matsue, Japan. And that I'm bringing Cousin Lafcadio's unpublished papers with me. I'll return them to the library when I'm through studying them." His expression turned wry. "Tell him I have a sudden interest in family matters."

Jianjun hunted for something unique and interesting about Japanese archeology or alchemy. If he could interest Michael in spending time in Japan, he could join him. But so far, he'd found no such material.

His phone buzzed and to his surprise the caller was Michael.

"I've left Wintersgate," Michael said. "I'm at the airport now."

"I'm shocked you stayed this long," Jianjun said. "Where are you going?"

"Have you ever heard of an author named Lafcadio Hearn?" Michael asked. "He's most famous for his Japanese ghost stories."

"Ghost stories? Nope. Never heard of him."

"You aren't alone in that," Michael admitted. "Anyway, I've been reading his books. A number of them are in my father's library, as well as letters Hearn wrote to my great-grandfather, Victor Rempart."

"So, this Hearn guy is dead?"

"Quite."

"Do I want to know why you're reading ghost stories by some dead guy no one has ever heard of?"

"He has his fans," Michael said. "A small group perhaps, but they exist. I learned Hearn might be a relative, and he lived in Matsue, Japan."

Jianjun was finding this conversation odd. "So... you want to learn more about this relative, I take it."

"Exactly. I've never spent much time in Japan—just a few quick trips to Tokyo. I think it's time to change that. Also, Hearn had an interest in alchemy. It shows up in his writings. I'd like to learn more about Japanese alchemy. I don't believe the Japanese ever took it seriously."

"With good reason," Jianjun muttered.

Michael ignored the comment. "I've always wondered if, when the Chinese alchemists talked about some special islands in the East, they meant Japan. Anyway, Matsue is just across the sea from China. And didn't you say that's where the guy who phoned you about the daimyo artifacts was calling from?"

"I did. Yamato Toru. But I called him and said you were too busy for him."

"Maybe I'm no longer so busy."

"He told me to call back if you change your mind," Jianjun said. "But don't you find it weird that out of the blue he calls you and now you decide to go out there? It's a strange coincidence. A troubling coincidence, if you ask me."

"Or, a lucky circumstance," Michael said.

"I somehow doubt that," Jianjun said. "Maybe I should join you, make sure things are on the up and up. I wouldn't mind seeing Japan again."

"You are such a cynic. It might just be a quick trip, but if I find anything worth looking into, I'll let you know."

"My fingers are crossed already!"

When the call ended, Jianjun stared at the phone. Michael didn't sound like himself. He sounded too upbeat and optimistic, but not legitimately so, more like he was trying to hide a deep hurt or disappointment. Jianjun wondered if going all the way to Japan was Michael's way of trying to flee from whatever was bothering him, and Jianjun suspected it had a lot to do with memories stirred up at Wintersgate.

William Claude sat scowling, arms folded, in his laboratory. He had just returned home and learned that Michael left for Japan. What the hell was going on?

William Claude had power, lots of it. He could control, deceive, and torment people continents away, but he couldn't affect his own son in his own home. Damn Michael to hell! Claude grabbed the vials of his latest elixir and poured them down the drain, then tossed the vials into the trash. They were all rubbish. Worse than rubbish. He paced back and forth across the lab.

When he first heard about the powerful philosopher's stone from Shang Dynasty China, he thought it was just a legend. Leave it to Michael to find it. Michael had the ability to become one of the best alchemists of all time. But first, he needed to accept his abilities and his role in using them.

It was ironic that the boy believed he had returned to Wintersgate of his own free will to learn more about Irina Petrescu and more about his mother's death. How ridiculous. Did he also think the nightmares that drew him here happened just by chance?

If so, he wasn't half as smart as he thought he was.

Michael had never learned all his father was capable of. But one day, before this situation with the philosopher's stone was over, he would find out.

And then he should stop wasting his talent!

William Claude was sure Michael had hidden the pearl somewhere near Salmon, Idaho. To hide it had to be the reason Michael and his Chinese friend went to that area last year after they left China. Claude found it especially curious, however, that Michael hadn't returned to the area given the problems that had resurfaced there. Didn't he care any longer about Charlotte Reed and Jake Sullivan?

William Claude had focused his attention on them, and then as a backup—an afterthought really—he decided to include that twit of a girl, the student Rachel Gooding. To his surprise, he found her rather delightful—young, intelligent, but needing to learn much more about the ways of the world. She was like a fresh new toy for him, her mind open and trusting. Maybe someday he would teach her about the world, the flesh, and the devil. He just might enjoy that. But at the moment he had other concerns.

Despite Michael's friends in Salmon feeling "troubled," and with death and weirdness all around them, they still hadn't convinced Michael to go back there to retrieve the pearl. What was wrong with the boy?

This Lafcadio Hearn business was an annoying wrinkle in William Claude's plans. He could understand Michael finding it interesting, even to the point of wanting to visit Japan someday. But why now? And why the sudden rush?

It made little sense. It was almost as if someone, or something, was trying to divert Michael's attention away from Wintersgate and Salmon.

Claude froze in mid-pace. That couldn't be, could it?

He stroked his chin. Was there a competing force, perhaps, that wanted the pearl? *His* pearl.

Or was something even more sinister taking place?

The old man's face was contorted with dark fury as he considered these possibilities, and an even deeper chill enveloped Wintersgate.

CHAPTER 14

SHERIFF JAKE SULLIVAN stared at the corpse of a man found two miles north of the Salmon River. Something had chewed his face to a pulp as well as his stomach. Jake's own stomach nearly flipped over at the sight.

But even worse, even more horrifying, the bite marks on the corpse appeared eerily human.

Jake had hoped that the meeting he'd held with the few ranchers who lived in and around the River of No Return Wilderness would be enough to sooth their nerves. He had expected wolves, or mountain lions, or even a grizzly or two had caused the strange livestock deaths. But whatever was killing animals out here had just moved to humans, and the situation had become a lot more serious.

A pair of hikers had found the body. They saw buzzards circling and thought the birds might be hovering over a spot where elk or deer had congregated. When they got there, they were horrified at what the buzzards had found.

The hikers did all they could to mark the location and then went to a fire service lookout station where they contacted the sheriff's office. Jake and Mallick searched the man's pockets for identification, but found only some loose 6.5 Creekmore cartridges, a good size for elk hunting. Since it wasn't hunting season, the assumption was that the fellow went out there to poach a deer or elk and probably planned to butcher it on the spot.

Whoever killed the man most likely took his rifle, wallet, and knapsack. Didn't sound like any animal to Jake.

The flies had become frenzied at Jake's approach, and he spent more time shooing them away than inspecting the body.

"I'll take pictures," Deputy Mallick said. "Can he have died from some accident? And then something tried to eat him?"

"Something?" Jake asked. He could tell by Mallick's expression that he saw the bite marks the same way Jake did.

"I'm not ready to say what," Mallick whispered.

"This was no accident," Jake said. "No animal did this."

The deputy looked scared. "We've seen this sort of thing before, you know."

The same thought had gone through Jake's head and he could only pray that everything that happened a couple of years ago wasn't starting again. "Shit," he muttered.

It was close to midnight when Jake returned home. He had learned the poacher's identity from friends concerned when the man didn't return from the backwoods. Brad Washington, unmarried, age 55, worked for the post office as a mail carrier in Twin Falls. He had gone into the wilderness area "to commune with nature" according to friends and had done it many times in the past. But there was nothing about him to indicate why he would be singled out for such a bizarre attack.

Forensic evaluation of the saliva found near the bite marks identified the attacker as human. DNA tests were being run but they would take time, and Jake knew whoever did this was most likely not a run-of-the-mill criminal.

Jake had stopped at the office and wrote out his report, annotating the areas he had searched and found nothing.

By the time he got home, he was hungry, tired, and irritated at the bizarreness happening all over his county. But then, everyone on the team was cranky and sore. Even Mallick had snapped at some volunteers.

His house was a short distance north of town in the hills. He loved the A-frame cabin-style home with lots of windows facing the mountains. It had a large "great room," a kitchen, plus two bedrooms, and a study.

As soon as he walked in the door, however, he knew something was wrong.

The house was dark, but Charlotte always left a light on for him when he worked late.

Sure, they'd been having troubles and not getting along for reasons not altogether understood by him, but he didn't think she was so angry she expected him to stumble around in the dark. "What the hell is wrong with her?" Jake muttered to himself as he hit the switch to turn on the living room lamps.

The side table next to Charlotte's favorite easy chair—an overstuffed one with a matching ottoman—was usually covered with books. Now, it was bare. He often had joked that he didn't know how she remembered which book was where, she had so many stacks.

Maybe she had put the books away ... finally.

He went into the kitchen. Not only were no lights on, there was no plate of food in the refrigerator for him. She always made up a dinner platter when he couldn't get home to eat with her. His stomach growled with hunger. Had she only cooked enough for one? Was it his fault he wasn't home on time? It wasn't as if he wanted to be out in the middle of the county because of a gnawed-on, maggot-filled corpse.

The more he thought about it, the angrier he became.

He stormed into the bedroom to confront her and froze. Her side of the bed was empty.

"Charlotte?" He called her name as he switched on the bed lamp.

Her side hadn't been slept in.

He walked to the closet. Most of her clothes were gone.

He phoned, but her phone went straight to message.

He phoned three more times. With the fourth, he demanded, "Answer the damned phone, Charlotte."

But she didn't.

In the living room, he saw an envelope with his name on it in Charlotte's handwriting. She had left it on the coffee table. He guessed he'd overlooked it when he was so stunned to see her books gone.

He sat and opened the letter.

Jake,

I've returned to Virginia.

Charlotte

That was it? After all their time together, she gave him no explanation? Not even a lousy "I'm sorry"?

Before he ever met her, her home in the outskirts of Alexandria, Virginia, had been destroyed in a fire. It had been insured, of course, and he assumed she would take the insurance payoff. Instead she opted to rebuild. Her new house was small but nice, an up-to-date version of the colonial farmhouse style popular in that area. They had gone there twice for vacations. Jake thought the area was okay, and Charlotte always said she liked going back to remember why she enjoyed living in Salmon so much. She also thought the Virginia house would make a comfortable winter retreat from the heavy snows of Idaho.

But now, Jake realized her not wanting to sell the land had been a clear sign of the beginning of the end.

He grabbed a beer—at least she had left him one of those—and plopped down on the couch.

They'd been happy together. Really happy, or so he thought.

But a few weeks earlier, something turned sour, and he didn't know why.

Charlotte claimed it was him—that he had changed.

He didn't think so. Yes, he was feeling cranky. And maybe that made him hard to live with. But it wasn't his fault.

He'd been having trouble sleeping. Not falling asleep, but staying asleep. And who the hell would want to sleep when every night he dreamed about a parade of dead people and zombies? It was as if they were hunting him again—those creatures he'd had to fight and kill to rescue the few surviving university students. But now in his dreams, the creatures were victorious.

Night after night he watched himself and Charlotte die.

He couldn't tell her that. He couldn't tell anyone.

All he knew was that he hated sleep, but without it he could scarcely function.

The biggest irony was that, because of his sleeplessness, he was drinking a lot of coffee. Since the coffee in the office was swill, he'd go to the coffee shop next door to the sheriff's station. And now, Charlotte thought he had taken an interest in its new owner, Emily Parker.

Of course he talked to the woman. And he enjoyed having a doughnut or bear claw in the morning. What on God's green earth was wrong with that?

It wasn't like Charlotte to be jealous, and he'd given her no reason to be. But it seemed they couldn't talk to each other anymore.

And the main thing they couldn't talk about was what was going on out in the wilderness. As soon as word of the unnatural mutilations hit, Charlotte told him to call Michael Rempart and get him out here to investigate. That was the last thing he wanted to do. It was nothing super-natural, he insisted, just some strange animal attack. Maybe a deranged grizzly. Who knew? Whatever it was, he told Charlotte he could handle it.

Maybe that was why he never told her about his nightmares.

But if he had, she would have nagged him even more to call "the great Michael Rempart."

He always suspected she was sweet on the guy. Two "academicians" and all.

How the hell was he supposed to compete with that?

In fact, he suspected she might have called him herself and he was too busy or something to run out here, because she suddenly stopped talking about him. Or, maybe he was waiting for her in Virginia?

Damn! He downed half the bottle of beer. He guessed Charlotte wasn't the only one suffering from jealousy. But he was right to be!

The best answer he could come up with was that Charlotte had grown tired of living in a town so small it didn't even have a Greyhound bus depot. He always suspected he couldn't keep a woman who had lived in Europe and the Middle East—whose deceased husband had been a CIA officer—and who was beyond brilliant in her own right.

She gave up her government job to stay with him in Salmon and to pursue her own studies. She claimed she was happy to do it—that being with him made her happy.

He hadn't imagined what a good liar she could be.

He was such a doofus he had even asked her to marry him. She had no interest in that, either.

Now, it all came together. Her accusations about him and Emily Parker were just excuses for her to get away. Well, the hell with her! If he never saw her again, it would be too soon!

But as quickly as it struck, his anger vanished. He tried to summon it back, but the only real anger he felt was directed at himself for having been dumb enough to believe her when she said she loved him and would stay with him forever.

CHAPTER 15

Rachel walked along a lonely dirt road between towns in a mountainous district in Western Japan. Her clothing, a black full-length robe and small brown bib-like garment worn over the heart, signified her as belonging to the Zen sect of Buddhism. As night fell, she realized she had taken a wrong turn, and was lost. She continued along the same path and eventually saw a light at the top of a hill. There, she found a small hermitage built for solitary priests, called an "anjitsu." Inside was an elderly priest, but the old man refused to give her a night's lodging. Instead, he showed Rachel the path to a nearby town.

When she arrived, she saw it wasn't a modern town, but an ancient one without even electricity. At the town's only inn, she found some forty people had gathered. Nonetheless, the innkeeper gave her a room. Around midnight, the sound of loud weeping woke her. She got up and gently pushed the sliding doors apart.

The young innkeeper said to her, "We did not mean to disturb you, but yesterday my father died, and the people with me have come here to pay their respects and mourn his passing. When you arrived, you looked so tired, we did not wish you to feel awkward about staying with us, so we didn't tell you about the death. Now, as is our custom, we are saying goodbye to my father. We will not remain in the house with him for fear of demons, and we will spend tonight at the home of a distant neighbor. But since you wear the robes of a Buddhist monastic, I'm sure you have no such superstitions, and will be comfortable remaining in the inn."

Rachel replied, "I have no fear of staying in this house. But since I am a Buddhist, I will say prayers for your father and remain beside his body until you return."

Everyone then left the house except Rachel, who sat with the body. She recited the Buddhist service for the dead and performed the funeral ceremonies. After that she began to meditate.

In the deepest part of the night, a dark shape entered the room. She watched, terrified, as it formed into a ghoul with long, sharply pointed teeth and finger-nails. She wanted to run but couldn't move as the ghoul lifted the corpse and ate. The creature started with the head and crunched its way through hair and bones and shroud, slurping up blood and all other bodily fluids as it ate. The ghoul then eyed Rachel.

Tears sprang to her eyes as terror filled her. She couldn't breathe knowing she was about to die a horrible death. The ghoul came closer. It howled, and the sound rippled through her body. But then, to her surprise and joy, it turned away and left the room.

When the funeral party returned, a stricken Rachel, too scared to venture outdoors, told them what had happened.

The innkeeper explained it was a flesh-eating demon. It tormented the town, and that was why they no longer dared sit with a corpse through the night.

Rachel's reaction went from fear to anger. "Why doesn't that worthless old priest who lives in the anjitsu on the hill perform services for your dead and try to rid this area of the demon?"

The innkeeper said there was no anjitsu on the hill, and no old priest anywhere nearby.

Much confused, Rachel returned to the anjitsu and confronted the old priest. She asked why he didn't help the people in the town who were being persecuted by a vile demon.

The old priest answered, "Because I am that demon. And now, you are one as well."

The priest grabbed her, his fingers mutating into vicious claws, and immedi-ately the hermitage, the priest, and Rachel vanished.

In their place on the high grassy area stood two ancient and moss-covered tombs. One showed the priest's name in Japanese characters; the other, in Roman letters, spelled out: Rachel Gooding.

Ceinwen woke Rachel because she was thrashing and crying out in her sleep. Her face twisted with terror. She had thrown off the covers.

Ceinwen rushed the few steps to Rachel's bed and grabbed her shoulders giving her a gentle shake. "Wake up, Rachel. You're having a nightmare."

Rachel opened startled eyes, seeming to not even recognize Ceinwen for a moment, but then threw her arms around her.

Ceinwen could feel Rachael's heart racing, pounding. The girl was drenched with sweat, shuddering. "Are you all right?"

No answer. Just a week sob.

"I'm here, Rachel."

No answer again. Another sob, but a weak nod.

"Tell me about it."

"It's too horrible," Rachel whispered.

"I could guess that."

Ceinwen could tell Rachel was regaining her composure. She was no longer panting, and the look of terror had changed to one of utter bewilderment. Rachel sat up, but still held onto Ceinwen's hand.

"Did I wake up anyone?"

"You didn't. God only knows why not!"

Rachel looked surprised, but then a wry smile crossed her face. "We are sound sleepers in this family."

Ceinwen joined her smile. "You haven't lost your sense of humor."

"No, instead, I'm losing my mind."

"It was a dream Rachel. Your mind was telling you something, warning you."

"Perhaps."

"Maybe it has to do with the ordeals you went through two years ago."

Rachel shook her head. "It was weird, I mean, completely different from any of my other nightmares and trances and whatever."

"How?"

"To start, I wasn't in Idaho. It took place in Japan, and I've never even been there. I hardly know anything about it. It was crazy. Not only that, I was a Buddhist! I don't know a thing about that religion."

Ceinwen listened with fascinated horror as Rachel told her about the flesh-eating ghoul who killed her.

A long time passed before they were able to go back to sleep.

The next day, Rachel's parents took "the girls" over to Yellowstone Park to see the "Old Faithful" geyser, massive herds of elk and bison, and boiling and bubbling mudpots. They said Ceinwen couldn't be that close to one of the most famous parks in the country and not see it.

The following day, Ceinwen, Rachel, and her two brothers rode out to the brushland surrounding the farm. They planned to picnic alongside a pretty creek.

While the boys splashed in the creek, Rachel and Ceinwen sat under a tree enjoying the warmth of the day. Suddenly, Rachel stopped talking and stared off into space. Ceinwen didn't like the way her eyes had gone flat and emotionless. She had seen this before. She shook Rachel, but it did no good. Rachel was breathing and didn't seem to be in any distress, so, as in the past, Ceinwen waited, hard though it was. Fortunately, again as in the past, Rachel came out of the trance about ten minutes later.

"Rachel?" Ceinwen said. "Are you all right now?"

Rachel lifted her head, straightening her shoulders, but then seemed to crumble. She covered her face as terrible, wrenching sobs tore from her lips. "God, Ceinwen! They were all dead! All of them."

Ceinwen grabbed her arm. "Who was dead?"

"My brothers and sisters. Their kids." She couldn't stop her tears. "I think I'm putting them in danger being here. I've got to get away."

"What do you mean? Why would they be in danger?"

She covered her face. "I can't!"

"Tell me!"

"I don't know why I said that. I'm having nightmares. That's all."

"Why do you think you've got to get away?" Ceinwen insisted. "It has to do with what happened two years ago, doesn't it?"

Rachel looked as if she were at a breaking point. Her hands shook, and her face had lost all its color. "I haven't been out in brush like this since I was lost in that strange area north of the Salmon River." She tried to wipe away her tears but her efforts did little good. "I can never forget it, no matter how hard I try."

"You've got to keep fighting," Ceinwen said.

"It's as if something is here with me – not only inside my head, but *in me*. It's something alien to me, and evil, causing me to see images and people I've tried hard to forget."

"What kind of images?"

"I found my family dead and knew I was the cause. I ran out of the house, through the land shrieking for them to take me, to kill me instead.

Then, somehow, dead friends appeared and told me I need to go back to Salmon. That they need me there. That without me there, everyone would really die—that it would be more than a nightmare. It would come true. Then, one of them took my hand and held it tight as I watched him die all over again, just as he died two years ago."

"My God." Ceinwen rubbed Rachel's arm, and when she felt the girl's hand, it was ice cold—as if she were already dead. "It was a dream, Rachel, a terrible nightmare. Nothing more."

"Was it? Look." Rachel held out her hand, and Ceinwen could see that it had turned red, and where Rachel wore a simple birthstone ring, the fingers around the ring bore its imprint as if something had squeezed her hand tight.

Ceinwen gasped. Rachel hadn't moved the whole time she was in the trance. Never did one hand touch the other. Never could she have squeezed her own hand to make it look that way.

"I've to go back, Ceinwen."

"To Salmon?"

"That's right."

Ceinwen drew in a shuddering breath. Once, not long ago, she had hoped for this. From the safety of Oxford, she imagined traveling to the River of No Return wilderness and seeing for herself where the terrible disappearances of two years earlier had happened. But now, faced with actually going there, she wondered if this wasn't a terrible idea. "If you really think you should go," Ceinwen said softly, "I'm going with you."

Rachel shook her head. "It's far too dangerous."

Soon, Ceinwen told herself, all of this will make sense—logically and rationally. With strong resolve she said, "I've come this far. I'm not stopping now."

CHAPTER 16

MICHAEL ARRIVED at the Izumo Airport in western Japan, rented a car, and drove to the nearby town of Matsue.

Lafcadio Hearn had traveled to Matsue in 1890, soon after arriving in Japan, to work as an English teacher. He rented a house near the Matsue Castle, a place he had called, *"vast and sinister in shape ... made up of magnificent monstrosities."* The massive, medieval castle had multiple roofs, and most of the exterior walls were painted black.

In Matsue, Hearn began to write *Glimpses of Unfamiliar Japan* in which he described his first experiences in the little-known country. He also began recording Japanese ghost stories which eventually grew to several collections.

Matsue's coastal location meant that in winter it took the brunt of cold winds off the sea and snow from the surrounding mountains. Hearn suffered terribly from bronchitis during his first winter, and dreading another winter in such a climate, he accepted a better paying job teaching English and Latin at a government college in warmer Kyushu. It was a decision he often regretted.

As Michael parked his rental car near the castle, he noticed a sign reading, "Lafcadio Hearn Way." It was the lane Hearn had used to walk between his home and the castle.

From there, Michael found himself strolling along a dusty, pine-lined street in the heart of what had once been the town's samurai quarter. A number of the samurai homes remained. They had been built in the traditional Japanese style, raised up off the ground, with sliding panels as walls, and shoji screens to let in light.

Among them was Hearn's residence. Beside it was a memorial museum. Michael had spent so many hours reading Hearn's books and letters, he felt strangely gladdened to see the respect the town gave to his maybe-relative. The museum displayed a number of photos and first editions of Hearn's books and magazine articles, and the museum prominently displayed Hearn's Japanese name, Koizumi Yakumo.

Michael went from it to Hearn's house which was quite small, but its peaceful, beautiful garden drew him outdoors. Hearn had loved his garden, and wrote an essay, "In a Japanese Garden," describing how enchanted he was by it. He was pessimistic about such gardens lasting, however. Michael remembered his words:

These are gardens of the past. The future will know them only as dreams, creations of a forgotten art.

As Michael stood enjoying it, a middle-aged Japanese man came up to him. "Are you Doctor Michael Rempart?"

"I am."

The man bowed. "I am most pleased to meet you. I am Yamato Toru. I spoke to your assistant, Mr. Li."

Soon, the two men pleasantly conversed about Hearn and his writings. Yamato's English was good, and Michael found him interesting. When they discussed how Hearn left Matsue for Kyushu, Michael said, "Perhaps that is the next place I should visit."

"No, not to bother. Hearn-*sensei* did not like it there and regretted to leave Matsue. He said he wished he could fly back against stream of time, to life of tiny villages. That, he said, was real Japan. That Japan he loved."

Michael could well imagine Hearn saying such a thing. "I understand he never returned to Matsue."

"Not to live. He needed more money than Matsue could pay him. He lived many places in Japan, but one place he most loved, that he kept secret from other foreigners and fellow teachers, was village called Kamigawa. It is only sixty kilometers south of Matsue, in hills with view of sea."

"I haven't heard that," Michael said.

"He never wrote of it. He was guest of family of a student. Nakamura family. Family was wealthy, descendant of daimyo. As I am sure you know, daimyo were similar to feudal lords of European history. Samurai protected them."

"Are there still many daimyo families?" Michael asked.

"Yes, of course. Daimyo lost power when Emperor Meiji regained control of country. It was around time of Civil War in your own country. So, not so long ago. Now, many daimyo families retain land and wealth."

"That makes sense," Michael said.

"I am certain if you go to Kamigawa, Nakamura family will be most happy to show you their many artifacts, and also to allow you to see house where Hearn-*sensei* stayed."

"It's not far," Michael said. "I can do that."

"If you'd like, I have cousin in Kamigawa. She is ... what do you call? Realtor. I will phone her. She can meet you and show you house. Maybe you like to stay there. Vacation, just like Lafcadio did."

The offer surprised Michael and made him more than a little skeptical. It sounded like a scheme to rent an out-of-the-way property to gullible tourists—a Japanese version of "George Washington slept here." But he was willing to meet the fellow's cousin and view the house.

After getting instructions about the route to Kamigawa, and where to meet the realtor, he got into his car and phoned Jianjun.

"I did some searches," Jianjun said. "I haven't been able to find anything about Yamato Toru or any daimyo named Nakamura. Both are common names, and not a lot of Japanese history from that area has been digitized."

"Not to mention that you don't read Japanese, and it uses simplified versions of many Chinese characters," Michael said.

"There is that," Jianjun admitted. "But still—"

"You worry too much, Jianjun. I'm finding it nice here—beautiful, and with helpful people."

"Well, that's good," Jianjun said. "Just saying, be careful."

CHAPTER 17

WADE COX OPENED his eyes to see the first light of dawn in the sky. He'd had a dream—a horrible, terrifying dream—and his heart was pounding. Something, some creature wanted to kill him, and he was trying to run, but couldn't.

With a start, he saw that he wasn't in his bed, but outdoors, lying on the cold ground of his pasture. He sat up.

"What the hell?" he muttered, wondering why he was out here freezing his ass off instead of inside the warm cabin. Had he started sleepwalking at his age? What kind of old fool was he?

His aging bones ached from the cold and the ground. In the distance, he saw a light burning in the cabin window. He always slept with a light on. It made him feel less lonely somehow. He'd lived alone some fifteen years, ever since his wife got sick of the desolation of their life and ran off. They'd never been blessed with kids. Good thing, all in all.

Something on his chest felt weird, and he looked down to see that his shirt was sticking to his skin. Something dark was on it, and the smell, acrid and sharp, almost tinny, was all around him.

Blood? He jumped to his feet.

He fumbled for the cell phone in his pocket. It didn't do much good here—there was rarely any service, but it had other useful items, such as a flashlight. He turned it on and aimed it at his clothes.

They were dark red with blood, as were his hands. And at his feet lay his seven-inch boning knife, also covered with blood.

He directed the light to nearby land. A large object lay a few feet away, and he crept toward it.

He stared in horror. It was the mutilated body of his neighbor, Mitch Ivansen. Well, not exactly a neighbor—Mitch's land was ten miles away. What the hell was he doing here, on Wade's property, in the middle of the night?

Wade stumbled backward. He felt the blood sticking his shirt to his body. Bile rose in his throat as he stared at Mitch's dead, glazed over eyes, at his slashed and torn torso. He'd been carved open like in those autopsies they liked to show on TV crime programs.

Only then did Wade remember the boning knife. *His* boning knife, covered with blood.

Had he done this? He shook his head. No. No. It wasn't possible.

But would anyone believe Wade was innocent of this murder?

Wade thought about the sheriff in Salmon. The guy always had it in for him—even made him stay in jail one night just for having a couple too many drinks. Jake Sullivan would lock him up faster than a bat out of hell. Probably not even give him a chance to say he had nothing to do with Mitch's murder.

And what about the other ranchers? None of them were ever close to him. Not that he cared. At least, he never cared before.

He didn't have a choice. All he could do was pack as much stuff as he needed to survive out in the back country and run for his life. He'd need to stay out there a couple years, he guessed. He hadn't lived on this land all his life and not learned how to survive off it. When the time was right, he'd make his way to some big city where he could get lost in the crowd. Portland maybe, or Seattle, or Reno. Anywhere outside Idaho. He'd figure that out later. Right now, he had to pack and get as far away, and as fast, as he could.

And at that moment he heard a deep, reverberating howl, a howl that sounded not so much like that of a wolf, not even that of a man, but of something strange, nothing he'd ever heard before.

Wade Cox dropped to his knees and cried.

In the morning, Rachel and Ceinwen set out for Salmon.

Ceinwen saw that Rachel's family did not understand the way her life was now. As much as her parents and siblings were proud that one of the best schools in the world had granted her a scholarship, they didn't recognize that returning to the farm wasn't what she wanted to do with her life. After listening to her mother, sisters, and sisters-in-law talking about nothing but their kids and local gossip, Ceinwen found herself puzzling over how different Rachel was from everyone else in the family. In a university filled with intelligent people, Rachel was one of the smartest. She had breezed through assignments with an ease and skill that had stunned her professors. Rachel had indicated that while she'd always been an excellent student, only recently had she learned to focus to a degree that made her senior year and now graduate school surprisingly easy.

Ceinwen couldn't help but wonder if this exceptional braininess wasn't another fall-out from her Idaho experience.

Judging from the way her relatives sometimes gazed at her—as if she was no longer the person they knew—Ceinwen suspected that was the case.

Rachel borrowed the old Ford Taurus she had used while a student at BSU, and soon the two women were driving along Highway 28, a desolate stretch of road, into the mountains around Salmon.

Ceinwen had thought Idaho Falls looked like a throwback in time, but it was nothing compared to Salmon. One- and two-story buildings dominated Main Street. A few were in red brick, but most were wooden and looked like what one might find in an old Western town, with high façades and covered verandas whose roofs jutted out to shelter the sidewalks.

The sheriff's station was on Main Street, and parking was plentiful. They walked in.

"I'm here to see Sheriff Sullivan," Rachel said. "Is he available?"

"Not right now, ma'am." The deputy did a double-take. "You're Rachel Gooding."

She stiffened. "I am."

"Deputy Mallick." He held out his hand to shake hers. "I looked at your photo so many times a couple years back, I thought I'd never forget it. You've grown up some since those days."

"Life has been different for me, I'll admit that."

Mallick gave her a gentle smile, one filled with concern. "Can't say I'm surprised. I don't think it's been easy for anyone involved."

Ceinwen stepped forward and introduced herself.

"Let me call the Sheriff," Mallick said, picking up his phone. "He's just next door at the coffee shop."

In less than a minute the door opened and Jake Sullivan walked into the station. "Rachel, how great to see you."

She gave him a hug. "I'm glad to see you, too." She introduced him to Ceinwen.

Jake led them into his office.

"So, are you all done at Boise State?" he asked Rachel after they sat.

"Not only that," she said. "Given all I learned two winters ago, I did well and managed to get a full scholarship to a graduate program at Oxford. Ceinwen is my roommate there."

His eyebrows rose. "In England?"

Rachel chuckled at his surprise. "The one and only."

"A full scholarship. Congratulations! What area are you studying?"

"Archeology," she replied.

"I should have known. I mean, after all that, what else could you be studying? That's great." He faced Ceinwen. "And you go there, too?"

"Yes. Another student of archeology."

"Did I catch an accent?" he asked her.

"To me, it's you who have the accent, Sheriff," Ceinwen said with a smile. "I'm from Cardiff, Wales."

He nodded. "So, what brings you two way out here?"

"I'm home for the summer, and decided to drive up and see how everyone is doing," Rachel said. "And Ceinwen has never seen this part of the world, so she came with me."

"Well, welcome," he said.

"I was also wondering," Rachel said, twisting the inexpensive ring she wore. "Is everything okay here? Or, out in the wilderness?"

Jake tilted his head as he watched her. "Well, you know how it is. Anything strange happens and everyone worries."

She frowned. "In what way, strange?"

His eyes narrowed as they went from Rachel to Ceinwen. "Is there something you want to tell me about? Charming as Salmon is, I can't imagine this area has much interest for someone getting a degree from Oxford. For either of you."

Rachel gave Ceinwen a quick glance, then said, "Ceinwen has read about the deaths out here. She was a journalist."

"*A journalist?*" He regarded Ceinwen with a scowl

"I can tell you aren't a fan of the profession, Sheriff," Ceinwen said.

"Don't worry. I'm giving all that up for the pleasures of digging around in the muck trying to find old chips of pottery. It's a much cleaner profession than the one I left."

"I can well imagine," Jake said, still frowning.

"I've been having dreams," Rachel told him.

"Go on."

"First it was … I guess you'd call them demons. Always after me. Scary stuff."

Jake nodded. "Not surprising given what happened to you. PTSD, some call it."

"Well … perhaps. But then the dreams became more specific. They were about the wilderness, the place we went to after we stepped between the pillars. I was back there. The dreams—or, I should say, nightmares—affected my work. My professors thought I needed a rest. So I came home."

"And it hasn't helped?" he asked.

"Not at all. I…" She stopped. After a long moment, she said, "The dreams made me feel as if I needed to return to Salmon. I don't know why. All I know is I kept feeling it was time for me to return. But now that I'm here, I have no idea what I'm supposed to do."

"Things have been kind of rough for you, I take it," Jake said softly. Ceinwen noticed a level of understanding and compassion in his eyes as he regarded Rachel. More than ever she wondered what had happened that affected both a hardened middle-aged sheriff and a naïve coed so completely. And what were these pillars Rachel said they 'stepped between'?"

Rachel drew in her breath. "Yes. It started just a few weeks back."

"As the land thawed after a long winter," Jake murmured.

Ceinwen stared at him a moment, wondering what made him say that.

Rachel nodded, then said, "I keep having this feeling that I don't belong here, that I … I'm fading away. And it grows worse each day."

Jake shook his head, worry and dismay at her words contorting his features. "I'll confess I don't like what you're sensing, or that something has drawn you here."

"I'm sorry," she murmured.

"Rachel has no need to apologize," Ceinwen said. "It's not her fault. She's suffering, Sheriff. And if being here can help her, I'm all for it."

"I agree." His lips tightened. "Something is happening. I can feel it, too.

We've had strange mutilations. Strange deaths of livestock and pets. And recently, a man."

A chill rushed through Ceinwen at his words.

"What about the other students?" he asked Rachel. "Have you contacted them?"

"I tried. Devlin dropped out of school and refuses to think about it, and Brandi thinks so much she can't cope and lives in drug-induced hazes. I don't expect either will show up here anytime soon. I don't fault them for wanting to bury the past. I tried to with my studies. But I couldn't." She paused a moment. "All I did was end up making a spectacle of myself at school. I had to get away because if any of my professors learned about this, they would tell me I've gone mad, and that I should leave and never return."

So, Ceinwen thought, she now knew what had happened to the only other student survivors. She wished she could pull out her notebook, but didn't dare. Besides, the sheriff acted willing and able to lock up anyone he considered a danger to his friends.

"I know what you're saying about not wanting to tell anyone," Jake said to Rachel, then cast a warning scowl in Ceinwen's direction. "You're the first one I've admitted my own uneasiness to."

Ceinwen found that an odd thing for him to say. "Have you kept in contact with any of the other rescuers?" she asked. "With Michael Rempart? Or Charlotte Reed?"

Jake looked surprised by her question, but then glared in Rachel's direction, probably thinking she had told Ceinwen about them. "Charlotte stayed in Salmon until last week. I can't help but suspect, now that we've talked, that she was affected by whatever is going on around here as well. It's like her to try to dismiss any occult signs as 'stuff and nonsense' that couldn't be happening to anyone rational."

"Where is she now?" Rachel asked.

"Back home in Virginia."

Ceinwen heard the heartbreak in his voice. Now she understood why a woman with Charlotte Reed's background had stayed in this small town —because of its sheriff.

"I'm sorry," Rachel murmured.

"So am I. But I'm glad you came here to try to work this out. I'll help you, Rachel, anyway I can."

Ceinwen suspected Rachel was proof for him that something real was happening around Salmon—that the problem wasn't him, and it wasn't

Charlotte. And it was strong enough to affect a person in another continent.

Ceinwen asked, "Sheriff, what do you think is happening here?"

"All I can say is people aren't acting the way they should, the way they always have, and that includes me. Even ... even the woman who was living with me, Charlotte, isn't herself. She came to believe it was over between us, and nothing I said or did could convince her otherwise."

"It's strange she wouldn't believe you." Rachel said. "That's not the Charlotte I remember."

"The problem is, whatever's scrambled Charlotte's reactions have scrambled mine, too. I've been acting like a son of a bitch, yelling at my staff, even at Charlotte when she was here. And I questioned her feelings. I've been irritable. Nothing pleases me. The only one I've been able to hold a calm, civilized conversation with for the past few weeks has been, weirdly enough, Emily Parker—the woman Charlotte thinks I've fallen for. Sometimes I suspect I like her company because she doesn't know a damn thing about the past, so she isn't constantly studying me for any hint that it might all be starting up again. We've all been touched, branded. It doesn't go away. Like some goddamn curse."

"No one in England knew of my troubles except Ceinwen," Rachel murmured. "Yet they plagued me there."

He cast a suspicious gaze on Ceinwen. "Is that so?"

"If I wanted to hurt Rachel," Ceinwen said, "it would have been much easier to do something in England than here. I believe you can trust me."

"I trust her," Rachel said.

Jake wasn't placated. "How do we know she doesn't want to find out what happened out here two years ago just to write up an interesting story?"

Ceinwen shook her head, but said nothing.

"Have you ever gone back?" Rachel asked Jake.

Ceinwen noted that Rachel didn't need to say where.

"I didn't. I couldn't. We lost too much out there. I don't ever want to see it again. It took months for me to get over it. When I think of how close we all came to being killed ..." He shut his eyes a moment, his mouth hard.

Rachel nodded as if remembering of her own struggles. "I need to see it once more."

He frowned. "Why? For God's sake, Rachel. Nothing's out there anymore. We don't want to remember, to conjure up..."

Rachel's lips pursed. "I've got to do this. I can hire a guide."

"And I'll go with you," Ceinwen said.

"No," Jake said.

"You can't stop us," Ceinwen snapped. "I've always heard that this is a free country, and as such, we have the right to travel on public property. I understand the area Rachel speaks of is protected for the public's use."

"Cut the lectures, lady," Jake said. "I'm not saying, 'No, you can't go.' I'm saying Rachel isn't going out there alone with some goofy guide and a mouthy Brit who probably doesn't know a real wilderness from a stroll through Hyde Park. I'm going with you ... if we can find it."

Ceinwen folded her arms and faced Rachel. "John Wayne still lives, doesn't he?"

Rachel smiled. "We'll find the right spot. I'll know it when I see it, but if nothing else, I'll feel it."

Jake gave her a sad gaze. "That's what I'm afraid of."

CHAPTER 18

MICHAEL FOLLOWED the stranger's directions and an hour later was in Kamigawa. Rows of traditional Japanese buildings in dark wood with curved eaves on rooftop corners made it look like a movie set for a samurai film.

Yamato told him to park at the first petrol station and his cousin would find him. Michael did so, and almost immediately, an attractive woman approached. He got out of the car.

"Mr. Rempart? I am Kazuko, Yamato-*san's* cousin." She was petite, with short, carefully coiffed hair, and looked as if she were in her late twenties. "I understand you wish to see the house where Lafcadio Hearn stayed."

"I would."

"Good. We can walk to the house. It is very convenient. Near shops and restaurant. We have one."

"One?"

"One restaurant."

Michael nodded. They went two long blocks and then turned onto a small street that led up a steep hill. As they walked, Kazuko proudly told him a little of the town's history, how it had once been an important place because a daimyo chose to live there rather than in the Matsue Castle during the days of the Tokugawa shogunate.

When they neared the top of the street, Kazuko stopped at a tall wooden gate within a six-foot high wall. She unlocked the gate and held it open.

Michael entered a small attractive garden with a gravel pathway leading to a "samurai" house.

"The house is old and small, but in good condition," Kazuko said. "Of course, we have many modern homes and apartments available. They may be more comfortable for an American if you wish to spend time in Kamigawa, perhaps to look at the Nakamura daimyo collection."

"I'm not interested in staying," Michael said, "although I may return to view the collection. But today, I just wanted to see the house." He stepped up onto what he would call a veranda that ran along the outside of the building under the roof line. Entering the house, he found himself in a small foyer with a cabinet of low shelves that held thin, backless slippers. The polished hardwood floors of the main part of the house were a step up from the foyer. Kazuko removed two pairs of slippers from a shelf, one large and one small. She placed the slippers on the hardwood floor and then, in a smooth motion, she stepped from her shoes into the slippers, taking care never to put her stockinged foot on the floor of the foyer, or *genkan,* as she called it. She waited for him to do the same.

He knew that wearing street shoes to walk on tatami, a woven reed, was the social equivalent of entering a person's home in the West and spitting on the carpet. He felt about as graceful as an elephant as he removed his loafers and stepped into the slippers.

Kazuko then led him from the hallway to a room with a tatami floor. The smell of the woven reeds was pleasant—a hint of nature—and helped the sense of bringing the outside in. As he took in the room devoid of furniture except for a low table and four large pillows around it, sunlight streamed through the white shoji screens, casting the room in a soft glow. Panels of sliding doors that could be opened wide made up the home's interior walls.

"Beautiful," he murmured.

She pitter-pattered down the hall with a pleasant sway to her hips. He followed her to a tiny kitchen, then to a Japanese-style bathroom with an *ofuro*—a steep-sided wooden bathtub. The toilet facilities were also Japanese, which meant floor level.

"Do not worry, Michael-*san,*" Kazuko said with a slight grin. She led him up the stairs to the second floor. It had a Western-style bedroom with a queen-size bed, and a bathroom complete with a Western-style toilet and shower. "Sometimes Westerners stay here for a brief visit. They are happy to have facilities they are accustomed to."

"Very nice," Michael said. The house was the type he would have wanted if he were to stay any amount of time in Japan.

"Now, I have a pleasant surprise," she said when they were back on the main floor. She stepped from the slippers into her shoes, and Michael did the same—less awkwardly this time. They walked around the house to the back garden, which was smaller than the one in front.

There, he saw a wooden shed-like building. She unlocked the door and opened it. "This little building has been set up to use as an office."

He looked inside to see a floor with a carpet, a desk, a computer, and even an ergonomic desk chair. Regular sash-windows were on two walls.

As he entered, she said, "Western businessmen who have rented this property have needed this convenience, so we provide it to all our renters."

"You've thought of everything, it seems." He put his hands on his waist as he looked over the space, and then walked around the back garden. It was less lush, although every bit as peaceful as the one in front. The peace and beauty of the setting were worming their way into his heart. He could imagine himself working out here and enjoying the traditional house at other times of the day.

Disappointment struck as he watched Kazuko lock up both buildings, and then the front gate. "Perhaps you would like some tea and something to eat before you head back to your hotel," she said with a warm smile. "Our restaurant has delicious sushi. Very fresh. Also, I can help you make an appointment with the Nakamura family if you would like."

"That sounds good," he said, not mentioning that he didn't yet have a hotel. There were plenty of places to stay back in Matsue, so he wasn't worried. But the thought of the house he'd just left intrigued him more with each passing minute.

They walked back to the main street. He saw a group of children get off a school bus and run towards their homes. They looked happy and cute in their public school uniforms.

When they reached the restaurant, the doors were open and inviting. Over tea and sushi, Michael asked about the cost of renting the house. When he heard how reasonable it was, that he could rent it by the week, and it was immediately available—he decided to take it.

Kazuko had him fill out rental papers as she spoke on her cell phone to the owners about their potential tenant. The town might have been remote, but the communications weren't, and Kazuko soon got an okay from the owners as well as Michael's credit card company as he put down a deposit. With that, she gave him the keys.

"I believe you will be happy there," she said. "I felt as if the Hearn house, as everyone here calls it, welcomed you."

He studied the keys in his hand. "That must be it," he murmured. "I didn't expect to like it this much."

"I'm glad." She used a napkin to draw a map to a grocery store in case he wanted to stock up on some food and such, and then promised to check in with him the next day to be sure everything was in order, and to answer questions he might have. "Since they now know where to reach you, the Nakamura's will contact you directly as necessary."

Michael wasn't sure why this was all happening so quickly and conveniently for him, but he felt good about the outcome. He didn't mind relaxing here for a week. How was such a place not well-known?

He stopped at the store for instant coffee, beer, and snack foods, and then picked up his car at the petrol station and drove back to the house. After unlocking the gate, he stepped into the garden—*his* garden.

Two men waited for him there. He stiffened, but both men placed their hands on their thighs and bowed low. When they stood upright again one man said, "Doctor Rempart?"

It took a moment for Michael to understand that his name was being said since the Japanese "r" was much softer than that used by Americans. "Yes I'm Michael Rempart."

"Please." The man handed Michael a note and then stepped back as if waiting for a reply.

Dear Dr. Rempart,

Welcome to Kamigawa. I am Nakamura Seiji, descendant of daimyo of Shimane Prefecture in the time of Tokugawa. I am honored to welcome you here. Please attend dinner at my home tomorrow at 5:00.

Nakamura

Michael read the note twice, then faced the two men. "Please tell Mr. Nakamura that I'll be happy to attend." At the blank looks on their faces, he shortened his answer. He remembered reading somewhere that "hi" meant "yes" in Japan, and "ohio"—like the state—meant "good morning." He wished he'd paid more attention. He gave it a try. "Yes. Hi."

"Ah, *hai!*" Both men smiled and repeated *"hai"* several times as they bowed and then left the garden.

CHAPTER 19

"I TELL YOU, the guy fucking disappeared. Right before our eyes. We were following his car along the coast, staying back a bit, sure. We didn't want him to pick up on being tailed. Anyway, the road curved and when we came around, his car was gone. We sped up, way over the speed limit, but couldn't find him. We went back to see if he'd turned off the highway, but there were only a couple side roads, and we didn't see him there either."

He waited, listening to furious ranting coming from the other end of the phone line.

"Of course, we were following the right guy. There aren't many 6'2" Westerners hanging around the Lafcadio Hearn Museum, believe me. We knew it was him the minute he showed up."

More ranting.

"Okay, okay. We'll ask at the museum, then will search. Up and down the highway, I know ... I know ... We'll find him. You can count on it."

Rachel and Ceinwen spent the night in an inexpensive Salmon motel. Both scarcely slept.

They met Jake before dawn at the sheriff's station. Only by getting a very early start would they make the round trip in one day. He had borrowed three quarter horses from a rancher friend, and a three-horse slant load trailer to move them.

"I guess I should have asked if you know how to ride," Jake said to Ceinwen. "If not, you could wait here for us."

"I've ridden," Ceinwen said. "We do have horses in England."

"That's right. You go after little foxes, don't you? Here, we go after grizzlies."

"Now he's Grizzly Adams," Ceinwen said to Rachel. To her surprise, Jake grinned at the comment.

Rachel sat between the two in the truck. They headed north to the Salmon River, and then westward along the Salmon River Road until it became no more than a footpath. There, Jake turned onto a fire road that was even worse.

Ceinwen was awed by the beauty of the Salmon and the high mountains edging it. "I never quite knew what you Americans meant when you sang about 'purple mountains majesty.' Now, I do."

Even Jake seemed pleased by that statement.

They rode in silence until Rachel faced Jake. "You didn't mention Michael Rempart. Have you heard from him?"

Jake flashed her a quick, cautious glance, then went back to watching the narrow roadway. "I saw him once last year. He came here with some weird ass story about a pearl with demons. I didn't understand half of it. Charlotte seemed to. More power to her, is all I can say."

"But you haven't heard from him lately?"

"No, and I think Charlotte would've mentioned if she had." But then he added, "Or, maybe not."

"What was that about a pearl with demons?" Ceinwen asked, ignoring his odd remark.

"It made no sense to me," Jake admitted. "The pearl supposedly gives demons power, so he wanted to keep it away from them."

"I should hope so," Ceinwen said dryly. The story sounded ludicrous.

Jake snorted. "Yeah, me, too. Even crazier, was that rare earth elements neutralize the demons. Since we have rare earth elements in the mountains of Idaho, I can't help but wonder if he hid the pearl here. Who knows? Maybe it's working. I haven't seen any red men with horns and forked tails scurrying about. Lots of other weird stuff, though."

"Strange," Ceinwen said. "I don't know anything about Michael Rempart, other than he was once popular enough for a show on American TV. Not sure if that's impressive or not. I've also been told he's quite a good archeologist, but seems to have retired since the strangeness out here two years ago. What's your opinion? Is he a weird duck?"

"Not really," Jake admitted. "Although a lot of what he says is gobbledygook to me. But Charlotte likes the guy—quite a bit, in fact. And she's usually a good judge of character."

"I wonder if Michael has retired," Rachel said. "My professors were saying he's been quiet since finding a Han tomb in Mongolia. Anyway, maybe he'll come back here and help us figure out what's happening."

"You'd have to ask Charlotte what he's up to," Jake said gruffly. "In fact, I wish you would. And tell her all you told me. I think she'd be interested. Maybe if Michael was going to show up, she'd come back."

Rachel cocked her head slightly at his tone. "I'll do it. Of course."

He grimaced. "Oh, happy day."

Ceinwen wondered what all the sarcasm was about. "Do you really think he might come here?"

Jake rolled his eyes.

"I don't know how to get hold of him," Rachel said. "If I did, I certainly would let him know something's going on. He's the one who saved … I mean, he understands a lot of this stuff."

"Understands what? And saved what?" Ceinwen asked. "Are you saying whatever happened here had to do with archeology?"

"Well, no," Rachel said. "Not exactly."

"Hell," Jake muttered. "We'll try to get Michael here if we need him, okay? Then you, and all the other women within a hundred miles can come see him. I don't know why all you women like those dark, moody, brooding types. Not when there are guys like, well, *me* around."

Ceinwen and Rachel couldn't help but laugh.

"Ouch! That hurt, ladies," Jake said, clearly trying to lighten the mood. "But, anyway, I guess the guy's pretty much okay. Most of the time."

"Frankly," Rachel said, "he kind of scared me."

Jake snorted. "I hate to admit it, but there were times he scared me, too."

A scary archeologist? As Ceinwen thought about her nerdy professors, she couldn't begin to imagine such a thing.

When the fire trail ended, they led the horses from the trailer and saddled them up. The horses would quickly and easily get them to the site Rachel both feared and yet felt eager to see once more.

As they rode northward, Rachel admitted to being glad Jake had accompanied them. She would have been completely lost if she had tried to direct a guide out here.

The land was dotted with pine and fir trees, and low-lying scrub brush. Because of the heavy snows of winter, strong winds, high altitude, and harsh terrain, little vegetation grew, and few animals of any kind lived there. Not even the various Indian tribes that made Idaho and Montana home had ever inhabited that particular area, and when forced to cross it, they would travel as quickly as they could to make their way out of the inhospitable, dangerous land.

The three rode for a couple of hours before reaching a cliff that overlooked the small valley they searched for.

"I remember the wonder I felt when I first stood on this cliff and looked out at the valley," Rachel said. "In its center was what looked like a perfectly shaped symmetrical mound of earth in the form of a pyramid with the top lopped off. It was some twenty feet tall and forty feet across. At the top, two granite pillars soared high into the sky. The pillars were stark and frightening, and at their very tops were Egyptian hieroglyphics."

"Did you say hieroglyphics?" Ceinwen asked. She was dumbfounded at Rachel's description. All she saw, now, was a small, flat valley.

"That is *not* for publication!" Jake insisted.

"Of course," Ceinwen agreed.

He went on. "Charlotte is a scholar of ancient Egypt, so she recognized a few of the symbols, but no one could explain how such symbols—let alone the pillars—came to exist in the middle of Idaho."

As Ceinwen looked at the landscape, she couldn't imagine the scene they were describing. Still, something eerie and surreal hovered over the land, and it was clear to her the two were telling the absolute truth. Or, what they *believed* was true. She couldn't help but wonder about the true depth of Charlotte Reed's knowledge. Egyptian hieroglyphics in Idaho? She didn't think so.

Still, as she studied the valley the hair on her arms seemed to stand on end. "This place is creepy," she admitted. "What happened out here? Where are the pillars and the pyramid-like mound now?"

Neither Rachel nor Jake answered.

She drew in a deep breath as she followed them down the steep hillside to the valley floor, taking care to find a route that the horses could easily walk.

Up ahead, Jake suddenly stopped and dismounted. Rachel and

Ceinwen did the same, then holding the reins, approached to see what troubled him.

The land before them was shaped like a giant bowl or basin with steep, sloping sides. The ground was black, as if it were a field of charcoal rather than soil. They inched forward and saw that in the center of the "bowl" was an enormous round hole. It was as if they were ants standing on the edge of a funnel. From where they stood, although the sun was high in the sky, they couldn't see how deep the hole went. Jake took a couple of steps onto the lip of the funnel, but when he did, the rocks slid under his feet and he had to scramble back up to the flat land. Ceinwen grabbed his hand to steady him. It looked as if anyone who went over the side would very likely slide, unable to stop, into the hole.

Jake found a rock and heaved it as close to the hole as he could. It didn't make it all the way, but as they suspected would happen, when the rock landed the burnt coals gave way and slid toward the hole, taking the rock with them. The three listened for the "kerplunk" that told them it had landed.

They never heard it.

They glanced at each other and backed away.

"Let's get out of here," Jake said.

"Do you see that black cloud?" Rachel murmured, staring straight ahead.

"Where?" Ceinwen scanned the sky, but didn't see anything.

"What is it?" Rachel cried, her voice filled with fear.

"Look, it's over there!" Jake said, eying the area to his right as he drew his Smith and Wesson. "Let's go! There are too many."

"Too many *what?*" Ceinwen cried, looking where he indicated but seeing nothing.

They were about to mount their horses when they heard a loud gunshot. It sounded quite close. The horses whinnied and reared in fright.

Rachel couldn't hold on to her horse and he ran off. Ceinwen threw herself onto the saddle, holding on tight as her horse bolted to follow Rachel's.

She glanced back to see Jake struggling to calm his horse at the same time as he was trying to reach Rachel.

Ceinwen's horse didn't slow down until it reached a narrow stream. Only then could she regain control. Rachel's horse was in the water taking a drink. Ceinwen managed to take hold of his reins along with her own horse's.

She took out her cell phone and, as expected, had no service. She couldn't even send a text. Around her was nothing but rocks and a few scraggly bushes near the water. A feeling of panic struck. What if something happened to Jake and Rachel? Who knew she was out here? What if no one could find her?

She fought to stay calm, but thoughts of the University group that disappeared came to her. There had been eight of them, and they could not be found. She was only one.

All the words about this area: roadless, wilderness, uninhabited, deadly, came at her in all their full, frightening meaning.

She didn't even know which direction to go in. The hillside they had descended wasn't visible, and she realized how completely alone she was out here. Not even the sound of a breeze broke the complete silence. Her heart pounded with unnamed fear and her mouth turned dry as she considered her options. They weren't great. The best thing to do, she believed, was to wait.

Two very long hours later, she began to think waiting was hopeless, and she might need to try to find her way back alone. She stood, doing all she could to muster her courage when she heard a faint cry.

She held her breath, listening. Again … it was her name. Yes, her name!

She answered, loud as she could, and soon spotted her friends in the distance. She waved her arms, running toward them.

"Are you all right?" Rachel called. She was seated behind Jake and slid off his horse when they reached Ceinwen.

"I'm fine, and beyond glad you found me," Ceinwen said, breathless and joyful as she gave Rachel a big hug. "But that was the damnedest thing. Did you see who was shooting at us?"

"It wasn't a gunshot," Rachel said, her eyes wide with fear. "It came from the black clouds."

"Clouds?" Ceinwen repeated.

"I think she means clouds of dust," Jake said. He, too, sounded nervous and even a bit shaky. "They were some real bad asses, and all carried massive cudgels."

Rachel stared at him with confusion. "What are you talking about? The cloud surrounded a coven of witches, horrible creatures. Somehow, they were able to fly and zoomed toward us, cackling and throwing fireballs that made booming noises. I don't know how they didn't catch us."

"Flying witches?" Jake scoffed. "What did they use? Broomsticks?"

"You saw them, too!" Rachel insisted. "You ran from them!"

"Not from witches," he said. "I saw something, yes—huge, strong ... ogres, I think they're called. More than a dozen."

"And I saw none of that," Ceinwen said as her gaze swiveled between them. "But it sounds as if you both saw your scariest fantasies come to life."

Jake looked stunned by her words, but quickly recovered. "All I know is, we need to get the hell out of here. Whatever's out there probably wants us dead."

"Maybe you have enemies out here," Ceinwen said, "who may or may not want you dead. But I saw and heard nothing, while you two rattle on about witches, ogres, and thunderbolt ICBMs. Either you two have serious traumatic delusions from your previous ordeal, or you're having flashbacks from having been drugged back then."

Jake made no reply. He spat on the ground and turned away. He was obviously both angry and frustrated.

Rachel moved closer to Ceinwen. Her eyes held a stark intensity as she spoke in a low, solemn voice. "This place is like no other. It's an intersection where two planes of reality meet and interact, one trying to dominate the other. I don't understand it, but it is real. As real as our favorite pub in Oxford. Jake and I and others have lived in this reality and in a way it's always, always with us. Be glad you don't see what we see. You're free."

Rachel broke eye contact and backed away. For one of the rare times in her life, Ceinwen was speechless. Her well-honed skepticism was shocked, outraged. But in the back of her mind, she couldn't deny the force of Rachel's words, or that they held a ring of truth.

Finally, she mumbled, "Okay. Okay, I'll think about it. A lot. But now, like Jake said, let's get the hell out of here."

CHAPTER 20

MICHAEL AWOKE the next morning to discover that the power was out. It must have gone out during the night because his cell phone's battery was dead. Fortunately, the house had gas for cooking, so he could make himself coffee.

The electricity remained out all day. The shops, where he went to stock up on food and supplies, must have run on generators. No one seemed surprised or worried about the power situation, so he guessed it was a frequent problem here. In fact, he enjoyed the time away from the internet.

As dinnertime approached, Michael found he need not have worried about locating the Nakamura house. All he had to do was to say "Nakamura" and people pointed up the hill from the Hearn house. He walked and soon reached a large estate with a view of the entire town at its feet.

Michael was near the front gate when a man wearing a dark brown *yukata* over black slacks ran out to him, bowed low, and led him into the house where an elegant, middle-aged woman met him. She wore a silk dress with a Western style cut, but the delicate bamboo pattern on a sky-blue background was pure Japanese. She waited while Michael switched to slippers, and as soon as he stepped up to the tatami floor, she bowed and said, "Thank you for coming to my home." Her voice was low and pleasant. "I am Nakamura Haruko."

"Thank you for the invitation," Michael said.

"First, I must apologize that we are without electricity. A power pole has gone down. It should be back sometime tomorrow, but often one such problem leads to others. Kamigawa is remote, and our infrastructure old, so these things happen frequently. The good news is it will give you a sense of living in old Japan. Also you'll find gas lines for cooking and kerosene lamps, as well as battery-powered lamps and candles throughout your house."

"It's not a problem at all," he said.

"Good. Thank you for being understanding. Now, I will bring you to meet my son, Nakamura Seiji—oh, excuse me, I should say Seiji Nakamura in the Western manner. If we were still a daimyo family, Seiji would be called Lord Nakamura, daimyo of this entire region."

She said the words proudly, but Michael also recognized that she was explaining the family situation, and that she was widowed. He nodded to show he understood.

Her voice was hushed as she added, "Also, you should know, my son is very ill."

"I'm sorry to hear that."

"The doctors cannot say what is wrong with him, but I fear that he will die if we do nothing. His affliction came over him one year ago, and it has steadily grown worse."

"I imagine," Michael said, not sure how proper it was to talk about this, "you've taken him to some of the world's top specialists."

"Of course." She dropped her gaze a moment before adding, "Switzerland, the US, France, China—we tried everywhere. Some doctors said he needed psychiatric help, that he suffered some psychosis that is causing him to make himself ill." She stared hard at Michael. "Such doctors are fools."

Her vehemence surprised him.

"I am hoping you can help him, Doctor Rempart."

Michael couldn't have been more shocked. "Me? I'm so sorry, but I'm not a medical doctor. I've been a visiting professor at several universities. It's a tradition there for those of us with a doctorate—mine is in Archeology—to be called doctor. It seems you may have been misled. If so, I'm sorry."

"I know exactly who you are. And *what* you are. As I said, medical doctors have not helped us. Psychiatrists were less than useless. Once we ruled out any physical issues, my son and I were forced to face what we both know." She raised her chin defiantly. "My son is being attacked by a demonic presence."

Michael drew in his breath, stunned that she would make such a declaration so openly, without apology or embarrassment. "Most people contact a Catholic priest when they feel that way."

Mrs. Nakamura's eyes turned cold. "This situation has nothing to do with Christianity."

"Demons don't care what the beliefs are of a person they possess."

"I have an idea what is trying to harm my son. Our family goes back centuries, and many strange stories are told about us. One legend said that demons were brought here by early emissaries from China, and that they were the reason our family's most powerful daimyo went mad."

Michael regarded the woman carefully. She appeared serious. "Why tell me this?"

"A friend of my family was in China last year. He heard a strange tale of an archeologist who found the perfectly preserved body of a Chinese woman in a two-thousand year old tomb in Mongolia. It was an intriguing tale involving alchemy. Later, this same archeologist was accused of leaving China with a pearl that once belonged to the Mongol emperor, Kublai Khan. They say the pearl is really a philosopher's stone with the power to control demons."

"You can't believe everything you hear," Michael told her.

She smiled. "Nor can you believe all denials. I know you are that archeologist."

"How did you find me?"

"It wasn't easy. And then, even after we found you, we knew it would be impossible to convince you to come to Japan unless something here was of interest, so we decided to offer you the chance to go through our family's collection of treasures. We believe some date back to the ninth or tenth centuries." She smiled. "I suspect that's why you're here."

"Actually, it had more to do with an interest in Lafcadio Hearn."

"Of course it did." Her words made his nerves stand on end. But then she smiled. "A fortuitous coincidence, perhaps. My hope, now, is that we aren't too late to help my son."

This scenario suddenly bothered Michael and reminded him of Jianjun's skepticism of the "coincidences" that brought him here. "I'm afraid you've wasted your time." His words were firm. "I should leave."

She placed a delicate hand on his forearm. "Don't judge me too harshly until you meet Seiji and see what I'm dealing with." She cocked her head slightly. "Please come with me."

She led him down a long corridor and then slid open the door and said a few words to the people inside. She stepped aside for Michael to enter.

The same two men who had visited him the night before sat side-by-side near the far wall. Dominating the room was a young man surrounded by pillows. He leaned against the wall behind him.

"This is my son, Nakamura Seiji, heir to all the Nakamura holdings."

Michael stepped closer to see a pale young man, so thin Michael could all but count the bones of his face. He looked like he might be, at most, in his early 20s. A greenish undertone colored his ivory skin, and his eyes held no luster. "It's good to meet you," Michael said with a bow of the head. "Thank you for asking me to your home."

"The pleasure is mine, Doctor Rempart," Seiji said. His voice was reedy and weak. "I have heard much about you. Please have a seat."

Michael folded his long legs to sit on the floor pillow. "Most of what is said about me is not even half true. I hope you won't be too disappointed."

"I'm afraid I have suffered the same fate." A brief smile touched the young man's face. "People expect me to be as strong as daimyo were in the past. But that's not me, I'm sorry to say. I'm glad I have no such power, and would not wish it. That troubles people."

"It shouldn't," Michael said.

"Perhaps." Seiji nodded. "Nevertheless you must understand that because of my position in this community, we must keep quiet about my illness and what I believe is behind it."

"Yes," Michael murmured.

"We will give you access to our family's collection of artifacts," he continued. "And all we have learned about alchemy."

"I've never heard that alchemy was practiced in this country," Michael admitted.

"There is much you, as a Westerner, will not have heard about. But if you help me, those secrets will be opened to you. That is my pledge."

"And if I say 'no'?"

"That is your prerogative. But I assure you, you will spend the rest of your life regretting it and wondering what you passed up."

At this, Michael grinned. "You've done your homework. You've found out that one of my worst faults is an abundance, perhaps an overabundance, of curiosity."

"And so, we agree?"

"We agree."

"Sumimasen." Mrs. Nakamura stepped forward. She faced Michael and bowed. "I am sure this conversation has tired my son. He slept poorly last night in anticipation of meeting you, wondering what you would be like, and if all our preparation will have come to nothing. He must rest. Also, the dinner we promised you is ready."

Michael could see that the young man was exhausted. He stood.

"Will you come back tomorrow?" Seiji asked.

"If you would like," Michael said.

"How about noon? We can eat lunch and talk."

Mrs. Nakamura said, "I'm sure my son will be much stronger tomorrow."

Michael gave Seiji a slight bow. "I'll see you then."

After their goodbyes, Michael followed Mrs. Nakamura to a beautiful room with a tatami floor, a rich teak table, and an intricately painted scroll in an inset in the wall.

He sat at the low table, Mrs. Nakamura across from him. A young woman knelt between them and poured sake.

"I hope you like what we have prepared," Mrs. Nakamura said.

"I'm most grateful for your hospitality."

"We are happy to have you here. It is a comfort to have someone to share the burden of what is happening to Seiji. He is a sweet and gentle boy, but this thing inside him is quite different." Her lips tightened, and she looked down as if she might have already said too much. "In any case, we will send you breakfast and dinner each day. For breakfast, is a Western one to your liking? Perhaps eggs, bacon, pancakes, corn flakes?"

Michael smiled. "Coffee and toast is all I usually eat in the morning. But you don't have to do any of that. I'll do fine between the shops and the restaurant."

"First of all," she said firmly, "our cook is much better than the one at the restaurant. And also, I remember reading how your relative, Lafcadio Hearn, thought he would 'do fine' when he first came to Japan. Between the harsh winter, and him not having any idea how to cook Japanese style or even to get around easily, he nearly died. It took a good woman to help him. Now, I'm not saying I will try to find you a wife, Doctor Rempart, but to avoid that necessity, you must allow me to do all I can to make your stay here an easy one."

Again, Michael couldn't help but smile. He found her a charming hostess. "Given those alternatives, I have little choice than to accept a light breakfast and dinner from you. But how do you know Lafcadio Hearn might be a relative? I only learned that over the past couple of weeks."

It was her turn to smile. "As I mentioned, we did a most thorough study of you." She then gave a nod to a woman standing in the doorway. "It is time, now, for dinner."

CHAPTER 21

BECAUSE OF THE misadventure with the horses, it was dark by the time Jake, Rachel, and Ceinwen reached Jake's truck. The road, or lack of road, was too treacherous to travel at night. Jake kept plenty of water and supplies in the truck, and Ceinwen had brought a goodly stash of chocolate and energy bars. They camped for the night. Jake made a fire, and they took turns keeping watch.

Idaho was far enough north that summer nights were short, and at first light, they started back.

They had spoken little the night before, too busy thinking about the strangeness they had witnessed, and what it meant. But that morning things were different.

"Whatever we saw back there," Jake said as they began the long drive to Salmon, "it wasn't anything like what we've seen in the past."

"If you don't mind an outsider's opinion," Ceinwen said, "I've got an idea."

"Go ahead," Jake said, his voice not exactly friendly.

"I think someone is trying to frighten the people in this area," she began. "In Salmon, where everyone is already nervous, that person or group of people have been going around mutilating animals in ways sure to freak out anyone who's used to working with and raising livestock for a living."

"That's a possibility," Jake frowned. "But why?"

"That, I can't tell you," Ceinwen said. "But I suspect that once they learned Rachel was in town, they could expect she would head for the spot we just left. They created something scary—the big hole—and then pumped a hallucinogen into the air when we got near it. There are hallucinogens that cause a person to think they see whatever is most scary to them. Obviously, this one tapped into your childhood fears."

"You're talking mind control." Jake scoffed. "I don't think so."

"No. Not mind control. Some type of drug. I've seen what they can do, although the drugs I saw were administered orally or intravenously. The only surprise here is the method of delivery—airborne."

"But you didn't see anything," he reasoned.

"And you've both spoken about nightmares. What if these people, who must know your past, hacked your computers or smart phones and are using a variety of mind-control means—flashing sub rosa images onto the screen, for example—to fill your minds with the stuff of nightmares and these visions?"

"I know what I saw," Rachel said. "And it was real."

"If it wasn't real," Jake faced Ceinwen, "how about that deep hole?"

"We don't know it was a deep hole," Ceinwen said. "For all we know, it's not in the least deep, and down there might be a mattress or something equally soft, so when you tossed the rock, it made no noise when it landed. Just look at the stuff movie sets can do. What they did out there is child's play to anyone who understands that stuff. The question is why is anyone going to the expense and trouble of all this? What's to be gained? It's got to be financially rewarding. Do you know, Sheriff? Is there anything out here that someone does *not* want others to find?"

"Not that I know of. The Salmon used to have gold, but it was mined out in the last century. I don't buy that this is all an elaborate trick."

"Come on, Sheriff. You, of all people, can't believe in witches and ogres." Ceinwen looked at him as if he would be crazy not to buy her theory.

Rachel spoke out. "I wish, Ceinwen, you were right. If we never saw the other things we did, I'm sure we'd be thinking the same as you. But what we saw was real. It's a different reality, a mysterious reality." Rachel's voice was intense, challenging Ceinwen to disagree. Ceinwen said nothing. Then, in a conciliatory tone, Rachel added, "You know, Jake, Charlotte is always looking for practical answers. What if you run Ceinwen's theory past her? Do you think we should call her when we get back?"

Finally, Jake's expression brightened. "If I know Charlotte, she'll love tackling it."

Ceinwen pursed her lips as she looked from one to the other. "Maybe if I knew what *other things* you two have seen, I'd be more accepting of your take on all this. But I don't know. When you're ready to tell me about it, about everything that happened two years ago, I'm all ears."

Their silence was a loud and clear reply.

When they reached the Sheriff's station, Jake gave Charlotte's phone number to Rachel. When she called, Charlotte answered.

Rachel explained to Charlotte that she and a girlfriend were in Salmon with Jake, and she was putting the call on speaker. She then told Charlotte about the nightmares she had been having, talked about going to the spot where the pillars had once stood, and how something there had tried to attack them.

"What do you mean, something?" Charlotte asked.

"I can't really say," Rachel confessed. "I mean, if I said I saw something that looked like a group of flying witches, you'd think I'm crazy, right? But Jake also saw something—an army of ogres—but Ceinwen didn't see a thing. Anyway, all I can say is that we were scared, they moved fast, and if we didn't have horses, they would have caught up with us. Now, I should tell you that Ceinwen, who has spent most of her career as a journalist writing about and debunking supernatural phenomena, is as rock-solid a realist as you'll ever want to meet." Rachel gave Charlotte a quick explanation of Ceinwen's theory of airborne hallucinogens.

"Hmm—that's an interesting position," Charlotte said. "But, a journalist?"

"She's okay," Rachel said. "I trust her. Also, Jake has had several strange animal deaths out here, and now he's investigating the death of a poacher. I can't help but think everything is related to what we saw today."

"So, it wasn't just me feeling that something odd is happening out there," Charlotte said.

"Jake feels it, too," Rachel said.

"He does? Why in the hell didn't the big oaf tell me that?"

"I don't know," Rachel murmured. She couldn't help but smile as Jake winced.

"Rachel, you said your nightmares brought you back to Salmon, correct?" Charlotte asked.

"Correct."

"But if Ceinwen is right, why would these tricksters, whoever they are, want you back there?"

"We don't know," Rachel admitted.

"It's bizarre." Charlotte sounded skeptical.

Rachel asked if Charlotte knew how to contact Michael Rempart. Charlotte promised to text his number and also that of his assistant in case Michael was at some out-of-reach dig site.

"Thanks," Rachel said. "And do you think you'll be back in Salmon soon?"

There was a long pause. "I'm not sure," Charlotte said.

They soon said their goodbyes, and Rachel hung up to find a dismayed Jake.

"I wish she seemed more willing to come home," he lamented.

"I expect she will. Give her time." Just then, she received Charlotte's promised text.

Rachel read it. "I guess I should try to reach Michael." Her call didn't go through, and her text had no better luck.

"No reason to be surprised," Ceinwen said. "As a journalist, I was often in a place without cell service or internet. And worse, were the many spots where we purposefully turned off our cell phones and Wi-Fi because we were afraid of being tracked and killed."

"No wonder you left that job," Rachel said with a shudder.

"I guess you should call Rempart's assistant," Ceinwen said.

Rachel hesitated and faced Jake. "Do you know this Li Jianjun?"

"Afraid not." He seemed now to be sulking over Charlotte's lack of response about returning to Salmon.

"Okay." Rachel called the number. She expected a voice message when someone answered.

"Hello?"

"Li Jianjun?" she asked.

"Who's this?" He sounded sleepy.

Rachel quickly explained who she was, and then asked for a way to contact Michael.

"I wish I knew!" Jianjun exclaimed, finally awake. "I should know better than to worry about the guy, but I haven't been able to reach him either."

"You haven't?"

Jianjun explained about Michael's trip to Japan, and that they last spoke as Michael was about to leave to see Lafcadio Hearn's house in

Kamigawa. "The town is so small I can't even find it on a map. Then Michael asked me to look into a couple of names, but I'm not having any luck with them either."

Rachel took down notes of all the names Jianjun spoke of. After hanging up the phone, she explained all she'd learned to Ceinwen and Jake.

"That's a really strange story," Ceinwen said, hands on hips. "Why would Michael Rempart be interested in Lafcadio Hearn? And why now?"

"I've never heard of him," Rachel said.

"I love his work—weird stuff. Lots of Japanese ghost stories. In fact, I'd be very tempted to go to Japan to find out what Rempart is up to." Ceinwen stopped then, as she suddenly remembered one of Rachel's dreams took place in Japan ... and in the dream, a demon killed her.

"You would?" Rachel looked shocked.

"In a heartbeat."

"If you went, I would, too."

Ceinwen's eyebrows rose in surprise. "Even though the place gives you nightmares?" She tried to sound as if she were joking, but failed.

"Especially because of that," Rachel said softly.

Ceinwen felt a sudden chill.

At that moment, the Jake's phone rang and he answered.

Ceinwen noticed him growing increasingly agitated as he listened to the call, answering only with a guttural "yeah" or "okay" from time to time. Finally, he hung up and faced her and Rachel.

"It's getting worse," he said, then drew in his breath. "Mitch Ivansen's been found dead. Murdered, gutted like a deer." His fists tightened. "Another rancher out in the backcountry, Wade Cox, is also missing. But who know? He might have done it. Or he could be dead, too."

It was as if the inexplicable was closing in, bringing nightmares, shattered relationships, and death to the area. The three said no more, but retreated into their own thoughts ... and fears.

CHAPTER 22

Rachel Gooding trudged along a steep incline of the Kumano Kodo, an ancient pilgrimage trail that wound through the quiet mountains of Japan's Kii Peninsula.

Crumbling stone deities beside the path displayed the Shinto origins of the route. Under Shinto, the Emperor of Japan was considered a god, a descendant of the goddess Amaterasu.

Moss-covered stones formed makeshift stairs on the mountainsides, while decades of use smoothed the wooden bridges. It was a place for contemplation and spiritual renewal.

Rachel didn't know how she came to be here. She was alone except for a young woman up ahead standing at the edge of a fast-rushing stream. The woman wore a flowery Japanese kimono. As Rachel neared, she saw that the woman was weeping bitterly. No one dressed so beautifully should be that unhappy, Rachel thought.

She stopped and offered assistance. But the woman continued to cry and moved closer to the water's edge. Rachel feared she might throw herself into the stream and drown. "Please listen," Rachel said. "This is no place for you. Step away from the water and tell me how I might help you."

The woman straightened, but kept her back to Rachel, holding her arm up so that the sleeve of her kimono hid her face as her sobs continued.

Rachel touched her shoulder. "Please, don't cry."

With that, the woman dropped her arm, and stroked her face with her hand. She then turned around.

She had no eyes. No nose. No mouth.

Rachel screamed and ran. A demon, she thought. A demon had followed her to this sacred place.

She left the Kumano Kodo and hurried toward towns and people. She hadn't gone far when, along the side of the road, a man had set up the stand and was selling soba, a noodle-based soup, to passers-by. Rachel flung herself at the feet of the soba seller and told him what she saw.

"Ha!" The soba seller laughed at her. "Did she show you something like this?"

He stroked his face, and his features disappeared.

Rachel cried out and again turned and ran. When she felt as if her heart would burst if she took another step, she stopped. Breathing heavily, she reached her hand up to touch her own face.

As she did, she felt no mouth, no teeth, and then her sense of smell vanished. All her features were gone, her face felt absolutely smooth and round. As much as everything told her not to do it, she reached up and touched her eyes.

Everything went black.

CHAPTER 23

A SERVANT from the Nakamura estate brought Michael a basket of fruit and rolls the next morning. Included was a note from Mrs. Nakamura:

Power line has been damaged. Expect power out all day. Soon fixed. Please do not worry. See me if you are inconvenienced. –H. Nakamura

He wasn't inconvenienced, and in fact, found it rather nice to be cut off from the outside world—for a while, at least, in this idyllic corner where past and present met perfectly.

At noon, he returned to the Nakamura estate and spent a pleasant and interesting afternoon with Seiji and Haruko Nakamura talking about Japanese history and artifacts.

They also gave Michael several English-language books on the subject, ordered in anticipation that he—or someone else—might be willing to help them with their collection, and knowing the local bookstore would be unable to help.

By four o'clock, Seiji was exhausted, so Michael returned home eager to begin reading the books. He went out to the office with them. Until the power was on and he could use the internet, his knowledge of Japanese artifacts would be limited to what they contained.

The little he knew of early Japan had come from his archeological studies, such as the country's earliest documented era being the *kofun* period, from roughly 300 to 700 A.D.

Kofun were mounds of earth and stones built over a grave. These mounds were similar to those he had worked near in Mongolia and were found throughout the Asian steppes, known as *kurgans*. A big difference was that many of the *kofun* in Japan were built in the odd shape of a keyhole. The largest *kofun* was the tomb of the Emperor Nintoku, near Osaka, which is said to be the third largest tomb in the world, after the Great Pyramid at Giza, and the tomb of Qin Shi Huang with its terracotta warriors in Xi'an, China.

During the *kofun* period the Emperor reigned supreme. Not until the twelfth century did the imperial family grow weak, and the power of the regional feudal lords expanded. The leader of those daimyo became known as the Shogun, a hereditary position that meant "Commander-in-Chief." The emperor continued to be worshipped, but he had no real power.

Time would tell which historical era the Nakamura items were from. But Michael wanted to have a good understanding of the artifacts, despite his being well aware that they were simply an excuse for the Nakamuras to get him here.

He hated the real reason.

He didn't ever want to become involved in anything demonic again. He had watched too many friends, and even his brother, die because of demons and alchemy. But when he thought about Seiji Nakamura trying to fight the demons on his own, and his mother, Haruko, a kind and generous woman, watching her son slowly waste away, his heart went out to them.

Now, at home for the evening, he went to the kitchen and made himself a cup of tea. The evening was warm, so he removed his 'indoor' slippers for 'outdoor' ones—woven sandals with a fabric thong that fit between the toes, and went to his front garden. The realtor, Kazuko, had bought the zoris to him as a "housewarming" present that morning. He was getting used to this constant changing of shoes and slippers.

Surrounded by a high wall as the garden was, with a small koi pond and bushes and miniature trees, he felt as if he were in paradise. More than ever, he understood Lafcadio Hearn's essay on such gardens.

Michael sat on a small stone bench by the pond and sipped his tea.

The night was still. Perhaps the fish were already asleep, he thought. Even his neighbors were quiet, and no cars rolled by on the street.

He found this garden, this house, so peaceful, he wondered if he had found a place to call home, much as his wandering cousin had done many decades earlier. Wintersgate and the heavy shroud of sadness that permeated it seemed worlds away.

His visit with his father had convinced him their relationship was irredeemable. He would learn nothing more about his mother's death, but at least he had found her diary. Through it he came to know her a bit as a person, even though he had been saddened by much of what he discovered about her life.

Also, his desire for finding out the full story of what had happened with Irina had ended with her passing. As much as he would have liked answers, that was the stuff of fiction. In real life, a person often had to accept that they might never know "why." He needed to forget about the past, and move on.

He felt a hint of hope that here, he might do that.

As he gazed into the koi pond, a woman's face appeared. It was blurred just enough that he couldn't make out her features. He straightened and peered over his shoulder, expecting someone had crept up behind him. No one was there.

He stared, again, into the water. The face was still there. Then, it moved. He jerked back and eyed the area all around him once more. But the garden was empty.

Someone was playing a trick on him. Who? How?

He reached into the water, trying to find a camera or screen of some sort. The ripples caused the face to vanish. He couldn't find any instruments or wires.

He pulled his arm out and waited until the water settled. When it almost stopped moving, the face reappeared, and became clearer.

"No." He dropped to his knees. It was the face of his mother, the way she had looked when he was a boy: the very long, dark brown hair, her sad, brown eyes. "Who's doing this?" he shouted.

This time, he stepped into the knee-deep pond. As before, the face vanished.

He felt around the sides and bottom. They were solid. Then he scanned every nearby bush, tree, and rock, expecting to find some projection device.

He got out of the pond. His trousers and shirt sleeves were dripping wet.

Whoever was doing this was clever.

But then, in the back of his memory, this all seemed somehow familiar, as if he had seen or read it somewhere. But where?

He needed to change his clothes to something warm and dry, and to make some hot tea to ward off the chill, but he remained at the koi pond.

He drew in his breath, wondering if he had just imagined everything. Of course he had. That was the only reason the vision had seemed so alive, why it felt as if the woman was looking at him, just as he was her.

And then her face reappeared.

He stared. Her lips moved, as if she were saying the same thing over and over. He tried imitating the movement and ended up with ...

"Remember me," Michael whispered. The words stabbed at him, as if she somehow knew what he had been thinking.

She made no sign that she heard him.

But then he saw a dark shadow behind her. The shadow seemed to grow larger as it neared. Michael saw a head slowly form, a body. It opened wide what might be arms.

"Run!" he yelled, but she still didn't hear. He pointed, hoping she would turn around, see what was behind her. "Run, *RUN!*"

Her head turned. The shadow vanished. And so did the face of his mother.

Michael stared at the water a long while, his heart pounding.

But she was gone.

And then he remembered why it all seemed familiar. He had read something similar, a story by Lafcadio Hearn. In the story, a samurai had seen a man's face in a cup of tea. It was the ghost of a man he had killed and forgotten ... a ghost that came back to haunt him.

At least part of the message was clear. Memory and not forgetting were the key to unlocking the mysteries of the past and present. And he was being guided, not haunted by guilt, but to what end? He had been guided to Kamigawa for a reason but, again, to what end?

CHAPTER 24

THE TRIP to the Izumo Airport took well over twenty-four hours. From there, Ceinwen and Rachel took a shuttle bus to the train station. They discovered trains left frequently for Matsue, but when they asked about Kamigawa, they were met with blank looks. Finally, they bought tickets to Matsue, hoping to learn more at the Lafcadio Hearn Museum. As they stood on a platform waiting for the next train, Rachel spotted a sign over a distant track that was flashing the name "Kamigawa" as a train approached.

Ceinwen couldn't see it, but Rachel was insistent. With Rachel leading the way, the two ran for the track, and made it onto the train just as its doors shut. To their surprise, the car was empty. They guessed the other passengers had all chosen to sit in cars closer to the front.

The train barreled along without stopping for over thirty minutes when a mechanical voice announced "Kamigawa." When the train stopped, they were the only passengers to get off.

It was late afternoon. The station was empty except for one man wearing a uniform and standing by the ticket counter. Rachel and Ceinwen walked to the street. They saw a few shops, but had no idea which way to go.

Ceinwen marched back to the station attendant. "Can you tell me if there's a hotel in town?"

The agent gazed at her, perplexed, not understanding a word she was saying. He pointed to a small building on the sidewalk near the station. "*Koban*," he said, which she didn't understand until he pondered a moment then said, "*O-mawari-san,* ah, 'cop.'"

Now Ceinwen understood. "Thank you." The *koban* looked like a one-man police station. The door was open, and a uniformed officer sat inside.

"Hello," Ceinwen called, and pulled a photo of Michael from her handbag. "I'm looking for this man."

The young policeman looked at the photo and nodded. "Ah, America-*jin?*"

Thank God! Ceinwen thought. "Yes. Where can we find him?"

He looked doubtful and then angled his hand leftward. "*Hidari.*" Using his fingers he counted, "*Ichi, ni, san.*"

"Ah! Left, three blocks?" she asked.

"Eh … yes. Left, three." He seemed to be thinking, then switched so that his fingers pointed in the opposite direction. "*Migi.*" Then he held up two fingers. "Up!"

"Then, right, two blocks? Up?"

"*Hai.* Up." He made a walking motion with two fingers.

"Up." Ceinwen and Rachel nodded, guessing it would make sense once they got there. "Thank you."

He gave a quick nod. "*Do itashimaste.*"

Ceinwen hoped the policeman's words meant "good luck," because she feared they would need it. "Thank you! *Arigato,*" she said back, wracking her brain for any Japanese she might have picked up over the years. There wasn't much.

So far the trip had been easy because the airport and the train station both had great signage in Japanese and Roman script, and they had no trouble making their way through them.

Now, however, everything was different. On the one hand, the lovely, picturesque village looked like something out of a Kurosawa movie. She half-expected to see samurai and geisha walking the streets, and no Roman script corrupted the view. On the other hand, there were a number of small cars and people dressed much like her. Or, if truth be told, most outfits were more fashionable and expensive looking than the jeans, boots, and jackets she and Rachel both wore. They might have been wearing signs reading "College Students R Us."

At least they were wheeling suitcases and not shouldering backpacks.

The blocks were curved and longer than she expected. She hoped they were guessing right as they crossed two intersections. When they reached the third, they turned.

"Uh, oh," Ceinwen murmured, and stopped.

Ahead was a steep hill with a narrow, curving street. They now understood what the policeman had meant by "up." But also, the road forked, and they didn't know which direction to take. They were debating it when two high-school-aged girls approached.

"Help has arrived," Ceinwen said as she took out the photo she had showed the policeman. For sure, in a small area like this, a good-looking single man and a foreigner would stand out.

"Excuse me, please." Ceinwen smiled at the girls. "Do you speak English?"

The girls giggled and nodded, murmuring, "Yes."

"Good. I hope you can help us," Ceinwen said. "We're looking for the home of Michael Rempart. Doctor Michael Rempart, an archeologist." She showed them his photo.

The girls whispered together.

"The American man? Friend to Nakamura-*sama?*"

"Yes, he's an American," Rachel answered for Ceinwen.

"We will show you."

The girls walked faster than Rachel and Ceinwen expected, and they had to hurry, the wheels of their suitcases bouncing high on the bumpy pavement.

When they turned onto another narrow, steep street, Rachel and Ceinwen glanced at each other with worry, but soon, the girls stopped at a tall wooden gate, faced the women, and bowed.

"Here is house, *the* house," the taller of the two girls said.

Rachel and Ceinwen bowed to the girls. "Thank you."

The girls giggled again and then shouted "goodbye" as they waved and ran down the hill.

Rachel watched them go and nervously pushed the buzzer. Nothing.

She tried again. Still no response.

"I'll knock." Ceinwen rapped hard on the gate.

A woman came out of the house across the lane and said something to them in Japanese. "Sorry," Ceinwen said with a shake of her head, then asked, "Michael Rempart? Is this his home?"

The woman nodded. "Rem-pah-to *sensei. Hai.*"

It took Ceinwen a moment to realize the neighbor was saying Michael's last name. She hoped the rest of the words meant he lived there.

The woman then showed her small wristwatch and made a motion as of time passing.

"I get it," Ceinwen said. "He'll be back tonight."

They thanked the woman and decided to find a restaurant to eat and then freshen up before returning to wait for Michael. Ceinwen hoped the mysterious Michael Rempart would be half as helpful and pleasant as the strangers she'd met so far.

CHAPTER 25

Seiji Nakamura had invited Michael to dine with him and his mother that evening. To Michael's surprise, they also invited the realtor, Kazuko Yamato. She had stopped by the Hearn house several times already to make sure everything was acceptable to him. It was more than acceptable. He was enjoying the simplicity of his life even though the town was still without power.

Two days earlier, Mrs. Nakamura had brought him to the wing of the house where porcelain, pottery, and artwork had been carefully stored for centuries. The years had done little damage to the pieces. Michael needed to work equally carefully as he unwrapped and then rewrapped the items. With each, he numbered the item and used the Nakamuras' powerful Nikon camera to take photos to help with later identification and cataloging. He was finding the job both fascinating and challenging.

The rarest artifacts had been placed in a storage facility that was temperature and humidity controlled. They were being delivered to Kamigawa, but hadn't yet arrived.

After a sumptuous dinner, Kazuko and Mrs. Nakamura left the two men alone for a while. "As pleasant as I find it here," Michael said, "I'm not doing anything to help cure this illness of yours, and I know that's the primary reason I'm here. I'm not an alchemist, but even if I were, alchemy isn't medicine. It can't cure ailments, not even demonic ones."

"How can you say that? You and I both know there are things in alchemy that modern medicine can't explain," Seiji said. "You need to call on its occult arts. Alchemy opens the door to the world of spirits. Demand that those spirits help me! Only you can do it."

"I don't practice such arts," Michael said.

"Please," Seiji whispered. "If you want me, the heir of the daimyo, to beg you, I will do so. Gladly. Please help me."

Michael knew the young daimyo's eyes would haunt him. They were the most desperate eyes he had ever seen in his life. "I—"

"Don't lie to me," Seiji whispered. He looked on the verge of passing out, his voice so weak Michael had to bend low to hear him. "You've faced them. You thought you defeated them, but you haven't. You slowed them down, but that was all. And now, because of you, they're after me."

Michael found the words astounding. "What are you saying? I have no part in what's happening to you."

Seiji's eyes turned hard, evil. "Don't you? Ask ..."

At that moment, the sliding door opened, and Mrs. Nakamura and Kazuko reentered the room.

As Michael stared at Seiji, he heard a whispered voice. It didn't come from afar, but came from deep inside his head. The voice whispered, *"Ask your father."*

The words, Seiji's continuing gaze, were chilling. Demons were here; they were real, and they were persecuting Seiji. But bringing up his father had to be a meaningless ploy.

He stood. "It's time for me to leave. I have work to do tonight."

Kazuko bowed to Seiji and Lady Nakamura. "I should leave now as well. And I'll walk with you, Michael-*sensei.* My car is at the bottom of the hill near your house."

With that, everyone said their goodbyes.

The sun was setting over the tiny town. Refreshed, Rachel and Ceinwen had returned to Michael's house, but an hour had passed with no sign of him.

"Maybe we should go back to the station and try to find a hotel, or if none, return to Izumo," Rachel suggested.

"Let's wait a little longer." Ceinwen realized Rachel was nervous about encountering the archeologist. "The later it gets, the more likely Rempart is to return home."

Rachel nodded as she peered up and down the street. "Okay, maybe another half hour will ... oh! That's him! I'd know that long-legged stride anywhere."

Ceinwen followed Rachel's gaze to see a tall, slim man walking down the hill. He was conversing with a Japanese woman hanging onto his arm and spending more time looking up at him than where she was going which, on the uneven pavement meant she kept bumping into him. Or, noticing how good-looking he was, Ceinwen couldn't help but think the woman was doing it on purpose.

His face registered surprise when he noticed two women waiting by his gate, but once he recognized Rachel, he smiled. He had, Ceinwen noted, a disarmingly nice smile.

As he reached the house, Michael pulled his arm free from his companion. "Rachel Gooding! I can't believe it." He strode toward her and gave her a quick hug.

"You remember me!" Rachel sounded happy at the greeting Rempart gave her and hugged him in return.

"Of course I do." His dark eyes glanced at Ceinwen and he gave a friendly nod before returning to Rachel. "What are you doing here?"

Rachel pulled Ceinwen forward. "This is my college roommate, Ceinwen Davies."

Ceinwen held out her hand. "Hello."

"Good to meet you," he said as they shook hands. His grip was strong and warm, and he stood a little taller than her. She could see why he had been on TV with his wavy black hair, pronounced cheekbones, straight nose, and nicely shaped lips. Being a popular archeologist was the icing on a fine cake.

"Oh, this is my realtor, Kazuko Yamato," he said. "Kazuko, this is an old friend, Rachel Gooding, and her friend, Ceinwen Davies."

Kazuko shook hands. "I should go, Michael. You are busy tonight." She gave him a quick hug, cast a suspicious frown at both women, and then continued down the street.

"I think we interrupted something," Ceinwen said in a loud aside to Rachel.

Rachel looked horrified at Ceinwen, then back at Michael to see his reaction.

He gave Ceinwen a bemused smile. "It's not a problem," he said.

Ceinwen grinned while Rachel looked like a student caught cheating on a test.

"Something troubling is going on in Salmon." Rachel blurted.

Michael's eyebrows rose. "Charlotte Reed phoned me a week or so ago. She mentioned strange things, but didn't sound overly concerned."

"She was wrong." Rachel's voice quavered.

"Have you been there?" Michael asked.

"Yes, we both were," she answered. "We saw Sheriff Sullivan."

Michael's scowled. "Did he tell you to come here?"

"Well... no." Rachel, flummoxed, turned to Ceinwen for help.

"We decided to come here on our own," Ceinwen explained. "We spoke to your assistant. Mr. Li said he also couldn't reach you by phone, but told us how to find you."

Michael nodded. "Electricity and all cell service has been out for several days."

"Several?" Ceinwen found the thought horrifying.

"Oh, before I forget," Rachel continued, "Mr. Li needs more information about some names you gave him. He's not finding the information you requested."

He gave a quick nod. "It's no longer an issue. Things are fine here except for the problem with the power grid. I could charge and use my phone if I left town and found some electricity, but frankly, I've enjoyed the peace and quiet."

Ceinwen couldn't take another moment standing out there on the street. "We first arrived here this afternoon. Fortunately your neighbor kindly told us you wouldn't be back until evening. Thanks to her, we've only been standing out here about an hour waiting for you."

He looked taken aback by the mild dressing down but also guilty by his lack of manners. "Sorry. Do you have a car?"

"We got here by train," Rachel said.

"Then you can stay here tonight. There are no hotels in Kamigawa."

"We don't mean to impose—"

"It's okay. Come inside."

Ceinwen followed him and Rachel to the house. Inside the foyer, he switched from shoes to slippers quickly and smoothly, and placed two pairs of slippers on the polished hardwood floor.

"You can use these slippers," he said. "Your boots need to stay in the *genkan.*"

"You must have tatami floors in this house," Ceinwen said.

"I do. Where are you from, by the way?" Michael asked, as Ceinwen and Rachel sat on the landing to remove their boots.

"You mean I don't sound as if I'm American?" Ceinwen asked as he offered a hand to pull her to her feet.

"Not in the slightest," he replied. As she then stepped up to the hardwood, she noticed the tiniest of smirks on his face as he picked up her suitcase as well as Rachel's. "Somewhere in England, but I can't quite tell where."

"You're close. I was raised in Wales, but haven't lived there for some years."

"That explains it," he said.

Ceinwen watched Rachel step onto the hardwood floor and put on slippers. When she looked up again, Michael was gone.

To the left was a hallway, and in front of them was a pretty room with paper panels as walls and a floor of tatami. Ceinwen angled her head toward the tatami room, and they entered.

A low table with pillows on each side made up the room's furniture. One wall had a nook with a Japanese scroll hanging in it. Below the scroll were an ikebana tree and a jade carving of a Japanese woman. It was all very peaceful and beautiful.

Ceinwen and Rachel stood and waited, not having any idea what they should do.

Soon, Michael returned. "This house is tiny. Only two bedrooms, so you need to share."

"I'm so sorry about this," Rachel said. "Tomorrow, we'll take the train to a larger town and find a place to stay. Today just seemed to get away from us."

"You're here now. Let me show you your room."

His voice was gruff, and they followed him down the hall to a small, nearly empty space. "This is yours. Your beds, *futon*, are rolled up in the cupboard, along with blankets. I suspect you're more than ready to freshen up. The W.C., as they often call them in Japan, is in the back of the house, down that hallway past the kitchen. But, until you get used to Japanese style toilets, you might want to use the facilities upstairs."

"Thank you," Ceinwen said. "As Rachel mentioned, we'll find other accommodations as soon as we can."

Michael stared hard at her, his mouth in a slight frown. "I'm afraid you two have come a long way based on wishful thinking. I hope you aren't too disappointed."

Ceinwen stiffed. His words, his tone, stung. "I absolutely agree," she said.

His gaze leapt between Ceinwen and Rachel, then he proceeded down the hall.

"The kitchen is here, next to your room." They followed him. "Help yourself if you're hungry. Next to it are the stairs to my bedroom and the Western-style bathroom. Feel free to use it anytime. That's it for the house. My office, where I spend most of my time, is in a separate building out back. I have a few things to do out there now, so make yourself at home."

He turned and walked out of the room.

Ceinwen and Rachel gawked at each other. "Do you feel as chilled as I do by that reception?" Ceinwen asked.

"I told you he was different."

"Different? Or an asshole?"

CHAPTER 26

Jianjun phoned Charlotte Reed, who Michael regarded as a scholar and a friend. When she couldn't give him any information about Rachel Gooding's whereabouts, he phoned Sheriff Jake Sullivan.

"Have you heard from Rachel Gooding since she went to Japan?" he asked.

"No," Jake said. "I wasn't even sure she'd gone. Why? What's happening?"

"I don't know. That's the problem. I told her what little I knew about where Michael might be, and she promised to call and let me know when she got there, but now I haven't heard from her either. I've tried calling, but I get the same 'not in service' message as when I try to reach Michael."

"Could it simply be bad cell service?"

"Maybe, but I thought one of them would have contacted me by now," Jianjun said.

"True."

"Tell me about Rachel. Do you trust her?" Jianjun asked. "And what about this friend of hers? Ceinwen. Where's she from? And what's her interest in Michael or any of this?"

Jake told him what he could about Rachel, vouching for her character. He knew a lot less about Ceinwen, except that she had been a journalist—a position that made him nervous. He said both were students of archeology in Oxford.

"So I heard. It's an expensive school," Jianjun said.

"Apparently, Rachel was given some kind of full scholarship."

"Interesting."

"That's as much as I can tell you."

"Please call me if you hear from anyone in Japan, and I'll do the same," Jianjun said, then hung up.

He put in a call to a cousin in London who worked in the Administrative Offices of the Imperial College where they had a lot of international students who used scholarships and grants. He asked his cousin, Li Chinwo, called "Chuck," to find out what scholarship an Oxford student named Rachel Gooding had been given. Chuck was always on the lookout for money to give to students trying to attend "his" college instead of going elsewhere and was happy to do it.

While waiting for a call-back from his cousin, Jianjun did an internet search on Ceinwen Davies. Born in Cardiff, thirty-three years old, she had a journalism degree and had worked for the past 11 years for the UK's Daily Mail and had written several magazine and online articles for publications such as *Fate, Paranormal Underground, Skeptic, Fortean Times,* and *Skeptical Inquirer.*

He found a number of articles by her on the internet about strange phenomena—from the "Face on Mars," to remote viewing, to the death worm in the Mongolian desert, a bunch on crop circles, and even more on supposed hauntings. She wrote most of them with tongue firmly in cheek and a heavy amount of skepticism.

Jianjun also found pictures of her with a number of men. She was striking with thick shoulder-length auburn hair and large green eyes—and she was single. He couldn't find anything that put up red flags, other than her having been an investigative journalist. She was likely a master at getting people to like and trust her for the sake of her reporting. He needed to warn Michael.

Three hours later, his cousin called back.

"Holy shit, Jianjun," were the first words from Chuck's mouth.

"What are you talking about?"

"You're going to find this fucking interesting. Your gal, Rachel, was the first to receive a new scholarship for the Archeology Department, and it went along with a $100,000 grant to the University in honor of one of its top alumni, your boss, Michael Rempart. The scholarship was to be given to the most deserving student from some place called 'Idaho.' Where the fuck is Idaho?"

"Michael gave the scholarship?" Jianjun asked, astonished.

"Not Michael, dipshit! It was in honor of him. Some dude named William Claude Rempart, who must be a relative, paid for the scholarship."

"Yeah," Jianjun said, his mind churning with the news. "It's his father."

CHAPTER 27

CEINWEN AWOKE to the pastel sky of dawn. In the kitchen, she found a French press coffee maker set up and ready for use. All she had to do was boil water. "Thank you, Lord," she muttered as she turned on the burner.

"Good morning. Did you sleep well."

She jumped at the sound of Michael's voice and spun around. "Considering I was lying on the floor without even a mattress, it was quite comfortable."

"That's the tatami," he said, entering the small room. "I take it Rachel is still asleep."

"She is. Sleeping soundly with nary a cry for once. She's been troubled by nightmares."

"She's not alone in that," he murmured. He placed a wicker basket on the kitchen table and folded back the cloth covering its contents. "Would you like some eggs? We also, as you can see, have fresh fruit, biscuits, butter, and breakfast pastries."

"No eggs, but those pastries look delicious. Where did you get them?" she asked as she made herself and Michael some coffee. She ran her fingers through her hair and wished she had taken the time to style it or put on make-up. She feared she looked a sight, while he looked even better than the food.

"My landlady sends a basket here each morning. I doubt you'd care for a traditional Japanese breakfast of rice and fish, sometimes with a raw egg. It's the one thing I'd never get used to here."

She handed him coffee and he thanked her. He was much more pleasant than he had been the evening before, and she hoped that meant he had gotten over his irritation at their unannounced visit. Maybe she had been harsh in her initial reaction to him.

"Tell me what this is about," he said as they ate. "Rachel said you're her college roommate, but you don't seem like a student."

"I'll take that as a compliment." She noted how uncomfortable he looked assessing her. "I've gone back to school after a wayward youth and some crap jobs. I'm taking some archeology courses at Oxford."

"Back when I was there, wayward youths rarely got admitted, and crap jobs didn't pay enough to afford it." He angled his head and waited for an explanation.

She owed him none, smiled, and then took a big bite of a scone.

He lifted his brows. "I didn't know Rachel was going there."

She swallowed. "She's already making a name for herself. Things come easily for her—almost too easily, if that makes sense. But she's paying a price for it."

"What do you mean?"

"We're here hoping you can tell us. She's troubled but it's difficult to tell how, or even why. I suspect it has to do with what happened to her in Idaho, but I don't know enough about it to judge. All I can say is, she's made me curious, and I've spent too many years looking into things that made me curious to stop just because I'm back in school. "

Michael's eyes narrowed. "How do you know what happened in Idaho? Did Rachel tell you?"

"She's said very little. She's been a good little trooper in keeping what actually happened out there a secret. Same with Sheriff Sullivan. But that doesn't mean I've given up trying to figure it out. You can explain right now, in fact."

He studied her a long moment. "You ask questions boldly, and follow up on answers. One of your crap jobs was as a journalist, right?"

She grinned. "Am I that obvious? I was supposedly a foreign corre-spondent. I had expected to work on world news and politics. Instead I was the one they sent to anything bizarre, wanting me to debunk it. Find a weird crop circle or sheep mutilation? Send Ceinwen to write about it. After all, she's from Wales, and aren't they all about crops and sheep? And now, the area upsetting Rachel has sheep mutilations. Strange world."

Michael seemed to choose his words carefully as he said, "I imagine there were few phenomena you couldn't debunk."

What, she wondered, was he hiding? "You're right. But that's all behind me."

"You aren't a journalist any longer?"

"Not at the moment. That part of my life is over, Doctor Rempart." Her words were true as far as they went. She had taken a leave of absence, and if she did well on a book deal, she wouldn't return to writing silly articles about the paranormal.

"Call me Michael," he said.

"Michael," she repeated. She found herself growing increasingly uncomfortable under his strange scrutiny, but that didn't stop her from studying him as well—the sharp profile, the overly long, wavy but rebellious hair. At the same time, she sensed an odd remoteness about him. She was glad to move past his questions since she had plenty of her own. She began with something neutral and non-threatening. "So, tell me, how did you ever find such a nice house to rent?"

He explained his meeting with Yamato Toru at the Lafcadio Hearn museum in Matsue.

She frowned. "That was certainly a round-about way to get help cataloging artifacts."

"It turns out there's another reason they want me here."

She waited, not speaking, but staring into his dark eyes. The moment stretched out until he said, "Nakamura Seiji, the descendant of a daimyo, wants to know more about the paranormal and demons. He ties my name to such nonsense."

She sensed how upset that made him. "Because of the events in Idaho?"

He drew back as if to physically as well as mentally distance himself from her. "That, and a few other things earlier in my career."

Her eyebrows rose with curiosity even as she realized how different he was from what she had expected. Once more she waited, detecting in him a strange undercurrent of sorrow.

He replied with complete seriousness. "Those close to him believe he's possessed."

She stared. "Do you?"

His jaw worked, then he confessed, "Yes."

She didn't believe him. "That's bollocks." She felt anger building.

"You're making fun of me because of my former 'news' articles. What are you really doing here?"

"That's it." He sounded befuddled by her dismissal of his explanation.

"Well, if that's it," she scoffed, "you should consider leaving this crazy daimyo and taking care of Rachel and the people back in Salmon."

"But—"

She was irritated. "Look, Rachel, the Sheriff, and I went out to the place where there were once supposedly some Egyptian pillars—impossible though that is to believe. Someone has gone to a lot of trouble to convince the locals that there's bad mojo happening all around them. People are scared, including the sheriff. They seem to think you would understand the situation more than most people. But instead of helping them, you're here playing exorcist to a wealthy nutcase. People in Salmon, God help them, want you to go there. I suspect, with a little hand-holding, they'll come around."

Now it was his turn to scoff, his tone filled with mockery. "Do you really think that all Rachel and the others need is hand-holding?"

She cocked an eyebrow. "If the right hand is doing the holding, yes."

A sleepy voice came from the doorway. "Holding what?"

After a startled glance at each other, both turned to see Rachel enter the kitchen.

"Michael was telling me about a descendant of a daimyo who lives here and fears he's possessed by demons," Ceinwen said in a velvety yet bemused voice, very different from the sharp tone she had been using. She busied herself making Rachel a cup of coffee as Rachel joined them at the table.

"It seems there's a lot of that going around," Rachel murmured.

"Would you like eggs for breakfast?" Michael asked, sounding equally pleasant.

"No, thanks. I'll just have a little toast. Or is there still no electricity?"

"Afraid not."

"The scones are great," Ceinwen said.

As Rachel ate, Ceinwen faced Michael. "So, can we meet your 'ailing' daimyo friend?"

Michael gave her a quick glare, but dropped it before Rachel noticed. "I'll introduce you to Lady Nakamura, and let her know you two might be visiting here a day or two. Then, it's up to her."

"A day or two?" Ceinwen said. "You mean you aren't giving us the boot?"

"I wouldn't inflict you two on Japan," he said with a straight face.

"Oh, ho! Listen to him, Rachel," Ceinwen said.

Rachel's gaze darted from one to the other.

"And why do you call your landlady 'Lady'?" Ceinwen asked Michael.

He shrugged. "You can call her Mrs. Nakamura if you'd like. I don't find that lofty enough for this family. If you meet them, you'll see what I mean. In Japanese, they use an honorific, Nakamura-*sama*. It best translates as Lord and Lady Nakamura—a kind of feudal system."

"I don't know that I want to meet anyone who thinks he's possessed by demons," Rachel said.

"You may be right." Michael's demeanor filled with concern as he faced her. "To meet him could be dangerous."

"Good lord!" Ceinwen couldn't hide her disdain any longer. "You can't believe such nonsense. Demons! Hah!"

"You don't?" Michael asked.

"Of course not!"

"So then, they can't possibly exist?" Michael folded his arms, an eyebrow cocked. "If a tree falls in the forest and you aren't there to hear it, it has no sound?"

She could all but feel steam pouring from her ears. "Thank you, Bishop Berkeley. What I'm saying is that in every case of possession, there's been an underlying reason the person under attack is acting up."

"Ceinwen," Rachel said, "you saw what happened north of the Salmon River. The creatures Jake and I saw were real."

"I saw that you two were scared," Ceinwen admitted. "But since I saw nothing beyond that, and you didn't see the same thing as the Sheriff, it was a psychological phenomenon, not a physical one."

Michael looked interested, but before he could ask about it Rachel spoke up. "Michael, about the young daimyo—has he seen doctors?"

"Many, throughout the world. It's a sad situation. I wish I could help, but I don't see how."

"And I imagine doctors can't help him," Rachel said. "How terrible."

Michael eyed her. "Are you agreeing he might be possessed?"

"Why wouldn't I? I often feel the same way."

Ceinwen was stunned to hear Rachel say that, and even Michael appeared taken aback. "Be ready in one hour," he said. "We'll all go up to the manor and I'll introduce you both to Lady Nakamura."

CHAPTER 28

LADY NAKAMURA EYED Rachel and Ceinwen with skepticism but then gave her assent for them to meet Seiji.

The young man sat up against a multitude of pillows, but he looked so weak, Michael doubted he would have had the strength to remain upright if the pillows were taken away.

The women's eyes were wide as they took in the understated opulence of Japanese high society. Natural materials and carefully selected time-worn rustic objects that showed perfection in their placement, gave the room a Zen-like calmness. They followed Michael as Seiji's retainers scrambled for two more floor pillows for them to sit on.

"How do you feel today?" Michael asked.

"The same. Who are these lovely newcomers you have brought?" The man's voice scarcely rose above a whisper.

Michael quickly introduced them.

Seiji's eyes were red and watery as he faced Rachel. "Why are you here, Miss Gooding?"

Rachel looked startled by the question. "I came here to talk to Doctor Rempart."

"About?"

She shifted. "Some … something back in the States."

"And have you?"

Michael answered for her. "She's just arrived. We'll have a lot of time to reminisce later."

Seiji turned to Ceinwen. "And what about you, Miss Davies? Why are you here?"

"I'm Rachel's friend. I hope to help her."

"And nothing else?"

Ceinwen raised her chin. "What could be more important than that?"

Michael didn't like the answer, and he noticed, neither did Seiji.

"Many things, in fact." Seiji replied. As he studied Rachel, curiosity filled his eyes. "Do you, Miss Gooding, believe in demons?"

Rachel glanced at Michael. He remembered that, despite the craziness around them, she and the others had never spoken directly about such issues. But then she said, "I don't need to 'believe in' them because they are a fact, as real as the floor beneath me, or the walls surrounding us."

Seiji winced. His back arched and one hand went to his chest as if something was hurting him. His other hand reached outward as if searching for a way to ease his pain. Without thought, Rachel grabbed it, and held it tight in hers. The young lord turned his head toward her and their gazes seemed to lock.

But then Michael heard Rachel gasp, saw her eyes grow wide and frightened. She tried to pull free. Seiji's hand clamped hard, holding her tight. Michael was about to intervene when Seiji's spasm passed and he let Rachel go. He dropped back against the pillows.

After a moment, he faced Michael. "She is strong," he whispered. "Perhaps, with her strength ..."

As his retainers rushed to check on Seiji, his pulse, his heart, Rachel cast a worried glance toward Michael, as if she realized Seiji was putting hope in her—hope that she could help him. Now, Michael guessed Rachel could understand the dismay he felt over a similar hope the young daimyo placed in him.

Michael also noticed that Ceinwen was contemplating Seiji with suspicion. He didn't know what to make of her. She was attractive and carried herself with proud self-assurance. During their contentious breakfast conversation, he found himself so foolishly attracted to her animated, expressive face it was difficult to look anywhere but at her. She was irritating and quarrelsome, but with a fiery disposition and boldness that was fetching and rare. Too bad she was a mystery, and that he didn't dare trust her.

He drew in his breath and tried to concentrate on anything but Ceinwen Davies.

Seiji's eyes shut, and his retainers stood to signal it was time for the visitors to leave. The men gave Michael and the two women harsh glares, then bowed their heads and kept their gazes on their young lord. Michael could see the despair in their faces at his illness.

"Michael," Seiji called, barely able to speak. "I'm weak today. Perhaps tomorrow you will return? All of you?"

"Of course," Michael said.

Seiji smiled and slumped deeper into the pillows as he whispered, "Good."

They left the house, and when they were on the street leading down to Michael's place, Ceinwen took Rachel's arm. "What happened to you back there? You reacted so strongly, I feared you would topple over and we'd be setting you up on pillows like our young daimyo friend."

"That poor young man," Rachel murmured. She hesitated, then said, "I saw it."

Michael and Ceinwen exchanged glances. "The demon?" Michael asked.

"I felt as if it looked at me. Is that possible?"

"When?"

"When I held Seiji's hand. When our eyes met. At first I saw the sadness in him, and I was filled with sympathy. But then, it seemed a mask lifted and his look turned evil. Pure evil. It scared me. I tried to pull my hand free, but couldn't. He was strong. But as quickly as it came, the evil look vanished and Lord Nakamura was back. I don't know how he bears having such a thing inside him."

"He fights it, and it seems it's killing him for doing so," Michael murmured.

"Yes," Rachel said. "I believe you're right."

Michael added, "His retainers told me never to touch him. I haven't. I saw them jump when you took his hand, but they let you. You being a woman. I wonder if you surprised even the demon."

Rachel thought a moment, and said, "If I did it once, perhaps I can again."

Once back at the Hearn house, Rachel felt tired and went off to take a nap, while Michael said he was going out to his office to read some books that Lady Nakamura had lent him about Japanese history.

Ceinwen decided she wanted a proper, Western-style shower, even if it meant going into the sanctum sanctorum of Michael's bedroom.

Once there, her journalistic curiosity took over, and she found herself looking through his drawers and closet trying to get a sense of him. After all, she was staying in his house. If he was a criminal, some kind of madman, or a sex pervert, she ought to, at minimum, know about it. Be prepared was her motto. And don't trust anyone.

She found quite a few notebooks and papers that had to do with archeology. Did he always work? Then she turned up some old hand-written papers that seem to have to do with Japan, and a green leather-bound journal. She flipped through it. A diary? Did he keep a diary? Did any man she ever knew keep a diary, come to think of it?

She put everything else back into place, sat on the bed, and opened the diary to learn it wasn't his, but belonged to someone named Jane Addams.

Her curiosity ran rampant now as she wondered who the woman was, and why Michael would bring her diary all the way to Japan.

She read it quickly.

When she finished, she took a deep breath and then put it back where she found it. Her heart had ached for Jane Addams Rempart, and she wondered if Michael's mother was still alive and still married to William Claude.

One thing was certain, reading about his parents, about the house he had grown up in, explained a lot to her about the way Michael Rempart was now.

That evening, Michael stepped out onto the veranda. He saw Ceinwen sitting under a loquat tree reading a paperback. She had pulled her hair back into a ponytail as if she couldn't be bothered with it. Her face had the bone structure that could handle such severity, and in fact showed how lovely she was.

She put the book down as he approached. She gave him an odd look—not filled with the hostility he had come to expect around her, but softer, almost gentle. In fact, he found those large green eyes disarming. Maybe because he had no idea what she was thinking or was about to say.

"Our dinner has arrived," he announced.

"Our dinner?"

"The Nakamura family sends a dinner to me each day."

"Breakfast and dinner. I'm impressed."

He grinned. "Tonight, we've been sent a big meal. I think the one impressed was Lord Nakamura."

Her brief chuckle was a bit husky. "Or he realized that Rachel and I ate nothing but airplane food trying to get here and took pity on us." As she walked toward him, he couldn't help but admire her long-legged, curvaceous figure. He drew in his breath; his thoughts really should not go there.

Yet, as she changed her outdoor *zori* to indoor slippers, he took her arm to steady her and then led her to the main room. There, two women knelt on the tatami by the dining table. They had placed several small bowls filled with soup and various tidbits onto the table, followed by a platter of sukiyaki.

Rachel stood waiting for them. She had been lying down since returning from the Nakamura manor.

As they sat on *zabuton,* the servers poured them tea and sake and then bowed and shuffled out of the room, shutting the shoji screens behind them.

"Look at this food! How nice to be a daimyo's guest," Ceinwen said, once they were alone. She wielded her chopsticks to put food on her plate. "I could get used to being treated this way."

"It looks delicious," Rachel added. She struggled with the chopsticks but stuck with them.

As they ate, Michael said, "Tell me about Salmon, Rachel. You said something is wrong there."

Rachel nodded. "I felt it; I dreamed it. And I was right."

As she spoke, something flashed before Michael's eyes. A dark funnel shape, whirling round like a cyclone. It was in the room. He shut his eyes a moment, and when he opened them again, it was gone.

"I was having dreams," Rachel continued. "Nightmares. I'm not sure what they were, but I knew I had to see Jake and Charlotte." Rachel filled him in on how everyone in the area seemed on edge, ready to argue and fight for no good reason. She also talked about the livestock mutilations and that two men had been murdered, and last they had heard, a third man was missing. Michael listened intently.

When they finished dinner, Rachel and Ceinwen helped Michael bring the dirty dishes out to the kitchen. "I asked that they not wait for me to finish eating," Michael said, "but to pick up the dinner dishes when they bring breakfast in the morning. That way they can have more time at home with their families."

Ceinwen feigned surprise. "You mean there are still people who enjoy home and family?"

Michael smiled. "Apparently so."

"Excuse me," Rachel said. "I'm tired and going to bed."

Ceinwen's eyes were troubled. "Rest up, girl. We've got to get you healthy again."

Michael and Ceinwen got themselves beer and went out to the garden. The night was warm, the air heavy with humidity. A few crickets chirped, and now and then a splash sounded from the koi pond. Michael went to the pond and stared at the water a long moment before glancing over at Ceinwen. She was seated on a plastic patio chair, and he took the chair beside her. He had to admit he found her beautiful. When she smiled at him, he felt a stirring deep inside.

"You know what you need?" she said.

Given his last thought, the question jarred. "What?"

"A couple of big easy chairs. Or even recliners. The ones where you push a handle and the back goes down while a footrest pops up."

He chuckled. "No kidding! I was glad to find these patio chairs in the local general store. My knees ache with all this sitting on the floor."

Ceinwen nodded in agreement. "I've often suspected that Japanese people move humongous easy chairs into their homes when no one is looking, along with a big-screen TV and a remote control."

"You may be right."

"I usually am," she said smugly.

"Well in that case," his expression turned serious, "any idea what's wrong with Rachel? She doesn't look well at all."

Ceinwen drew in her breath and then told him about the nightmares and the catatonic episodes. She knew of three of them. The first, at Oxford, saw Rachel rushed to an infirmary and given lots of fluids. It lasted, at most, five minutes. The second occurred at Heathrow Airport as they waited for seats to the US, and the third lasted fifteen minutes, and happened when they were at her parent's farm in Idaho.

"These episodes worry me, Michael. Rachel once told me she felt as if she doesn't belong here, even that she feels she's fading away. She was talking about her life. It was really chilling. What do you think is going on?"

"I don't know," he said.

"Well, shite!" She blurted out the British euphemism. "Here, we came all this way because you're supposed to be the expert on such stuff."

He wasn't in a smiling mood. "I seem to be disappointing all kinds of people these days."

Her face fell. "I'm sorry, Michael. I didn't mean that. I have the feeling people put too much of a burden on you. I certainly don't want to add to it."

He held her gaze and saw genuine dismay. It surprised him. "It's all right," he murmured. "This is nothing you should ever need to understand."

Ceinwen soon said goodnight to Michael and headed to her room, expecting he would like time alone in the house.

Rachel was sound asleep so she tried to be quiet as she unrolled her futon, covered it with sheets and a blanket, and then got under the covers.

Michael weighed heavily on her thoughts—his eyes, his voice, his presence. She didn't know why he troubled her even as something about him drew her toward him. With the peculiar work she had been doing, she had learned to see the reality behind words being spoken. She had taught herself not to listen so much to what was said, but to seek meaning in the eyes and gestures of the person talking to her. "Tells" were a fascinating subject, and the number of people who made odd gestures with their hands or eyes when lying was astounding. At times, she felt she was carrying on two conversations simultaneously—one with words and logic, the other with eyes and heart. The duplicity she often witnessed was shocking.

She didn't find any such duplicity in Michael. What she found was a man filled with echoes of sorrow, a lonely desperation, a man who was surprisingly vulnerable. Yet, she had learned in her research, he was often accused of having a recklessness that bordered on the suicidal. From the outside, he had everything, yet within him, she sensed more emptiness than most people could bear.

CHAPTER 29

Jianjun entered the Lafcadio Hearn museum in Matsue, Japan. "I'd like to speak to whoever is an expert in Hearn's life," he said to the ticket-taker.

"You can go to the museum supervisor, Mrs. Ishigawa." She pointed out the office's location.

Jianjun was greeted by an older woman with short, gray hair, curled to frame her face. "A colleague of mine was here a while back," he said. "And I'm trying to follow-up on some information he was given. I'm looking into the daimyo family that lived in the area."

"I'm sorry, but there were no longer daimyo when Lafcadio Hearn lived in Matsue," she explained.

"Yes. I know. But I understand Hearn became friends with the family of the last daimyo, and that they lived somewhere other than in Matsue."

"The last daimyo was from the Matsudaira clan, and they lived here, in Matsue Castle."

"What about Kamigawa?"

Her brows wrinkled in thought. "I don't know any Kamigawa."

"But you must," Jianjun insisted. "The daimyo from the Nakamura family let Lafcadio Hearn stay in a house in Kamigawa. Maybe it had a different name back then, but I've heard it called Kamigawa now."

Her expression changed from confused to sad as she shook her head. "I don't know where you are getting such information, but I've never heard of such a thing. I also don't know of any Nakamura associated with the ruling class in this part of Japan, and there is, and was, no place called Kamigawa in this area."

Jianjun looked at her as if she might be mad—and noticed that she was looking at him the same way. In fact, the way she was sizing him up, he decided the best thing would be to leave. Now.

Outside the museum, he headed for the house where Hearn once lived.

He couldn't believe so many days had gone by with no word from Michael or Rachel. And after he read several articles by her roommate, Ceinwen, he became even more troubled. He was certain she wasn't traveling with Rachel purely out of goodwill or to sightsee, but to write a major story about the cover-up of the Idaho disappearances.

He didn't trust Ceinwen and wanted to let Michael know that. Michael had a reputation to protect. Any news story about him and weird supernatural phenomena could jeopardize his future studies and grants, not to mention, end Jianjun traveling with him to exotic places on digs.

When Jianjun reached the house, he strolled through it and its garden. He asked a couple of people if they had any idea where Kamigawa was. They didn't.

He then headed to the Matsue Castle and spoke with the castle archivist and historian about the Nakamura clan. They had never heard of any Nakamura daimyo. When he asked about Kamigawa, he received the answer he had become accustomed to.

Finally, he mustered enough bravery to go to the Matsue central police station and explain that he was trying to find an American friend who told him he would be staying in Kamigawa. "Apparently, Kamigawa isn't a town," Jianjun said. "But I'm wondering if it's a district, or a park— or anything that will give me a clue where my friend might have gone."

"Did your friend say anything about how far from Matsue he was going?"

"Less than an hour's drive."

All the Matsue police could suggest was that Jianjun go back to the Izumo Airport police and ask them. They often dealt with foreigners and might have more ideas. They took down Jianjun's name and phone number, as well as Michael's, and said if they heard anything, they would call him. Jianjun then threw in Rachel Gooding's and Ceinwen Davies' names.

As soon as the police learned a man and two female companions went missing, they weren't inclined to open a formal missing person's report or do anything more at that time. As they put it, "Foreigners are always fine in Japan. It's a very safe country. Your friends will show up when they're ready to be around other people." They all but smirked in Jianjun's face.

Jianjun drove around some smaller towns, including going into the mountains. He hoped the people there knew more than the local police.

CHAPTER 30

THE NEXT MORNING, Michael received a message from the Nakamura house that two storage chests filled with artifacts from the eighth and ninth centuries had been delivered.

They held little interest for Rachel although she knew her colleagues were excited over their arrival. Michael was glad that, even if he couldn't help Seiji, he might at least be able to provide assistance in cataloging the family treasures. And Ceinwen was curious about anything new and different.

When they arrived at the house, Lady Nakamura greeted them. The chests had been brought to a concrete, temperature-controlled outbuilding cooled by massive generators since the power continued to be off. The three went to visit Seiji, but it was obvious that Michael and Ceinwen were anxious to leave. Rachel said she preferred to stay with Seiji.

"Let us go outside," Seiji said to Rachel when they were alone. "The day is too beautiful to remain indoors."

"It is."

He leaned on the arms of his two retainers who helped him to a pond with water lilies surrounded by ferns and other greenery. Rachel couldn't get over the gorgeous landscaping.

"How do you feel today," she asked. A blanket had been spread for them, along with a pot of tea and some rice crackers.

"When my time comes, Rachel, I hope I am in this very spot. I would like this to be my last vision of this world."

"I saw the demon when I held your hand," Rachel said softly. "And then it backed off. I won't let it take you. I'll help you fight it."

As he inhaled, his breath rattled. "It's not possible. It's too strong for me. For you, as well, if you are not careful. It is an evil *kami*—a god—and a mere man cannot fight *kami*."

"Don't give up, please," Rachel murmured.

"Will you hold my hand again? I feel stronger when you do."

She moved to his side and did as he asked.

"Can you hear him?" he asked. "He is speaking of danger to you. Can you see him?"

Rachel watched a greenish-black aura build near Seiji. It swirled around him as if to capture and crush him. "I see it," she whispered.

Seiji's eyes changed from his black orbs to eyes that were serpentine and yellow—the eyes of a snake. Frightened by how quickly he changed, Rachel let go of his hand.

Seiji laughed at her and tried to grab her hand again.

She shoved him, but no sooner did she touch him than Seiji's retainers grabbed her arms and dragged her off the blanket.

"Stop!" he ordered. "It wasn't her fault. Leave her and go!"

Clearly unhappy, the retainers let her go. She stood up as they bowed to Seiji and hurried off.

Rachel warily watched him. His gaze was despondent. "You see, now, how strong he is," he whispered. "He takes over my body, does things I would not. I fear that, someday, I won't be able to come back. He will own me completely."

Rachel didn't know if she dared stay there, or if she should run from this man. But at the same time her heart ached for someone who had to deal with a strange possession. She wondered if she seemed equally out of control when she was having a nightmare or was in a trance.

At that moment, she saw Lady Nakamura rushing toward them with two serving women.

"I heard you might not be feeling well, Seiji," she said. "We've brought you some lunch—both of you. Come, Rachel. Sit and eat with him."

The women spread a variety of sushi, shu mai, and spring rolls, with sweets made of gelatinous rice called *mochi* for dessert. Then Lady Naka-mura and the others left.

The two ate in silence, eying each other as if they had a shared secret. Neither had said a word about the demon Rachel saw in Seiji's eyes.

By the time the meal was over, Seiji had a little more color in his usually pallid face. "I'm glad you agreed to stay with me today. I hope you aren't missing too many exciting artifacts."

"I'm happier being here, and I'm happy to see you looking so well," she said with a shy smile.

"So, Rachel-*san*, tell me about yourself. You're quiet when Michael is here."

"That's because I have little of interest to say." She felt her cheeks reddened.

"Maybe ... everything about you interests me."

She drew in her breath at his sweet words before deciding he was simply being polite. She never spoke of her bizarre experience of two years ago, and didn't with him. Instead, she told him about being raised LDS, her life on an Idaho farm, and how she had received an invitation to apply for a full scholarship to Oxford, and then, amazingly, had been awarded it.

She thought it was terribly boring, but he seemed interested. He had encountered LDS missionaries in Tokyo and didn't know what to make of them attempting to convert Japanese people to such a very American religion. He had been raised Buddhist, with a heavy dose of Shintoism because of his family background.

He told her, "There is a popular saying in Japan, 'Born Shinto, marry Christian, and die Buddhist.' People here enjoy Shinto rites for children, they prefer Buddhist funerals, and love Christian marriage ceremonies."

Rachel could scarcely believe what she was hearing.

He laughed at her shocked expression.

"I must say it's quite different from the way I was raised, which is the need to follow the one true path to salvation, the path revealed in the Book of Mormon."

"You see how difficult a task your missionaries to this country have."

"Perhaps impossible," she admitted.

Before long, Seiji ordered sake, which he called *o-sake*, or "honorable sake." He sat even closer as he kept her cup filled.

After the sake, Seiji switched to beer. His cheeks grew fiery. She was sure hers were as well, but she had to admit she was enjoying his company. They talked about him attending Tokyo University where he was studying Japanese history until he grew too weak and had to come home. He was only 21 years old, while she was already 24.

"Ah, a woman of the world," he joked.

She chuckled at the absurdity of that. "Right, that's me."

"I think you are," he murmured, studying her.

She didn't find the thin, sickly young man at all handsome, but she saw a lot of kindness and gentleness in him. Still, his words made her uneasy, so she went back to an earlier topic. "Tell me about the possession you fear has overtaken you."

His gaze searched her face. "I don't know how to describe it. I try to fight this depression, or whatever it is, every minute of every day. I'm fighting him now." He rubbed his temples. "He doesn't want me to talk to you for some reason. Even sleep gives me no rest. I dream of him constantly. He's a fearful, ugly monster. This constant battle has worn me down. Sometimes, Rachel, I wonder if I shouldn't give up."

"Don't say that," she cried. "Although, I understand the feeling. I have nightmares. Horrible ones. I've had fewer here in Japan, but they still occur."

Seiji lightly stroked her arm. "Do you think demons plague you as well?"

"I do," she admitted.

He seemed to ponder her words. "Would you try an exorcism? Or, maybe I should ask, do Mormons do exorcisms?"

She all but laughed aloud at the image that conveyed. "The most I've ever heard is a laying on of hands and giving a person a blessing, while praying that the Holy Spirit will drive away evil."

He frowned. "So then, I must believe in a Holy Spirit to get rid of this demon?"

She nodded. "It would help."

He took a deep breath and turned to stare out at the garden. "I don't think this is the kind of possession the Christian religion thinks of. This possession doesn't have demons shouting at me and wanting to pull me through the Gates of Hell. Instead, he whispers, convincing me I would enjoy doing evil, debauched things." He faced her again, his expression odd, almost tortured. "He doesn't seek to destroy me, but to corrupt. There is no right and wrong as with the demons in the West. My demon only seeks pleasure—pleasure in perversion, in pain, in anything that good humans deny themselves out of a sense of decency. My demon has no decency. It's almost as if ... as if he's jealous that you're here with me."

Rachel shuddered. "I wish I knew how to help you," she whispered.

"You are good and pure," he said, taking her hand and sitting shoulder to shoulder. "I think you protect me by being near."

Her pulse quickened. "I'm not as good and pure as you think. I try to be, but I often fail."

"I can't imagine." He turned over her hand, palm up, and pressed his lips against it. She felt the delicate touch of his lips, his breath, down to her toes. He wrapped her hand in both of his. "If only Doctor Rempart would use his pearl, his power, to take away the demon persecuting us," he whispered. "We would both be saved, Rachel. I know they persecute you as they do me."

She stared at him. She remembered Sheriff Sullivan saying something about a pearl that could control demons. "I don't know what you mean."

"But you do. I see it in your eyes." His hand skimmed the side of her face.

"No," she whispered.

"Rachel." The hand slid to the back of her neck as he drew her closer.

"Please. Don't." She placed her hand against his chest to stop him.

"You've heard something about the pearl," he whispered. "You know it will help, and you need to ask him where it is. For me. For us both."

She tried to break free of his hold. "It's time for me to see how Michael and Ceinwen are doing."

His arms tightened around her. "Don't go." A darkness spread over Seiji's face, and it took on an expression she hadn't seen before—almost as if he were a different person. Knowing eyes drifted over her body. "Stay with me and let us enjoy the moment. Enjoy each other."

She couldn't move. *You know you want me.* The voice reverberated through her body, but it wasn't Seiji's voice ...

Stay with him. Love him. It's what you want. Do it! Her own voice filled her even as a cold chill crept along her spine. Her own demons ...

"You see," he whispered in a forceful voice that was not his, "how strong I am. How strong *we* are."

"No! You're not him. Seiji, let me go!"

His arms loosened enough for her to twist free and scramble to her feet. She backed away to the door, but before leaving she faced him once more. "There's got to be something we can do."

"Yes, there is," Seiji whispered. His voice, the way he was looking at her, had become dangerously seductive. He held out his hand. "Come back to me, Rachel."

She hesitated only a moment, then turned and hurried into the house to look for Michael and Ceinwen. She didn't know exactly what was happening, but she found the demonic Seiji far too attractive.

———

Rachel was shown to the area where Michael and Ceinwen worked. They were both over the moon about many of the extremely old and rare artifacts they were finding. Rachel waited outside as they said their goodbyes to Seiji and thanked Lady Nakamura for allowing them to view such important pieces.

At dinner, while Michael and Ceinwen talked at length about their finds, Rachel noticed a new awareness flowed between them, an electricity that caused their eyes to spend more time on each other than anywhere else.

When they asked Rachel about her day with Seiji, she said only that she found him to be a pleasant young man, but his demons scared her.

She realized how exhausting being with him had been, and finally, although it was relatively early, she said goodnight.

CHAPTER 31

I<small>N A VILLAGE OF</small> M<small>USASHI</small>, *in the days of the Tokugawa Shogunate, there lived two woodcutters: Nakamura Taishi and an old man named Mosaku. Taishi was only eighteen years old. Every day the two went to a forest to do their jobs. To get there, they needed to cross a wide river by ferry.*

One cold evening, a great snowstorm overtook them as they worked. By the time they reached the ferry, the boatman had gone, leaving the ferry on the other side of the river. The woodcutters took shelter in the ferryman's hut, glad to have found any kind of shelter, even though there was no brazier in the hut, and no place to build a fire. The two men fastened the door and lay down to rest with their straw raincoats over them. At first they did not feel terribly cold; and they believed the storm would soon be over.

The old man immediately fell asleep; but Taishi lay awake for hours listening to a fierce wind and the snow smacking hard against the door. The river roared while the hut swayed and creaked like a junk at sea. The temperature dropped in the little hut. Taishi shivered under his raincoat as, eventually, he also fell asleep.

A showering of snow on his face woke him. The storm had blown the door of the hut open, and the light of the moon on the snow brightened the hut. He saw a woman in the room—a woman all in white. She was bending above Mosaku, and blowing her breath, a bright white smoke, upon him. The next moment she eyed Taishi.

She floated toward him. He tried to cry out, but she was so beautiful he couldn't utter any sound, couldn't do anything but watch her. And want her.

Rachel found herself in a ferryman's hut. She wore a long white kimono. Her gaze met the simple woodcutter named Taishi, but the face that looked back at her was Seiji's.

This Seiji was strong and healthy. And desirable.

She was herself, but not herself. She felt attractive, alluring, and strong— nothing she had ever felt before.

The air was bitter cold, yet heat traveled through her body from the fire in Taishi's eyes when he looked at her. She bent down over him, lower and lower, until her face almost touched his. She could feel how much he ached for her, as she did for him.

She stared hard at him, and in his eyes she saw lust, but also fear. It emboldened her.

She ran a long fingernail over his brow, down his cheek, and across his lips. Then she lifted the coat he had used as a blanket and lay beside him, taking him in her arms. Through the long, stormy night she brought him to erotic heights he had never before known.

As dawn broke, she dressed and whispered, "I had intended to treat you as I would any other man and kill you for the liberties you have taken and that I have allowed. But I cannot help feeling pity for you because you are so young. You are a pretty boy, Taishi. So I will not use you and discard you. But, if you ever tell anyone at all about what you have seen or done this night, I shall know it; and then I will kill you. Remember what I say!"

With these words, she kissed him one last time, then turned, and passed through the doorway.

Taishi sprang to his feet and ran after her, but the woman was nowhere to be seen; and the snow was driving furiously into the hut. Taishi closed the door and secured it. He thought that he might have been only dreaming, a wonderful, lustful dream. He called to Mosaku, but the old man did not answer. He put out his hand in the dark, and touched Mosaku's face. It had turned to ice. His friend was dead.

Soon, the storm was over; and when the ferryman arrived at his station a little after sunrise, he found Taishi lying senseless beside the frozen body of Mosaku.

In time, Taishi recovered from the cold that terrible night and returned to his job, going alone each day to the forest. He never told anyone about the woman in white, and he never forgot her.

CHAPTER 32

"Rachel? Rachel!"

Ceinwen shook her, but she couldn't rouse her friend.

"Michael!" Ceinwen ran through the house, calling him. She found him out in his study. "Come quick. I can't wake Rachel."

He joined Ceinwen trying to rouse Rachel, but had no luck.

His cell phone still didn't work, and he was about to run to the Nakamura home to ask where he could find a doctor or a hospital when there was a knock at the door.

He opened it to see Lady Nakamura standing before him.

"My son is under a spell," she said, breathing heavily, her brow furrowed with worry. "We cannot wake him. The doctor has looked at him, and there is nothing wrong that he can see. It is as if Seiji is asleep and doesn't wish to wake. I'm wondering if you have ever encountered such a thing."

"Not before a few minutes ago," Michael said. "I wonder if Rachel is suffering from the same problem." He invited Lady Nakamura into the house to see her.

Lady Nakamura touched Rachel's forehead, then spoke in Japanese to one of the men who accompanied her. He ran out of the house.

"He will bring a doctor who is very discrete about this situation with Seiji. Unfortunately, if word got out, people would believe he is mentally ill."

Lady Nakamura studied Rachel a while and shook her head. "Yesterday, she and Seiji seemed to have a good conversation. Her helpful attitude encouraged him, but I know at one point something happened that concerned Seiji's retainers. Some sort of spell seemed to come over him. That happens with more and more frequency these days."

"Rachel said nothing about that," Michael said.

Lady Nakamura nodded. "I wonder if something happened that created a connection between Seiji and Rachel and whatever is going on now. It's my belief that there are many levels of existence in this world. Perhaps they are somewhere, now, together."

Ceinwen brought Lady Nakamura some tea as they sat in the main tatami room waiting for the doctor to arrive. He did so in less than twenty minutes and went straight in to see Rachel.

He checked her over, listening to heart and lungs, taking her pulse, and then stood back and stared at her with a sigh. "Look at her eyes."

Her eyes were shut, but some movement of the eyeball was visible, the sort of movement seen when someone is in a deep sleep. He faced Lady Nakamura. "Like Nakamura-*sama*," he said, "she is not in a coma, but asleep. We could wait, as I suggested with Nakamura-*sama*. In time, she will become hungry and thirsty and her body should awaken. Or, we could give her a shot of adrenaline to attempt to wake her. It should not be harmful."

Michael realized the doctor feared testing his solution on the daimyo heir. He looked at Ceinwen. "What do you think?"

"Some of her dreams have been terrifying. I say we try to wake her."

The doctor nodded. "I would agree."

He gave Rachel a shot and in moments she opened her eyes and looked around, confused.

Ceinwen touched her shoulder. "You were in a deep sleep, dreaming, and we couldn't wake you. Lady Nakamura called for her doctor."

"I was sleeping?" She bolted upright. "What are you saying? That was no dream! I saw ..." She looked from one to the other. "How long have I been asleep?"

"About ten hours," Michael said. "It's morning."

"My God! It's crazy. Too crazy!" Tears came to her eyes.

"What is it?" Ceinwen asked. "Rachel, talk to me."

She shook her head, but her skin had turned chalky. "It's nothing. I'll be fine."

A short while later, one of the Nakamura retainers came to the door.

Lady Nakamura's aide went to talk to him and came back into the room with a smile. "Nakamura-*sama* is also awake now. He is asking to see his mother."

All expressed their thanks to Lady Nakamura and the doctor as they left the house. Before going, the doctor assured them that Rachel should be just fine. Perhaps there was some allergen in the garden where they spent the afternoon that caused a mild version of "sleeping sickness" to strike.

They all hoped that was the case.

Ceinwen was in the kitchen having coffee with Michael when Rachel entered the room. She had taken a shower in the upstairs bathroom, and her hair was still wet.

"How are you feeling?" Michael asked.

"I guess I was tired. I feel fine now."

"Lady Nakamura sent some breakfast pastries and fruit," Ceinwen said, doing her best to sound cheerful.

Rachel shook her head. "I'm not hungry."

"You need to eat to build energy," Ceinwen said. "It's quite delicious."

"No thanks. Just some tea."

Michael spoke. "We understand from Lady Nakamura that there was a strange episode involving Seiji yesterday. Can you tell us about it?"

"There was a moment where he was feeling … possessed, I guess. But it soon passed. We had a nice time."

"That's good news," Michael said. "Did anything happen that was at all worrisome, or odd?"

Rachel blanched. "Has Seiji ever mentioned a pearl to you? A pearl that can attract demons?"

Michael's brows crossed. "No, although his mother has."

"Attract demons?" Ceinwen used a mocking tone although she remembered Jake Sullivan's worry that Michael might have brought it to Idaho. "Where is this magical stone?"

"Well hidden," Michael said.

Rachel added, "Seiji believes the pearl can help him."

Michael's head snapped toward her. "He said that?"

"He was insistent." Rachel cried, tears welling up in her eyes. "What if he's right? What if the pearl can rid him and me and the people in Salmon of the demons persecuting us? If it could control demons once why not again? *Why won't you help us?*"

"Hold on, there," Ceinwen said. "You're being unfair."

"Me? I don't think so!" Rachel shouted.

"The pearl is dangerous," Michael admitted, his voice low and filled with sadness. "Yes, it lures demons, and was used to capture them. But it took a number of strong men to do it, and many lost their lives trying."

Rachel studied him, and then lowered her gaze, wiping her tears away. "I don't understand any of this." She spoke softly. "I don't know what's happening to me."

"Rachel," Ceinwen said gently. "Please tell him about the strange dreams you had. The ones in which you were in Japan—in old Japan." She then faced Michael. "The strangest part was that the dreams began before we came to Japan, before we even learned you were here. It was as if they were some sort of premonition."

He found the news startling. "You dreamed about Japan?"

Rachel nodded and told him about the corpse-eating ghoul.

His brows crossed. "Any other dreams?"

"I dreamed I stood at a bridge and saw a woman sobbing as if her heart was broken. I offered to help, but when she turned around, she had no face."

He made a sharp intake of breath, then with a hushed voice asked, "Did you dream that you then went to a soba-seller?"

She stared at him and nodded. "He, too, had no face. And soon, neither did I."

He felt chilled to the bone. "You must have read ghost stories by Lafcadio Hearn, and simply forgot that you did." When Michael explained why he chose to live in this house, Rachel claimed to have never heard of Hearn.

"Anything is possible, but I really doubt it. Why?"

"Because those are two of Hearn's stories."

Rachel and Ceinwen gawked at him.

"That makes no sense," Ceinwen said. "I would say it's this house, but Rachel had those dreams before we ever got here."

Michael turned to Rachel. "Anything other dreams?"

She bit her lip, then shook her head. "No."

He frowned. "Are you sure?"

"There were a lot of dreams that were 'simply' demons chasing and scaring me."

Michael studied her a moment, then said, "You haven't told us what you dreamed last night."

She blushed. "It was nothing I can remember."

CHAPTER 33

"Michael, I'm glad you're back," Seiji said, shaking his hand before greeting Ceinwen. He was enjoying the sun near the koi pond. Michael noticed the look of joy and more that filled Seiji's face as he gazed at the entrance to the garden. "Where is Rachel? She's coming, isn't she?"

Michael was puzzled. In the time he'd known Seiji, he rarely shook hands, and never with such a strong grip. "She's home, resting after a troubled night's sleep."

"I'm sorry to hear it," Seiji said. "I would have liked to see her today."

A servant brought Michael and Ceinwen glasses of cold beer. "You're looking strong today, Seiji," Michael said as they sat.

"Yes. I think such a long sleep agreed with me. Please forgive my mother for troubling you about it. I must have been fighting off a virus. That explains why I was so sleepy."

"Perhaps Rachel, as well," Ceinwen said.

Seiji nodded. "Perhaps."

"Rachel told me you asked her about a pearl that could control demons," Michael said.

"I'm most fascinated by it," Seiji said. "I couldn't help but hope it has the power to help me with this … problem."

"I doubt it," Michael said. "Besides, I don't have it."

"Can you get it?"

"No."

"I suspect, if you needed to, you would find a way," Seiji said, his voice icy. "It has to do with alchemy, doesn't it? I know, Michael, that's what interests you. As it does me."

"There's no alchemical tradition in Japan, and in the artifacts I've viewed so far, I've seen no such symbols."

"You will, in time. It existed in this area because, in the days when my country was young, we had many ties with China, particularly here, on the western side of the island." Seiji lifted his chin as he continued. "My ancestor, daimyo Nakamura Taishi, ruled this entire area. One of his many envoys to China was an alchemist. He brought much information back here, and Taishi learned from him how to become immortal. There are many stories of how Taishi has returned to visit later daimyo and give them advice. And also that, over time, he refused to leave."

"What do you mean, refused?"

"They say Taishi became a *kami*, a god, and that he helped the generations of Nakamura daimyo that followed."

Michael waited. There was clearly more to the story.

"At the same time," Seiji continued, "whispers began that Taishi hadn't become a god or an immortal man, but he had turned into a demon."

"So," Michael said, "do you think Taishi is a god or a demon?"

Seiji shook his head. "Who knows? I don't want to believe in such things, but it's all I'm left with. I'm told that you rid the world of three vicious demons. I need you to take away my one. Only one."

Michael glanced at Ceinwen who was intently watching him, then back to Seiji. "I can't."

"With the pearl, you can do it."

"What makes you insist I have such a pearl?"

"Because I trust those who told me of it. I implore you, help me."

"If you continue to appear stronger, you won't need the pearl."

Seiji glowered, breathing deeply, then said, "You should leave now. I am not pleased with you today. I wish you to reflect on the pearl, and that it may be needed here soon. For Rachel as well as me."

The young daimyo's words stunned Michael and Ceinwen. It wasn't a threat. It was a prophecy.

CHAPTER 34

WILLIAM CLAUDE MIXED an elixir containing gold, mercury, sulfur, and a few shavings from a philosopher's stone he once created. He knew it wasn't a powerful stone, but that it existed at all was, to him, quite an achievement.

As the elixir boiled, it cast off fumes which he breathed in, filling his lungs. He held it, letting its magic seep through his blood.

He concentrated first on Michael, opening his mind to his son. But he still could not penetrate his defenses. He then focused on Rachel. He knew she had gone to Japan looking for Michael. With her was a friend, her roommate – another young chit of a college girl, he imagined. Someone he doubted would interfere with his plans in any way.

His mind connected with Rachael's. He gasped as a new panoply of images swirled into his brain. The strongest was demonic. Some thing or *things* wanted her—wanted to draw her away from this world and into its own.

William Claude opened his eyes. His mind raced. Whatever held her frightened him with its power, its sheer forcefulness. His first reaction was to protect her. But then, a different line of thought came to him. Perhaps she was more useful to him if possessed.

Michael would want to protect her, to rid her of the demons. Being face-to-face with Rachel, wanting to help her, the only way to do that would be to use the philosopher's stone. And since he didn't know how, he would need to ask his father for help.

William Claude smiled. "I'll make him realize he needs my help every bit as much as I need his." William Claude spoke aloud to no one and everyone. He rubbed his hands. "I know my son. He'll come back here with the stone, and together, we will use it!"

He picked up his pitiful substitute of a philosopher's stone—one he thought was acceptable until he learned more about the stone Michael owned. He should have realized his stone was inferior since it had yet to turn him into an immortal.

"You, stone of little worth, must now help me create a new, stronger stone." He needed one whose sole purpose was to open Rachel to possession, to weaken her defenses.

As always, his first step was to free himself of all impure thoughts by concentrating on the Emerald Tablet, written by Hermes Trismegistus, the father of alchemy, some 3000 years earlier. William Claude didn't bother with all of Hermes' many platitudes, but concentrated on the five he liked best. He chanted them aloud:

"I speak not fiction, but what is certain and most true.

What is below is like that which is above, and what is above is like that which is below.

Its father is the Sun, its mother is the Moon, its nurse is the Earth.

It is the cause of all perfection throughout the entire world.

Thus were all things created."

Then, like Hermes Trismegistus, William Claude began the process of creating a new philosopher's stone. His face was filled with determination; there was no boundary he wouldn't cross, and no law of man or God he wouldn't violate. After all, were he to be immortal, would he not be a god?

CHAPTER 35

ONE EVENING in the winter of the following year, Rachel stood by the road waiting for Taishi as he made his way home. She was the Snow Woman. A demon.

To her surprise, she had never forgotten the gentle young man although she had toyed with many other men since having had him.

Finally, she saw Taishi and found him even more sensual and arousing than she had a year earlier. As he passed, she fell into step beside him. She had left behind the Snow Woman's white kimono, and appeared as a young peasant close to him in age.

When he asked her name, she replied, O-Yuki, which meant snow. She told him she was an orphan, on her way to Edo to find work. Taishi was immediately charmed, and the more he looked at her, the more beautiful he seemed to find her.

He asked her whether she was yet betrothed. She laughed and said she was quite free. She then asked Taishi if he was married or pledged to marry; and he, too, said no. After these confidences, they walked on for a long while without speaking, but they cast quick, meaningful glances in each other's direction.

When they reached the village, Taishi asked O-Yuki to join him at his house to rest a while before continuing her journey. After some shy hesitation, she went there with him. Upon entering the house, they rushed into each other's arms. He couldn't bear to part with her, and in a matter of days they married.

Hidden behind the name O-Yuki, the Snow Woman, Rachel came to love Taishi. And soon she learned she was expecting a child.

In the morning, Ceinwen again could scarcely arouse Rachel. When she did, Rachel looked around, dazed, confused. She drew in a ragged breath. "No," she whispered, then louder, "No! God, no!"

"What's wrong?" Ceinwen was alarmed at this reaction.

"It wasn't a dream!" Rachel cried, then burst into tears.

Ceinwen helped her get dressed and out to the kitchen where she made Rachel tea and cooked her some scrambled eggs. She was a believer that food could cure many ills.

Michael joined them, and in a hushed voice, Ceinwen told him what had happened that morning.

Rachel took one bite, then pushed away the plate. Both Ceinwen and Michael tried to get her to explain why the dream had upset her so badly.

"The dream wasn't upsetting. The dream was fine," she said finally.

"What then?"

"I don't know how to explain. When I think about it, I don't understand."

"Tell us."

"I was in old Japan. In the dream I was"—she drew in her breath, then blurted out—"I was a demon, a beautiful demonic woman who would pursue men, have sex, and then kill them. But then I met a young man, a woodcutter, who looked like Seiji except that he was healthy and handsome and ... virile. His name was Taishi. And I didn't kill him. I pretended to be a mortal woman, and I married him." Her words hung in the air until she added, "I loved him. I mean, I truly loved him. And he loved me. No one has ever loved me like that. We were expecting our first child when I was awakened."

"That was some dream," Ceinwen murmured.

Rachel glared at Ceinwen. "I hate you for waking me!"

Ceinwen gasped and couldn't reply.

Rachel put her fists against her eyes, then to her temples, trying to calm herself. "It didn't feel like a dream." She tried to explain. "I spent a night with Taishi and vanished for a long time before coming back as a woman. But then, over a period of three months, I spent every day with him as a lover, a wife, and to our joy, as a mother-to-be. I lived those days and those nights—each and every one of them. And you know what was the strangest part of all?"

The other two shook their heads.

"I was so very happy. I don't know if I've ever, at any time in my own life, felt as filled with joy and love as I did for the three months in my dream. To think, to know it was only a dream makes me so sad I can hardly bear it. I want that life not this one. And I ache for all I've lost, and the child I will never know."

Ceinwen and Michael glanced at each other. "Rachel, I'm so sorry," Ceinwen said.

"His name was Taishi Nakamura?" Michael asked.

"Yes." Rachel fought tears. "If you told me I'd been asleep for months, I might have believed you because in my dream, I lived that amount of time. And it was all so very real ..."

"Was your name in the dream Yuki?" Michael asked.

Rachel clasped her hands so tightly her knuckles turned white, and she shouted at Michael. "My dream, my life, was not another of your damned Lafcadio Hearn stories!"

He didn't even flinch at her reaction, but stated, "It's called 'Yuki Onna.' It means Snow Woman."

"*No!*" The word was a scream, a loud, heartbreaking, terrifying scream.

"I'm sorry," he whispered.

She stood, ready to run from the room when she stopped and stared at him. With a shuddering breath, eyes wide, she asked, "Was that the end of the story?"

"No. There's more."

"What?"

"You don't want to know."

Rachel froze there a moment, horrified at the implication of his words, then ran out of the room.

Michael returned to the Nakamura house to work a little on cataloging the artifacts and to check on Seiji, but Ceinwen felt she needed to stay at the Hearn house with Rachel.

At the Nakamura estate, Michael could scarcely believe how strong Seiji appeared—much more so than Michael had ever seen him. Even Lady Nakamura was thrilled as this sudden recovery.

"Perhaps just being around interesting people close to his age is doing wonders for him," Lady Nakamura happily exclaimed. "And his obvious interest in a certain young woman also seems to help his blood flow more strongly."

Michael had to wonder about that, along with Rachel saying her lover was named Taishi – the same name Seiji used for the daimyo thought to have become a demon.

Michael went into the temperature-controlled building and tried to concentrate on some interesting pieces of pottery, but his mind wasn't in it.

In Rachel's eyes, Michael saw the early stages of possession. He hoped he was wrong, but he was especially troubled when he saw how strong Seiji looked while Rachel grew weak. If Taishi was the demon possessing Seiji, and the creature was using Rachel to draw strength, she was in grave danger.

Sexual demonic attacks were well known in Greek and Roman mythology. The most common were succubi, female demons who used men for sex and drained their energy from them. But incubi also existed, male demons who would lie with sleeping women and have sexual relations with them. Sometimes the male demons would appear as satyrs or fauns, but they could take on any form—even that of a handsome Japanese wood cutter.

Michael's mind raced with things he'd read about such creatures. Rachel had dreamed she was pregnant, and many believed incubi had the ability to father demon children.

One of the many legends about the wizard known as Merlin, advisor to King Arthur of Camelot among others, was that he was a cambion: born of a mortal woman, and sired by an incubus. It was said he inherited his supernatural powers and abilities from the incubus. He was also said to have been an alchemist.

Michael tried to remember everything he'd ever heard about incubi. He couldn't remember much except that the *Malleus Maleficarum*, the *Hammer of Witches*, suggested such creatures had no fear and didn't respond to typical exorcisms.

He wondered if everyone was right, and that the only thing that could stop this demon was the pearl.

Demons were attracted to it. They couldn't prevent or stop that attraction and so would do anything to get it, including attacking a young woman who didn't deserve any of the horrors they might inflict on her.

He could feel the demon around Seiji, but couldn't see it.

Why could Rachel see it and not him?

And Ceinwen ... why did she seem immune to these demons?

Just then, the door to the room burst open. It was Ceinwen.

"When I returned from the grocery, I found Rachel asleep. And again, I can't wake her up."

CHAPTER 36

As Ceinwen and Michael rushed to leave the Nakamura house, the family doctor stopped them. "Nakamura-*sama* has once more slipped into a coma. Is Miss Rachel all right?"

"No," Ceinwen said. "I came to tell Michael I can't wake her. Will you come and see what's happening?"

The three hurried to the Hearn house. The doctor didn't hesitate to give Rachel a shot of adrenaline. But this time it had no effect.

"We should take her to a hospital," Michael said.

The doctor shook his head. "A hospital will be of no help to her."

At Michael's puzzled expression, the doctor added, "I have taken care of the Nakamura family for years. I understand the situation, and your friend has somehow become ensnared in it. I believe the best thing is to move her to the Nakamura estate. There, she will be given the best care, and I will be able to watch over both my patients at the same time."

"Do you have any idea how long this sleep might last?" Ceinwen asked.

The doctor rubbed his chin in thought. "Maybe an hour. Maybe a week. Who can tell? I will make sure they have nourishment and remain hydrated."

Ceinwen nodded and looked at Michael. He met her gaze and agreed.

"If I may," the doctor said to Michael, "Lady Nakamura confided in me that you have access to something that could deal with whatever is possessing her son and your friend. If true, and I leave it up to you to decide, I hope you are willing to do what is necessary to help these young people."

Michael's shoulders sagged. His expression grim, he nodded.

After the doctor left, Ceinwen sat alone in the main tatami room, worried and forlorn. Michael entered with two open bottles of beer.

"I've decided," Michael said as he put a bottle in front of her and then sat on a *zabuton.* "I'm going back to Idaho to retrieve the pearl. It might be the only thing to help Seiji and Rachel."

"So it is in Idaho," Ceinwen said, reaching for the beer. "I think it's time you explained what this pearl business is all about."

"You still don't know?"

"Not for lack of trying! To tell me it's a 'philosopher's stone' means nothing. My meager study of alchemy tells me the whole thing is a hoax and its supporters charlatans."

He looked dismayed. "I can see where you'd think that. Most people do."

"But you don't?" Her gaze was skeptical.

He didn't answer for a long while. "It all began last year. I was in Florence, and an old priest showed up at my door with something that looked like a reddish-pink pearl."

Michael explained that the pearl was an ancient Chinese artifact from the Shang dynasty—a dynasty so old historians had assumed it was mythical, until modern archeologists proved it really once existed. The pearl was a philosopher's stone. Demons desired it so that they could have power over mankind. Those demons destroyed the Shang empire, but eventually were defeated and captured within the pearl.

All remained quiet for centuries until Marco Polo made his famous travels to China over the Old Silk Road. He discovered the pearl, stole it, and then brought the pearl—and the demons within it—back to Europe, where the demons did much damage. Eventually, the pearl reached Michael with instructions to return it to the place from which it had been stolen. The demons battled to stop him.

Michael and others managed to overcome the demons and then he and Jianjun buried it deep in a mountainous area of Idaho with no roads, no people, few animals, and an abundance of rare earth elements. The ancient Chinese knew those elements somehow neutralized demonic power.

"I've heard of rare earth elements, but I'm not sure what they are," Ceinwen admitted.

"They're metals—ones you'll find listed near the end of the periodic table. They weren't valued until recently and now become more valuable each day. They're used in cell phones, computer hard drives, wind turbines, hybrid cars, solar panels, catalytic converters, and so on. Also, since they make other metals even stronger, they're used in airplane engines."

"They sound amazing," Ceinwen said.

"They are," Michael agreed. "Right now, China is heavily invested in mining the elements in what's called 'Inner Mongolia.' Whenever another country makes progress in mining their own supply, China drops the price until the competition goes bankrupt. Then, China once again raises the price of the elements.

"Also removing them from the ground is dangerous since they're often connected with toxic low-level radioactive elements that can be airborne as dust or leach into the water supply. In the US, mine operators must follow strict, expensive rules. That's why most rare earth elements there remain left untouched and unmined."

"And do they drain demons of power?"

"I've seen it work. Jianjun and I were certain the demons that we placed in that ground would be stuck there forever. But, perhaps, they weren't drained of as much power as we had hoped."

"You mean the demons might continue to be powerful?" Ceinwen cried.

"It seems something, perhaps demonic, is going on in Salmon. It might be because of the pearl, but I won't know until I'm there."

"That doesn't sound good," she murmured. "Is the pearl in a remote location?"

"Quite," Michael said.

"In that case, I'm going with you."

He grimaced. "Sure you are."

"Really."

"No. You aren't coming with me."

"If Rachel wakes up while we're in Idaho—"

"*We?* Didn't you hear what I said?" he asked. "It's dangerous."

"Obviously." Ceinwen looked at him as if he just didn't get it. "If it was a walk in the park, I'd let you go alone. But it's not."

"You'd *let* me?"

"You heard me."

He threw up his hands. "But what if Rachel—?"

"As I was saying," Ceinwen interrupted, "if Rachel were to wake while we're gone, she'll be well taken care of. And if she remains asleep, what good would it do for me to be here? Should I sit around here twiddling my thumbs? I don't think so!"

"First, since there are no roads out there, it'll be necessary to hike to the spot."

"I once did a story about yeti in the Himalayas, and I had to go to where they might be. I'm not some delicate flower, Michael. I can do this." Ceinwen gazed at him, then placed her hands on her hips. "I'm worried about you. You can't go there alone. Something strange is going on, and demonic or human, two would be safer than one."

"But you're no demon slayer."

"I'm better than nothing. I haven't been to war zones and other shitty places without learning how to protect myself. I've spent hours at a gun range, and I'm a good shot. A damn good shot actually. But," she hesitated, her mind at work, "what about your assistant? Maybe we should ask Li Jianjun to join us."

He sighed in defeat. She was headstrong. Determined. And maybe too brave for her own good. She was like no woman he had ever known... and mind-boggling as it was, he liked each and every one of those traits.

Taking her with him would be risky, but it appeared she wouldn't take no for an answer.

But was she wanting to go to debunk another mystery, to put another feather in her cap? Or, did she really want to retrieve the pearl in the hope that it could help Rachel?

He leveled a questioning stare at her. "Do you finally believe Rachel and me?"

"Ninety-five percent convinced." She grinned. "And weakening on the other five."

CHAPTER 37

"Pack your bags and meet me in Seattle. We're going to Salmon, Idaho."

Michael's phone call, made from the Izumo Airport, filled Jianjun with relief. His boss—his friend—was still alive. Jianjun had been on the verge of giving him up for lost, or maybe even dead. He barely heard Michael's rushed explanation about the power outage that made it impossible to receive or make calls. He was more interested in learning why they were going back to Salmon, only to hear Michael say, "I'll explain everything when I see you."

"You'll see me sooner than you imagine," Jianjun said. "I haven't been sitting around Vancouver wondering where the hell you've been, I've been in Japan looking for you. In fact, I'm not more than twenty minutes from the airport now, so reserve me a seat on your flights and you can start explaining within the hour." He didn't bother to tell Michael that he'd been searching for a place called Kamigawa, or that no one he'd met had ever heard it. There were too many strange things going on, all of which he hoped Michael could explain when they met for their flight.

Jianjun easily found Michael in the Izumo airport, and was stunned that Ceinwen Davies was traveling with him. But on the long flight home, he came to understand why. Outwardly they acted like exasperated colleagues, but Jianjun saw the attraction between them. He found it fascinating that she wasn't the least bit intimidated by Michael, when most everyone else who came in contact with the archaeologist found him formidable. Michael obviously cared about her thoughts and reactions to all that was going on.

Jianjun wasn't yet sure how he felt about her, but he loved that she had gotten Michael interested in helping with the situation in Salmon. He wasn't crazy about going into the Idaho backcountry, but it was preferable to returning home.

As he sat with them on the plane from Seattle to Missoula, Montana, the closest major airport to Salmon, Idaho, he couldn't help but think about the last time he went to that area. He had just received a message from Kira Holt saying goodbye. He understood why she sent it. It was his fault, not hers, but it broke his heart.

The ironic part was that he never really understood how they became a couple in the first place.

To call him a "nerd" was an understatement. He'd always been shy and awkward around women. His marriage had been arranged in the Chinese way, and he always felt that, had his parents not found him a wife, he'd probably still be a bachelor.

He was born in Beijing. When he was eight years old, his parents moved to Hong Kong, and later emigrated to Vancouver, Canada. Jianjun was now a proud Canadian citizen, but the Chinese tradition was strong in his family, and he had grown up with Chinese sensibilities.

He had been taught that women must be petite with smooth-as-silk jet black hair, ivory-toned skin, almond-shaped black eyes, and a tiny mouth and nose. Much, in fact, the way his wife, Linda, looked.

Kira Holt had everything wrong with her. That she was his height was bad enough, but on top of that, her hair was bright red, curly, and flyaway, her skin so pale it was almost translucent, and to make matters *much* worse, she had freckles across the bridge of her nose. Any Chinese woman would have died of shame, or at least gone somewhere to get the bizarre dots removed. And her eyes were big and blue.

Yet, he found himself liking the way her body was shaped, and intrigued by the way the sun glinted off her coppery hair. The delicacy of her skin made him almost afraid to touch it. The freckles on her nose, instead of ugly, he thought were cute, and her beguiling eyes had captured his heart as he found himself lost in their depths.

She was, to him, perfect.

But he was raised to be a dutiful son, and he had vowed to take care of Linda as his wife. To do otherwise would not only bring shame to her, but to his parents and all his ancestors. His parents knew he was unhappy, but their solutions were untenable. His mother had proclaimed a baby would bind him and Linda together in love. His father suggested if things with Linda were as bad as Jianjun made it seem, maybe a mistress was the answer.

But both solutions seemed manipulative and wrong—wrong for both himself and Linda. It was strange that his own parents, whom he had always felt close to, couldn't see that.

Every day he thought about Kira. She was a psychiatrist, working as a profiler for the FBI when he met her. She had turned him into a vat of Jell-O with just one glance. He could hardly get two sensible words out of his mouth when she was near. Yes, he had fallen hard for Kira Holt. Beyond hard, he loved her. And most amazingly, Kira seemed to care about him, maybe even loved him—a little, at least—except for the major problem that he was married. Because of that, and because he couldn't leave his wife, Kira had walked away and never contacted him again.

He tried to put thoughts of her out of his mind as they navigated the Missoula airport, but he guessed he wasn't doing such a good job of it because Michael patted his shoulder, as if he understood why Jianjun was unusually quiet.

Michael rented a four-wheel-drive Jeep for the three of them to travel from Missoula southward to Salmon.

For most of the three-hour journey, the highway edged a river east of the Bitterroot Mountains until, high in the mountains, they crossed the continental divide into Idaho. It was June, and the land was green and awake. As the heavy snows of winter melted, the river and surrounding creeks became swollen with frigid, rushing water. The landscape enraptured Ceinwen. The mountains were jagged and bold, and she swore she had never seen a sky as high as in Montana and Idaho—and she was a world traveler, as she liked to remind Michael. He told her the locals called it "Big Sky Country." She could see why.

"You'll be interested in knowing that Lewis and Clark, whose trails and historic landmarks you see all over this area, crossed the divide fifty or so miles south of here, at what's now called Lemhi Pass," Michael said.

"Hmm. I've heard of Petula Clark, Dick Clark, Clark Kent, but I can't think of any Lewis N. Clark."

He told her about Lewis *and* Clark making their way across the continental United States to the Pacific Ocean. She had all kinds of questions for him about the history of the area, most of which he could answer.

"I used to enjoy Longfellow's poetry about early America," Ceinwen said. "I've always wanted to see an area like this."

"Longfellow?" Michael said. "I didn't know he'd be popular in Wales."

"He's one of the few American poets we read. Let's see...

By the shores of Gitche Gumee,
By the shining Big-Sea-Water,
Stood the wigwam of Nokomis,
Daughter of the moon, Nokomis.

And why are you laughing, Doctor Rempart?"

"I'm sorry. It's just that *Hiawatha* spoken with a Welsh accent seems to lose something. It comes across as really ... uh..."

"*What?*"

"Hammy. Or should I say overacted, melodramatic—"

"Stop. I didn't think you were talking about a side of pork. What's your opinion, Jianjun?" She turned to look at him in the backseat, but before he could come up with a response, she added, "I'll have both of you know, I once starred in a school play."

"So, a star in our midst," Michael said. He wanted to add that he found her quoting the poem to be quite charming, but doubted she'd appreciate it. Instead he said, "What was your role?"

"I was a talking frog. The frog had the most lines, and I was one of the rare first graders who could not only memorize more than three words at a time, but was bold enough to say them in front of an audience."

"I can only imagine," he said with a grin.

"And you, Professor, would have gotten the role of a bump on a log."

"Just in time," Michael said as he turned onto Main Street, "we've arrived in Salmon."

He parked in front of the Sheriff's Office. It was afternoon, but a chill touched the air. Summer came late in the high mountains of Idaho.

Michael entered the office to find Deputy Mallick hunched over his desk staring at a piece of paper as if he were afraid it would come alive and denounce him.

"Mallick?" Michael moved forward.

Mallick nearly jumped out of his skin. "Sorry. I didn't hear you come in." His eyes widened with recognition and he stood. "Oh, my."

"Michael Rempart," Michael said as he held out his hand.

Mallick shook it. "Of course I remember you. It was such a strange time. I don't think I'll ever forget any of it. And Ms. Davies, welcome back," he added greeting Ceinwen.

Michael introduced him to Jianjun who, despite having been in Idaho in the past, had never met the deputy or the sheriff.

"I hope you being here doesn't mean that things are about to become as crazy as they did a couple of years ago," Mallick said nervously.

"We hope not as well," Michael said. "Is Jake around?"

Before Mallick could answer, the sheriff came out of his office and stared with surprise at Michael, Ceinwen, and Jianjun.

Michael walked up to him, his hand outstretched. "Jake, good to see you again," Michael said.

Jake caught him in a quick bear hug. After greetings and introducing Jianjun, Jake asked, "Where's Rachel?"

"She's ill," Ceinwen said. "Some kind of virus, we think, so she stayed in Japan. We're going back there soon."

Jake's face filled with concern. "Do I want to know what brings all of you here?" He ushered them into his office and closed the door. "Something tells me I'm not going to like it."

"It has to do with a pearl." Michael said. "A mysterious pearl that can lure demons. I think I told you about it last time I was here."

"Yes, you did. And something also tells me you may have left it among our rare earth elements," Jake said, arms folded.

"So you figured it out, did you? I should have known," Michael said. "Yes, I left the pearl because I believed it would be neutralized. But something is obviously going on here. I don't know if it has to do with the demons within the pearl, or other demons interested in it, but I'm going into the mountains to retrieve it. Hopefully, that'll solve your problems."

Jake's gaze met Ceinwen's. "I still can't get used to hearing this guy talk about demons as if they were as real as wolves, bears, and mountain lions."

"My sentiments exactly, Sheriff," she admitted.

"So, Michael, you want to retrieve it," Jake said. "But doesn't that mean you'll be exposing all of us to danger while the pearl is here but not contained within rare earth elements?"

"It would except that I'm hoping you'll help us get our hands on a small lead container that we can fill with rare earth elements. We'll put the pearl and its case into it before we move it anywhere."

Jake nodded. "I've got a buddy who works down at the Idaho National Lab in Idaho Falls. It's part of the DOE's Office of Nuclear Energy, so I suspect they have stuff like that. I'm pretty sure I can get him to send whatever we need up here by messenger as long as we're willing to pay the cost, which we definitely are."

"Great," Michael said, then turned to Ceinwen. "You'll be interested in seeing the bronze vessel the pearl is in. It's no bigger than an apricot and from the Shang Dynasty. It's a completely rare and unique piece, worth a fortune. I wish I could let the world know about, but all things considered, that's not a good idea."

Ceinwen's eyebrows rose. "How intriguing. It makes me even more glad I'm on this trip."

"So, Jake," Michael continued, "is there a way I can get my hands on some firearms? The demons should be contained, but who knows what else we might encounter out there in the middle of nowhere."

"Not to worry," Jake said. "I'm going with you. And, I'll ask a couple of deputies along. There are too many strange things happening in that backcountry, and the last thing I want is for you and your international friends to end up in the news because you've disappeared or been killed."

"Why, Sheriff, that's so thoughtful." Ceinwen's tone dripped with sarcasm. "You're really looking out for us, aren't you?"

Jake looked at Michael. "Why am I not surprised you've traveling with her?"

Michael grinned. "Just my luck I guess."

"Well, while you two are grinning like a pair of hyenas," Ceinwen said, "Jianjun and I will pack up the Jeep with whatever you think we should bring along."

"Tell you what," Jake said. "Let's go over to my house. We'll spend tonight gathering supplies, and make the trip first thing in the morning. By the way, Michael, how far are we going?"

"It's in the mountains north of the Salmon River and south of the Selway, off Highway 12."

"That's pretty far, and not much out there."

"I remember a sign for Selway Falls, but after that, there's nothing at all."

CHAPTER 38

JAKE WAS ready early the next morning. Two part-time deputies, Len Rosenfeld and Pete Grayson, volunteered to join them. They rode with Jake in his truck while the others followed in Michael's Jeep.

Ceinwen did her best not to think about where they were going or what they might find there, but it wasn't working. Her investigations had resulted in many unusual trips, but her earlier journey to a spot where Egyptian pillars supposedly once stood, not to mention Jake and Rachel's bizarre reaction to what they saw there, was one of the strangest. She feared this trip might make that one look like a Teddy Bear picnic.

She had scores of questions about the past, but since Michael would only give the barest details, she turned to face Jianjun in the backseat. "Were you part of the group lost out here two years ago?"

He glanced in Michael's direction. "I was spared that, I'm happy to say."

"But surely, you know about it."

"Yes, of course. I mean, Michael talked about it." At Michael's quick frown in the rearview mirror at him, Jianjun added, "When he needed to." He clamped his mouth shut.

"Have you traveled with Michael many places?" she asked.

"Many places. He's been my boss for a few years."

"So, tell me about yourself," Ceinwen said. "Are you married?"

"Yes. My wife is in Vancouver, Canada."

"Any kids?"

"No. No kids."

"What does she think of you doing a lot of traveling?"

"She's fine with it."

"Does she ever join you?"

"No way! I mean, traveling around, roughing it, she'd hate it."

"It must get lonely for you," Ceinwen said.

Jianjun looked to Michael for help against the barrage, but Michael was, or pretended to be, concentrating on his driving. "Not really," Jianjun murmured.

"No?"

His breathing quickened. "I mean ... there's so much work to do. Always. Who has time to think about being lonely? Ha, ha."

He gave as forced a laugh as Ceinwen had ever heard. "Sure," she said. She knew evasive when it slapped her in the face. But why? She stopped asking questions, realizing that to get real answers, she'd have to talk to Jianjun when he was alone.

The highway brought them into Montana before heading west, back to Idaho. At the tiny town of Lowell, they turned due south. Past Selway Falls, the road ended. There, they made camp.

"This is a far cry from what we ate in Japan," Ceinwen said to Jake as they shared canned beef stew and pan-fried biscuits. "But it's better than airplane food."

"Horse pellets would be better than airplane food," Michael said.

Jake's two deputies soon took their bedrolls and retired for the night as if realizing the old friends had a lot to talk about.

Michael and the others kept their voices low as they huddled around the campfire.

"What really happened in Japan, Michael?" Jake asked. "I can't believe you left Rachel alone there."

As Michael filled Jake in on everything that had happened, Ceinwen studied his expression. The amazing part was that Jake, just as Jianjun had done when Michael told him the same story on the flight from Japan, accepted everything Michael told him without question. More than ever, she wondered what in the world took place out here two years earlier.

She heard a low howl in the distance. "I hope that was a coyote with a very deep voice," Ceinwen said.

"We pronounce it 'KAI-yote' out here," Jake said. "Not 'kai-YO-tee,' but that's no coyote. I'd say it's a wolf. Don't worry, they know better than to come around people. Pretty much, anyway."

"I hope you're right. We rid England and Wales of wolves a couple centuries ago, but some people are trying to reintroduce them. I think the sheep farmers in Wales will have something to say about that. Textiles, my brothers' business, is still an important industry there." She stopped talking at the sound of another howl followed by an answering cry. She rubbed her arms against a sudden chill, and when she spoke, her voice was tiny. "It's been a while since I've slept outdoors. And never around wolves. And don't you have grizzly bears and mountain lions out here as well?"

"We do," Jake said.

She faced Michael. "Is it too late for me to bow out?"

At his stricken look, she laughed. "Just kidding. I wouldn't miss this for the world."

"So I've been told," Michael said. "And it's not four-legged creatures we need to worry about."

She nodded. "How are we going to do this?"

"First, we hope the pearl is still where we buried it. If not, we'll need to find it. It's too dangerous to let loose on the world."

She turned to Jianjun. "You've been involved with this pearl, haven't you?"

He drew in his breath. "I'm sorry to say I have. I was hoping I would never be again."

"Do you think it'll be possible for us to retrieve it and take it back to Japan?" she asked.

"That ... should be possible," he said.

"I hear hesitation."

Jianjun glanced at Michael, then said, "If there are demons around, and apparently there are, they'll want it. They'll attack, and they're formidable."

She gawked at him. "So ... you're saying you've been attacked by demons?"

"Hasn't everyone?" He deadpanned. Michael and Jake chuckled.

"Har, har," Ceinwen said. "But you, like Michael, believe demons are real."

"I *know* they are. I've had bruises to prove it." Jianjun hesitated a moment, then faced Michael. "That's why this worries me. What if the pearl doesn't work on whatever is hurting your friends in Japan? What if we can't control the demons and end up releasing them into the world again?"

"Don't talk like that, Jianjun. Michael can handle them," Ceinwen said. The words were no sooner out of her mouth than she thought, my God, now I'm believing all this!

"I'm worried, too," Michael admitted to her, his expression tortured. "You and Jake didn't see how strong and cruel they were. They killed a lot of people. For us to attempt to save two friends, who knows what harm we might end up doing to others?"

"But how can we sit back and do nothing when we might save them?"

Troubled eyes met hers. "But at what risk, Ceinwen? The last time, I couldn't have contained the demons alone. I had help. Men sacrificed themselves to help." His voice dropped to a whisper. "It was terrible."

"I'll do all I can," Ceinwen said.

"I know." He took her hand. "You don't need to be part of this. You could be safe at Oxford. What if something happens to you out here?"

Her fingers tightened. "It's my choice to be here. No matter what happens, remember that."

He nodded, then stood. "We should get some sleep. We'll make an early start in the morning."

The men spread out their bedrolls, and Ceinwen took a blanket and got into the SUV. Another wolf howled, and she shivered as if it were an omen.

"Michael," Jianjun whispered after Jake's snores told him the sheriff was asleep. "Are you awake?"

Michael sat up. "What is it?"

Jianjun move closer so as not to wake anyone. "I need to tell you something. I wanted to tell you on the plane long before we got here, but I didn't want to worry Ceinwen."

Michael frowned. "I'm all ears."

"When I went to Japan, I went in search of the place you told me you were going to--Kamigawa. First I went to Izumo, then Matsue. I talked with people at the museums, to the local police, to villagers, old *and* young, but I found no one who had ever heard of Kamigawa. I tried everything I could think of to find it. But it's not on any maps. It's *nowhere*. And then, when I talked to Japanese historians to find out about the Nakamura daimyo family, I discovered there was no such thing."

"That's impossible."

"It happened."

"Did you drive around or try the trains?"

"Both. I've concluded Kamigawa doesn't exist. At least not *in my world.* And no Nakamura was ever a daimyo ... *here.* What does that tell you?"

"Christ!" Michael said. "I'll admit I kept getting a sense that nothing was quite as it seemed. Things were too perfect and fell into place too easily. And when the power went out, I didn't even care. No one cared, in fact."

"I hate to say it," Jianjun said, "but I suspect something lured both you and Rachel there. How else could you two end up in such a place?"

"A place that doesn't exist on this plane," Michael murmured. "It could be like the area around the pillars in Idaho."

"You and Rachel were at those pillars together," Jianjun said. "That's got to be the connection."

"And it would explain why Ceinwen wasn't affected by any of it."

"Are you sure you can trust Ceinwen?" Jianjun asked. "I also researched her. She is what she said—an investigative reporter on paranormal phenomena, living in Oxford. But that's the problem—she's a reporter."

"I want to trust her, but I'm not sure," Michael said. "As you know, I've been fooled before."

Jianjun nodded, then dropped his gaze. "Haven't we all?" he murmured.

Michael knew what he was referring to. "Have you heard from Kira?"

"Not a word."

"I guess that's for the best."

Jianjun's mouth wrinkled. "Yeah. That's what I keep telling myself."

CHAPTER 39

THE NEXT MORNING, Michael tapped on the SUV's window. Ceinwen opened her eyes to sunshine. She groggily sat up and opened the door to see Michael looking fresh and well-rested, while she felt like something that should be put out with the trash. He handed her a cup of coffee.

"That smells heavenly," she said. She took a sip, then climbed out of the SUV and stretched. The back bench was soft but short, and sleeping on it wasn't the most comfortable thing although, as she looked at the ground where the men had slept, it could have been worse.

Jake and the deputies were eating, while Jianjun was sitting up in his sleeping bag, staring into space as if he wasn't sure where he was. His uncombed, thick, black hair stuck straight up.

But everyone soon pulled themselves together and were on their way once more.

This time, Michael took the lead. He drove over fire roads heading south as long as the Jeep could handle the terrain. Once on foot, everyone helped carry supplies and digging equipment as they hiked into the mountains. The two deputies hadn't been told exactly what was happening, but knew it could be quite dangerous.

Last year, Michael and Jianjun had marked the route as best they could, including taking photos of what they hoped would be natural signposts. Nevertheless, more than once they had to backtrack.

The second time that happened, Michael said to Ceinwen, "You're probably sorrier than ever that you're here."

"Not at all. This will work out. I trust you."

Her trust both warmed and bothered him. He had failed too many people he cared about. And, he had to admit, the more time he spent with her, the more he was learning to care.

Two hours passed before he called to Jake and the deputies, "We're near." Then, turning to Ceinwen, he pointed out a tall mountain up ahead. "Do you see a few reddish brown rocks up on that mountain? They're that color because they have rare earth elements in them. But those near the surface aren't worth mining—there are too few of the valuable elements."

She looked upward and blanched. "Do we have to climb all the way up there?"

"Only about half-way."

"There is a God!"

They went up single-file, Michael, then Jake, Ceinwen, Jianjun, Deputy Pete Grayson, and last, Deputy Len Rosenfeld.

After a while, Michael motioned Jake and Jianjun to go ahead and waited for Ceinwen.

"Doing okay?" he asked. She said she was fine, but he stayed with her.

"I have a basic question," she said after a while. "One I'm surprised no one has asked."

"Which is?"

"If, as all of you say, we're dealing with all-powerful demons, what's to stop them from grabbing the pearl from you as soon as you free it from the rare earth?"

"Easy. They can't attack whoever controls the pearl."

"Why not?"

"Damned if I know. But it saved me before."

She gawked at him. "So that's well and good for you, but what about me, Jianjun, and the others? What are we supposed to do while you're all safe and sound?"

"They'll have to go through me to get to you, and I won't let them. Demons are powerful but not omnipotent. They are subject to limits which is what tempts so many to engage with them. You do it at your own peril. They are deceivers. Jianjun has dealt with them before. He knows what we're up against."

Michael slowed. He shaded his eyes, studying the terrain. "I think we're getting close to the pearl."

"Yes?" Ceinwen asked.

He nodded slowly. Methodically. "I can feel it."

"What do you mean?"

"Jake. Jianjun. Stop!" He wrapped an arm around Ceinwen's waist and tugged her close.

"What's going on?" Jake asked, his voice hushed, as if he feared the answer.

"Up ahead." Michael pointed upward. "There, where the mountainside flattens out. See the dark shapes?"

"I don't see a thing," Jake said. "Not a damn thing." Yet his hand hovered over his gun.

The deputies also reached for their pistols.

Michael had buried the pearl near the area where the dark shapes waited. A part of him wanted to turn back, but now that they'd come this far, they had to go on. No matter what.

"I don't see anything either," Ceinwen said. "No dark shapes at all. Only the mountainside."

"I wish you could all see through my eyes," he murmured. "Believe me. They're just ahead, about ten more steps. Jake, you and your deputies stay here, but be ready for anything. Ceinwen, Jianjun, stay close to me."

He gripped Ceinwen's hand, felt her trembling, yet she followed him up the mountain, as did Jianjun, step for step. For the sake of everyone who'd come on this journey with him, he remained calm. "Let's hope my power as owner of the pearl still exists."

"Let's *hope?*" Ceinwen sputtered.

"Hope. Pray. Whatever works."

Jianjun put a hand on Michael's shoulder as the three of them moved forward, connected, almost as one. As they neared the darkness, the shapes floated to the side, opening a pathway.

"It's working," Michael whispered. "They're getting out of our way."

"I still can't see anything," Ceinwen said. "Are you sure?"

"Yes!" he insisted. He'd not only seen them, he'd felt their presence, thick and menacing.

When they reached the flat area, the dark shapes had vanished, but Michael didn't let down his guard. He looked back and gave the okay for Jake and the deputies to join them. The deputies regarded Michael as if he were hallucinating, but Jake acted as if they should trust the guy. They were seriously spooked, but Jake was no bullshit artist, so they followed.

"The pearl is right around here," Michael said. He continued to hold

Ceinwen's hand as he and Jianjun walked around looking for the burial spot that matched the cell phone photos they'd taken the year before. "We're so close," Michael said. "I feel its presence. It's weird. And powerful."

"This is it. Right here," Jianjun said, pointing at the ground. ""I'm certain."

Michael looked at the photo on his phone, at the placement of rocks at Jianjun's feet, and nodded. He then faced Ceinwen, Jake and the deputies. "Now for the bad news. Jianjun and I buried it over six feet down."

Ceinwen groaned.

"Give me that pickax," Jake said. "Come on, fellas. Let's get this taken care of."

Jake and the deputies made short work of digging through loose dirt and rock, clearing out a hole at least five feet deep, its width and length big enough to hold a coffin, or at least a couple of people brave enough to climb down into it to explore further. Michael jumped into the pit and in spite of his protests, Ceinwen followed, spade in hand. Michael's eyes went from the spade to her. "You're helping?"

"Of course. Stay back while I while I wield this thing." She stabbed the ground with the spade. The end went down about an inch.

"Maybe we should let Jianjun do it," Michael said.

"Who's the archaeologist-to-be around here? Besides, this pit isn't big enough for the three of us."

She and Michael dug through the dirt, being careful not to strike too hard or too deep. They had to go slowly and carefully. Damaging the metal box that contained the pearl could, perhaps, unleash the demons and doom them all.

Ceinwen shifted away from Michael as she tried to dig deeper. She was sweating, but he noticed her shiver as if struck by a chill. Suddenly, she screamed as some unseen force lifted her high in the air.

"Holy shit!" Deputy Grayson cried, unable to look away, as he fumbled at his side for his handgun.

Michael reached for her, but before he could grab her she was tossed like a rag doll towards the mountain's face. She managed to put her hands up to protect her head before she hit, and fell to the ground, stunned but conscious.

The two deputies stared back and forth from her to Jake, Michael and Jianjun, all but frozen in place, and not daring to believe what they had just witnessed.

Michael was climbing out of the hole when a whirling black cloud stuck Jianjun hard. It knocked him against Michael, and both fell back into the pit. A shriek of rage sounded around them.

Jake and the deputies tried to run to Ceinwen, but a strong wind pushed them to the edge of the flat area, then shoved them down the mountains slope as if they were featherweights. The deputies shrieked in terror over the invisible menace as they slid, rolled, and tumbled down the hill.

Jianjun was in a daze, but Michael couldn't do anything for him now. He had to get to Ceinwen.

Pulling himself out of the hole, he saw a multitude of black shapes swirling over her. They were no longer indistinct shapes. They'd sprouted heads and hands and arms. They were grotesque. Menacing. And even more vile when one turned toward him, opening its cavernous mouth to howl, and flashing long fangs and a flicking black tongue. It then turned and swooped toward Ceinwen, blood and saliva dripping from its lips onto her face.

"No!" Michael shouted, rushing at the evil being as it sank its teeth into her neck.

He threw himself at the dark silhouette, but instead of knocking the demon from Ceinwen, he ran through it, as if it were mere air.

Was there no stopping the thing?

Again he tried to yank it away from Ceinwen, but it was like grabbing handfuls of smoke. All he could do was to cover her with his body, hold her tight, and do his best to shield her from the black, nightmarish apparitions.

Ghouls spun in furious swirls around and around him and Ceinwen. For long minutes evil swarmed and howled, pulling at him, tugging, and clawing. But then, almost as if he had snapped his fingers to make it end, the apparitions vanished. Demonic chaos was replaced with empty silence.

Michael looked down at Ceinwen. Her eyes were wide with fright. "Are you all right?"

He began to lift himself off of her, but she grabbed his shirt, holding him close. "I saw them this time," she whispered. "Black, like charcoal. I saw their glaring red eyes. It was horrible. I don't understand, Michael. It's not possible. But it was all too real—and not of this world."

"Shh, don't talk. I've got you. You're safe now." He helped her sit up, and then checked her over as best he could to make sure no bones had been broken when she was tossed against the mountain.

"There were so many of them," she cried, shaking her head. She was bruised and there was a superficial wound on her neck, but she appeared to be otherwise unharmed. Still, he would watch her for signs of concussion or internal injuries.

"They're gone for now."

"My neck ... it feels as if it's on fire." She lifted her hand toward her neck.

"Don't touch it," he warned, seeing the torn skin and blood.

But she had already placed her hand on the wound, and when she drew it away, her fingers were red. At the sight, she passed out cold.

When Ceinwen awoke, she discovered Michael had tied one end of a rope around her waist, and the other end around his. They were back in the pit and she lay at his side as he dug through the earth.

"What's this?" She started to sit up.

"Stay down," he said, placing a hand on her shoulder. "I don't want you to scare me again. I've heard of people who faint at the sight of their own blood, but I've never seen it before. You went out like a light."

She felt woozy and decided that lying down was best for now. "Where are Jianjun and the others?"

"Jake and the deputies are scouting around, completely freaked out, I'm afraid. And Jianjun is the one who came up with the rope idea. As we suspected, it seems any kind of connection with me—as owner of the pearl—stops these demons from doing serious harm. For whatever reason, you're the one the demons fixated on. They pushed the others out of the way to get to you. It was scary ... although not as scary as when you fainted."

"It's not like I fainted on purpose." She lightly fingered the bandages on her neck.

"Thank goodness the blood stopped flowing." He winked down at her. "We might have run out of bandages."

"How compassionate! How did I get down here?"

"Jianjun helped me move you. You're no featherweight."

"You really know how to make a girl feel great about herself, don't you?" She sat up now but was too dizzy to try to stand.

"Don't move. I can handle this." He continued to push the dirt away with his hands.

"And the demons are now leaving me alone because of this little rope?" She eyed the rope linking the two of them.

"So it seems. It's probably also that the rare earth elements around us have made them weaker than they would normally be. They were surprisingly easy to run off. I'm afraid the bite you received would have gone a lot deeper and probably been a lot worse if they hadn't been weakened."

"When I saw their fangs, worse wasn't on my mind. Fatal was."

He stopped digging and sat back on his haunches to look at her. She was trying hard to act brave, but he couldn't miss how scared she was. His hand lightly caressed the side of her face. "Damn, but I shouldn't have let you come out here. I knew it could be bad. I'm sorry, Ceinwen."

Their eyes met and what began as a gesture of comfort quickly grew to something more. Something neither of them needed right now.

He drew his fingers from her face

"It's all right," she whispered, attempting a smile. "It wasn't as if I wasn't warned over and over again."

At her attempt at bravery, he wanted nothing so much as to kiss her, right there in front of Jianjun, the demons, and even the sheriff and his men. He didn't care. His gaze never leaving hers and throwing caution to the wind, he shoved the spade into the ground to the left of where he'd been digging and heard the slight "ding" of metal against metal. He froze. It took a moment for the sound to register. "Did you hear that?"

"Yes."

He pulled out the spade and dug his fingers into the ground. "I feel something! This could be it."

He lifted out the small metal box he'd buried the pearl in a year earlier. He opened it cautiously, and inside, wrapped in silk cloth, was a small bronze vessel with a lid and three legs. It was the size of an apricot and cast with a monster design with large round eyes, c-shaped horns and an s-shaped mouth.

"It's incredible!" Ceinwen gasped at both the intricacy and the obvious age of the bronze piece.

Michael nodded at her, smiling at the treasure, then stood.

"We found it!" he called to Jianjun. "Get the lead container."

"Will do."

Michael sank back down into the excavation, resting on his haunches. The vessel had a clever opening, and Ceinwen watched his every move as he twisted two of its three legs. Inside the container were the metallic ores known as rare earth elements. Michael carefully brushed aside some of the metals and Ceinwen managed to sneak a brief glimpse of a pinkish stone before he covered it once more. "I knew it." He sighed with relief. "It's still here."

"May I see it?" Ceinwen asked.

"No." Michael shut the lid. "When you look at the pearl, it will look back at you. I don't want the demons trapped inside it to know anything about you."

"Don't you think they already do?"

"Some do, but hopefully not these. They were once strong enough to bring down an entire Chinese dynasty. We don't want to take them on."

"You really do believe in this pearl's powers, don't you?" she said.

"After all this, how can you doubt it?"

"It's strange," she murmured. "My eyes believe what I'm seeing, but my brain still says it doesn't compute, like it's insulted by this other reality."

"It is another reality," Michael said. "An evil one. And we have to stop it."

A moment later, Jianjun handed Michael a rare earth-filled lead container. He put the bronze vessel in it and handed it back, then helped Ceinwen up and out of the hole.

"I can't help but think," Michael said, after climbing out himself, "that when we get this pearl away from the rivers and these mountains, that the demons that are causing so many problems for this area will leave as well."

"Where would they go?" Ceinwen asked.

"They may follow us all the way to Japan." He turned to Jianjun. "Want to come along?"

Jianjun grinned. "I thought you'd never ask."

Just then, a shot rang out. Deputy Sheriff Pete Grayson fell over, the top of his head torn open as blood and brain sprayed out.

CHAPTER 40

RACHEL FOUND herself once again in the small village with the handsome husband she loved. Joy filled her. Here, she felt happy, and accepted.

The years passed slowly and joyfully for her and Taishi. Six healthy children were born to them. And much to the surprise of everyone who knew them, O-Yuki, as Rachel was known to the village, never aged. She stayed as youthful and beautiful as the day Nakamura Taishi married her.

But then, one night, after the children had gone to sleep, Taishi took his wife to his futon. Their love-making was even more passionate than usual.

When it was over, Taishi lay on his side and gazed at her with adoring love as a stream of moonlight fell on Rachel's face. He leaned close, kissed her, and said, "To see you lying there with the light on you reminds me of a strange thing that happened when I was but a boy of eighteen. No one could ever be as beautiful as you are, but the strange woman I met back then came the closest. She was radiant —just as you are in this moonlight. Indeed, when I think of her now, she seems very much like you."

Without facing him, Rachel whispered, "Tell me about her. Where did you see her?"

Taishi told her about the terrible night in the ferryman's hut, and how old Mosaku had died in the freezing cold. But then he spoke of the Snow Woman who had held him, loved him, and kept him warm and safe through the night. "Asleep or awake," he said, "that was the only time I ever saw a being who came close to *your beauty. Of course, she was not human; and I was afraid of her, very much afraid. Indeed, I have often thought she must have been some kind of demon."*

At those words, Rachel jumped up from the futon, loomed over Taishi, and shrieked at him. "You fool! That woman was me! O-Yuki!"

He stared a moment, then whispered, "No, O-Yuki. What are you saying?"

"I told you then that I would kill you if you ever said one word about it!"

He looked at her with horror as he remembered those very words spoken by the Snow Woman. "Please, you wouldn't..."

She was beside herself with fury. "But for the children asleep in this house, I would kill you this very moment! And now you had better take very, very good care of them. If, for any reason, they complain about you, I will not hesitate to kill you as I said I would, just as I killed old Mosaku that night so many years ago."

"It can't be true," Taishi cried, as tears rolled down his cheeks. "You aren't her, and you aren't a killer. Some madness has come over you! I love you, O-Yuki."

Listening to his plea, her expression went from anger to sorrow. Soon, her own tears fell. "Why did you do it, Taishi? Why didn't you keep your promise to your wife, your demon?" As she spoke, her voice became thin, like a crying of the wind. Slowly, she melted into a bright white mist that spired up to the roof-beams, and then vanished into nothing.

CHAPTER 41

THE MOUNTAIN OFFERED them no cover. Michael grabbed Ceinwen and pulled her with him toward the upslope, and the two lay flat. Jianjun followed.

Jake and the other deputy, Rosenfeld, had drawn their sidearms as they dropped to the ground and tried to figure out where the shot had come from.

"Drop your weapons," a voice shouted from below. They couldn't see him. "We don't want to kill anyone else. We only want the pearl."

Deputy Grayson had carried a rifle, one Jake and Rosenfeld might need. Rosenfeld made a sudden break for it, but as he ran, a shot was heard and he fell, hit in the leg.

"We warned you!" the voice said.

Jake saw that the shot came out of a patch of sagebrush on the downside of the mountain. He returned fire over and over. As he did, Michael crept then sprinted toward the rifle, picked it up and ran to Jake's side, diving for cover as rifle shots from below filled the air.

"The warnings go both ways," Jake called. "Show yourself."

"Look back here," yelled a different voice. "And if you shoot, those two will die."

Jake and Michael looked behind them. On rocks high overhead, two men stood, one with a long rifle, the other with a crossbow, aimed at

Ceinwen and Jianjun. The men wore hats, dark glasses, and what—even from a distance—looked like fake beards.

"Here I am." A tall, stocky fellow stood up from behind the large sagebrush where he'd crouched and now walked toward them, the stock of his rifle at his shoulder and a finger near the trigger. He wore a green baseball cap, dark glasses and had a beard. But his beard was graying and looked real. "Now, toss the pearl this way, along with your rifle and guns, then my men and I will go. If not, we can always shoot you and take the pearl, anyway."

"How do you know about the pearl?" Michael called.

"I'd say that's the least of your worries."

"If your men shoot, you won't make it off this hill alive," Jake said.

"Maybe. Maybe not. But I'm counting on you fellows to be reasonable." His voice was gruff, but had a cloying, whiny quality to it. "Is some pearl worth all your lives? And mine, too? I don't think so. Toss it down! Or you—"

From behind them, Michael and Jake heard a series of shots. They turned their heads to see as the spokesman stopped talking and stared past them.

Ceinwen was firing a 9 mm. Above her, one of the two gunmen dropped his rifle, clutched at his midsection, lurched forward, and fell. The other began firing wildly at Ceinwen and Jianjun, hitting Jianjun, before running for the cover of nearby heavy brush.

Michael turned from the gun battle on the upper slope to the spokesman who recovered his wits and took aim at Ceinwen. Michael raised his rifle and fired. Surprise and anger flared on the gunman's face as he turned to run for the dense sagebrush. He seemed to stagger, than stumbled into the brush in full flight.

"God damn, I think you winged that running-off-the-mouth bastard," Jake yelled.

"Yeah, I hope so," Michael growled.

"Hey, up here!" Ceinwen was shouting. "I've got two wounded!"

As they heard horses riding away, they ran up the slope as Jake groused about the ones that got away.

Michael rushed to the wounded Jianjun. The shot to his back hit his lower rib cage. He was bleeding and unconscious.

Ceinwen had removed Deputy Rosenfeld's belt and wrapped it around his leg as a tourniquet.

"I'm sorry," Ceinwen said to Jake as she pulled the strap tight. "Maybe

I've watched too many American shoot-'em-ups, but when I realized Jian-jun, who was shielding me, had a revolver, and no one expected that I'd know how to use it. I saw a chance and took it."

"There's nothing," Jake said as he gawked at her, "to be sorry about."

Jake used his satellite phone to call Mallick and get a Medivac helicopter to fly out to help the wounded and retrieve the dead. At the same time, Michael and Ceinwen compressed Jianjun's wound to try to stop the bleeding.

A little more than an hour later, the helicopter arrived.

Jake rode in it with his men and Jianjun, giving Ceinwen the keys to drive his truck back to Salmon. He could scarcely speak over the death and the serious wounding of his deputies.

Michael was also devastated. He remained quiet as he and Ceinwen made their way back to the fire trail where they had left their vehicles.

"There was nothing else you could have done," she said, after a long while.

"I should have come here alone."

"And then you'd be dead."

"The deputy had a wife and kids. I've got … no one."

Ceinwen's breath caught at the bleakness of his words and the sadness with which he spoke them. "I know one thing for sure," she said. "Those weren't demons shooting at us. Some very human person wants that pearl. Who could it be? Who knows we're out here?"

He shook his head. "It's got to be someone following my movements, someone who realizes I've decided to get the pearl, and that's why I'm out here. But who? Those in Japan know I'll bring the pearl to them."

Ceinwen thought a moment. "You'd bring it to the Nakamuras. But what if some other person there wants it for himself? They knew what you were up to. They could easily have found a way to track your phone and then hire mercenaries to be ready to attack as soon as you retrieved the pearl. Who knows how many people Lady Nakamura told about all this."

Michael nodded, lost in thought between what she was saying and the guilt weighing down on him, the guilt of being his father's son.

They reached the vehicles and drove through the night to Salmon, stopping only for a couple of hours sleep before facing the long, winding road over the Bitterroot Mountains. They arrived in Salmon early the next morning.

Jake and Mallick were already at the sheriff's station.

"How are they doing?" were Michael's first words upon seeing Jake.

"Len Rosenfeld and his wife have gone to one of the hospitals in Boise, and Jianjun is being treated at the medical center, just a few blocks away. He had surgery, and the doc sounded pretty positive. A couple of ribs are worse for wear, but they deflected the bullet from hitting anything vital. But, good God, he lost a lot of blood."

"I'm glad for the basically positive report," Michael said, but then his shoulder sagged and he bowed his head. "I never meant to bring any of this on you. I'm so sorry."

Jake gripped Michael's arm. "Whatever is going on started before you ever got here. You aren't to blame." He let go as he added, "We've had deaths, mutilations. We saw what was out there, human and … not. And like always, it's the human element that's the most dangerous. I can't help but wonder if the things spooking us here in Salmon weren't done by those shooters. The way they killed my deputy, a really good man, with no warning, nothing, shows pure viciousness. Plus, they had guns, supplies, horses. That isn't the sort of thing they could get at a moment's notice. It means they've been lurking around Idaho a while."

"Good point," Michael admitted.

"Damn straight. In fact, I'm thinking this was all a set-up. They were probably nearby, watching and waiting for you to come back to Salmon, somehow knowing you'd have to come back for the pearl. And when you did, they were ready."

"But how did they know where we were going?" Ceinwen asked.

Jake shrugged. "As soon as I found out, I talked to the deputies who might have told their wives. I told Mallick, had to say a bit about where we were going to the INL to get the rare earth elements. Anyone could have told the wrong person or had their conversation overheard. It even"—he glanced quickly toward Ceinwen—"might have been one of us. Anyway, if those guys took a bush plane out of Salmon, they'd have arrived well before us and waited at Selway Falls. I'll be checking small airfields around here for three or four men."

"Four?"

"I figured there had to be four. Three do the dirty work, one to tend and protect the horses for a fast getaway, and to act as backup. Things happened too fast for him to get in on the action. A break for us."

"Makes sense," Michael said. "But I also know none of that would have happened if I hadn't brought the pearl here to begin with. I honestly thought it would be safe since it's surrounded by metals that are supposed to neutralize it."

"But it's not the demons in the pearl that have caused the problem," Ceinwen pointed out. "It seems they were neutralized. So you weren't wrong. The problem came from outside forces—from very human outside forces."

Jake nodded in agreement. "That sounds right."

"But you can't deny there were also demonic forces out there," Michael said.

"I don't want to believe in such things," Ceinwen said, "but I know what I saw attack me out there, and we know Rachel's problems aren't being caused by men on horseback in Idaho."

She looked so forlorn, Michael found himself putting an arm around her shoulders and drawing her to his side. He then faced Jake. "We're going to have to leave, Sheriff. Once the pearl is out of your state, I bet you'll find things get a lot quieter here. But we'll come back, and when we do, we'll make whoever is behind this pay for all they've done."

Jake nodded. "Just be careful."

To both men's surprise, Ceinwen gave Jake a quick hug. "You be careful, too, Sheriff. You're a good man, even if you don't know me well enough to trust me yet. And I'm sure *she* has not stopped loving you. Woman's intuition."

"I'm listening and hoping," Jake said with a grin.

CHAPTER 42

MICHAEL AND CEINWEN learned Jianjun was still in the ICU after having had surgery, but they were able to talk to the doctor who performed it. He had repaired most of the bone, muscle, and nerve damage, and expected there would be little if any lasting damage to Jianjun. But the blood loss had weakened him, and his left side was going to be stiff and painful for some time to come.

He wasn't able to see non-family visitors until the next morning.

"I'm not leaving Salmon until I talk to Jianjun," Michael said.

Ceinwen saw his heartbreak over his friend. "Of course," she murmured. "Should you call his wife and let her know what's happened?"

Michael thought a moment. "I'll let Jianjun do that. But there is someone I should call."

They left and ate breakfast at the coffee shop next door to the sheriff's office, then booked rooms in the hotel where Ceinwen and Rachel had stayed. Michael didn't want to impose on Jake's hospitality any more than he already had. He knew Jake needed time alone to grieve for his friend.

They were both exhausted from their all-night drive back to Salmon. Michael said a quick goodbye to Ceinwen and went to his room.

Around ten that night, Ceinwen tapped lightly on the door to Michael's hotel room.

He opened the door.

"I didn't want to wake you if you were still sleeping," she said, then held up two bottles, one of tequila, the other a Margarita mix. "But since you're not, fancy a drink? I've come to like this mix. It's not popular at all in Europe."

"Sure. Come in. I even have a bucket of ice." He took the bottles and mixed them both drinks.

"How are you doing?" she asked.

"I've been better," he admitted, handing her a glass.

She sat on the only chair in the small room while he took his glass and sat on the bed. "This is good," she said after tasting the drink.

He nodded, but remained quiet.

"Do you have any idea who might be behind all this?" she asked.

"I do." His voice was hushed.

"Do you want to tell me?"

He shook his head. "I'll need some proof. Too many feelings and past history are involved to be objective. Right now, I have other things to think about, to worry about. Like will my best friend be all right? He still could get an infection. Did they get all the bone and bullet fragments? He could still die."

"He's in good hands," she said. "And given the remoteness of the area, he was in the operating room surprisingly quickly. The doctor sounded confident that he's got a good chance of coming out of this well."

"I wish I could walk away from all this," Michael murmured. "But when I try to, it follows me. If I was the one hurt, it would be fine. Instead, it's people close to me." Pain-filled eyes caught hers. "Never get close to me, Ceinwen. I'll ruin your life. Trust me on that."

She moved to his side on the bed and placed her hand on his arm. "You've brought on none of this."

He stood. He needed to keep away from her, away from her touch. He took a few more steps and then faced her again, his mouth firm. "I'd like you to leave—not only me, not only Salmon, but all this. Go home. I'll do what I can for Rachel and Seiji—if there's anything to be done."

"Home? Where's home for me, Michael?" She asked. "All I know is I'm here now, with you. And it's where I want to be."

He shook his head. "Too many people around me die, Ceinwen. You need to understand that."

"No." She walked up to him, green eyes capturing his. "I understand that you're afraid. So am I. But my fear isn't because of demons. It's because of you."

"Don't." He lifted his hands as if to push her away, but instead, she took hold of them, intertwining her fingers with his. Then she lowered their hands as she stepped closer and kissed him lightly.

"Ceinwen, you don't want this."

She let go of his hands and raised hers to his shoulders. "But I do."

He couldn't resist and kissed her as gently as she had him, planning to then back away and show her the door.

But her arms slid around his neck and she pressed the soft contours of her body against his as she briefly touched her lips to his. The feel of her, her taste, everything about her in his arms, was even better than he had imagined.

Just one more kiss, he told himself, letting his arms circle her.

And soon, he had neither the strength nor the will to push her away again.

CHAPTER 43

THE NEXT MORNING, Michael and Ceinwen went straight to the hospital. Jianjun was sitting up in the bed.

"How are you feeling?" Michael asked, after their greeting.

"Like I've been hit by a truck. It's amazing what one little bullet can do."

"Thank goodness it wasn't a lot worse," Ceinwen said.

"And thank you for being our own Annie Oakley," he said.

"Annie ... ah, your Wild West sharpshooter," Ceinwen said. "I do believe I like that comparison!"

Jianjun and Michael smiled. "Good," Jianjun said, then heaved a sigh. "At least some day this big scar on my side might look kind of cool. And I can tell all sorts of tall tales to wow the ladies."

Michael chuckled, glad his friend could joke.

"So," Jianjun said. "What now?"

"We go back to Japan," Michael said.

"And what about whoever is behind those hit men?"

"I'm working on it."

Jianjun nodded. "I wish I could go to Japan with you, boss. The doctors say I'll be laid up for at least a week or two. Two days here, but then I need bed rest, some light activity, and not to do anything that might cause internal stitches to tear or infect the wound."

"Don't worry, Jianjun," Ceinwen said. "I'm going with him."

"I've told you, that's a terrible idea," Michael said. "You should wait here with Jianjun."

"No."

Jianjun smiled at Michael's stunned reaction to her simple word.

"You were almost killed on that mountain!" Michael roared as he remembered the many bruises he'd seen on her body and the demon bite on her neck. Each had torn at him.

She looked him in the eye. "I'm coming with you."

He couldn't argue with the proud determination or strong defiance of the woman he had held in his arms throughout the long night—a night filled with thoughts of death, with guilt, and with an aching sorrow for the man who died, and those injured. Somehow, her presence, her warmth, her passion, had helped him through it. He didn't understand her, but he wouldn't have her any other way.

He faced Jianjun. "Looks like she and I are both heading to Japan."

"Good. And while you're there, as the Sheriff and his men find evidence about the attack, I'll hack into every database I can think of to help figure out who did it. We'll get those bastards."

Michael nodded. "Jake couldn't ask for better behind-the-scenes help than you and your computer."

Just then, there was a light knock on the door. "Come in," Jianjun called.

The door opened, and Kira Holt stepped into the room. She saw Michael first and nodded, then Michael stepped aside so she could see Jianjun.

She didn't move, but just stood there and looked at him.

Jianjun sat up straighter and didn't say a word, just stared back at her, only her.

Ceinwen nudged Michael and they quietly left the room.

CHAPTER 44

CONVINCING airport security in Missoula not to attempt to open the small Chinese container that held the pearl had been the most challenging part of the flight back to Japan. Michael explained that it was an ancient, very expensive Chinese artifact. But the lead container and dirt made the TSA agent suspicious, and he tried to pry open the bronze with a penknife. Michael finally convinced him that it obviously hadn't been opened in two thousand years. After a sniffing dog and wand scan found no problem, the agent let it through.

At Izumo, Michael rented a car, and he and Ceinwen headed for Kamigawa.

"This is weird," Michael said after about thirty minutes. "I was sure that the first time I drove this way, by the time I reached this area, I was seeing signs with the name Kamigawa."

"Are you sure this is the right road?" Ceinwen asked.

"It's the only road that goes along the sea. I can't imagine having taken any other."

"Maybe signs will show up soon," Ceinwen said.

They continued on, settling back into the comfort of the car and glad to be away from airplanes, airports, and crowds of people.

"Do you think you'll be staying long in Japan?" Ceinwen asked.

"If I can't help Seiji Nakamura, I won't be welcome," Michael said.

"I'm sure the pearl will be able to help him and Rachel," she said.

"I'm glad someone is." He pulled off the road. "Something's wrong. We've driven an hour and haven't seen a sign yet. It took much less than that the first time."

"Maybe they changed the signs while we were gone?" Ceinwen said, but even she couldn't believe that had happened. "Let's ask how to find it at the next town."

They reached the town five minutes later and stopped at a bento stand. They asked the man selling box lunches which way to Kamigawa. He had spoken English when they bought the lunch, but now he seemed perplexed. Ceinwen got out her Japanese phrase book and said, "*Kamigawa wa, doko desu ka?*"

He shook his head. "Kamigawa? *Wakaranai.*"

They guessed he was saying he had no idea where it was. They tried asking a few more people. One of them spoke enough English to say there was "no Kamigawa."

They saw a train station and went into it. The route map was so complicated they couldn't understand it. Ceinwen went to a ticket attendant, put 10,000 yen on the counter and said, "Ticket, please."

"*Hai!* Where to?"

"Kamigawa."

The attendant frowned. "There's no town with that name here."

"Yes. Two weeks ago, I took a train from Izumo to Kamigawa."

"Must be someplace else. No Kamigawa here."

Ceinwen glanced at Michael who looked every bit as puzzled as she felt.

"This makes no sense," she said as they walked out of the station.

"Just like Jianjun indicated," Michael murmured, then explained. "Jianjun came to Japan when he couldn't reach me or Rachel by phone or text, and the emails he'd sent weren't opened. But he couldn't find the man named Yamato Toru who first told him about Kamigawa. Yamato's phone number had been disconnected. Even stranger, he discovered the Nakamura family isn't listed as a daimyo family."

Ceinwen gawked at him. "That's crazy. Rachel and I found Kamigawa with no trouble at the Izumo train station. Although, now that I think about it, we had no luck at first either, but once on the train platforms, Rachel saw the right sign. I never did. But the train took us right there."

"And was it a normal train?" Michael asked. "By that, I mean there were a lot of people and stops."

"I don't know what's normal for Japan," Ceinwen admitted. "But Kamigawa was the first stop, and we were the only ones to get off."

"Did you see others on the train?" Michael asked.

Ceinwen thought a moment. "Come to think of it, no. But we were in the last car and assumed others were up front."

"Strange," Michael said.

"If all else fails we can go back to Izumo and find the train Rachel and I took to Kamigawa."

"I don't think that'll help," Michael said. "Not if Jianjun was right. Let's drive along the coast. We're sure to see something that looks familiar."

"I don't understand," Ceinwen said. "What are you thinking?"

He waited a long moment, then said, "That Kamigawa is in a different plane of existence from this one. It's like what we encountered ... uh, in the past."

"In Idaho?" she asked, shocked at what he was suggesting.

"Maybe."

"You're talking different dimensions. Isn't that Einstein territory, or somebody like him? But that's all theoretical."

Michael nodded. "I know."

They got in the car and headed back along the main highway toward Izumo. Michael hoped to find something familiar. After about fifteen minutes, he reached a small town and stopped. "I'm sure I drove through this town," he said as he peered up and down at the small street. "A road sign to Kamigawa directed me to head up into the mountains."

"Let's find that road," Ceinwen said.

They easily found it and drove into the mountains.

"Does this look familiar?" Ceinwen asked.

"No. But let's see where it leads."

It led to a dead-end.

Michael stopped the car. He and Ceinwen got out and studied the area around them. "This has to be the place," Michael said. "I spent a lot of time looking at the mountains as I walked from the Hearn house to the Naka-mura manor. It was those mountains, right there, that I saw."

Ceinwen eyed the landscape. "But I see no sign any town was ever here."

"Which means it—Kamigawa—was all an illusion," Michael

murmured.

"But it wasn't! We were there," Ceinwen said. "No matter what, *we were there*. And Rachel still is."

Michael took a deep breath. "In Chinese tradition, there's a land where alchemy works, and the dead don't die. Over two millennia ago, the alchemist Li Chao Kuin learned to transform the powder of cinnabar to a yellow gold that gave prolonged longevity. People with such longevity live among the blessed *hsien* on the island of P'eng Lai. There, it's as if they are immortal. I always suspected the island spoken of was part of Japan. Now, I can't help but wonder if Kamigawa isn't a part of that land."

"I won't pretend to understand any of that," Ceinwen said. "But you talk as if such a superstition is real."

"Would you believe me if I told you I once met someone who lived there? She was a fine woman who died an unfortunate death, at far too young an age."

"You knew a woman who claimed to be immortal?" Ceinwen asked softly.

"Not only claimed. She was. She saved my life, in fact." He paused a moment as if thinking back to that strange time, and ignored the confused, troubled way Ceinwen was looking at him. "But right now, the important thing is for us to reach Kamigawa. We know demons want this pearl, which gives me an idea."

He took the lead container from his duffel bag and then lifted out the bronze vessel. "I've brought the pearl to Kamigawa," he called into the wind and the land around him. "I know you want the pearl. It's here. And now, I need to see Kamigawa, to see my friends. Only after that will I open this container and free the pearl."

He placed the bronze, unopened, on the ground.

And waited.

Nothing happened.

When the hour grew late, Ceinwen got into the car and fell asleep.

At first light, Ceinwen awoke to the call of nature. She stumbled from the car, and then froze.

"Michael! Wake up!" He was asleep on the ground, the bronze in his hand.

He opened his eyes.

"Look."

He sat up to see Kamigawa in the distance, and at the top of the hill overlooking it stood the Nakamura estate.

CHAPTER 45

As Jianjun watched Kira get ready for bed, he couldn't believe she was with him. If it took a bullet to get her there, he was glad to take it. He had come to think of it as Cupid's bullet, but he didn't need to be shot with it to know how he felt.

He had been released from the hospital that morning, and Jake Sullivan had invited them to stay at his house. Well, not exactly Jake. His lady friend, Charlotte Reed, after learning all that had happened, flew "home" to Salmon. She wanted to be there for Deputy Grayson's funeral, but also to help Jake in any way she could. Jianjun had heard all about her, though he had never met her face-to-face.

She had suggested Jianjun move into their guest room, with Kira staying there as well. But much to Jianjun's relief, Kira had already found accommodations in a lodge on a rise overlooking the town. The suite had a separate sitting room and a private deck. Jianjun happily joined her there to recuperate.

They spent a lot of time catching up on the past year. He learned that although Kira had lost her job as an FBI profiler, she was once again working as a psychiatrist in private practice. She had been asked to join an established team of doctors, and her business had quickly picked up. It included a number of former patients who were glad she was practicing again.

She basically liked her work, although several patients thought their lives were a lot tougher than they really were. She was often tempted to ask them if they wanted to hear about *real* problems and *real* life-threatening situations. If so, the stories she could tell!

But she didn't.

He laughed with her. It felt good to laugh, even to smile. He done little of either the past year. Sometimes when he was alone he'd shut his eyes and relive the complete elation he felt when she walked into his room in the Salmon hospital.

"Kira," was all he could say.

She gave him a shy smile. "I hope you don't mind that I'm here. When Michael told me you were hurt ..."

He wanted to jump for joy, despite the tubes, pain-pills, and everything else that tied him to the hospital bed. Instead, he calmly said, "He shouldn't have bothered you."

"Yes, Jianjun. He should have."

His heart filled his throat and he had to wait a moment before he could speak. "It's good to see you again."

"You're probably thinking that I still can't pronounce your name correctly." Her eyes grew shiny and moist.

His mind raced with a thousand things to say to her—and another thousand that he should never say. "I like the way you say it."

She drew in her breath. "How are you feeling?"

"Much better ... since about a minute ago. The doctors have a good prognosis, fortunately."

She pulled the chair to his side and placed her hand atop his as he explained briefly about the attack.

"That damned pearl," she said. She was one of the people with Michael as they had faced down the demons connected to the pearl. "I had hoped we would never hear anything more about it."

"All of us hoped that."

She took a deep breath. "Is your wife here yet?"

He shook his head. "I didn't even tell her about this. And I doubt Michael did either."

"Why not?"

"She wouldn't have cared. Not really."

Kira's lips tightened. "I see."

"What about you?" he asked. "Are you seeing someone? Someone special, perhaps?"

"I'm afraid not." Her expression was wry. "After you've battled crazed

Chinese demons side-by-side with someone, everyone else you meet seems a bit dull."

He beamed and both his hands wrapped around hers. "God, Kira. I can't believe you're here. I turned away from you once, and a bad situation has only become worse. I don't know how you feel about me. I don't know how any of this will turn out. But, if you're willing, I want to be with you. Only you."

She flashed him a broad smile. "I'm here, aren't I?"

Every night in the hospital he had relived that scene before he fell asleep. Now, in the lodge overlooking Salmon City, she got into bed beside him and kissed him. In his drugged state, with medicine and bandages, that was as much as he could handle. But he didn't think he'd ever gone to sleep with a broader smile on his face.

CHAPTER 46

CEINWEN WOKE up a few hours later in Michael's bedroom. She had to admit, as comfortable as the futon had been in the room she had shared with Rachel, it didn't compare to the nice mattress she'd fallen into when she and Michael reached the house around five that morning. Nor did it compare to having Michael in the bed with her.

She sat up. Where was he?

She made her way down to the kitchen. He sat at the table with coffee. Pastries and fruit were on the counter, and food was in the refrigerator. "Good morning."

"Did you sleep well?" he asked.

"Once a certain someone left me alone long enough to fall asleep. Not that I'm complaining, mind you."

He pulled her close for a quick kiss.

"This is all too strange." Ceinwen got herself some coffee, and then tore a croissant in half. It wasn't the least bit stale. "Hmm. I wonder if I dare eat this."

"It's as if everything has been in suspended animation waiting for us to return," he said.

She picked up a peach and washed it. "Demons, do you think? Or do I sound like you now, seeing demons in every nook and cranny?"

He grinned. "I don't know what's behind it, but whatever it is, it wants the pearl."

She nodded and ate the peach in silence.

Soon, they left for the Nakamura home.

They had just stepped onto the street when a dust cloud rose up. They squeezed their eyes shut and waited. When the storm passed, nothing seemed to have changed, and they headed up the hill.

When they entered the gate, one of Seiji's retainers came out to greet them, bowed low, and then ran back into the house. Lady Nakamura rushed to meet them.

"Michael-*sensei*! And Miss Ceinwen! I'm so glad to see you both again." She was breathless. "Please, come and sit. I must tell you all that has happened. I, we, need your help."

"What's going on?" he asked, studying her face.

"*O-cha!*" She commanded the maid to bring them tea. "Sit, please." She directed Michael and Ceinwen to the *zabuton* by the low table. The two sat, and then she joined them.

Michael and Ceinwen said nothing. Finally, Lady Nakamura spoke. "Seiji and Rachel are gone. They have left this house."

Michael and Ceinwen glanced at each other. "Do you know where they went?" Michael asked.

"I have no idea."

"Any hint, or guess from something they might have said?"

"You must understand. They both slept for a long time—several days. And then, they suddenly woke. When they did, they hugged and held each other. Rachel could not stop crying. They try to act happy to be alive and awake, but after a few days they stopped. Both said they had left too much behind. I don't know what they meant. But they didn't want to be here, not at all. They said ... they said they must return, and that they'd rather be dead to this world. It makes no sense that they would speak such words."

"Return where?" Ceinwen asked, but Lady Nakamura only shook her head.

"I can't believe Rachel saying she'd rather be dead," Ceinwen cried. "That's not Rachel."

"Isn't it?" Michael quietly asked.

Ceinwen paled.

Lady Nakamura wiped her tears. "What can I tell you? I have no idea where they could be. We have searched and have offered large rewards. But no one has seen them."

"If it is at all possible," Michael said, "We will find them."

"Thank you," Lady Nakamura said. "But also, there were two things that troubled me. I don't know how to explain them."

"Go on," Michael told her.

"First, Seiji had grown healthy again. Not only that, but he was stronger, much stronger, than he had ever been. It was as if someone else had taken over the body of my son, but at the same time, he was Seiji. He was the same dear boy I have always known and loved. I don't understand it."

Michael nodded. "And the other thing?"

Lady Nakamura bit her bottom lip and looked away a moment. Then she slightly raised her eyebrows. "When they thought they were alone, when they thought no one was listening, I heard her call him Taishi, and he called her O-Yuki."

Lady Nakamura insisted Michael and Ceinwen join her for a simple tempura dinner. Afterward, they talked to the retainers and maids in the Nakamura estate to see if any of them ever saw or overheard anything that might give any clue as to where Seiji and Rachel might have gone—and none had. They then returned to the Hearn house.

It was evening, and they sat by the koi pond as the sun set.

"Why do you stare at the pond so intensely, Michael?" Ceinwen asked. "I've seen you do that a number of times."

He lifted his gaze. "It's nothing. Sometimes, the water forms an interesting pattern. But it's nothing."

Ceinwen waited for Michael to bring up Seiji and Rachel, but when he didn't, she asked, "What do you think?" She didn't have to say about what.

"If the two were as unhappy as Lady Nakamura believes, it's probably because they reached the end of the Snow Woman story and learned she leaves Taishi and their children because he breaks a promise to her. In the story, it's very sad."

"That's the end? She just leaves him?"

"Actually, she had threatened to kill him if he broke his promise, but because she fell in love with him, she spared his life. Still things couldn't continue as they had, and she was the one who had to disappear."

Ceinwen looked appalled.

"It sounds as if they wanted to somehow overcome the separation that was forced on them by the Snow Woman tale," Michael said. "But I don't know how they could have done it."

Ceinwen thought a moment. "You've said that every one of Rachel's dreams came from a Lafcadio Hearn story. Maybe we need to find out where his stories went next."

Michael looked intrigued. "You may be right. I like it. I know Snow Woman was a story in *Kwaidan* which was published in the year of Hearn's death. He died of a sudden heart attack so that could mean that whatever he was working on next is among his unpublished papers."

"If such papers still exist," Ceinwen said.

"They do, and I have a bunch of them here. If we find nothing, we can try the Hearn museum in Matsue."

She was surprised. "How did you get your hands on Hearn's unpublished writings?"

His lips pursed. "My interest in Hearn wasn't altogether by chance. When I was visiting my father, I discovered the papers, and that Hearn was very likely a relative."

"Your father ..." She thought about the diary she'd read. "So your parents are still alive? And do you visit them often?"

"Only my father is. My mother died when I was very young. And it was during the first visit I'd paid to my father in many years that I found those papers."

She drew in her breath, wanting to ask what had happened to Jane, but not daring to. "I'm sorry," she murmured.

"These things happen in families."

"Yes," she said as she pieced together all he had told her. "So, if I have this correct, you may have some genetic connection to Lafcadio Hearn. Rachel has some odd connection to you. And your father was the keeper of all Hearn's books and papers. That's bizarre."

Michael nodded. "That's one word for it."

CHAPTER 47

LATER THAT NIGHT, seated on pillows by a kerosene lamp in the tatami room, Michael and Ceinwen went through Hearn's papers. The only fiction was a bare-bones draft of a story that took place in a haunted forest, a forest filled with ghosts of suicide victims. In it, a *ronin*—a samurai without a daimyo master—traveled with his fellow *ronin* to a forest known as a place for suicides and filled with ghosts of the dead. They planned to kill themselves because they had failed to protect their master. But when they reached it, the daimyo appeared before them. He was a ghost and wanted revenge on his enemy—the usurper and his family—who had killed him and took over his fiefdom. The ghost then possessed the *ronin*, but at that point the story abruptly stopped.

"This story is genuinely creepy," Ceinwen said after they had both finished reading it.

Michael paced, lost in thought.

"It would have been a hell of a story if Hearn had lived to tell it," Ceinwen said. "A forest that's home to ghosts of the dead. Wow. But does that fit with the demons? I don't think so."

"I disagree." Michael cast bleak eyes her way. "It could be the next phase in the journey of Taishi and O-Yuki."

"A suicide forest?" Ceinwen was appalled. "I hope they aren't thinking along these lines. I'll go along with the idea that the two are possessed, but that means none of the things happening around them are real. We've got to be sure they understand that."

"We can try, but it sounds as if Rachel and Seiji believed it was real," Michael said. "And what are beliefs and feelings anyway, but nebulous things?"

"It's up to us to show them they're wrong," Ceinwen cried. "If you're right, we've got to find them as quickly as possible."

Michael agreed. "We need to find the forest Hearn was talking about."

"You know, a few years back, I saw a horror film about a forest in Japan," Ceinwen said. "Did you see it?"

"No."

"Don't you scholarly types get out at all?"

"Obviously not enough to watch Japanese horror films, besides *Kwaidan*, of course," Michael said.

"I'll have to fix that." Ceinwen's mouth wrinkled as she continued to page through Hearn's papers. "Who would have thought that something written over a hundred years ago could affect a young American girl now?"

She stopped and stared at a page, her face turning ashen as she read. "Oh, no. Michael, read this. Now, I know we have no time to waste."

She handed him one of Hearn's studies on the Japanese character:

Falling in love at first sight is less common in Japan than in the West ... Love suicides, on the other hand, are not infrequent....

The suicide is not the result of a blind, quick frenzy of pain. It is not only cool and methodical: it is sacramental. It involves a marriage of which the certificate is death. The twain pledge themselves to each other in the presence of the gods, write their farewell letters, and die. No pledge can be more profoundly sacred than this.

CHAPTER 48

EARLY THE NEXT MORNING, Michael and Ceinwen visited Lady Nakamura and asked if she knew a place called a "suicide forest" in the area. She paled and nodded, then rushed off. A short while later she was back with a map showing an area called "Aokigahara." It was about an hour's drive deeper into the mountains. Soon after, several servants appeared carrying a supply of food, water, and some light camping gear. They loaded everything into Michael's car and Lady Nakamura bowed deeply, wishing them good fortune as they set off.

They were surprised to find that the forest had a specific entry point that wasn't some remote, isolated spot, but had a gift shop, food, drinks, and a parking lot filled with cars.

"This is getting stranger every minute," Michael said as he parked.

"I can't imagine anyone committing suicide around so many people." Ceinwen got out of the rental and lifted the backpack to her shoulders. "Maybe the Hearn writings caused us to overreact."

"A lot has changed in the past hundred years," Michael said.

Ceinwen noticed that some cars had amassed quite a bit of debris in the slot where the windshield wipers were. The leaves and grit had piled up onto the windshields, as if the cars had been parked there a while. As she wondered why anyone would leave a car here that long, an answer to the question came to her, causing a chill along her spine. She hurried to Michael's side, refusing to let herself think more about it.

They saw a yakisoba stand and decided to eat before going into the forest. Ceinwen couldn't help but flash back to one of Rachel's nightmares. Fortunately, this soba seller had a face.

At the stand, Ceinwen picked up a pamphlet about the forest. She read it as they ate. "The forest is called 'sea of trees' or *jukai*," she said as she perused the information, "because the trees are so thick they look like a sea. It's around fourteen square miles. That sounds huge. Anyway, the forest was created only a thousand or so years ago after a nearby volcano erupted."

He frowned. "That means it has a lot of lava on the ground. It'll interfere with compass readings and even GPS."

Ceinwen read aloud, "*In the 19th century, people practiced what they called* ubasute, *which was taking a sick or old relative into the forest and leaving them to starve to death.* Sheesh. That's not good. *They say their ghosts haunt the forest to this day.*" She shuddered. "It sounds like assisted suicide, where the 'assistance' was not necessarily requested."

"A good reason for a haunting," Michael added, looking bemused at Ceinwen's reaction to the area's history.

"Oh my! Listen to this," she said. "*In the 1960s, a book called* Tower of Waves *by Seichō Matsumoto ended with a couple that couldn't stay together deciding to commit suicide inside this forest. It was a romantic, popular book, and brought unhappy couples here to kill themselves.*"

"Who said romance is dead?"

Ceinwen scowled at him before continuing. "*When the suicides rose to over two a week in 2003, the government stopped reporting the number, feeling the suicides were being sensationalized. However, many bodies have not been found to this day, and many mysteries surrounding the forest remain unsolved.* My God, that's disgusting." She put the pamphlet down. "Are we sure we want to go in there?"

Despite the gloomy statistics, as they approached the forest, Ceinwen felt a surge of hope about finding Seiji and Rachel and getting them out of there safely. The forest was green and lush, and she remarked on its beauty as they followed the foot path to the entry point. A crowd of people were entering at the same time, and many of them were talking and laughing.

Once inside, however, the crowd turned quiet. Lining the pathway were pairs of shoes—men's and women's—looking as if they were waiting for their owners to come and get them. But judging from the discoloration and conditions of the shoes, the owners never did.

Everyone hurried past the sad and lengthy display.

The abandoned shoes cast a pall as Michael and Ceinwen followed the crowd deeper into the forest. They hadn't gone far when they saw a large sign on the side of the trail. It was written only in Japanese, which was rare in Japan, where almost every tourist spot included an English translation.

Ceinwen hushed her voice. "I read somewhere in the brochure that signs in the forest tell people not to kill themselves and to think of those they'll be leaving behind. I suspect that's one such sign."

Michael quickened his step, and they hurried past it.

After about twenty minutes, the trail was still wide and well-trodden, but the crowd had thinned. As they continued, the trees grew thicker, blocked the sunlight, and made the air chilly.

They stopped at a spot with a rope strung across it. A "No Entry" sign hung from the rope.

"We need to leave the main path," Michael said. "In there is most likely where we'll find Rachel and Seiji, if they're here."

Ceinwen shuddered as she stepped over the rope. The trail soon vanished.

They walked single-file, eying the ground with each step. Dried volcanic magma was so hard the tree roots couldn't bore into it and lay twisted above the ground. The shallow roots caused many trees to topple, creating their own kind of hazard. Leaves and vines many inches thick covered the ground, and more than once Ceinwen took a step thinking the ground was solid, and stepped into a hole.

Near the forest entrance, birds chirped and sang, and they heard ripples from mountain streams. But as they went deeper, the thick canopy of trees darkened the land, and all was silent except for the crunch of leaves with each step they took.

"What's that?" Ceinwen said, pointing at something pink and yellow. "Over there."

They approached to see a small bouquet, now wilted, propped up against a tree. A box of chocolates lay beside it. "Someone must have died here." Michael's words were scarcely more than a whisper.

She could feel the sadness in the air. Their expressions grim, they continued on.

Michael checked his cell phone. "As expected, there's no cell or GPS out here." He took off his backpack and reached for his compass. It spun, never settling on magnetic north. "And no compass. We'll need to find a spot where there isn't much lava to get our true bearings."

"Do you think there are many such spots?" Ceinwen asked.

Michael swallowed. "Probably not."

"As much as we can, we keep going straight," Michael said as they walked again. "As long as we don't let ourselves go in circles, we'll be all right."

A few steps further, they saw a blue tape tied to a tree and then stretched out and tied to a second tree. "What's that?" Ceinwen asked.

"It's a smart way to keep from getting lost if you don't intend to go very far," Michael said. "Whoever did it wanted a means to find his or her way back. After a while, all these trees look the same, and it's easy to get turned around."

"They already all look the same," Ceinwen admitted.

"The tape is a good idea," Michael said. "We should have brought some, but since we didn't ..."

He cut the tape, but left the piece tied onto the tree. He took hold of the loose end and gathered it as he followed it to the second tree. There, he tied some tape to the trunk, and gathered tape as they continued on to the third tree.

"If we keep this up, will have enough tape to help us mark our own route," he explained.

"Good!" Ceinwen exclaimed.

But when they reached the last strand of tape tied to a tree, they found a rope hanging from a limb. The end of the rope was frayed as if someone had cut it.

They met each other's eyes and silently searched through the nearby leaves. It didn't take long to find what they had feared: a noose.

Ceinwen took a shuddering breath. "I guess whoever strung the tape didn't use it to find his way back, but as a means for others to find him." She gazed up at the tree, contemplating the level of despair it would take to kill oneself that way.

"Let's keep going," Michael said, his expression troubled.

As the forest grew even darker, they knew it was time to make camp. It was an eerie, unsettling place to sleep.

With the aluminum poles, stakes, and clips, they set up the lightweight tent Lady Nakamura had given them, and then put their bedrolls in it, side by side. They slept with their arms intertwined, feeling better inside the enclosure than outside in the forbidding forest.

CHAPTER 49

MICHAEL WAS COOKING biscuits when a yawning Ceinwen joined him by the campfire.

"Hey, sleepyhead. I didn't hear you stir all night," he said.

"I slept soundly despite my dreams. They were weird."

"I had the same problem," Michael poured her some coffee. Just then, they heard a bone-chilling scream far in the distance. They couldn't tell which direction it came from, or if it was human, bird, or animal.

They remained still, but the sound didn't come again.

"This really is the forest primeval," Ceinwen said.

"Ah, yes, 'Evangeline,'" Michael said. "It was a favorite of my mother's:
This is the forest primeval. The murmuring pines and the hemlocks,
Bearded with moss, and in garments green, indistinct in the twilight..."

"Yes. A sad poem, that one is. It's as if Longfellow knew this place," Ceinwen said. She rubbed her arms to ward off the cold.

After eating, they started out again in the direction they believed would lead them deeper into the forest.

They saw no trail, so they tried to walk in a straight line. But felled trees, high roots, and the holes of burrowing animals, forced them to make turns. Michael continued to use the blue tape, tying it to trees to mark the trail.

They found a tent and sleeping bag covered with leaves and dirt as if they had been abandoned for some time. Michael was searching for a clue as to who they might have belonged to when he noticed a woman wearing a white kimono walking among the trees. "Wait! *Chotto matte!*" He'd been asked to "wait" often enough by Lady Nakamura that the expression came to him now.

He ran after her, but soon realized she had disappeared. He stopped and waited for Ceinwen to catch up to him. "Did you see her?"

"Just an instant," Ceinwen said. "All in white—like a bride."

"White is the traditional color of death in Japan," Michael said.

"We should go back to the abandoned tent and mark the trail," Ceinwen said.

They returned in the direction they had come.

"We should be able to see the tent by now," Michael said after a while.

"Maybe we ran faster than we thought we had," Ceinwen suggested.

"If we were just a bit off as we backtracked," Michael pointed out, "we'd miss it. And the farther we go, the more distant from the tent we'll be. We'd better mark a new trail from here."

"Wherever *here* is."

They continued on and found a tree with a piece of paper nailed to it. It was written in a stylized Japanese script. "I suspect it's a suicide note," Ceinwen murmured. "This forest is truly getting on my nerves. What a horrid place!"

Michael agreed. It was almost making him physically ill. He took a step back from the tree and heard a "snap." He pushed back a few dried leaves and found a woman's comb—a fancy type worn as a hair ornament. His footstep had broken it in half. He stared at it, saying nothing.

"How sad," Ceinwen whispered.

"It reminds me of the haiku I once read," Michael murmured, then quoted:

"What piercing cold I feel!
My dead wife's comb, in our bedroom,
Under my heel."

Ceinwen shuddered. "No more poetry from you!" She grabbed his arm. "Let's get away from this spot."

They eventually stopped for lunch. When they started out once more, they spotted one of their blue ties on a tree trunk up ahead.

"Shite!" Ceinwen cried. "Did you tie that on the tree? None of this seems at all familiar."

"I agree." Michael put his hands on his hips looking around them with dismay. "This isn't working. I think we need to give it up. This forest is too big, too crazy. We tried, Ceinwen. I don't know what more to do." He searched for another blue tie to lead them back to the park entrance. "There it is," he said, and started walking toward it.

"I see it, too," Ceinwen said, and headed in a slightly different direction. Then both stopped.

"We're both right," Ceinwen said.

Then they saw a third tie. Slowly, as they pivoted in a circle, they saw that they were surrounded by trees with blue ties … with no way to tell which would lead to the entrance.

"We are so screwed," Ceinwen murmured.

"They're playing with us," Michael said grimly. "This damned forest, or whoever's in it, is having fun. But they won't get away with it. Let's go that way." He pointed to the tie he first saw, and walked toward it, Ceinwen following. It led to another tie, and another, and soon, Michael stopped.

"I think we're going in circles," he said.

"Don't say that!" Her breath came in short, unsteady bursts.

"Have you noticed that there are no animals around? No birds, lizards, squirrels, not even ants. Nothing lives here. Nothing at all."

"Yes," she whispered.

"That explains the quiet and the thickness of the ground cover. It's as if nothing decays. It's all static." His dark eyes searched the forest. "Alchemically speaking, it's an anomaly—an impossibility, in fact. In alchemy everything that is not 'perfect' will change—not only animals and vegetables but also rocks and minerals. In the process of turning cheap metals into gold, the alchemist's job is to speed up nature's slow progression. It's just as coal, over time, becomes diamonds. But here, in this forest, we have the anti-alchemy. Nothing changes. This is wrong, Ceinwen. Completely wrong, and unnatural."

"What can we do?" Ceinwen asked. "I refuse to give up!"

"We won't. We'll stay put," Michael said, "and stop traipsing all around like rats in a maze."

"In other words," she whispered, "if the demons want us, we'll be here waiting for them?"

"Right."

She swallowed hard, then nodded in agreement.

They built a warming campfire, a part of them hoping that it might bring a forest ranger or some other person who might be able to show them the way out. They quietly sat facing it, eating just a little of their food, knowing they needed to preserve as much as they could. Ceinwen leaned against him, needing to feel his warmth.

"I wonder if there's ever been a forest fire here," she said.

"It doesn't look like it," Michael replied, drawing her close.

"That, in itself," she murmured, "makes this a strange place."

Ceinwen was awakened by a loud knocking sound. She saw Michael putting on his shoes and a jacket, and quickly did the same. "I hear it, too," she whispered.

They crept out the tent and aimed their flashlights into the trees. They saw nothing, but the knocking stopped.

Michael put more logs into the fire pit and lit it. "I don't know why I'm even trying to sleep."

"I agree. This is an incredibly sad place. Ever since we've come in, I feel as if some weight is pushing down on my shoulders, and a pressure behind my eyes as if tears should fall."

"It makes sense—the sadness of all the lives lost here."

"That's probably why there are no fires," She said. "It's too damp from tears shed."

"From loneliness," Michael added. "People who came here to die believed there was no hope, no one for them. Little did they know how often someone was left behind that grieved their loss."

"Sometimes," her voice was soft, but her gaze intense as she said, "people build barriers around themselves that stop others from getting close—and they don't even realize it."

He made no response, but added kindling to the fire.

Jianjun had made it clear to her that Michael had allowed her into his life to a remarkable degree. At the same time, despite their new physical closeness, she could feel the emotional wall Michael kept around himself. She wondered if she or anyone could ever break through it.

Having learned a bit about his past from his mother's diary, that his mother had died when he was young, and that he had been raised by his cold and strange father, helped Ceinwen understand some of the reasons for his hesitancy to let anyone close to him.

She reached over and took his hand. He glanced up at her, and looked as if he were about to speak when he suddenly started, his gaze fixated on something over her shoulder. She spun around and gasped.

It wasn't a black blob-like shape or a mouth with sharp, bloody fangs as in the past. But it was an entire being. It looked like a young man, and it also looked dead.

Michael and Ceinwen stood. He pushed her behind him.

"What is it?" she asked.

"This forest is supposedly haunted by ghosts of the people who have killed themselves here, people who have died with such strong passions such as jealousy, rage, and hatred, that their souls are unable to pass on. Instead, they seek vengeance for the cruelty life bestowed on them."

One by one, other creatures stepped out of the dark nearer the fire and moved toward Michael and Ceinwen. Both male and female, they were wraiths. They looked frightening, perhaps evil, perhaps dangerous, but they also appeared completely downtrodden. Most of them had killed themselves by hanging, but few of them knew how to tie a noose in a way that would snap a neck and bring instant death. Instead, they dangled from the rope until it strangled them, which meant their faces were bloated, their eyes and tongues bulging, and their heads at strangely lopsided angles.

"Let's get out of here," Ceinwen said, backing up, her hand reaching for Michael's.

"When I give the word, run," Michael said. "Now. *Go!*"

The two ran from the wraiths. As soon as they dared, they stopped. Running in the dark was treacherous and more than once one or the other stumbled and nearly fell. They saw nothing around them. The thick canopy of trees that blocked the sunlight now blocked the moon and starlight. They switched on their flashlights and saw…

The dead, even more of them, now surrounded them.

Once the flashlights were switched on, the rotting corpses began to move. The wraiths stretched out their hands, palms up, as if begging for something. But what? Surely not food, water, or money. What could the dead possibly want from them?

"We have nothing for you," Michael said. "Leave us. Go!"

But they moved closer.

One reached out and touched Ceinwen's hair.

"No!" She shouted and struck the creature's arm with her flashlight.

It recoiled, but others charged forward, reaching for them, touching their faces, clothes, bodies as if they couldn't believe Michael and Ceinwen were there, and alive.

The two fought, wielding their flashlights like cudgels to get the wraiths to back off. Michael forced his way through them using his fists, his arms, his body to break through the crowd.

Ceinwen stayed as close to him as she could, fighting off anyone—anything—that tried to attack from behind.

Suddenly, Michael grabbed her arm. "We're free. Let's go."

They kept their flashlights on this time and didn't stop running until they crossed a small stream. Looking around them, it seemed they were finally alone.

"My God," Ceinwen cried.

"They didn't hurt you did they?"

"Surprisingly, no." She took a deep breath. "We just seem to be getting deeper and deeper into this damn place. And now, we've left our food and…" Ceinwen's light focused on a yellow tape. Their tapes had all been blue. "What's that?"

"Let's find out," Michael said, turning to follow the tape as it stretched from one tree to the next.

"And hope it doesn't lead us to our death," Ceinwen added. "I've come to realize, you can't trust demons."

They followed the tape, despite Ceinwen's sense of a rising panic. She felt her heart beating faster and heavier, her lungs working hard to simply breathe as the air seemed to thicken and the forest to weigh down ever heavier on them. She continued to follow Michael.

"I see a bit of light," he said.

He switched off his flashlight. Not until she did the same could she see what he was referring to.

It was the last few glowing embers of a campfire, one that had been allowed to burn out rather than safely extinguished. They crept toward it. At first, they thought the camp had been abandoned. Not until they were near did they see two bodies, their arms around each other.

"God, no," Ceinwen cried. She and Michael rushed forward.

It was Rachel and Seiji, but not as they had looked while alive. Rachel wore a kimono, and her hair had been pinned up in a Japanese style. By her hand, lay a dagger.

Seiji wore the rich, colorful robes of a samurai … or a daimyo.

Blood streamed from the area around Rachel's heart, darkening and nearly hiding the cut in her clothes where the knife had gone through.

Seiji's robes lay open down to his belly, and the slice across it showed he had performed *hara-kiri*. But his neck also had a gash where someone had severed the artery.

"I don't understand this," Ceinwen cried, falling to her knees beside her friend. "Did someone kill them?"

Michael shook his head. "Cutting open one's belly is a slow, painful way to die. Often a second person cuts the neck, making death quick. I can't help but suspect Rachel did that for him, and then killed herself."

"No, not Rachel." Ceinwen reached out and touched the girl's hand, but it was icy cold. "She was one of the kindest people I've ever known. She couldn't do that to him, or to herself."

"Perhaps not, but the demon Snow Woman could do it."

Ceinwen's tears flowed. "How could they do this? It's crazy."

"Is it? They couldn't live in his world, and not in Rachel's. We can only hope they've found a place to be together."

He helped Ceinwen stand, and then led her away from the horrific scene.

"Maybe...," Ceinwen swallowed hard, "maybe Rachel will live if we take her body back to 'our' world?"

He shook his head. "The people who died in the strange part of Idaho where the pillars existed were also dead in our world."

"Are you saying there's no hope for her? Or him?" Ceinwen cried.

He brushed back her hair. "And Rachel would have known it. She saw it all before."

"No! I won't accept that." Ceinwen pushed him away and started back to Rachel and Seiji, but stopped. She couldn't face them either. She turned to Michael. "I thought I was protecting her." The words were like a desperate sob. "I convinced her to go places, do things, she never would have. If it weren't for me, she might still be at Oxford, studying and awing people with her brilliance. Instead this. I feel as if I killed her!"

Michael put his arms around her, trying to offer comfort. "I also remember Rachel saying that in the land of her dreams she was happier than at any other time in her life. She knew things we don't, Ceinwen. She went places and made discoveries we have not. Especially if this is part of those strange islands with the blessed *hsein* of Chinese alchemy, where people can live forever, maybe the good in those two young people overcame the demons in them."

Ceinwen lifted her head and studied his face. "It's too much, Michael. She shouldn't be dead!"

"In the end," he whispered, "it was her choice. All we can do is pray that she found the life she hoped for."

"Pray?" She let him lead her away from the bodies. "Do you believe in prayer, Michael?"

"Of course. You can't have seen the things I have and not be a believer." He kissed her lightly. "We've got to keep going, to find our way out of here. We can't help them now."

CHAPTER 50

ANOTHER DAY PASSED with Michael and Ceinwen walking in circles. Their food was gone and they had no choice but to drink the water found in streams. They hoped no dangerous parasites were in it. They tried to find their way out of the forest, or even back to the campsite the wraiths had driven them from, but could find neither. The gloom and suffocating atmosphere of sadness in the forest of the lost was weakening them more than the lack of food.

It was as if the forest were conspiring against them.

They gathered logs and built a fire as the sun was setting. Not that they could see the sun, but the ever-shaded forest simply grew increasingly dark, until all light vanished completely.

Hungry, tired, and scared, they lay in each other's arms to sleep, in Ceinwen's case hoping, and in Michael's praying, that they would find a means of escape the next day.

Michael didn't know how long he'd been asleep when he opened his eyes to see a large figure standing near.

It looked like a troll or an ogre from a child's book of mythological tales. Its eyes glowed red; the canine teeth were as long as a wolf's, and its forehead was huge and bulging, with two horns growing from it. The skin was blue and a thick pelt of fur covered its chest and shoulders.

He sprang to his feet, staring at the monster, then stepped between it and Ceinwen.

"I want the pearl." The demon spoke those words in a low, hideous voice that reverberated in the pit of Michael's stomach. It reached out its hand, but instead of a hand, it was a paw with long, curved claws.

"Who are you?" Michael asked.

"Can't you see us? We are all around you."

"I see nothing but one pathetic blue monster. You are nothing and not worth giving up the pearl." He glanced down at Ceinwen. To his surprise, she was still asleep. Hadn't she heard their voices? Or was he dreaming? Was this another nightmare?

"Then we will take the pearl from you and kill you and everyone you care for."

"You can't touch me."

"But we can touch them."

Michael stepped closer to the beast. "No. She has my protection. The protection of the pearl."

"But the others don't. Your father doesn't. Nor does the woman you love. Irina."

"Irina is dead."

"No. She isn't. We've found her. We'll torture her until you give up the pearl."

"You're lying."

"Oh? Look."

A vision of a woman walking on the sidewalk of a bridge over a river filled Michael's head. She wore a heavy coat and a warm woolen scarf covered her head. He couldn't see her face. The water was a river, and across it, to his surprise, was the Peter and Paul fortress which contained the burial place of the Romanovs, the last Russian dynasty. He'd visited the spot several times in St. Petersburg.

"That's not her," he whispered, his heart pounding. "This is all a trick. A vile trick."

"Is it? Do you dare to test us?"

In his vision, the woman stopped and leaned against the metal railing, her head bowed. The Neva River was wide, and the bridge high. A jump would most likely be fatal.

"Stop it! I don't know who the woman is, but whoever she is, there's no reason for your madness to kill her."

"You still don't believe us? Say her name, and you'll see. Say it!"

"Irina," he whispered.

"Louder!"

"Irina!"

The woman peered over her shoulder as if she heard someone call. It was the face, older now, but still the face Michael had remembered all these years. "No. You're causing my mind to play tricks. Of course it's her face I'm seeing. It's her face I *expect* to see. But she's no more Irina than you are!"

"Well, you thought she was dead, so why not make your dream come true?"

She turned back to look at the river, and then her hands tightened on the rail. She leaned forward as if to boost herself up.

"Stop it! Let her go," Michael said. "We can negotiate this."

"Ah, so you do believe us."

"I don't want to see her killed. Not even in a dream."

The demon laughed. "Let's 'negotiate.'"

"Bring Nakamura Seiji and Rachel Gooding back to life and I'll give you the pearl," Michael said.

"There's much I can do, but power over life and death is not one of them. But you shouldn't mourn for them since you are dead now as well. You've entered our world."

"Demons lie, and that's what you're doing."

"If demons lie, it's because they've learned it from humans. From people like me."

"You?" Michael didn't understand.

And then a swirling cloud appeared, wrapping the demon in a haze. When it ceased churning, the clouds drifted down to the ground and vanished. In place of the demon stood a small, thin, gray-haired man with a shattered eye.

"I didn't mean to trap you here," he said softly. "I'm quite sorry. Still, I do want to take the pearl from you."

"Hearn?" Michael asked.

"Not exactly. A form of Lafcadio, perhaps." He put a hand on his narrow chest and looked down at himself. His features were Caucasian, but he wore a man's kimono in brown and black. "I don't really know myself. All I know is I used to 'play' with alchemy. That was a foolish thing to do."

"You turned into a demon?" Michael asked.

"I'm not sure what I am anymore. But yes, a demon is one form. It usually frightens people into doing whatever I want. You surprise me, *cousin.*"

"I don't understand," Michael said.

Hearn chuckled. "It baffles me, too. You see, I once had a friend who was a sorcerer as well as a descendant of Nakamura Taishi. I believe you've heard of him."

"I have," Michael said.

"But I doubt you know that centuries ago, Taishi led an armed revolt against a daimyo family, hoping to overthrow him. He failed, and he and his samurai were all killed."

"He led a rebellion?" Michael was trying to fit that in with what he'd heard from Seiji.

"And lost," Lafcadio said. "So, I wrote my stories and then, using my friend's alchemy, I built a world where all of my characters could live. In it, Taishi won his battle, and the Nakamura clan prevailed. I called my land Kamigawa, which means River of the Gods, and it was to be a wonderful place. I thought it would be a happy place where I was not mocked or scorned or abandoned, and where I, my stories, and my family could live forever. But alchemy is a black art, and I forgot about that. Or ignored it. The Taishi I created was a demon, and the land, demonic. From the outside, it looked idyllic. But inside, it's decayed and fetid. My good wife was horrified by what I had done. She burned my story about Kamigawa before it was ever published, hoping that would destroy the land I created. It didn't."

"You couldn't find a way to destroy it?" Michael could scarcely believe what he was hearing.

"No," Hearn confessed. "But I was cautious. Fearing unsuspecting men might become trapped in it, I sent my papers to the other side of the world, to my cousin, Victor Rempart. I was quite sure he would never bother to read them. I didn't want anyone to use my work as a gateway."

"But someone did," Michael said with a sigh as he contemplated the way he had read the papers. That simple act must have brought him—and then Rachel—to Kamigawa. As he remembered the day he first discovered Hearn's writings in the library, a detail came back to him, something he had all but forgotten. "I wonder if something didn't purposely lead me to your work. Kwaidan fell from its shelf. I picked it up and began to read."

Hearn looked at Michael with sadness. "I have watched that house with interest from time to time over the years, perhaps because you are relatives, and certainly because you are alchemists. Your returning home has turned the wheels of your destiny. Consider how your connection to your mother has been reawakened ever stronger, how your discovery of me in your family history has opened new directions, and how you now better understand your father's terrible ambitions. All these agents of your fate have brought you here now. Each has played a part, largely unbeknownst to each other, and imperfectly understood."

Michael shook his head. None of this made sense to him.

"It's the cost, Michael, of forbidden knowledge. Your own mother may have had a hand in bringing you here. She knew the evil that infested your home, and that you might be the one to break the spell it exerts."

"Your words are nonsense," Michael said. "You know she's dead."

"So? Aren't I as well? Really, cousin, you know better than that. The dead are always with us."

Michael sighed as he acknowledged the truth of Hearn's words. "I've always felt there are ghosts in that house."

"And there are, as well as demons. Your mother, unfortunately, had no way of knowing about Taishi," Hearn continued. "But as soon as you began to read my stories, Taishi sensed you and learned about you and the pearl. He had to be the one who put everything in place to draw you to Kamigawa, to my creation.

"When you read my stories, it opened a gateway between the world I created and the one in which you live. You—and those close to you—have the ability to pass from your world to this one." As he spoke, Hearn's eyes widened, and the whites took on a reddish glow. "You have the ability, I believe, to become one of the greatest alchemists of all time, possibly the greatest. But use the power wisely. We don't truly understand it or fully control it. We hope, but our best intentions can and do create evil."

"That won't happen." Michael's voice was firm. "I've seen the destruction alchemy has caused, the lives lost because of it. I want nothing to do with it."

Hearn shook his head. "I fear it's too late for that. You possess what may be the most powerful philosopher's stone of all time. And they know it."

"They?"

"From the moment you began to read my stories, Taishi and his minions worked to draw you here, to this land peopled with my thoughts, the world of my creations. Surely, you don't rush off to every place in the world you read about, do you? Of course not. You knew this was special even if you didn't know why. And so did the demons. They want you here. They've done everything they could to make you happy here."

Michael looked at Ceinwen. Strangely, she still slept. Was she a part of this demonic plot?

"Who are the demons you speak of?" he asked.

"Taishi's samurai. They fought and died for him, and their payment was to watch the leader that they loved turn into a demon and torture this town and the people in it. He possessed Lady Nakamura's son because the boy was weak and gentle, two attributes Taishi hates."

"But now he's with Rachel—he's no longer evil," Michael said.

"No, no, no. For Rachel and Seiji to overcome the evil within them both and be together, they couldn't remain in my world, or in yours. Where they've gone isn't for us to know. A better place, I think. They are dead, but perhaps not lost. It's Seiji, a healthy Seiji, who is with her. Not Taishi. The demon is here, and he is evil.

"His own samurai know that. That's why they want the pearl. They want to use it to trap Taishi and free them from his power. They're coming here now. Coming for the pearl. You must take it and run."

"Aren't we on the same side?" Michael asked. "We both want to rid the world of Taishi."

"You must understand, Michael. *They are demons* and will do horrible things. They will gladly kill you and your companion to get the pearl. I'm warning you. You must leave, now. Hurry."

"Wait. What about my father?"

Hearn became crest-fallen. "Your father is the most dangerous of them all."

And as suddenly as he had appeared, he vanished.

Michael knelt by Ceinwen and shook her. "Wake up. We've got to leave."

Startled, she looked around and quickly rose. She stood, but then froze, staring past him in horror. Michael spun around to see a group of eight samurai marching toward them.

The demons quickly surrounded Ceinwen and Michael, blocking their escape.

"Give us the pearl," a samurai demon roared as the others slid long, curved swords from their shafts and then raised them high over their heads, two hands gripping their hilts, ready to attack. "In this land, you are in our power, and you cannot fight us."

"Stop!" Michael said, holding a hand outward as if to stop them. They stood still watching him. He slowly took the lead box from his jacket pocket and unfastened the clasp, but didn't open it. The pearl remained encased in the rare earth. He could feel the samurai demons lean toward to it. "The pearl draws you forward," Michael said in a hushed voice. "You have no power to resist it, but it already has demons trapped in it; demons who have persecuted many more people than you. The ones in the pearl are pure evil. You don't want to face them."

"You will give us the pearl," the samurai demanded, "or watch your loved ones die."

With that, a fire sprang up out of nowhere, close to Ceinwen. She and Michael tried to move away from it, but it followed.

"Give us the pearl!" The samurai demons chanted the words at different times, at different speeds, creating a babel of sound.

"The demons trapped inside the pearl find pleasure by watching other's pain. Yours as well as mine," Michael warned.

"They cannot hurt us."

"You think not? Do you scorn them because they're trapped like rats?" The box in his hands quivered slightly at these words.

"They're nothing!" the samurai bellowed. "We are all powerful!"

Michael could feel the lead box vibrating hard now—a vibration of pure, demonic rage. He opened it and removed the bronze vessel. "It's in here," he whispered.

The samurai demons' desire to grab the pearl emanated as a wave and pulsated through him. He knew they would soon attack.

Ceinwen watched him, her eyes wide as she grabbed hold of his jacket with both hands.

"Take the pearl," Michael shouted as he opened the lid. "If you can!"

Immediately, a black cloud-filled ribbon of pure fury streamed from the box. It whirled free for a moment, upward through the trees, and Michael feared the demons from the pearl would escape. But then they turned and swooped downward over the samurai. They stretched out as if they were a long rope and began to wrap themselves around the samurai.

The samurai yelled in support of each other and slashed at the demonic attack with their swords. The demons from the pearl continued to wrap themselves around the samurai.

They spun round and round, knocking into and uprooting trees, stirring up the campfire into a wall of flame, and hovering over Michael and Ceinwen. Michael realized he had guessed correctly. The demons' anger at the way they'd been insulted made them want to punish their detractors more than escape, but with rare earth elements so near they didn't have the fullness of their strength. If they did, they would have made quick work of these samurai.

Finally, they began to squeeze the samurai as if they were a boa constrictor killing its prey. Michael waited until the samurai had been crushed into something about the size of a baseball, and then he took a handful of rare earth elements from inside the lead container and dumped it on them.

The samurai screamed and slowly shattered into ever smaller fragments and then into nothingness.

Michael then lifted the pearl out of its bronze container.

Ceinwen saw it for the first time. It was pinkish red with a bright luster creating a halo of light around it. She was unable to take her eyes from it. It was beautiful, hypnotic, and enticing.

With his arm outstretched and the pearl in the palm of his hand, Michael walked away from her. He spoke in a strong, firm voice. "The power of the earth's rare elements have weakened you as well as the samurai. You will return to the pearl. And you will protect and obey me. Only me."

Michael felt the pull of their demonic power fighting against his command. He felt his hold slipping.

"I am the keeper of the pearl. You will serve me and heed my commands," he ordered. "Enter the pearl. Do it. Now!"

A rainbow of colors shot out from the stone, and with it a loud, terrible wail filled the air. Ceinwen covered her ears, bending over in pain. The stone seemed to grow larger.

Furious, the demons rushed at Michael, wanting to attack, but could do no more than to swirl around him and form a gray-black churning mist, paler and less powerful than the mist that had surrounded the samurai.

Ceinwen backed away, then ran to the thickest tree she could find and hid behind it. She couldn't believe anything she was seeing and felt as if her mind might snap.

Michael held his hand higher, even as the mist buffeted him and tried to squeeze the life from him just as it had squeezed the samurai.

"Enter the pearl!" His voice boomed and, as if from some innate part of his soul, some collective unconscious memory, ancient words that were unknown to him spilled from his lips, weakening the demons.

Peculiar lumps appeared under the skin of his hands, arms, and face, distorting his body, as if something had been drawn under his skin and was fighting to break free.

Ever so slowly, the mist vanished. The contortions under Michael's skin shrank, and the pearl returned to its original size.

He fell to the ground, his eyes shut.

Ceinwen continued to hide behind the trees. She was scared. Her mind couldn't process what she had witnessed. What kind of man was he? If he even *was* a man. What had the pearl done to him when he called upon its powers?

She didn't know what to do, which way to turn.

Of all the strange things she had once written about, of all the witnesses she had mocked and dismissed as being crazy when they tried to convince her of unexplained phenomena they had seen, this was the worst ever—and real.

Michael lay on the ground, hurt, possibly dying. She had held him in her arms, had loved him, had let her body, her being, be filled by him, and now…

Somehow she forced herself to step toward him, slowly at first, but then she ran. She cared about him, more than she was ready to admit. She couldn't let him die.

"Wake up!" she cried, touching his face, shaking his shoulders. "Please. Michael, come back to me! They've gone now. We've got to get away!"

She couldn't rouse him.

She saw that he continued to clutch the pearl in his hand, and that the bronze vessel lay on the ground. She wasn't sure what to do. When she looked at the pearl, she felt its pull, a feeling so strong it scared her. Despite Michael's warnings about the power of the pearl, she hadn't been prepared for the pure, visceral desire it caused her. She not only wanted it, she *craved* it. Michael had said it was evil, and she understood, now, what he meant.

Something told her she needed to get it out of his hand and back into the vessel … and that she didn't dare look at it any more closely.

She picked up the open bronze vessel, held it in one hand, and then shut her eyes tight. Using her sense of touch, with the other hand she took the pearl from him. But as soon as she touched it, her fingers burned, as if the pearl were a ball of fire. She pressed her lips tight against the pain, not daring to cry out, not daring to drop it, but as quickly as she could, she placed it inside the bronze, and then twisted the bronze legs as she had watched Michael do to shut it.

Only then could she breathe again. When she looked at her fingertips, she expected to see burnt skin and blisters. But despite the pain that had raged through her body, she saw no marks. She cradled her painful hand in her arms and couldn't suppress a groan.

Yet, despite everything, if only briefly, she had been the master of the pearl ... and she had loved the sense of power it gave her.

"Ceinwen," Michael murmured, blinking as he opened his eyes. "What happened? Are you hurt?"

He was weak and she shifted so that he could lay his head on her lap as she stroked his brow. "I just learned the truth of the old saw that if you play with fire, you'll get burned. I think I've been getting too close to the flame."

He stared at her, trying to understand. Then he looked down at his hands, and then searched the ground. "The pearl! Where—"

He tried to get up but she stopped him. "It's in the bronze," she said. "And they're gone. You did it Michael. I'm not sure how, but you did."

He looked around. The samurai were gone, and there was no sign of the fight that had just taken place.

They heard the chirping of crickets. "It's going to be all right," he whispered and shut his eyes again.

Exhausted and spent, she helped him lay back down, then curled up beside him and held him close until the light of dawn seeped into the forest, bringing a new day.

CHAPTER 51

MICHAEL AND CEINWEN returned to the area where they had left Rachel and Seiji's bodies, but they were no longer there. They walked all around, but could find no sign of them.

As they searched for a tree with one of their blue ties, they stared in shock as a member of the park service strolled by. He was one of many employees tasked with showing visitors out of the forest if they got lost, and to be constantly on the lookout for potential suicides.

They shouted and ran to him. He didn't speak English, but it was obvious from the way he looked at them that they had the appearance of those who had been in the forest too long. He gave them water and energy bars, then indicated that they needed to follow him. They gladly did in the silence.

They walked for nearly two hours before he pointed to a rope with a "No Entry" sign—the same rope they had climbed over when they first arrived at the forest. And then he left them to go in search of others needing help in the forest of shadows and sorrow.

Once they had stepped over the rope, they knew they were back at the path that would lead them out of the forest to the land of the living. A sense of relief and even a strange sense of joy at having survived filled them as they rushed to the exit, past the sign warning people not to kill themselves, and even past the shoes waiting for owners who would never return. Finally, as they reached their car in the parking lot, they held each other for long minutes, glad to be alive, and happy to be together.

They drove back in the direction from which they'd come, back toward Kamigawa. But when they arrived there, they found no Kamigawa.

"How can this be?" Ceinwen said.

"Somehow, we're free of it," Michael said.

"What now?" Ceinwen asked.

"I can take out the pearl and try to find it, or we can leave it where it is, if anywhere. Do we really want to bring back that world? It was ultimately a place where evil had power."

"We have no reason to go back there. But what do we tell Rachel's parents?" Ceinwen murmured. "We can't say she went off to Shangri-La."

"Maybe we tell them just a bit of the truth—that she found someone she loves, and she's happy, and the two of them went away to be together, just themselves, but we don't know where. Maybe someday she'll return from the other world to them. I doubt it, but who knows."

"'There are more things in heaven and earth, Horatio, than are dreamt of in your philosophy,'" Ceinwen murmured.

"Thank you, Princess Hamlet." Michael smiled.

Just outside Izumo, they found an attractive seaside resort and checked in. This time, they only booked one room. When Ceinwen went into the shower, Michael joined her. Not until sometime later did they wander out to the private veranda overlooking the Sea of Japan.

Michael was happy that his cell phone finally worked again. He phoned Jianjun, and let him know he had the pearl, and the demonic threat was over ... at least for the moment. He told Jianjun he'd explain everything when they got together, and that he and Ceinwen would be on their way to Salmon the next day. He was glad to learn Jianjun was doing well and was ecstatic to still be in Salmon with Kira Holt.

When Jianjun asked about Rachel, Michael only said she'd met a man, fallen in love, and the two had gone off to parts unknown. Jianjun sounded surprised, then said he wished her happiness. Michael and Ceinwen thought their white lie might work after all. And it had to be better than a truth that no one would believe.

The next morning, Michael and Ceinwen left the hotel to head for the airport. They were on their way to their car when a black van pulled in front of them and stopped. The side door opened and two men jumped out, guns drawn.

Michael had grabbed Ceinwen's hand, ready to run, but the guns stopped him.

"Get in!" one ordered. "Both of you."

Ceinwen glanced at Michael. Reluctantly, he nodded. As she stepped near the van, a third man grabbed her arm and pulled her inside, while a fourth remained at the wheel. Michael recognized one of the gunmen as the stocky murderer from the Idaho mountains. He had no choice but to follow the order, and also entered the van.

He noticed the big man moved slowly and winced with pain as he did. Michael had wounded him in the shootout in Idaho. He now wished he had killed him.

They were driven to a barren area near a beach, then stopped. Michael's breathing came sharply as he tried to determine how to break free and get Ceinwen away from these bastards. But one man held a gun to her head. When Michael was told to get out of the van, he glanced first at Ceinwen. Raw fury struck as he saw how scared she was.

As soon as he climbed from the van, two of the armed men faced him. The big fellow was, as always, the talker of the group. "You can give us the pearl now, and we'll let you two go. Or, we can kill you both and then search your belongings until we find it. No one wants either of you dead. We only want the pearl. It's your choice."

Michael knew how ruthless these men had been in Idaho and didn't doubt their threat. He couldn't take the chance of them hurting Ceinwen.

"All right," he said. "It's in my carry-on. I'll get it."

A gunman grabbed the carry-on and tossed it to Michael. "Open it, then dump everything onto the ground. Don't get cute or she dies."

Michael did as told. With no weapon in the bag, he could do nothing but point to the lead container. "It's in there. I suggest you keep it in that lead box. The pearl can be very dangerous if mishandled."

The gunman scoffed. "Dangerous? It's a pearl!"

"Open it, if you don't believe me," Michael said. "Unless you're afraid to."

"What? Afraid of this?" One gunman lifted the lid of the box.

"No!" The big fellow shouted. "Shut that! Don't chance it. This whole job is way too goddamn crazy. The name 'pearl' might be a code name for something. If it's stored in lead, it could even be radioactive. Take it and let's get the hell out of here."

Heeding the warning, the others agreed. One man tossed their suitcases from the van and told Ceinwen to get out as well. She rushed to Michael as the other thieves jumped inside the van and sped away.

Michael held Ceinwen close as they watched the three men disappear.

"What do we do?" she asked.

"I've got a good idea who's behind this," he said. "There's only one person who knows so much about me and our movements, and at the same time, doesn't want us killed."

"Who?"

"Have you ever been to Cape Cod?"

CHAPTER 52

CEINWEN AND MICHAEL reached Boston at midnight. The next morning, since Ceinwen had never seen the city, Michael drove her to some historical sites. They ate brunch near Paul Revere's House and walked a bit of the Freedom Trail before making the long drive to Cape Cod.

As pleasant as it was, Ceinwen was sure Michael had played tour guide more to delay facing his father than anything else. He had said little to her about his family home or his life there, but what he didn't say spoke volumes. Now, as he drove toward that home, the taciturn but tough loner who kept everything bottled up inside was back.

She, too, fell silent.

Her thoughts turned once again to his mother's diary. It had been beyond cheeky for her to read it, but she had been in a strange country and in the house of a man she didn't know. Or maybe that was just an excuse for journalistic nosiness.

She had never told Michael she'd read the diary, and hoped she would never need to confess it. At the same time, she was glad she'd read it and could now understand why Michael was so apprehensive about this visit.

She had to admit she felt much the same. There was an aura of evil attached to everything about his father.

After reaching what Michael called "Outer Cape Cod," they left the highway and took a narrow lane toward the ocean. Michael stopped at tall iron gates with a large, scrolled "R" medallion in gold on each gate. He tapped a code onto a keypad, and the gates slid open.

The length of the driveway surprised Ceinwen, but it was nothing compared to her reaction to the house itself with its elaborate cornices, fan-shaped molding above the windows and doors, castle-like turret, and grotesque winged monkeys parading above the entrance.

"Welcome to Wintersgate," Michael said wryly.

"So I see," she said. "Someone had a fondness for Gothic manor houses."

He tried to grin, but it came out more as a grimace as he rubbed his forehead. "My sentiments exactly," he said softly.

"Headache?"

"They seem to hit whenever I come home." He blinked a few times, as if the sunlight itself was bothering him.

They were removing their suitcases from the trunk when an older skeleton of a man approached. Michael introduced the valet, Stedman, to Ceinwen. He took her suitcase, and as they proceeded toward the house, he asked Michael, "Will the Green Room do for your guest?"

"That's fine. I suspect we'll only be here a couple of nights. Is the old man home?"

"He's in his laboratory at the moment. I'm sure he'll be happy to learn you're back," Stedman replied as they entered the foyer. "Dinner will be served at seven tonight. Would you like some tea or coffee after your drive?"

"Iced tea for me. Ceinwen?"

She was so busy taking in the home's interior, it took a moment for the question to register. "Same, please. Thank you."

The massive entry hall reminded her of a once beautiful woman who had grown old and didn't realize that her makeup was now garish, and her clothes frayed, faded, and misshapen. It was as if no one cared anymore about the house, and, in revenge, it had turned ugly and uninviting.

They followed Stedman up the stairs. He passed two doors along the hallway and then opened the third. "This is for you, Miss Ceinwen."

"Thank you." She looked at Michael before going into it.

"My room is next door," he said, indicating the room at the end of the hall. "Head downstairs when you're ready for your tea. Take your time. It may be a while. I'll be down after I say hello to my father."

Stedman entered the room ahead of her and placed her suitcase on a bench at the foot of the bed, and then quietly left, shutting the door behind him.

She knew Michael's family had money, but she never expected anything the size of this home and property. The guest room had a queen-size four-poster bed with a lush bedspread in green and gold. Green floral wallpaper covered the walls. The furniture appeared to be museum quality antiques. The room was clean and had been dusted but the air was stale. She flung open the windows and a brisk breeze entered. She hadn't realized how close the house was to the water.

She was exhausted, but knew if she lay down, she'd probably fall asleep. Instead she took a shower and washed her hair, glad to find a hair dryer in the room. Not everything was antique in the house.

Michael took a few Motrin with water, and lay down awhile, eyes shut, but that didn't help his headache at all. He suspected there was only one cure, and he went in search of his father, starting at his laboratory.

William Claude put down the vial he was holding and looked up, his face contorted in a frown. "So there you are. I was wondering if or when you would venture up here."

"Stedman told you I'd arrived?"

"Yes, but I didn't need him to," William Claude said with a frown. "You surprised me. I expected it would be another sixteen years before you bothered to come back here."

"Things have changed."

"Yes, they have." William Claude focused on measuring a portion of a blue liquid.

"You should be pleased," Michael said, even as his head throbbed worse with each passing minute.

"About what?" He mixed the liquid with a clear substance in a beaker.

Michael knew William Claude wasn't about to confess to having anything to do with the robbery of the pearl. He rubbed the ache between his eyebrows. "I've brought a friend with me, Ceinwen Davies. I want her to see the house and to meet you, to get an idea of who I am, and what I'm all about. No woman would believe me if I tried to explain my childhood. This was the best thing I could think of."

William Claude's eyes narrowed. "She's that important to you, is she?"

"Time will tell."

"I see."

Michael waited for more comments. They weren't forthcoming.

"What are you working on?" Michael asked, blinking against the pain.

"It's quite interesting. Not many years ago, some scientists at Los Alamos discovered that cell-like organisms—primitive vesicles made up of polyaromatic hydrocarbons and fatty acids, to be precise—were able to capture metal ions and harvest protons. In other words, they could draw energy from the environment and thus create life."

"Create life? Impossible."

"But that's the point—it isn't. They discovered the chemical origins of life on earth."

"No," Michael insisted. "They discovered the chemical *elements* for life on earth. That's different from creating it."

William Claude looked disgusted. "Don't you see? Simply by adding silicon protocells, we'll have cells that function like a carbon-based life form."

As ever, William Claude's knowledge of chemistry was far beyond Michael's. "So what?"

William Claude held up his forefinger—always a preliminary step to his making a grand pronouncement. "Combining all that with the creation of perfection by means of alchemy will give us an immortal man who can also regenerate living body parts."

Michael found the concept horrifying, something befitting a modern-day Dr. Frankenstein. William Claude didn't seem to notice the disgust on his face. Or, didn't care.

"What good is being immortal if, for example, your legs cease to function due to some accident or even a bacterium or virus?" William Claude asked rhetorically. "My creation, once I finish my work, will take care of that problem."

"Except for one major problem." Michael stared hard at his father, his eyes squinting against the bright laboratory lights. He didn't know if he could handle much more of this. "You haven't yet completed the first step: how to make a man immortal."

William Claude's eyes flashed with a savage fury. But almost as quickly as it came, it vanished and his lips curved into the small, secretive smile that Michael had seen him use on many occasions. "In time, my boy, in time. Now, let me show you what I'm doing here."

Ceinwen went downstairs to the breakfast room. Stedman appeared so silently, he startled her. He had a definite Boris Karloff air about him—yes, she knew a few classic American movies.

He gave a curt nod, walked to the table in the center of the room, and pulled out a chair for her. "I'll bring your tea."

"Thank you." She sat, and then looked out on the cliffs and ocean beyond. "This is beautiful. Has Michael been down yet?"

"He's with his father."

"I see. How is his father?"

Stedman appeared surprised at her question. He stiffened and said, "He was a bit under the weather, a migraine seemed to come on him suddenly. But I'm sure, with Master Michael back, he'll be better."

"I'm glad to hear it," she said, pondering this sudden outburst of severe headaches.

She wondered what was happening between Michael and his father.

Before long, Stedman brought her a tall glass of iced tea with lime, and a plate with one eclair and one Napoleon, saying they were to tide her over before dinner.

She hadn't thought she was hungry after lunch, but the pastries were so delicious, she ate them both. She was licking her fingers when she heard, "Well, I'll have to inform cook her desserts are a big hit."

She looked up to see Michael approach. She smiled with relief to see him looking much less stressed, and she suspected the meeting with his father went well.

He bent to kiss her. "You look nice sitting there. Would you like something stronger than tea?" he asked as he went to the bar in the room. She declined as he made himself a whiskey and soda—heavy on the whiskey. Maybe it hadn't been such a great meeting.

"We should go outside," he said. "The weather's good today."

Just past the patio was a stone bench on a lookout with a wide view of the ocean. They went there and sat.

"How did it go with your father?" she asked.

"He was mainly curious as to why I've returned. I said it was because I brought 'a young lady' with me."

"Oh? Does that happen often?"

"Never."

That surprised her, but she tried not to show it.

"He told me about some chemical experiments he's working on," Michael added, his voice low.

"Anything interesting?"

"Just the origins of life."

She studied him to see if he was joking. He wasn't.

"When you meet him," Michael continued, "I'm sure you'll find him to be a pleasant older man. Nothing more, nothing less. But don't let that fool you. A devious nature and a black heart hide beneath all his so-called charm."

"I think you need to tell me more about him," she said.

He nodded faintly as if he had expected her to say that. "What would you like to know?"

"Oh ... things like why you and he seem to have been at odds most of your life. I have the impression you've scarcely seen him."

"That's true." He drank some whiskey.

"Why? What happened?"

He stared out at the water. "Has anyone ever told you that you ask far too many questions?"

"All the time. It doesn't make me want to know any less, however."

"It's a boring story."

Her eyes slowly traveled over his handsome face. "I don't believe anything about you would ever be boring."

He met her gaze, then spoke in a low voice. "Sometimes I have to wonder how it happened that I just met you in Japan, and now you're here with me in my family home."

She paled. "What do you mean?"

He looked puzzled. "Nothing. Just that it's odd ..."

"Why?"

"Well ... you're a journalist, and I'm—"

"My God, Michael." She felt as if she'd been hit in the face with ice water. "You still don't trust me, do you? After all this, you think because I was a journalist—"

"No. That's not it." He exhaled sharply, then folded his hands and gazed out at the ocean.

Heart pounding with both fury and dismay, she forced herself not to run, but to wait for an explanation ... if such a thing were possible.

"If you must know," he began cautiously, "I've carefully taught myself not to trust anyone. Ever. Everyone I ever have, except Jianjun, has proved I was wrong to do so."

His words stabbed at her. "I'm sorry."

"There's nothing for you to be sorry about. The problem is mine."

Is it? She couldn't help but think about the way she had lied to Rachel, and about the way she had searched his room, even read his mother's diary. Maybe he'd been right not to trust her. The realization caused her anger to vanish and filled her with shame.

She intertwined her fingers and stared at her hands. She chose her words carefully. "I come from a loving family of honest, straightforward people. Once I became a journalist, I entered a world where people pretend to be friends to get a story. Men I dated and thought cared about me were more interested in my sources, or what I'd found in my investigations."

"I didn't mean—"

She wouldn't let him continue. "I'll admit I had to practice deceit at times. But once things became personal, I stopped. If you think I'm with you because I'm after your story, you're wrong. I would never betray your trust. It's hard to prove what I'm *not* doing, so if you'd like me to leave..."

When he didn't respond, she stood.

"Wait." He caught her arm. "Sit back down, please."

She did, but pulled her arm free. She was angry, hurt, guilt-ridden, but also sad that she didn't know how to get through his walls. They were stronger than the Tower of London. "You don't have to tell me a thing. But I want you to know I do care about you. Believe me, I wish I didn't because you're close-mouthed, suspicious, secretive, and enigmatic."

He actually did a double-take. "What?"

"You apparently have some freaky powers, and you live a life filled with the kind of occult beliefs that I've spent the last few years debunking as hoaxes."

He gaped at her, stunned and speechless.

Her lips pursed. "Unfortunately," she took a deep breath, "I also find you fascinating, intelligent, loving, and sexy. So, I'm a conflicted mess, and half my brain tells me to run, not walk, away from you because this thing between us can only end badly for me. For *me*, Michael."

To her surprise, he put his arms around her. "I can't argue with any of the negative stuff you said. But I wish you'd stay. For some reason, I do trust you. Journalist or not."

Her eyes met his. "Maybe you shouldn't."

He smiled, and it was enough to weaken her. Unsure what to so, she pulled herself from his hold and then shifted so that she faced the ocean. They sat silently watching the waves roll in.

After a while, he spoke. "Years ago, just out of college, I wanted to marry a woman and my father objected to her. She left me because of that."

She gawked at him. "She left you because your father objected? Why did she care what the old codger thought?"

"For it to make sense, I'd need to start at the beginning. I don't think you want to hear all that."

"Ah, Michael," she sighed. He still didn't understand how she felt about him. "I'm here, aren't I?"

He nodded, but dropped his gaze. A long moment passed before he spoke again. "Her mother, Magda Petrescu, had been our housekeeper. After my mother's death, she pretty much raised me. Irina is—was—five years younger than me. We played together growing up. Then one summer, I came home from college to find that our housekeeper's scrappy little daughter had grown into a beautiful woman. We spent our summers together and planned to marry when I finished at the university. Finally when I was twenty-six-years old, with a Ph.D. in Archeology, I returned home. She was gone."

"Gone? Without a word for you?"

His voice was low, hushed. "My father had seen to it that she walked out of my life."

Ceinwen could scarcely believe what she was hearing. "But, if she loved you?"

He shrugged. "Apparently, she loved money more."

The coldness of his statement took her aback. "Money? Your father paid her off?"

"God, this is actually embarrassing," he admitted, looking away.

She clutched his shoulders and made him face her again. "You should never be embarrassed around me, Michael Rempart. I would have hoped we were past that."

He kept his gaze fixed on her, even as his eyes turned bleak. "My father showed me a check he'd written to her for two million dollars. Her signature, endorsing it, was on the back. Seeing that, I left Wintersgate and didn't return until this summer."

Her jaw dropped. "Two *million?*"

Her astonishment made him smile. "Having a family full of alchemists has to be worth something. And in my family's case, it's hundreds of millions."

Ceinwen drew in her breath. "Bloody hell! Well, all I can say is, your father did you a favor! I can't imagine a woman leaving you for any reason!"

He touched her cheek lightly, his thumb brushing over her lips before he dropped his hand. "That's not what you said a few minutes ago, but I'll take it. And, who knows what really happened? I never saw her again, and I've only ever heard my father's version of the story. But no matter how much I searched, and believe me, with my income I was able to do a lot of searching, I never found her."

"This has been a question since you graduated from Oxford?" Ceinwen asked. "That's a long time not to know what happened."

"I decided what my father told me was true and moved on. My youthful heart had been broken, but that seems to be a pretty common occurrence. Besides, if she had loved me, the way I did her, she would have thrown the check back in his face. At some point, she would have tried to find me, to give me some explanation."

"I agree. Are you saying something changed?"

"Last year, I tracked down Irina's mother, Magda. I learned there was much more to the reason Irina left than I thought, and it had something to do with my father. Magda wouldn't say, so after much thought, I came here to find out from him. Instead … instead I learned that Irina is dead."

She gasped, not only from the harshness and despair in his voice as he explained what had happened, but the immense sorrow it caused him. She drew back as she realized that one of the many walls around him, perhaps the highest and thickest, had a name: Irina. "I'm so sorry. Do you know what happened to her?"

"A car accident, apparently."

She took a deep breath. "How awful. What a terrible shock."

"It was, but it's a story from long ago. I don't want to talk about it." Michael put an arm around her and drew her to his side. "I'd much rather hear about that family of yours in Cardiff."

She could tell he was trying to get past his tale of Irina and was failing miserably. But she was willing to play along. "My da owns a pub, my mum sometimes helps out in the kitchen, and my two older brothers run a textile mill that they love. They make fine Welsh woolens, and when the economy is good, they do okay. When it's bad, they struggle—a lot. From the time I was a young girl, I wanted to get away from that life and become a foreign correspondent to see the world. At times I wonder what possessed me. Maybe it was one of the demons you're so familiar with."

Michael smiled sadly, his fingers playing with a lock of her thick auburn hair. "Do you ever wish you had stayed at home?"

"What, so I could have married Gwydion Evans who's been panting after me since I was in the eighth grade? No thank you. I'll take demons over the boredom of Cardiff."

"Poor Gwydion. But how do you feel about this life you're living?"

"Sometimes, I feel in control, but other times, I simply have no idea what's happening, not even who I am anymore."

"That's how I felt when I learned about my family of crazy alchemists. Does hearing about us make you want to get on the next plane back to England?"

Enough talk. She decided it was time to show him how she felt. "Not on your life." She kissed him, and his arms tightened around her as he returned her kisses.

An "Ahem" sounded in the distance.

Stedman hovered by the edge of the patio. "Dinner is ready, Master Michael, if you and Miss Ceinwen would like to come inside."

"Will my father be joining us?" Michael asked as they stood.

"I'm afraid not. He'll be eating something light in his room tonight. He's sure he'll feel much stronger in the morning."

CHAPTER 53

THE NEXT MORNING, Ceinwen awoke to an empty bed. Michael had joined her in her room, saying the bed in his was far too small for two.

She showered and dressed, then went down to the breakfast room. Stedman heard her enter and approached.

"Have you seen Michael?" she asked.

"Yes. He and Mr. Rempart had a light breakfast, then Mr. Rempart went up to his laboratory, and I believe Master Michael went out for a walk. I'll bring you some breakfast if you'd like."

"Thank you," she said.

Before long, he brought out a carafe of coffee with an omelette and toast. She had finished and was thinking about going out to see if she could find Michael when a tall man with pure white hair worn long and combed straight back off a high forehead stood at the table. His eyes were almost black, as were his eyebrows, and the contrast with his hair was startling. Remembering her manners, she quickly stood, nearly knocking the chair over as she did, but catching it just in time. "Good morning. I … I didn't hear you approach."

"You must be Michael's friend." He smiled and then faced the valet who was now also in the room. "Stedman, some coffee for me."

Ceinwen wasn't sure what to do, so she held out her hand. "Yes, Ceinwen Davies. I'm happy to meet you, Mr. Rempart."

He shook it with a fast, loose grip, saying nothing as he took a seat across from her.

She quickly sat again. "Michael has told me much about you."

"Oh?" He placed a napkin on his lap as Stedman brought him a cup of black coffee. "But he's told me almost nothing about you—although I can hear a trace of an accent. Welsh, although I can guess that from your name. Ceinwen, a traditional Welsh name I believe, meaning beautiful, fair, and blessed." He flashed her a smile with surprisingly white teeth for a man his age—whatever that age was.

"'Tis so," she said in the thickest Welsh accent she could muster. "I'm surprised you know so much about a name that, frankly, is a burden everywhere outside of Wales. Few have any idea how to pronounce it, let alone spell it."

To that admission, William Claude gave a hearty laugh. "I can see why Michael has kept you to himself. Of course, Michael and I don't talk much. Where did you two meet?"

"Only a short while ago in Japan."

He quizzed her a bit about the experience and then talked to her about Wales which he had visited a couple of times over the years.

His coffee finished, he stood. "Why don't we take a walk down to the beach? It's a beautiful day. A bit breezy, but when isn't it by the ocean?"

"I'd love to."

He took her arm. The gesture felt both gallant and part of the old-style charm that went along with a house like this.

Michael had warned her time and again about his father, and everything she had read about him in Jane Addams Rempart's diary was fresh in her mind, but still, she was finding him gracious. She wondered if the years had mellowed him.

The wind was up, causing her hair to fly about. She tried to get hold of it, and twist it into submission. "No, no. Let it go," he said. He lightly ran his hand along the side of her hair, then lifted some of it, and watched it slip through his fingers. "It's been a long time since anyone with such beautiful hair has been out on this terrace."

She had always thought of her thick, hard-to-manage hair as the epitome of boring.

He smiled. "There's nothing boring about you, Ceinwen."

The comment astounded her. He couldn't have read her mind, could he? And his pronunciation of her name was perfect—as if he were from the old country.

"What's wrong with my son that he doesn't tell you what a beautiful woman you are?" He tucked her hand in the crook of his arm as he led her to a narrow, sandy footpath.

She was telling herself she had either misheard or misunderstood the man ... although he was right, Michael rarely let a compliment pass his lips. "I should make it clear to you, Mr. Rempart, that Michael and I haven't known each other very long. Although, on my part, I would like to get to know him better."

"Call me, Claude, please."

"Claude," she repeated.

"So, you say you and Michael don't know each other well, yet you've traveled half way around the world to meet his father, and he's slept in your room. It sounds as if you know him quite well," he said with a sparkle in his eye.

She realized the housekeeper or Stedman must keep him informed about everything that happened in the house. "I'm not saying I'm immune to your son's charms," she admitted. "But we won't tell him that, will we, Claude?"

He grinned and patted her hand. "Definitely not. And I'm glad you aren't one of those rough young starlets Michael used to date, much to my displeasure."

Rough young starlets? She didn't know about them.

Soon, they reached the sandy beach.

"Ah. Here we are. I hope you like it." He waved his arms as if presenting the ocean to her.

"This side of the 'pond' as we call it, is lovely," she said.

A wooden bench was nearby. "I'll sit here. Feel free to remove your shoes and walk barefoot in the sand. It's not easy to walk on with heels. Not that I've ever tried it, mind you!"

His laughter was strangely infectious, and she joined him as she took off her shoes and knee-length hose. She rolled up the bottoms of her linen slacks and headed toward the water. When she reached wet sand, she dug in her toes, enjoying the sensation. The wind was brisk, and she used both hands to capture her hair, and pull it forward over one shoulder. As she did, her body twisted slightly, enough that she caught a glimpse of William Claude watching her. The look on his face was one of pure, masculine pleasure.

She found it unnerving, but it didn't displease her.

After a few minutes, she headed back to him.

She sat on the bench to put her shoes back on, but he took hold of each foot and used his handkerchief to brush away the sand before she put on the stockings. "You won't be comfortable with sand in your shoes," he said.

"Thank you, Claude." The way he had held each foot and brushed it with his handkerchief felt strangely erotic. What, she wondered, was wrong with her? Even stranger, he no longer seemed as old as he had earlier. The hair was still white, but he looked far from frail. She tried to laugh off her uneasiness, but couldn't.

Instead of taking her arm, he put his hand on her waist, his grip firm, as they walked along the narrow path back to the house. She found herself leaning against him as if enjoying his touch ... as if she had no control over such feelings. Too soon, it seemed, they were back indoors.

At the staircase that led up to her room, he faced her, standing close. "Thank you for a pleasant walk. I'll see you at dinner time. Oh, and if you'd like to explore the house, please feel free. It's a lovely old place and hasn't had such a delectable young woman in it for far too many years. It's a complete delight to have you here. Make use of anything you'd like in the house, and particularly in your room." He then made a slight bow and walked down the hall.

As she watched him go, the bizarre magnetism she had felt when he was near slowly faded. She felt as if she had been standing in the midst of some kind of fog, and when she thought back on her reaction to Claude's "charms," it all felt weirdly off-kilter.

Back in the guest room, Ceinwen went to the window and searched to see if she could spot Michael. She couldn't. She wondered where he could have gone for so long.

She wandered around the room, but thoughts of Claude's invitation to look over the house beckoned.

She bypassed Michael's room, but checked the other rooms on the floor. Two were unused guest rooms, and the third was filled with old paintings and sculptures. Next to it was what appeared to be Claude's bedroom—she quickly shut the door—and, at the very end of the hall, the opposite end from Michael's room, was his father's laboratory.

Beside the laboratory was a narrow, stone staircase leading up to the third floor. Curious, she went up the stairs and found herself in an enchanting room.

The room was round, the walls stone, and the side of the room that faced the ocean had large windows on both sides of French doors that lead out to a deck. She was in the turret.

Where most rooms in the house were spacious, with few objects anywhere, and nothing out of place, this one was filled with a hodge-podge of belongings that gave it a used, lived in, and even a much-loved feeling. A feeling of warmth.

This must have been Michael's mother's room, she thought. Her private retreat, perhaps.

She slowly toured the space. There were several bookcases, with books that looked as if they'd actually been read. Tucked here and there among them were knickknacks and display items that were frilly and far more feminine than anything else in the house.

Near the bookcases was an open cupboard filled with multiple skeins of yarn in deep, rich colors, mostly reds and blues and creamy shades. She touched the yarn. Its exceptional softness told her its quality.

A corner of the room had a large sewing cabinet, with an older sewing machine and, beside it, piles of fabrics in plaids and floral, and threads in a rainbow of shades and sizes. A stack of cloth had been cut to form quilts, and a quilt top that looked about half-finished, hand-sewn with a fine stitch into an intricate star pattern, lay carefully folded to one side. Near it, was a garden scene done in needlepoint, again little more than half finished. The handwork was beautiful.

She was surprised that, not only were the furnishings not covered with sheets, but the room was free of dust. Someone was taking care of it as if the owner might come back at any moment.

No, she thought, not "the owner," but Jane Rempart. Ceinwen felt as if she had gotten to know Jane through the words of her diary, and she had ached for her as she read of Jane's unhappiness in her marriage and her life. And now, she was here among Jane's possessions.

Near the French doors were two comfortable arm chairs, one with an ottoman. On a side table lay a book. She picked it up. It was a well-worn, illustrated edition of Longfellow's "Evangeline." She remembered Michael saying his mother had loved the poem.

She opened the French doors and went out to the deck. A stone railing ran along its edge. The view from up here was breathtaking.

She was enjoying the sun and the ocean view when she heard a voice calling from below. She leaned forward and saw Claude on the patio waving up at her. She waved back.

He said something, but she couldn't hear over the ocean's roar, and stretched, leaning forward as far as she could.

Suddenly, arms circled her waist and dragged her backward, away from the rail.

"What are you trying to do?" Michael roared. He spun her around to face him. He was breathing hard, his face flushed.

"What are you talking about? What's wrong?"

He grabbed her upper arms hard. "What are you doing out here?"

"You're hurting me! Your father said it was okay for me to look around the house. This room is—"

"Is nothing! It should be locked." He let her go, his eyes filled with a black anger.

"It's a lovely room." She lowered her voice, hoping to calm him. "I know it was your mother's, and that these were her things. But someone has cared for it all these years." She reentered the turret and picked up a needlepoint she admired. "Look at the work she did here—the fine, tiny stitches. And over there, those beautiful quilts. It shouldn't be locked up at all."

His face looked strained. "She fell from that balcony."

The words were blunt, but through them Ceinwen understood his strong reaction to seeing her out there, leaning over the balustrade. "I didn't know," she murmured.

He shut his eyes a moment. "That was where she died. I was walking into the house when I saw you out on the deck. I came up to see what you were doing here and when you leaned so far forward..."

She saw a shudder go through him. She tried to put her arms around him, but he turned away and went to the door. He held it open; his voice like ice. "Coming?"

She hurried past him down the stairs and into her room without another word.

That afternoon, Michael phoned Jianjun to check on how he was doing. He had phoned him every day since leaving Japan, and was glad to hear he was healing well, and the infection that had flared up was now almost gone. He was also glad to learn Kira was still with him.

Michael also called Jake.

Jake had sent a couple of deputies to work with experienced investigators and crime scene analysts from Boise and Coeur d'Alene to help gather evidence. So far, nothing had panned out, and the investigation was widening. They learned that the morning Jake, Michael, and the others drove to Selway Falls, a private plane had been used to fly four men from Salmon to a small airfield in that area. A car awaited. No one could trace the owner or pilot of the plane, or the car.

They were now zeroing in on where the attackers might have gotten the horses they had used in their getaway. Someone had to rent or sell them, and most likely it was some rancher who lived fairly close to Selway Falls and was trying to make extra money.

Michael hung up feeling good about the progress being made in Salmon, but he continued to feel guilty and responsible for the loss of life and suffering going on.

And now, he had to add guilt for the way he was treating Ceinwen. He had stupidly allowed himself to get too close to her. He let his heart open the smallest bit—and she marched right in. She was fun, kind, warm, and with her feet firmly on the ground—all the things he wasn't and never could be. With her, life felt exciting, maybe even be worth living.

But bringing her to this bizarre house, subjecting her to his own and his family's history, made him realize that the kindest way to express his growing feelings for her would be to make her run from him and not stop until she was far, far away.

CHAPTER 54

WHEN CEINWEN SAW that the doors to the formal parlor and dining room stood open and the table had been set, she expected that night's dinner would be a special occasion. She pulled her hair back into an elegant chignon. She might not have brought a beautiful dress to wear, but she had packed a nice black skirt and sea-green top.

The jewelry box in the room beckoned, along with Claude's words that she was welcome to use anything she wished. Inside were several lovely pieces of jewelry, but a pair of dangling earrings with green stones that sparkled like emeralds caught her eye. The thought crossed her mind that they might have been Michael's mother's earrings, but she dismissed the idea. Mrs. Claude Rempart would wear nothing but real gems, and they wouldn't have been tossed in a guest room jewelry box.

She put the earrings on. They brought out the green of her eyes, and she knew she had to wear them.

Downstairs, Michael waited for her in the formal dining room, a cocktail in his hand. He was wearing a black jacket and slacks, white shirt and blue tie. She had guessed right that dinners with Claude Rempart were formal occasions.

"You had a suit here?" She asked lightly fingering the rich wool and cashmere blend of the jacket.

"Stedman brought it to me. Don't ask," was his only comment.

"Well, I wish he could have worked his magic with women's clothes," she said "I never dreamed I'd be anywhere that I'd need a dress."

"You look beautiful," he said. "Beautiful, as ever. And I apologize for the way I acted this afternoon. I was startled—and scared for you. I just don't know what will happen from one minute to the next in this house."

Beautiful ... his use of the word hearkened back to William Claude's comment. She shoved the thought aside. "It's understandable. I had no idea or I wouldn't have gone up there."

"No. It's all right. I think she would have liked you appreciating her things. I used to spend a lot of time there with her."

I know. She was tempted to say that, to confess what she had read. Instead, she said only, "I'm glad you were happy with her. I'm sure she loved you very much."

He looked at odds as to how to respond. "Can I get you a drink? Bourbon? Chardonnay? Pinot noir?"

"Red wine sounds good."

He nodded and went to the sideboard and poured her a drink.

She searched for new topic. "By the way, I met your father."

His brows raised as he handed her the glass. "And?"

"He was quite nice to me. Charming, even."

Michael's brows knitted for just a moment, then he took a gulp of his bourbon and poured himself a bit more.

A voice from the back. "Go easy, there, Michael. You don't want to give the young lady the wrong impression about you."

She turned around to see William Claude looking quite dapper in a black suit with a black bow tie. The black made his hair look like spun silver. She smiled at him.

"I'm so glad you found those emerald earrings, my dear. They belonged to my mother. But I must say, they've never looked better." He walked to her side, took both her hands and kissed her cheek in greeting. "I want you to keep them."

The two continued to hold hands. "They were Michael's grandmother's? Oh, my. I couldn't possibly keep them, but I love wearing them tonight."

"In this house, they'd stay hidden away in a drawer. Besides, I have plenty of pieces of her jewelry." He reached up and touched an emerald. "And they wouldn't do justice to anyone else. They highlight your captivating eyes. They must have been waiting for you, and here you are. Wouldn't you agree, Michael?"

"They're perfect for her." Michael walked to Ceinwen's side, put his hand on her waist and led her to the dining table. "Take them," he whispered. "He wants you to have them."

She looked from the son to the father, then said, "Thank you, Claude. I'll always cherish them."

She noticed Michael's surprise at her calling his father "Claude."

William Claude nodded and then took his seat at the head of the table, Michael on one side, and Ceinwen on the other. They had an elaborate meal during which different wines were served with the soup and the entrée, and an after dinner wine with the dessert.

Both Michael and William Claude were on their best behavior and the resulting scholarly conversation was one that Ceinwen might have dreamed about, but had never before experienced.

When William Claude asked her if she'd given thought to her thesis, she was stunned that he had heard anything about her supposed attendance at Oxford. And since it was essentially a lie, she hesitated to respond. "I'm not sure how long I'll stay at the university." Her brain wracked for an excuse. "I wanted to take some classes to see how dedicated I felt, but then other things happened, and now I'm not sure what I want to do."

"Well, since you've been accepted to Oxford, getting a Ph.D., or D.Phil. as they call it, would open all kinds of doors for you," Claude said. "It's nothing to be tossed aside lightly."

She nodded. She had never told anyone that her "acceptance" to Oxford was simply to audit some classes. She felt terrible about not admitting the truth to Michael. But this wasn't the time or place.

She buried her head in her meal.

"Since she's obviously got an interest in alchemy and Japan," William Claude said, "she should think about alchemical symbols found on Japanese tombs and in their pottery. I suspect it's a topic that hasn't had much research, if any."

"Not a bad idea," Michael said. "In fact, if she doesn't want it, I might have to give it some thought."

The two launched into ways to find out where such symbols had been discovered, and what they could do to learn more about them.

Between the wine and the conversation, Ceinwen's head was spinning, But she was enraptured by the evening with the two brilliant men.

"You'll need to excuse us a few minutes," Michael said to Ceinwen as they walked from the dining room to the parlor, another room reserved for formal occasions. He remained in the doorway. "My father wants a private word with me—something about this land. It shouldn't take long."

"Certainly," she said.

"But the night is young, Ceinwen." William Claude brushed past Michael to take her arm and escort her to a sofa. Then, he murmured words for her ears alone. "Please wait for me. I'll be back."

"Of course." She found herself puzzled. "I'll see you both soon."

He smiled. "There are many books in this room you might find interesting."

Ceinwen hadn't noticed a bookcase until William Claude gestured toward it. She thanked him as he left the room. Going over to it, a book on alchemy immediately caught her eye.

Ceinwen had fallen asleep, waking only when she felt a hand touch her shoulder. She was surprised to find William Claude sitting beside her on the sofa, the book of alchemy on her lap.

"I'm sorry it took us so long." His tone was gentle, caring. "Michael thought you had already retired for the night. He's gone to his room."

Again, she felt charmed by the man, at ease around him. She stretched lightly, covering her mouth to stifle a yawn. "Too much wine and good food. It made me sleepy."

His fingers brushed her thigh as he lifted the book. "Alchemical tales. I should have known." He placed it on the coffee table. "Does this interest mean you have come to believe in alchemy?"

"Not exactly."

"Oh, but you will, my dear. Believe me, you will."

She thought about his words. "You know, they say 'seeing is believing.' Maybe I need to see an alchemical experiment actually work."

He grinned. "That can be arranged. It all starts with the philosopher's stone."

"Some say that. Others, I've read, say it ends with the philosopher's stone. That you need something called a 'prime agent' to start the process. I've never been able to tell exactly what a 'prime agent' is."

"Why can't it be both?" William Claude said. "Let me show you."

He reached into this pocket and took out a reddish stone, about the size of a gumball. "This is a philosopher's stone." His thumb was brushing over the stone as he spoke. Then he placed it in the palm of his hand and held it in front of her.

She bent forward to see it better.

"Look at it carefully." He moved closer, and then placed his hand on the nape of her neck, his long fingers near the spot where she'd suffered a demon's bite. It began to sting. "Isn't it beautiful?"

She picked up the stone to study it. At the same time, he began to rub the area of the bite, and the stinging sensation not only eased, but the warmth of his touch surged pleasantly through her body.

"It is quite beautiful." She was confused by the strange sensations, but still stared at the stone.

"You feel its pull, don't you?" He whispered in her ear.

She tried to move back a bit.

The hand by her neck clamped down hard. "No. You must regard it. Let it come to you."

She did as told. With that, he lifted his hand from her neck and allowed it to course slowly along her spine to her hips.

Even through her clothes, she felt heat where his hand touched. Her limbs grew heavy. "I don't understand what's happening."

Dark eyes studied her. "I know. But you will ... in time." He moved his head closer to hers and dropped his voice. "I've felt that about you, felt something that you aren't yet aware of."

"What do you mean?" she asked.

He took the stone from her and held it before her eyes. "Let them see you."

Some deep sense of self-preservation caused her to try to pull away again, but his arm tightened around her back, holding her still. His strength shocked her. "Stop! I ..." The stone began to glow.

With its brilliance, an all-consuming desire flowed through her body. All she could think of was how much she wanted it. She wanted everything about it—and alchemy. She wanted to learn it, practice it, relish in it.

She wanted the immortality it could give. "Claude," she breathed, leaning into him.

"Yes." He drew her closer, placing his lips against her temple.

She had no interest in him. It was the stone she wanted. What was the possibility she could snatch it from him, keep it, and learn to use it?

As if he'd read her thoughts, he leaned away from her temple, just enough to see her face. His eyes mocked her, eyes that had changed, blackened to an onyx shade, yet with a smoldering fire deep inside.

His eyes ... they reminded her of something.

"You can't steal it, Ceinwen." He put his head next to hers. "You must accept it and let it take you. Then, together you can do anything, be anything, *have* anything you desire."

He kissed her, but something in his kiss, its scent, its taste, was stale and corrosive. She turned her head away even as she allowed him to lay her down on the sofa. She welcomed his kisses along her jaw and neck and lower. When he placed his mouth over the spot that the demon had bitten, fire radiated from it throughout her body. She gasped from the pain, but with it came pleasure, an overpowering, orgasmic pleasure that made her want him, made her want far more from him.

With that thought, his body began to change. Without fear, she faced him as he stood over her as a beast, a massive, glorious monster with greenish-black scales and the wings of a bat. It spoke. "You are here to help me."

"Of course," she said, and ran her hands over its hips, and along its thighs. The demon's red eyes responded to her touch with lust.

There was no emotion on her part, only an all-consuming physical desire. A demonic desire. She ached for this monster, this demon, as it ran its scaly hands over her.

"You are mine," he growled, shoving her skirt up above her hips.

At that, some rational part of her warned her to stop this, warned her to push him away, to cry out, but she had no strength left. "Please, Claude, if you're still there," she cried. "Don't do this."

"It's too late," the beast murmured. "Too late for us both."

CHAPTER 55

"CEINWEN, you're having a nightmare. *Ceinwen! Wake up!*"

She gasped, opening her eyes to discover that she was in her room, in her bed. Michael switched on the lamp. He was standing over her, a worried frown on his face.

Images from moments earlier came back to her, horrible, frightening images. She rolled to the edge of the bed, reached for a small wastebasket on the floor beside it and threw up. Her stomach kept heaving, over and over, until it felt emptied of all the horror she had seen and felt and endured.

Michael gave her a wet washcloth for her face, and then he removed the wastebasket to the bathroom.

She lay back on the bed.

He gently brushed her hair from her face and sat beside her. "Are you sick? Do you need a doctor?"

"No. I'll be fine. Something ... upset my stomach."

"Obviously." He rubbed her arms.

After a while, she calmed a bit. "How did you ...?" She wasn't even sure what to ask.

"After I finished an inane discussion with my father about his land grants, I went to look for you. Stedman told me you said you were sleepy and had retired early. I thought I'd check to make sure you weren't ill and found you tossing about and crying out."

"You left your father and immediately looked for me?" she asked, sitting up on the bed now.

He looked surprised. "Of course. Where else would I go?"

She thought about telling him what had just happened. No, it hadn't happened. It was a dream—a vile, disgusting dream. "Hold me," she whispered, throwing herself at him again.

"I am." He kissed her hair, her brow. "What's wrong, Ceinwen? What is it?"

"Nothing." After a while, she drew back, and as she did, she noticed she was wearing a thin, lacy negligee. "What in the world?"

He touched the delicate material. "You must have found it in a drawer here." It was thin enough to be revealing, and he seemed unable to keep his hands off what was revealed. "I must say, I approve. It's beautiful. You're beautiful."

"But I don't remember finding it or putting it on." Alarm sounded in her voice.

Michael tried to calm her. "Stedman did say you were tired."

"I wasn't that tired! All I remember is finding a book about alchemy in the bookcase in the parlor. I sat down to read it and ... and the next thing I know, you're here, waking me."

He studied her eyes. "There is no bookcase in the parlor."

"But ..."

Worry tinged with a dark fear filled his face. "Damn, Ceinwen. I can only think of one explanation for all this. My father. He's dangerous. If he's hurt you ... I've got to get you away from here."

She shook her head as the images from the dream came back.

"Your nightmare," he said. "What was it about? A demon? What?"

"I don't know," she whispered, but then admitted it. "Yes. God, Michael!" She folded her arms and curled up. She began to rock at the horror of her memories, and at her own participation in them.

He held her tight. "It'll be all right. We'll stop them. I'll find a way."

"I'm sorry," she cried, unable to stop her tears. "I don't know what's happening, what's wrong with me. Rachel had dreams of demons. And now she's dead!"

"Rachel wanted to be with her demons, she wanted that life. You're strong, Ceinwen. You can fight them."

"Can I?"

"Yes! Definitely. Now, lie down." He smoothed the covers over her. "We should try to get to sleep."

"Don't leave me."

"Never." He shut the light, then kicked off his shoes and lay beside her, atop the covers, his arm over her, protecting her, until she fell into a restless sleep.

CHAPTER 56

CEINWEN SLEPT until nearly ten o'clock, and woke to a sweet note from Michael, saying she seemed to be exhausted and should rest in her room that day, that he would be back to check on her soon.

She clutched the note as a talisman as visions of last night's demonic dream played over and over in her brain.

A knock on the door startled her. "Who is it?"

Stedman came in with a breakfast tray, saying he understood from Master Michael that she was feeling under the weather. He told her to leave the tray in the hall so he needn't disturb her again.

She ate a little of the breakfast, and was feeling better, but still didn't care to leave the room. The thought of seeing Claude again made her stomach churn.

As she dressed in casual slacks and a top, her gaze lingered on the lacy nightgown she had worn. Where had she found it?

A highboy chest of drawers was in the room. Most of the drawers were empty, but one was filled with stoles and scarves, and another had several beautiful négligées.

Last night, she must have opened that drawer to find the one she had worn. But why? And most disturbing, she didn't remember doing it at all.

The drawer held a number of exquisite lingerie pieces. As she looked through it, in the back of the drawer she found a book. It had a green leather cover, the same as Jane Rempart's diary. She opened it to find it was written in a fine, familiar hand, but the writing was smaller, terser, more adult, than the diary she had previously read.

The first page showed "Property of Jane Rempart."

Ceinwen felt no hesitancy this time. She needed to know all she could about this family, this house—and how dangerous William Claude might be.

CHAPTER 57

Jake Sullivan joined the investigators out near the Selway River. He had been flown there by bush plane to meet the daughter of a rancher who had rented four horses and two double horse-trailers for a good sum of money.

The daughter didn't live on the ranch, but near Hells Canyon. She told him that her father had contacted her because he felt nervous about a business transaction.

The week before, he had called her to say that four strangers had come to him saying they wanted to rent horses for five days to ride and hike deep into the backcountry. They claimed to be from Salmon, and that they knew how to handle themselves and horses out in the wilderness.

The rancher swore they didn't look like "dude ranch types," but were tough and leathery skinned—as if they had spent plenty of time in the wilds. Still, it struck him as odd that they showed up the way they did. People usually rented his horses for day trips only. But, along with IDs and credit cards, the men gave the rancher the phone number of their business in Salmon. He had checked into it. The business appeared to be legitimate.

Finally, when the men offered to pay double the rental rates, and in cash, the rancher gave his okay.

Still, he had been worried, and for that reason called and gave his daughter all the information he had collected.

His daughter was convinced he'd been right to have been nervous. After she couldn't reach him for a couple of days, she drove out to the ranch and found him dead, shot to death.

She was sure the four strangers had something to do with it.

The woman showed Jake the numbers her father had given her from the men's Idaho driver's licenses and credit card. Jake would check to see if they were real or fake. But when she gave him the name, address, and phone number of the Salmon business her father had contacted, Jake knew it was legitimate. It was the coffee shop next door to the sheriff's station. The daughter said that when her father phoned there, the woman who answered claimed to be the wife of one of the hikers: Emily Donahue.

Jake could scarcely believe what he was hearing.

When he returned to Salmon, he found that Emily was gone. That very morning, Jake had told her he was heading out to the Selway River because he had a lead on someone who may have rented horses to Deputy Grayson's murderers. Apparently, that news caused her to close the shop and leave town.

Jake couldn't help but wonder what else he might have inadvertently revealed to her about his investigation.

He checked phone records to and from the coffee shop, as well as the personal phone of Emily Parker, or Emily Donohue, or whatever her name really was. More than one call had originated from somewhere in Massachusetts.

"You're right, Jake," Jianjun said. He and Kira had joined Jake and Charlotte for dinner that night at Bertram's on Main Street to fill each other in on how the investigation was going. "I did some tracking of Emily Parker or Donahue. Neither are her real name. It's Emily LeGrand. She's not married and has a record. Felony burglary. It was the key to tracking her."

"Great," Jake muttered, still steamed by the way he'd been taken in by the woman.

Jianjun continued. "She received ten grand to report what was happening in Salmon. She was a go-between for the people in New England and those in Central Idaho. Various unlisted phones were used, but satellite phones have much stronger footprints than regular cell phones, so I was able to dig up at least this much information."

"Ten thousand dollars doesn't seem like enough for something this big," Charlotte said. "Not when murder charges are now on the table."

"Maybe it sounded like a fortune to her," Kira suggested, "when she thought all she had to do was to listen and make some phone calls."

"And me and my big mouth gave her all the help she needed," Jake said. "Damn me!"

Charlotte squeezed his hand. "How could you know? And why would you suspect her? Look at how badly my wires crossed about that woman."

"Actually," Jake said with a cocky grin, "I kind of like it that you were so jealous."

She swatted him with her napkin.

CHAPTER 58

CEINWEN WOULD HAVE LOVED to have dinner brought to her room just as lunch had been. The last thing she wanted to do was to face Michael's father. As the dinner hour approached, however, and she heard nothing more from Michael or anyone, she stiffened her spine and headed downstairs. She refused to spend the rest of the visit hiding in her room, and decided to get the encounter over with.

On the sideboard she found enough food to feed at least six people, but no one else was present.

She was wondering what to do when she heard Stedman's voice behind her. He had approached as quietly as ever. "Mr. Rempart may be a bit delayed. He said not to wait for him."

Relief filled her. "Thank you. Have you seen Michael?"

"I'm afraid not."

She filled her plate and had begun eating when William Claude entered the room. She froze as memories of her dream came back to her.

But Claude greeted her with ease, looking directly at her with no sign of anything untoward having occurred between them. He sat across from her as Stedman prepared his plate.

"Don't tell me that son of mine has abandoned you already?" Claude said. "What's wrong with that boy?"

Her mouth felt dry and her throat had all but closed. Somehow she forced out, "He does seem to lose track of time."

Claude nodded. "It comes from living alone, I'm afraid. I suffer from it as well. We are much alike, although the boy hates to admit it."

No, you aren't at all alike, she wanted to shout. They ate in silence. Ceinwen kept hoping Michael would show up, but he didn't. When Stedman cleared their plates and brought them some after-dinner coffee, Claude said, "So, has Michael told you much about the amazing Chinese pearl he found last year?"

She drew in her breath, remembering Michael's warnings not to even think about what was happening with the pearl. "Very little," she said. "Does it interest you?"

"Of course! I'm sure Michael told you I'm an alchemist, and that the pearl is a powerful philosopher's stone. How could I not be interested?"

She frowned. "Perhaps because alchemy is a hoax."

He snorted. "Men and women of today are amazingly close-minded. All of you think you know 'truth,' which you define as whatever you happen to believe."

"Narcissists, are we?"

He grinned. "Absolutely. The civilized world knew alchemy worked from the time it was discovered around three thousand years before Christ up to the twentieth century when scientists convinced people it didn't. Keep in mind, these are the same scientists who can't tell you how Tylenol works. At least they haven't decided that everyone who takes a Tylenol and says it helped relieve their pain is a charlatan or a huckster. But that's what they've done with alchemy, even though many of the most brilliant minds of the past were alchemists, including Sir Isaac Newton, the father of modern physics and the inventor of calculus. He had a closely guarded blueprint, or recipe if you will, for creating a philosopher's stone."

"I thought philosopher's stones simply existed."

"Not at all. Man creates them, and man perfects them. And once man creates a valuable philosopher's stone, he can perform untold miracles with it."

"But have they? Has any man?"

"Oh, yes," William Claude said, clearly relishing this conversation. "Newton's contemporary, a giant in the world of chemistry, Robert Boyle, also was one such believer. Based on work of men like him, the world has learned to create new alloys, invent apparatuses for distillation in making perfumes and whiskeys, developed the concept of the atoms centuries before modern atomic theory, and provided a template for the scientific method by running controlled experiments."

"Uh huh," Ceinwen murmured, her tone dripping with skepticism.

"You can mock it, but the list of famous men who at least dabbled in alchemy goes on and on," William Claude continued. "Of course, there's our family's famous ancestor, Edward Kelley, associate of the famous Elizabethan occultist, John Dee, and the Frenchman, Nicolas Flamel, who succeeded in creating enough gold to build a children's hospital—and he had been a poor bookseller before that. The Bishop of Cologne known as Albert the Great or Albertus Magnus, was also said by many to have created gold. His work laid the foundation for St. Thomas Aquinas' work on alchemy which discusses the manipulation of matter in a laboratory. You also have Roger Bacon, George Ripley, Villanova—"

"You can stop now," Ceinwen said.

"The list goes on, and as you can see, those men aren't lightweights. I believe many of them were far more brilliant than our so-called scientists today. How many of today's scientists can compare with, say, Sir Isaac Newton?"

"All that is true, but the achievements you cite are because alchemy was the foundation for chemistry," Ceinwen said. "Much of what is said to have 'arisen' from alchemy has nothing to do with creating gold, and especially not with immortality. It developed through what we now call chemistry. You are mixing the two to make a point that, scientifically, you cannot make."

"I completely disagree!" he bellowed. "It's you whose mind is closed to what really happened. Alchemy is the expansion of chemistry, not its genesis."

"You expect me to believe that?" she scoffed.

"Of course! I can prove it in my laboratory."

"Sure. You'll rig something up to impress me. I know how that works. I might have been born at night, but not *last* night."

He chuckled. "Why don't we go up to my laboratory? I can show you now. No time for 'rigging.'"

She stood. "I think it's time for me to say good-night. I'll visit your lab some other time."

He suddenly gave her a look that, if he were a younger man, would have curled her toes. In a voice low and knowing, he all but purred, "I look forward to it."

She hurried from the room to look for Michael.

Michael sat in the tower room, in the chair that had been his mother's favorite. Just as during his last visit to his strange ancestral house, he had heard the sound of his mother's music box. And once again, the sound led him to this room.

He found it odd that his father hadn't emptied it of all his mother's things years ago, and especially that he had the housekeeper keep the room vacuumed and dusted. He wondered if it was a sign of guilt over the way his mother had died, or a sign that his father really had loved her. But it was hard for him to believe William Claude ever loved anyone except himself.

"Michael?"

He turned to see Ceinwen in the doorway. "Come in. It's okay. What brought you up here?"

"I was looking for you and heard soft music. I followed it."

"Music?"

She looked perplexed. "I don't hear it now. Strange. Maybe ... my imagination."

"Do you know the piece?"

"It was familiar, but..."

He whistled the first few bars of Für Elise.

She stared at him, clearly upset, and then nodded. "That was it. How did you know?"

"It brought me up here as well," he said. "But I don't know why."

"Where is the sound coming from?"

"It was from a music box my mother once owned. I have no idea where it is now."

"Your mother?" she whispered. She sat in the chair facing him. Ironically, it was the chair he used to sit in as a boy. She had a strange expression on her face.

"What is it?" he asked.

"I wonder if I know the reason we're both here. But it's too crazy." She inhaled sharply. "You aren't going to like this..."

He waited.

"When we were in Japan and I was trying to find out about all the strangeness going on, and about you, I came across a diary and read it. It was your mother's."

He gaped at her, then quietly murmured, "I see."

"I didn't realize who it belonged to when I started, but I was immediately brought into her world. She was a fine person, Michael, and she loved you so very much. More than once my eyes were filled with tears by all she said."

He didn't say a word, but simply stared coldly at her.

Her heart sank. "I'm so sorry. There's no excuse for what I did. I was curious, and you're right to be angry. But I'm not sorry I read it. It explains a lot about you, about this house," Ceinwen said. "About your parents."

He wouldn't even look at her.

She swallowed a couple of times and then continued. "I'm glad I read it because in the room I'm using, I found the second volume."

Michael leaned forward in the chair as he took in her words. "A second volume?"

"Yes. It was in the back of the drawer under the lingerie."

"I wonder if my father even knew it was there."

"I somehow doubt it." She couldn't know, but if William Claude had read it, she suspected he would have taken delight burning it, page by page.

"Maybe I should read it."

"Or, maybe not," Ceinwen said. "These pages ... they have some information you might not want to know."

"I won't know that until I see what they're about."

"If it were up to me, I'd advise you not to read it. Let those unhappy ghosts rest in peace."

"But are they in peace? Something drew me into this room, and did the same to you. Maybe the diary is the reason."

"Yes, I can't help but suspect that as well," she said, rubbing her arms as if feeling a ghostly presence. "But trust me when I say, if you were to read it, it will color your opinion of your parents, of both of them."

"Where is it?"

"In my room."

"Let's get it." He stood.

"No." She stood as well. "I'll bring it up here. There's no better place than this for you to learn Jane's story. The complete story."

CHAPTER 59

"I'll leave you alone," Ceinwen said, handing the diary to Michael. Their fingers brushed lightly.

"Stay," he asked, but Ceinwen shook her head, her eyes filled with concern.

"As much as I'd like to be here with you, the diary, the words Jane writes ... I think you'll want to be alone as you read them." She kissed him softly. "But I hope you'll join me later."

His eyes followed her as she left the turret room. When she closed the door behind her, the warmth she'd brought into the space dissipated. The temperature seemed to drop a good ten degrees.

He stared at the book in his hands, thinking of the warning in Ceinwen's words, of her advice that he not read it. But he needed to know.

He opened the diary, noting the date. The entries began when he was seven, and his mother could no longer put off sending him to boarding school.

His heart ached as he read of the many tears she had shed over his leaving. After he left home, she was unable to rid herself of her depression. Finally, knowing how much she liked ancient Greek mythology and literature, after the Christmas and New Year holidays ended, Claude sent her away to a Greek island where she could spend the long months until the boys returned again for summer vacation.

As he read the heartfelt pages, he quickly realized he could get through them only by distancing himself, by thinking of her only as "Jane."

April 8th -

Today is Michael's eighth birthday. I should be with him, but Claude refused to allow him home for such an "unimportant" occasion, so I decided to remain here, thousands of miles away.

I was sitting on the beach, tears streaming from my eyes at the thought of my boy, when a kind fisherman came by. He asked me if I was hurt. When I said, "Only my heart," he sat down and talked to me. His name is Constantin, and he is originally from Romania, now living in Greece, on the mainland. He was quite nice and, I'll admit, very handsome. It did me good to talk to him.

April 9th -

I went back to the beach where I sat yesterday, and again, today, Constantin came by. He brought me some cascaval, a Romanian yellow hard cheese, and some bread with which to eat it. I was quite taken by the man's thoughtfulness. He told the story of how he and his wife managed to sneak out of Romania last year, and how he now made a living as a fisherman, traveling between the various Greek islands. His story was thrilling, and I can't believe how brave he must have been to flee the military in his home country.

April 15th -

Constantin is back! He was far from here fishing for a few days. Fortunately, he doesn't smell fishy at all. He brought some dried fish, bread, and cascaval cheese. It was like a picnic. I felt bad because I had brought food for him for a couple of days, but then stopped, assuming I'd never see him again. I must ask him to give me some idea of his schedule.

The diary entries continued in that vein for the rest of April and deep into May. Michael noticed how much more cheerful Jane's entries became whenever Constantin entered the picture.

May 20 -

I told Constantin that I must go home to Massachusetts tomorrow. I couldn't bring myself to tell him any earlier. I'm stunned at how hard it is to leave him, even though I'm going for the best of all possible reasons. He is a married man, and I know I'm finding his company far, far too agreeable. I must think of the bright side, that I will be home when Michael returns for the summer. How I miss my dear boy.

But to my surprise and shame, tears came to my eyes as I said goodbye. They shouldn't have. I'm sure Constantin never suspected my feelings because I've done all I could to hide them from him, and he knows I'm also married. He looked stricken and gave my hand a quick squeeze before he hurried away.

What must he think of me, other than I'm a silly, lonely woman in a bad marriage? It's not as if we're having an affair or anything. We're simply lunchtime friends. Actually, making such a spectacle of myself has made it easier for me to leave Greece.

The diary was almost embarrassing for Michael to read as Jane told of the joy seeing him brought her, and that he made everything else worthwhile.

When summer ended, Jane returned to Greece and bought a home on the island she had visited the year before. She shipped a number of her books there, and loved the freedom that went with life in the area. She even began studying the Greek language, but classical, not colloquial. She returned home for Christmas, and then went back, once more, to Greece.

March 28 -

Yesterday, I found a spot on the beach and was reading one of Longfellow's poems, "Evangeline," when a shadow came over the pages. I looked up and saw Constantin. I don't even know how it happened, but in the next moment I was in his arms and he was kissing me. I have never known such pure ecstasy. We came back to my house. Loving him was more I had ever imagined. I've spent a lifetime reading the Romantic poets and never knew, until this afternoon, what they were truly writing about.

When he left, he said he would be gone for three days. I smiled as he left, but when he was gone, all I could think of was one of my favorite poems by Caroline Norton:

I do not love thee!—no! I do not love thee!

And yet when thou art absent I am sad;

And envy even the bright blue sky above thee,

Whose quiet stars may see thee and be glad.

Michael read of her liaison with Constantin through that spring.

It was clear she had fallen head over heels in love with the fisherman, even as she marveled at how unlike they were, and often quoted from the Elizabeth Barrett Browning, *Unlike are we, unlike, O princely Heart! Unlike our uses and our destinies.*

But none of that mattered to her. She found his oneness with nature and the sea, his courage, his sheer earthiness as something to cherish. With him, she discovered she could still laugh.

Her only dread was that someone would tell William Claude, but it seemed no one did.

She was sad when the time came to leave, but once back at Wintersgate, she happily wrote of her summer with Michael and Lionel.

When they returned to school, the time came for her to return to Greece.

It was the third year she had gone there.

April 19 -

A month has passed, and although other fishermen are here, Constantin is not. Although I'm sure others know about our secret, I have never spoken of him to anyone on this island, nor have they talked to me about him. It has been almost as if everyone is in on our illicit secret, and none of them care. Some of the women eye me strangely. But that doesn't matter. Nothing matters except that Constantin return.

April 28 –

I've begun taking the poem "Evangeline" with me to the water's edge, praying for a repeat of the day we first acknowledged our love. But it hasn't happened.

At the mention of "Evangeline," a sense of foreboding wrapped around Michael. His very flesh tingled, as if surrounded by a presence, but it had to be his imagination ... perhaps because his mother's diary made her feel so close, so close that he was compelled to keep reading, no matter what.

May 2 -

As I stood by the piers today, I saw a fishing boat that Constantin had worked on. I went to the captain and firmly asked if Constantin Petrescu was working for him this year.

Michael stared at the page. This was the first time Jane had mentioned the last name of the man she loved. Petrescu was Irina's family name. His mouth went dry, and he quickly read on.

The captain looked at me sadly, and then he spoke the words that ended my life. "I'm sorry, but Constantin is dead."

Somehow I managed to remain standing as I calmly asked how it happened. He had heard that Constantin was attacked late one night—probably a robbery— and he was stabbed to death. It had happened in February, and no one was ever caught. No charges were brought. Nothing was done.

And my love, my life, is no more.

I came back home and began to pack to return to Wintersgate. I don't know how I can live there, but I can't bear staying here where everything reminds me of happiness, of love. At least there, no joyful memories will ever plague me.

She scarcely wrote about her return to Wintersgate, except that it happened. But then ...

June 3 -

He knew. That is the only conclusion I can reach, and with it comes the terrible suspicion that Claude had something to do with Constantin's death.

Suspicion? I wish it were mere suspicion. No, I know it in the depth of my soul.

I can scarcely write what has transpired, but I'll never forget the look he gave me as he told me about our new housekeeper and her child.

"I've done a good thing," he announced when I entered the breakfast room this morning. "I've hired an immigrant to our country to help with the housework. Manuela is too old to do it anymore. I've given her a good severance pay and sent her on her way. The new housekeeper has a young daughter, but I've been assured the girl is very quiet and well-mannered."

I was shocked that he would send off Manuela so easily. She had seemed like family to me. But as he continued talking, it all became clear. "The woman has been recently widowed. She and her daughter are from a poor village in Greece and are looking for a new life. I heard about them and, knowing how much you

love everything Greek, I decided we could use some fresh blood around here, espe-
cially someone willing to work hard. And her child might be nice to have around.
The girl is five years old, and should be a good playmate for Michael."

In late afternoon, the woman arrived. Her name is Magda Petrescu, and her
daughter is named Irina. Claude brought Constantin's wife and child here, to my
house, to remind me every day that Constantin hadn't belonged to me alone.
From the way Magda spoke of her deceased husband, it's clear his marriage
wasn't as "over" as he had told me it was. Every day, I'm forced to look into
Irina's eyes and see the eyes of the only man I have ever truly loved. And to be
reminded of his lies ... to his wife, and to his lover.

There the diary ended, but even if it hadn't, he wouldn't have had the strength to read further.

He shut the book, sick at heart.

He could scarcely imagine how Jane had felt when William Claude brought Constantin's widow and child into his home. Such cruelty to his wife was unimaginable. Of course, there were probably those who would side with him. After all, Jane was having an adulterous affair. But having read the diary—having lived in this house with her and William Claude—Michael understood why.

He'd never been given any details about his mother's life. But now he learned more than he had ever dreamed. He couldn't help but wonder if she hadn't hidden the diary away in a drawer William Claude would never look in as a way, possibly, for Michael or someone else to find it. And then, by reading her words, to understand her.

He was glad, actually, that the diary ended when it did. He was old enough to remember what came next—his mother's descent into a black depression. It was bad enough to witness; he didn't know if he could bear to read about it.

And then one afternoon while supposedly alone in the tower, she fell to the stone patio below and died. No one knew for certain if the fall was an accident, if she was pushed, or if she jumped.

He stood up. He had to leave the turret. Being here was all but unbearable.

He needed to find Ceinwen. She was warm and caring—why, he had no idea. But he was not only glad to have her with him, he was grateful for the way she put up with him and the madness that seemed to follow wherever he went.

But before leaving here, he ran his hands over the journal. His mother was always too much of a romantic, and the harshness of the world—of her own husband—had crushed her. Less than a month after the last entry, she was dead. He had spent hours with her that month, often in the very room he sat in now.

He had never imagined she would have taken her own life ... never, until now.

CHAPTER 60

MICHAEL LAY AWAKE deep into the night. Sleep refused to come.

Ceinwen lay curled beside him, one arm across his chest. She breathed softly, and he was glad to see she slept peacefully without a recurrence of the horrific dream she'd had the night before. It had been too reminiscent of what he had watched happen to Rachel, and as he looked at the sleeping woman, he knew he couldn't bear it if anything like that happened to her.

His thoughts kept spinning round and round about the diary and all he had learned about his mother, his father, and even Irina.

He couldn't get over learning that Irina had come into his life as a way for his father to persecute his mother for her infidelity. It was beyond anything he could have imagined. He wondered how much of the story Irina and Magda knew. And if they knew it, was that the hold William Claude had over them? He could well imagine his father telling Irina that if Michael ever found out about Jane's love for Constantin—and that it might somehow have contributed to Jane's black depression and ensuing death—any feelings Michael had for Irina would vanish.

Had William Claude convinced Irina of that? Could that be why Irina took the money and left?

Michael honestly didn't know how his twenty-six-year-old self would have reacted to such news. Even at this age, he found it both perverse and repugnant.

But at the same time, why wouldn't Irina at least have talked to him about it, to see what his reaction would be? She should have known there was no way he would have considered her to be at fault in that sad history.

He guessed there was more to it, but he didn't know what that could be.

And probably never would.

But this was about much more than him and Irina. Why were he and Ceinwen both hearing "Für Elise"? He didn't remember seeing the music box anywhere in the house since his mother's death, and had no idea what might have happened to it.

It was almost as if his mother drew the two of them to her tower room, as if she wanted him to read her journal and perhaps to find out what had happened in this house. He couldn't stop his mind from going to the darkest possibility: to discover that she had been murdered, and if so, who did it.

No, he told himself. That was the sort of wild idea a person got at three in the morning and then rightfully scorned in the light of day.

Ceinwen stirred. She rolled to her other side and he followed, spooning her against him, relishing her warmth. His eyes were finally growing heavy. Sleep was coming soon. Blessed sleep, when he no longer needed to think about diaries or murder or the messed up existence within the walls of Wintersgate.

He closed his eyes. He was drifting into sleep and then ....

Did he just hear someone's voice?

Had Ceinwen wakened? Had she said something? No, she still breathed softly. She was sound asleep and beautiful in the moonlight coming through the window. He didn't understand, at all, why he was so comfortable around her, or why she put up with him. All he knew was that she had found a way into his heart, and he was glad of it.

He drew her even closer, her curves melding perfectly against his body.

And then he heard the sound again. Voices.

He quietly slipped out of bed. Throwing on some clothes, barefoot, he crept downstairs.

A lamp was on in the breakfast room. He tiptoed to the door, keeping out of sight, all but holding his breath.

"I think the elixir will fully work by the time we meet them." He recognized his father's voice.

"I hope so." That voice belonged to Stedman.

"Just to be on the safe side, put on the° ankle holster for this little revolver. I should be able to control their minds, but if, as I suspect, their minds are somewhat feeble, it might be more difficult than I anticipate."

"I understand, sir."

"It's time. We should go now."

Michael hurried back up the stairs and into the bedroom. He woke Ceinwen. "Something's up. My father and Stedman are leaving the property. I'm going to follow them."

She immediately got out of bed, picked up the clothes she'd worn the day before, and stepped into her shoes. "I'm ready. I'll dress in the car."

"It might be dangerous. You should—"

"We've been through this before," she said fiercely. "And we've no time to argue."

As Michael suspected, Stedman was a slow, cautious driver, which was a good thing since Michael had to follow the Bentley with his headlights off for some distance. Not until they reached US-6 could he put the lights on without causing Stedman, or worse, William Claude, to realize they were being followed.

As he drove, Ceinwen called Sheriff Sullivan in Salmon and told him Michael suspected his father was on his way to meet people involved in the deputy's murder. Jake needed to know which city or county they were going to before contacting a local police department to alert them that potential cop killers were in their town.

So far, all Ceinwen could tell him was that William Claude Rempart and another elderly man named Stedman were in a black Bentley. They weren't close enough to the car for her to make out the license number, but a Bentley should be easy to spot wherever they went. She hoped.

When Stedman reached Hyannis and turned off the highway, Ceinwen let Jake know where they were headed. "Thanks for the heads up," he said. "I'll fill in the chief of police in Hyannis and also give him your number so his officers can contact you directly for details. But keep me posted. Please."

In the summer months, Hyannis was filled with tourists. Even at five in the morning, the streets weren't completely empty. Stedman drove onto the parking lot of a 24-hour CVS. He parked near the front of the store, several spaces away from any other cars. He and William Claude remained in the car.   ·

Michael stopped at the unlit corner of a side street, hidden from view.

They watched in silence, but nothing was happening. The Bentley sat motionless.

He could hear Ceinwen breathing deeply. He felt his own heart beating hard in his chest. There was nothing they could do but wait and hope the cops would call. Jake had been a cop a long time. He knew what he was doing—and hopefully the Hyannis police would listen to him.

At long last, Ceinwen's cell phone rang. She jumped at the sound, even though the volume was turned low. He couldn't hear what was said to her, only Ceinwen's reply. "They've parked the Bentley at a CVS. They're just sitting there. No. Wait. A large black SUV just pulled into the lot. It's going really slow. I can't quite make out the license number—"

The moment she said that, Michael grabbed the phone from Ceinwen and gave the officer the information.

"We've just dispatched several patrol cars to your location," the officer told him. "Stay in your car, and stay on the line with me. Don't try to approach them."

Michael had no intention of getting out of the rental car. He and Ceinwen had been through enough hell lately. Instead, he relayed everything that was happening. The SUV remained running as the driver opened his door. William Claude did the same. Michael told the police that a boxy package had been handed off from the SUV driver to William Claude, who then passed the man an envelope.

A moment later, the SUV tore out of the lot.

"Damn," Michael shouted into the phone. "They're getting away." He handed the phone back to Ceinwen, who was so surprised to find it in her hand that she accidentally cutting off the connection.

"Just wait, Michael. The cops will find them."

"We can't take that chance." He shoved the car into gear and as he sped around the corner. At the same time, he noticed the Bentley backing slowly and carefully out of the CVS parking space. His father and Steadman appeared to be in no hurry at all, but Michael was. Steadman and William Claude were no doubt going back home; Michael and Ceinwen were going after the SUV.

He tried to follow at a reasonable distance, but few other cars were on the road and it wasn't long before the SUV's odd maneuvering made him pretty certain they'd been noticed.

"Ceinwen, reach in the back. There's a gun case."

She did as told and opened the case to see a nine millimeter automatic. "Where did you get—?"

"The Remparts have always kept a small arsenal at the house. And from the time we first arrived there, I figured if the trigger-happy guys from Idaho showed up, I wanted to be prepared."

He turned once more, but this time, he didn't see the lights of the SUV up ahead.

"Michael, behind us!" Ceinwen cried.

He looked in the rearview mirror to see the SUV bearing down on them. A passenger reached out the window, gun in hand, and fired.

"Shoot back!" Michael ordered as he swerved the rental from side to side.

Ceinwen eased off the safety and fired toward the SUV as best she could. Her first shots missed as both vehicles twisted trying to outmaneuver the other.

Michael had to slow to turn at the corner and when he did the SUV rammed his back bumper. Ceinwen fired again, and this time they heard a "plunk" as the bullet hit steel.

But the SUV didn't stop. Its bumper once more slammed into the back of Michael's smaller, lighter rental. The SUV's size and strength overwhelmed the rental car and pushed it forward. Michael turned the steering wheel, but the SUV was powerful enough to give him little chance to control the direction they were going. The car shuddered as the front tires were unable to stop the forward momentum.

A barrage of shots flew at them. Ceinwen was forced to duck down as the back window shattered into a thousand shards. Michael stomped hard on the brakes. The tires locked with a shriek that slowed but didn't stop the car's forward progress.

He could hear the wail of police sirens, but up ahead, the street curved, and they were headed straight at a row of parked cars. He feared they would be crushed between the parked cars and the SUV. Airbags did little good in that type of accident.

"We've got to jump, Ceinwen," he shouted as he unfastened his seatbelt. "Get out and run before we hit."

She looked stricken but disconnected her seatbelt. With one more glance at him, she opened the passenger door.

"Wait!" he shouted. Through the rearview mirror he saw that the SUV had braked and then turned into an intersection.

As he pulled the rental car to a stop, safe at the side of the street, they saw a stream of police cars, their sirens blaring, in hot pursuit of the SUV.

Michael reached out for Ceinwen's hand, holding it tightly, as they waited for the police activity to quiet down around them. "You okay?"

"I've fought demons. A big black SUV doesn't hold a candle to that."

Michael laughed softly. As soon as he no longer saw any police cars near, he shoved the battered, bruised, and dented car into gear and pulled away from the curb. It would be hell to pay when they returned the rental, but he'd worry about that later. Also later, he suspected they'd need to give statements to the Hyannis Police.

But right now, they needed to return to Wintersgate.

CHAPTER 61

WINTERSGATE WAS dark when Michael and Ceinwen arrived, but as soon as they entered, something felt very wrong.

"Do you think we beat them home?" Ceinwen asked.

Michael opened the door to the breakfast room. A candle burned near the windows, which was a surprise. Candles were never used in that room—never anywhere in the old house for fear of fire.

Michael was about to blow it out when other candles suddenly lit all around him. "What the hell?"

With the entire room ablaze, William Claude and Stedman entered. William Claude placed the Shang dynasty bronze on the table.

"Look familiar?" he asked Michael with a sly grin.

Michael's lips pursed. "I knew you were behind its theft. Do you know you're also responsible for the death of a deputy and others in Idaho?"

"Nonsense. Now, about this little bronze object, I'm sure there's a trick to opening it," he said, glaring at Michael. "Do it, or I'll break it open."

Michael knew he wasn't joking. "By removing the bronze vessel from the rare-earth elements in its lead container, you've already strengthened the demons trapped inside it," Michael said. "They were once strong enough to bring down an entire dynasty in China, and whenever they were out and about could manipulate much of world history. Are you sure you want to let them loose on the world again?"

"I'm in control of them now, so I'm safe," William Claude said. "All I want is for you to help me use the pearl to create immortality, then I'll give it back for you to use however you wish."

Michael shook his head. "The harm would have been done, and the demons unleashed."

"If I destroy the container, the demons will certainly be released. I suspect they're already very angry with you. They'll want you to pay. And all demons love to watch people suffer." William Claude then faced Ceinwen. "Don't they?"

The bite on her neck began to burn. She put her hand to it, crying out at the sharp pain. She grabbed hold of a chair to stay upright, the pain nearly blinding her. Tears filled her eyes and her breath came in short gulps. "Stop, please."

"Leave her alone!" Michael lunged at William Claude, but Stedman grabbed his arm and held him back. He had no idea Stedman had that kind of strength—superhuman strength. But he couldn't think about that now, he had to help Ceinwen who had crumbled to the floor. "You're killing her. Stop this!"

"Open the bronze," William Claude commanded. "And then go with me to the laboratory where we will create immortality."

"Only if you stop torturing her."

"Open the bronze, and I will stop ... and if you don't assist me in the following steps, the next pain she feels will make this seem like child's play."

Michael couldn't bear seeing Ceinwen suffer. He opened the bronze.

A cloud of black smoke streamed upward from the pearl and hovered over the room.

At the same moment, Ceinwen fainted.

"You are my demons now," William Claude cried as he snatched the pearl from the bronze and held it high in his hand.

Michael grabbed the bronze vessel and then ran to Ceinwen. But Stedman had already reached her. He lifted her in his arms as if she were no more than a doll.

"Let her go!" Michael ordered.

"We're taking her to the laboratory with us," William Claude said. "I wouldn't want you to forget the reason you're helping me. After all, I couldn't harm the flesh of my flesh. But I could certainly harm his cheap little girlfriend."

"You'll pay for this," Michael warned. "You're a sadistic bastard. No wonder you fear death's judgment."

William Claude only smirked as they went up to the laboratory. There, with a thick black pen, he drew a squared circle, a symbol of alchemy, on his laboratory table:

Around each point of the triangle, and at each point of the square, he place a potion. Then he stopped and studied the pearl. "Those demons you so feared, Michael, are amazingly quiet after their first minor outburst."

"That's because they're curious about you. They won't stay quiet for long."

William Clark chuckled. "We'll see. You really should have tried some alchemy with them."

"Why should I waste my time?" Michael replied. "Why should I be like you?"

"It does take a great deal of time," William Claude said. He sounded almost jovial now. "We will begin with the potions I've already created, and hope one of them works. If not, we will start over. That, I'm sorry to say, could take days."

Michael was filled with anger and self-loathing as his curiosity began getting the better of him. What was the old bastard trying to conjure? Then he glanced at Ceinwen, who had awakened but was pale and dazed from her ordeal. Stedman was all but holding her upright. "Let her sit down," Michael demanded.

William Claude nodded, and Stedman led her to a chair and seated her in a sweeping, effortless move. Michael went over to her and squatted down, meeting her at eye level. "How are you feeling now?"

"Do what you need to," she murmured. "Don't worry about me."

"But I do."

"I know," she whispered, and lightly touched the side of his face.

He kissed her forehead as he stood, and then walked back to a scowling William Claude. He could sense Steadman behind him, ready to pounce if he appeared at all threatening.

"Now that you've shown us how disgustingly pussy-whipped you are," William Claude said with a sniff, "we can proceed. Here, you see four stages. Each stage purifies the mercury more than the last, and at each stage the fire is twice as intense as that preceding it. The fire awakens the inner spirit that also must purify the alchemist without interruption throughout the process."

It was all Michael could do not to object to what his father was attempting. "So where are you in these four stages?"

William Claude picked up a flask, and then spoke like a lecturer to a slow student. "This first one is calcination, resulting in dark ashes, and so it is often called the Raven. Here, you see the Peacock's Tail, an explosion of colors. As I mix in other substances, all the black matter becomes white —a sign the work is moving in the right direction—and so it's called the Swan. It's also a symbol of the moon, or female. Last, are those potions that symbolize the sun. This final chemical wedding should create the philosopher's stone. I have created many such stones, but none has been strong enough to transmute me into immortality. Each stone only has a finite amount of power which can be used up. At that point, the stone dies."

"How do you know?"

"Alchemy gathers and concentrates energy to make its transformations. It amplifies and dramatically speeds up what happens naturally over eons but still, it must follow physical rules. Those rules can be bent and skewed as needed, but never broken."

Michael grimaced with boredom. "That's nothing new."

"Creating gold is simple, merely increasing the speed of a natural process. But to bend the process of mortality to create immortality, the stone must be massively powerful—as this one is." William Claude all but caressed the stone in his hand.

"So, now that you have the stone, what will you do with it?"

"For years, every day, I have taken a small portion of a philosopher's stone—one I created using my formula, dissolved the stone's shavings in wine and ingested a teaspoonful. The elixir energizes me, retards aging, and increases my psychic powers to an extraordinary degree, as I believe you've come to realize. When I take a tablespoon or two, I'm greatly invigorated, but only for a short time.

"Now, I intend to ingest a generous portion of this most powerful pearl. And doing so will, finally, make me more than human."

"Or," Michael said, "the increased physical energy in your body will cause you to go mad, if not kill you. The pearl has contained three powerful demons for centuries. How could you dare to ingest it?"

"I don't care about those demons." William Claude snorted with contempt. "This pearl is so powerful it will not only heal diseased, aged organs, but will allow such repair to continue time and again. It will be *as if* I am immortal. After one thousand or two thousand years, I won't really care." With that, he took the pearl and placed it in a vice. He picked up a diamond tipped chisel and solid gold hammer.

Immediately, the mist that had floated to the ceiling when the stone was removed from the bronze, now congealed into a black cloud. As William Claude studied the best place to strike the stone, the cloud began to swirl around the room.

"Stop!" Michael shouted. "Don't do it. You don't know what you're dealing with. If you strike it wrong and break the stone, those demons will no longer be drawn to it. They might escape both of our controls and wreak havoc on everything around them."

William Claude laughed. "As I expected, you want to protect the stone. That means, as much as you say you hate it, it has a power over you. With that connection, it draws the life-giving power of an alchemist from you. And now, as its new owner, it will be able to draw that power from me as well, making it even more powerful than I ever dreamed."

"Impossible."

"Is it?" As his father stared at him, his eyes turned bright red. "Clearly, you have no idea who you are dealing with."

Michael gasped at his eyes. "What have you done to yourself?"

"It's not what I've done, but what I've allowed. My elixirs have given me a sense of immortality, but it fades quickly. I want more. I want true immortality."

"You're beyond mad," Michael said. "You're evil."

He smirked and then glanced at Ceinwen. "She didn't find me evil the other night."

"My God," Ceinwen whispered. "You disgusting son of a bitch."

Michael felt sick at what his father was implying. "You attacked her, somehow using the bite of a demon. That's the only way you'd ever control her or anyone—make them sick and weak so they can't act on how disgusted they are by you!"

His expression turned smug. "And how would I know about such a bite?"

Horror struck at those words. "What do you mean?"

William Claude chuckled. "I never could watch you directly, but your sheriff friend was easy. That was your mistake. When he joined you to unearth the pearl, I concentrated on your location and invited some demons there to create havoc and weaken your defenses. You were right, Michael, the pearl did draw them. For a while, I could make them attack, but they were weak and easily scared off." He stopped bothering to explain as he, again, struck the pearl.

The sharp diamond chisel sliced off a piece that was the size of an eyelash. Claude picked it up and swallowed it. The black clouds swirled faster and faster around the room.

Scarcely a moment passed before William Claude clutched at the laboratory table. Holding it tight as he stared at Michael and gasped for breath. He seemed to swell; his face grew black and his features blurred and altered. The lights in the laboratory flickered on and off as half the time he looked like a man, and the other half he was a demon, a hulking creature with scales and wings.

"It can't be," Michael shouted.

"It wasn't a dream," Ceinwen murmured. "It was him."

Even Stedman backed up to the far wall in shock and horror.

The demonic Claude flicked a long tongue in Ceinwen's direction, causing a wad of spittle to fly from its tip onto her shoulder, hitting the bite wound. She screamed with pain.

"Do you want to continue with this argument, Michael?" Claude's voice filled the room, boomed in their heads, but the demonic Claude stood before them.

"You're a coward," Michael shouted. He had gone to Ceinwen, and was helplessly trying to comfort her. But then, remembering a gesture his father had made, calling on his innate power as an alchemist he pressed the palm of his hand against the neck wound. Immediately it seemed to give her some relief. "Take me on, not her!"

Claude once again turned human. "No. I may need you. Help me, or you'll watch more than one painful wound appear on her body." He took up the hammer and chisel and struck the pearl. The chisel slid off it, leaving the pearl unmarked.

The cloud of demons shrieked. Claude struck the pearl again, and once more, the chisel slid over it, leaving not a mark. The demons whirled around them, crashing into shelves, knocking over flasks, and causing beakers to fall to the floor and shatter.

"William Claude, *father*, by all you've ever held dear in your life, stop this!" Michael shouted over the hubbub. He pulled Ceinwen to a corner of the room and tried to shield her.

William Claude paid no attention to him or anything else. He aimed the chisel to strike more deeply into the pearl. He hit it and it left a tiny mark, but it was enough for the swirling demons to shriek even louder. The laboratory windows blew out.

But then William Claude's demon self took over, and with the creature's stronger strength, he hit the pearl again, cutting into it.

Michael drew on his power as protector of the pearl, and as an alchemist, and shouted at the demons. "He's going to destroy the pearl's beauty—make it a thing of ugliness and horror, just like he is! I've protected you. Not him. Look at the creature he is! He'll destroy you, use you. Do you want that *thing* to have power over you?"

The swirling demons' roar grew louder.

The demonic Claude again attempted to attack Ceinwen, but Michael was ready, and thrust out his arm between the monster's snake-like tongue and Ceinwen's body. It struck him and left not so much as a scratch. Michael felt power surge through him.

The demonic Claude focused again on the pearl. He chipped off a piece larger than the last, put it in his mouth and swallowed.

A roar filled the room, a roar so loud it caused the walls to shake and crack. Michael and Ceinwen covered their ears for fear of their eardrums exploding.

"Stop him!" Michael ordered, his voice strong as he used his authority over the unleashed entities. The battle for control was now between him and his father.

A small tornado-like cloud, what Michael called a "dust devil" as a child, suddenly appeared near William Claude. Where it spun, the floor caught on fire. The fire quickly sprang up and widened, soon reaching the wooden desk filled with stacks of research papers. The legs of the desk burned as the fire rose, reaching and igniting the papers. William Claude slapped at them, trying to extinguish the flames.

The tornado raced to the walls of the laboratory and then along them, leaving a trail of fire as it went.

"We've got to get out," Michael said to Ceinwen, and pushed her ahead of him out the door before the fire trapped them. Stedman had already fled the room.

At the top of the stairs, Michael turned to see the fire reach the laboratory door just as his father did. William Claude somehow managed to make it into the hallway unharmed. But then the fire flared out from the laboratory and grew into a wall between William Claude and Michael.

Beyond the flames, Michael saw his father glaring at him, his mouth distorted with hate as he spoke. "So you finally drew upon your power. And as usual for you, you're too weak, and too late." His father turned in disgust and walked away toward the stairs to the tower.

A snake-like trail of fire broke free, away from William Claude, and slithered along the ground directly toward Michael and Ceinwen. Michael stared after his father a moment, then grabbed Ceinwen's hand and ran down the stairs.

It was as if the fire had become an evil flaming serpent, with intellect and purpose, and once on the ground floor it veered from them and raced toward the library. "No!" Michael cried. "Damn. It has rare collections. Priceless knowledge." Michael grabbed a fire extinguisher from the kitchen and sprayed the flames as he ran into the library. He stood amazed to see that the fire had snaked directly to the shelf with Lafcadio Hearn's books and papers. They burst into flames as if fueled by gasoline.

He did what he could to save other books. Michael could hear in the distance, above the roar of the flames, Steadman phoning the fire department.

"Michael, you've got to get out of here," Ceinwen cried. "The fire is growing too fast."

He wasn't listening, but kept trying his best to save the library. He was managing to contain it in the location of the Hearn papers, but still, the fire had soared up the bookcase and was licking the ceiling. The sound of crackling and whipping of wind caused Ceinwen to grab his arm. "You're more important than the books. Leave them!"

Seeing her in danger trying to save him finally got through to him. He faced her, his eyes tortured and frightening.

"Come on!" she insisted, taking his arm and pulling him through the foyer to the front door. The St. George killing the dragon tapestry that he'd always hated was also in flames.

He followed Ceinwen outdoors and they ran a safe distance from the fire before they stopped and looked back.

When they did, the entire house appeared to be aflame.

They heard the sirens as fire engines approached. Stedman had already gone to open the gates.

As the firetrucks pulled up to the house, Michael saw the silhouette of William Claude at the windows in the tower room. The fire raged behind him. He could feel William Claude's hatred and contempt.

Michael yelled at him to get out of the house, and told the firemen his father was in the tower room. He pointed out the deck outside the tower, knowing that they had the equipment to climb to the top of the mansion.

But as they raised the ladder, the windows in the turret blew out. The interior had become an inferno and smoke billowed out into the starless night.

Still, two firemen climbed up to the deck to see if William Claude had somehow made it out. They found no sign of him, and the tower room burned so fiercely, they couldn't get close enough to attempt a rescue even if they had seen him. The clear assumption was it would have been a fool's mission to try.

CHAPTER 62

Michael and Ceinwen stayed on the property until the fire department was sure all flames had been extinguished. One of the EMTs wrapped them in blankets to ward off the nighttime chill and their shock at what they had been through, including the certain death of Michael's father.

When questioned about how the fire started, Michael told the fire chief his father had been working in his laboratory on the second floor, and the fire seemed to have begun there. He believed that was why his father hadn't run downstairs and out of the house, but had gone upstairs, hoping for rescue. But the rescue didn't arrive in time.

At daybreak, the damage to the house became clear. The second floor and the turret room had been gutted, but the first floor, except for a corner of the library and the tapestry in the foyer, had suffered incredibly little damage. The fire investigators couldn't hide their surprise at the bizarre way the fire burned. They had never seen such an usual pattern. One of them muttered that the fire had had a mind of its own.

As soon as it was safe to do so, the firemen made a more thorough search of the house. Soon, the chief came to Michael. His face showed his confusion.

"What is it?" Michael asked.

"There's no body. We searched everywhere, but we can't find your father in the house. It was a damn hot fire, but there should be remains."

Michael stared at him, speechless. "You're sure?"

"Absolutely. Are you positive you saw him on the third floor?"

"There was a lot of flame and smoke, but I know I did."

The chief stared for a moment and then turned away shaking his head.

Ceinwen put her hand on Michael's arm. "Stedman also seems to be gone," she said.

At her words, Michael went to the garages, which stood a good hundred feet from the house. The Bentley wasn't inside. Michael called the fire chief over to the garage. "It seems my father and his valet must have driven away. All I can think of is that my father felt guilty for having started the fire that did all this damage, and wanted time to himself."

The fire chief wasn't pleased. "But you said you saw him on the third floor. You told my men he was up there."

"I thought it was him," Michael said.

"It may have been a strange shadow," Ceinwen said. "I also thought it was William Claude, but obviously, we were both wrong."

The fire chief pursed his lips at the possibility his men had faced unnecessary danger, but he seemed willing to be satisfied with the explanation. Soon he and his men left the scene, warning that no one should enter the house. It wasn't safe, and fire and insurance investigators would be there later that day to take photos.

When the cook, Patience, arrived, Michael sent her back home, telling her he'd be setting up a stipend for all the years she had worked for his father, but that she would no longer be needed.

Finally, Michael and Ceinwen found themselves alone.

"I've always hated this house," he said, looking up at the ruins. "But I'm sorry to see it end this way."

"You can rebuild. The fire chief said the foundation is strong."

"No. Not now that I know its history and know that I wasn't the only one who had hated living here."

"That's true," Ceinwen said. "But this land is beautiful, and it deserves a happy home. Yours or someone else's."

His shoulders sagged. "Knowing what you know, what you've seen—and felt—how can you mention me and a 'happy home' in the same breath?"

"I've seen terrible things happening around you through no fault of yours. But they've happened because of your family, not you. They aren't anything to do with the kind of man you are. Stop beating yourself up. You're a good, loving person. In fact, given all you've had to overcome, I wonder that you aren't a complete misanthrope who, if around the nuclear button, wouldn't gladly push it and blow this world to smithereens."

He had to smile at her exaggeration. "Even now, after everything, you can make me smile."

"Good," she whispered, and kissed him. "Maybe we should leave. The investigators don't need us here."

"Wait one minute," he said, walking toward the house.

"You can't be of a mind to go inside. It's too dangerous."

"I'll be careful."

"Michael!"

He ran into the house.

Ceinwen paced and grew beyond anxious until he came out again.

"What were you doing in there so long?"

"Luckily, we left my jacket and your handbag in the breakfast room when we arrived back at the house. They're smoke damaged, but haven't burned, so we still have our passports and you have whatever else you women seem to fill your purses with. This thing is heavy." He handed the bag to her.

"Thank God," she murmured.

"And, I've got the pearl." He reached into this pocket and pulled out the bronze. "It was still in the vice in the laboratory. It's now back where it belongs."

She looked at the bronze she had once considered beautiful but now saw as purely ugly. "And the demons?"

"I don't know. If they're here, they're quiet."

"And if they aren't?"

Michael's jaw tightened. "I'm not sure."

They got into the small, banged-up rental car. Michael took one last look at the house. Where the window had once been in the stone turret, he thought he saw a woman with long brown hair gazing down at him. He recognized her and recognized the slight smile on her lips. He hadn't seen her smile often.

He dropped his gaze a moment, working to control the strong emotions he felt. When he looked up again, she was gone.

On the way back to Boston, Michael and Ceinwen stopped at the Hyannis Police Department to give statements. Jake had already offered explanations and filled in most of the details for the lieutenant in charge of the investigation, so they were quickly allowed to leave.

Michael scarcely spoke as he drove, and Ceinwen had no idea what he was thinking. She didn't ask, knowing he was a man of silences, that he needed time within himself to work through all he had learned, witnessed, and faced.

After parking near the Boston's North End, they bought beers and strolled along the Harborwalk. They found a place to sit while Michael phoned Jake. When he didn't get an answer, Michael sent a simple text: *We're okay. My father seems to have disappeared—a long story that I'll explain later. Thanks for all your help.*

Next, he called Jianjun and filled him in on all the horrid details about William Claude, the pearl, the demons, and the fire.

"Now I've got news for you," Jianjun said. "The two guys arrested by the Hyannis Police were among those who shot at us out on that mountain. I hear they're singing like birds."

"That's good news," Michael said.

"Before Jake rushed off to catch a flight to Hyannis, he told me they had been given access to three million dollars at a Seattle bank, and they claimed they were 'forced' to take part in a four-man team paid to steal the pearl in both Idaho and Japan, as well as to create havoc and scare people in Idaho."

None of that surprised Michael.

"They swore they had nothing to do with the deputy's death, the murders and mutilations in the backcountry, or the rancher whose horses they'd rented."

"Of course they didn't. It had to be the two other guys." Michael's words were purely facetious.

"That's what they're saying, all right."

"Something tells me they'll claim anything to escape multiple murder charges."

"Jake's going to look for your father, too. He's sure he financed and planned the reign of terror." Michael wasn't surprised by that, still, it was hard to hear.

"So," Jianjun added after a short pause, "what are you going to do with the pearl?"

"Good question."

"If you keep it, demons will follow you."

"But if I don't keep it, wherever I put it may be at risk, just as Salmon was."

"Not if your father is gone. He has to lay low, for a long, long time. He was the one who caused the deaths out here, not the demons."

"Wherever—and whatever—he is, I suspect he'll want the pearl again," Michael said. "He's powerful, evil, and mad with the desire for immortality. He's out there and will come at us when we least expect it."

"Which is why you need to find a way to destroy it or completely bury it. Somewhere no one will ever be able to get it again. I can work up some options for you if you'd like."

"Good. And I'll work on a few of my own. But more important than that, I have another task."

"Oh?"

"To find William Claude."

"But Jake says he's going to do that."

"He'll try, but I have better resources. You, for one."

Jianjun said nothing for a long moment, then asked, "So, how do you want this handled?"

"I have to know where he's gone to ground before he blindsides me again. The man has access to money and property all over the world. I suspect he has, or could easily obtain, fake IDs and passports. He won't be easy to find. And he's probably traveling with a companion, a man I only know as Stedman. I'll try to learn more about him."

"Any photos of them?"

"Old ones of my father. None of Stedman."

"I'll look at driver's license and passport files—see what I can turn up. Should we assume he's left the country or is still in the States?"

"I'm sure he's left. I'd begin looking at interesting cities in Europe, somewhere cosmopolitan enough that he won't be too noticeable."

"I'll get right on it."

"Thanks," Michael said. "By the way, is Kira still with you?"

"Yes." A pause, then Jianjun's words sped up as he confessed, "I really care about her. I mean, more than I thought possible. And she says she feels the same. Well maybe not quite the same. I mean, it's not like she loves me, I don't think. But it's a start."

"Jianjun, calm down." Michael laughed. "That you two love each other is obvious to anyone."

"You think so?"

"Definitely," Michael said, with a smile in his voice.

They soon ended the conversation. Michael put the phone in his pocket, and stared out at the water.

"It sounded as if you received some news," Ceinwen said.

"Jianjun is happy with Kira."

Ceinwen nodded. "I'm glad."

Michael drank some of his beer.

"What about you?" Ceinwen asked. He gave her a questioning look. "What will make you happy?"

He studied the ground a long moment before speaking. "I don't know."

She fell silent.

"And you?" His gaze met hers. "The airport is near. You can be back at Oxford in a matter of hours."

She bit her bottom lip. "I need to confess something. Something I should have told you a long, long time ago."

"Oh?" He looked worried.

"I was never a student there. I was allowed to audit a couple of classes —allowed to because some friends pulled journalistic strings for me. I did it to get close to Rachel. I wanted to write an article or even a book about what happened to all of you two years ago in Idaho. But not now, Michael. Not ever."

He looked a bit stunned, then accepting as he nodded but said nothing.

Tears filled her eyes, but she blinked them away. "Just think, you've been hanging out with an Oxford fraud." She struggled to make her voice light, even jocular. "Whatever will people say?"

"They'll say I was a lucky guy," he murmured.

It took a while before she could find her voice. "*Was.* That's the operative word, isn't it?"

"You don't want to be a part of my world, Ceinwen."

"Don't I?"

"You've seen how I live. You've seen the strange things that happen around me. You'd learn to hate the constant danger … to hate me, most likely."

"From what I've seen, you're the one who should be wanting me around to keep you safe. Just like your hero, Lafcadio Hearn. He had an arranged marriage so that Koizumi Setsuko could help him survive in a difficult world. I'm not saying you need to go that far, but I am saying you're in danger out there on your own. And with Jianjun's interest in Kira Holt, he might not be available as often as you think."

"Perhaps," he murmured.

She waited, but when he said nothing more, she stood. "I guess we all have choices to make. And by your silence, I see you've made yours. It doesn't include me, much as I might wish it did. Somehow, I think I always knew this whatever-it-is between us would end this way. Good-bye, Michael."

She walked away. She was about to hail a cab for the airport, when she heard him call, "Wait!"

He ran to her. "I'm a jerk, Ceinwen. I hate the thought of you going, and I'm too much of a mess to tell you that."

She said nothing, waiting.

He drew in his breath and continued. "Something tells me, if I let you go, it'll be the stupidest thing I've ever done ... in a lifetime of stupid mistakes."

Her expression remained serious. "You surely don't know how to flatter a girl, Michael Rempart."

He searched her face. "You're fascinating and beautiful. Lovable and clever. How's that?"

She smiled. "A good start."

"You already know that the smartest thing for you would be to run back 'across the pond' as you call it. But if you're willing to take a chance ..." He had never felt so tongue-tied in his life. "If we can give ourselves time, together, maybe we'll find that we're exactly what we want. And need. Together."

She put her arms around his neck. "Haven't you figured out by now how much I love taking chances?"

CHAPTER 63

One month later—

Michael was sitting on the deck looking out at Idaho's Lake Pend Oreille. He had a cup of coffee and was reading a morning newspaper when Ceinwen came out with a tray of food.

"Here's some breakfast," she said. "Welsh rarebit, which is nothing but a posh cheese on toast, seasoned and baked. It's time I tried a few of the cooking skills my mum tried hard to teach me."

"Not much else to do out here," he said.

"And I'm loving it," she added. She put his plate in front of him, then gave him a quick kiss before she took her seat. The bright blue of the lake was beautiful and invigorating, and they enjoyed watching the sea gulls circle it.

They had traveled from Boston to Salmon where they checked in on their friends, and then headed north to Idaho's panhandle, not far from the Canadian border. While driving around the lake, they spotted a large furnished home on twenty acres available for lease. It had a view of the water in one direction, and the Rocky Mountains in the other. They took it.

Over the past month, they were learning a lot about each other, particularly that two strong-willed, strong-minded people didn't always have smooth sailing. Simply being together, however, made it worthwhile. Ceinwen realized that what she thought was love had been an infatuation. As her feelings for Michael deepened, she was learning what the real thing was all about.

Michael remained wary of his feelings, but was slowing lowering his guard, and each time he let her get closer to him, the more he appreciated her patience, and even thought that she—dare he say it?—understood him. There were times he found himself marveling at the new emotions she caused him to feel, the kind of emotions others talked about, but he hadn't truly known for most of his adult life. Things like love and happiness.

Still, he knew that living here in Idaho was a temporary reprieve, not the way he or she expected to live their lives. He enjoyed being an archeologist too much for that, and he wondered if she'd be happy living in remote places, or going with him to even more desolate areas on digs. But that was an issue for another day. Right now, he was content here, and she seemed to be as well.

He had finished his breakfast, and found it delicious, when his phone chimed to let him know he'd received a text message. "It's from Jianjun," he said, his brow crossed.

"Take it. I'll handle these." Ceinwen picked up their dirty dishes and headed into the house.

For some reason, he hesitated. That's silly, he told himself, then opened the text.

I think I found your father in, of all places, St. Petersburg, Russia. I hired a PI, and he took a photo of the man at an outdoor café on Nevsky Prospect. If it's William Claude, we can talk about how you want to proceed.

Michael had expected he'd get such news someday, but not quite yet. He sucked in his breath as he enlarged the photo to better see the features. When he did, the phone nearly slipped from his hands. He picked it up again and stared hard at the photo Jianjun had sent.

Yes, it was William Claude, sitting at a small table having coffee. But he wasn't alone.

Sitting at the table with him, clearly engrossed in conversation, was a person whose face he knew he would always recognize no matter how many years had passed.

Sitting with William Claude was Irina Petrescu.

The demons had been right.

She was alive.

AUTHOR'S NOTE

Great liberties have been taken with many of the places mentioned in this book. For example, the Aokigahara Forest is a real place, but it is in the vicinity of Mount Fuji in the Eastern part of Japan's main island. It does have a long and colorful history involving suicides, and was featured a few years ago in a horror movie entitled "The Forest." The Kumano Kodo is a network of pilgrimage trails through the peninsula south of Osaka. They have been in use for over a thousand years and are the only pilgrimage routes besides the Camino de Santiago in Spain to be designated a world heritage site.

Lafcadio Hearn is a fascinating man with a small but dedicated following throughout the world. In Matsue, Japan, there is a museum dedicated to him, and it is near the samurai house where he once lived. If you're interested in learning more about Hearn, two great biographies of him are *A Fantastic Journey, the Life and Literature of Lafcadio Hearn* by Paul Murray, and *Wandering Ghost, the Odyssey of Lafcadio Hearn* by Jonathan Cott. Most of his works are freely available on the internet or in libraries and large bookstores. And, if you've never seen the art file, *Kwaidan*, which features the story of Yuki-Onna among others, you're in for a real treat. Many copies of the film have only three stories, but the full DVD includes a fourth story, called "A Cup of Tea," it's the story Michael remembers when he sees a face in the pond.

For pictures of those places, Lafcadio Hearn, and much more, be sure to visit my website, www.joannepence.com, where they can be found under The History of the Ancient Secrets Novels.

PLUS ...

ABOUT THE AUTHOR

Joanne Pence was born and raised in northern California. She has been an award-winning, *USA Today* best-selling author of mysteries for many years, but she has also written historical fiction, contemporary romance, romantic suspense, a fantasy, and supernatural suspense. All of her books are now available as ebooks and in print, and many are also offered in special large print editions. Joanne hopes you'll enjoy her books, which present a variety of times, places, and reading experiences, from mysterious to thrilling, emotional to lightly humorous, as well as powerful tales of times long past.

Visit her at www.joannepence.com and be sure to sign up for Joanne's mailing list to hear about new books.

The Rebecca Mayfield Mysteries

Rebecca is a by-the-book detective, who walks the straight and narrow in her work, and in her life. Richie, on the other hand, is not at all by-the-book. But opposites can and do attract, and there are few mystery twosomes quite as opposite as Rebecca and Richie.

ONE O'CLOCK HUSTLE – North American Book Award winner in Mystery
TWO O'CLOCK HEIST
THREE O'CLOCK SÉANCE
FOUR O'CLOCK SIZZLE
FIVE O'CLOCK TWIST
SIX O'CLOCK SILENCE
Plus a Christmas Novella: The Thirteenth Santa

The Angie & Friends Food & Spirits Mysteries

Angie Amalfi and Homicide Inspector Paavo Smith are soon to be married in this latest mystery series. Crime and calories plus a new "twist" in Angie's life in the form of a ghostly family inhabiting the house she and Paavo buy, create a mystery series with a "spirited" sense of fun and adventure.

COOKING SPIRITS
ADD A PINCH OF MURDER
COOK'S BIG DAY
MURDER BY DEVIL'S FOOD
Plus a Christmas mystery-fantasy: COOK'S CURIOUS CHRISTMAS
And a cookbook: COOK'S DESSERT COOKBOOK

The early "Angie Amalfi mystery series" began when Angie first met San Francisco Homicide Inspector Paavo Smith. Here are those mysteries in the order written:

SOMETHING'S COOKING
TOO MANY COOKS
COOKING UP TROUBLE
COOKING MOST DEADLY
COOK'S NIGHT OUT
COOKS OVERBOARD
A COOK IN TIME
TO CATCH A COOK
BELL, COOK, AND CANDLE
IF COOKS COULD KILL
TWO COOKS A-KILLING
COURTING DISASTER
RED HOT MURDER
THE DA VINCI COOK

Supernatural Suspense

Ancient Echoes
Top Idaho Fiction Book Award Winner
Over two hundred years ago, a covert expedition shadowing Lewis and Clark disappeared in the wilderness of Central Idaho. Now, seven anthropology students and their professor vanish in the same area. The key to finding them lies in an ancient secret, one that men throughout history have sought to unveil.

Michael Rempart is a brilliant archeologist with a colorful and controversial career, but he is plagued by a sense of the supernatural and a spiritual intuitiveness. Joining Michael are a CIA consultant on paranormal phenomena, a washed-up local sheriff, and a former scholar of Egyptology. All must overcome their personal demons as they attempt to save the students and learn the expedition's terrible secret....

Ancient Shadows

One by one, a horror film director, a judge, and a newspaper publisher meet brutal deaths. A link exists between them, and the deaths have only begun ....

Archeologist Michael Rempart finds himself pitted against ancient demons and modern conspirators when a dying priest gives him a powerful artifact—a pearl said to have granted Genghis Khan the power, eight centuries ago, to lead his Mongol warriors across the steppes to the gates of Vienna.

The artifact has set off centuries of war and destruction as it conjures demons to play upon men's strongest ambitions and cruelest desires. Michael realizes the so-called pearl is a philosopher's stone, the prime agent of alchemy. As much as he would like to ignore the artifact, when he sees horrific deaths and experiences, first-hand, diabolical possession and affliction, he has no choice but to act, to follow a path along the Old Silk Road to a land that time forgot, and to somehow find a place that may no longer exist in the world as he knows it.

Ancient Illusions

A long-lost diary, a rare book of ghost stories, and unrelenting nightmares combine to send archeologist Michael Rempart on a forbidden journey into the occult and his own past.

When Michael returns to his family home after more than a decade-long absence, he is rocked by the emotion and intensity of the memories it awakens. His father is reclusive, secretive, and obsessed with alchemy and its secrets—secrets that Michael possesses. He believes the way to end this sudden onslaught of nightmares is to confront his disturbing past.

But he soon learns he isn't the only one under attack. Others in his life are also being tormented by demonic nightmares that turn into a deadly reality. Forces from this world and other realms promise madness and death unless they obtain the powerful, ancient secrets in Michael's possession. Their violence creates an urgency Michael cannot ignore. The key to defeating them seems to lie in a land of dreams inhabited by ghosts … and demons.

From the windswept shores of Cape Cod to a mystical land where samurai and daimyo once walked, Michael must find a way to stop not only the demons, but his own father. Yet, doing so, he fears may unleash an ancient evil upon the world that he will be powerless to contain.

Historical, Contemporary & Fantasy Romance

Dance with a Gunfighter

Gabriella Devere wants vengeance. She grows up quickly when she witnesses the murder of her family by a gang of outlaws, and vows to make them pay for their crime. When the law won't help her, she takes matters into her own hands.

Jess McLowry left his war-torn Southern home to head West, where he hired out his gun. When he learns what happened to Gabriella's family, and what she plans, he knows a young woman like her will have no chance against the outlaws, and vows to save her the way he couldn't save his own family.

But the price of vengeance is high and Gabriella's willingness to sacrifice everything ultimately leads to the book's deadly and startling conclusion.

Willa Cather Literary Award finalist for Best Historical Novel.

The Dragon's Lady

Turn-of-the-century San Francisco comes to life in this romance of star-crossed lovers whose love is forbidden by both society and the laws of the time.

Ruth Greer, wealthy daughter of a shipping magnate, finds a young boy who has run away from his home in Chinatown—an area of gambling parlors, opium dens, and sing-song girls, as well as families trying to eke out a living. It is also home to the infamous and deadly "hatchet men" of Chinese lore.

There, Ruth meets Li Han-lin, a handsome, enigmatic leader of one such tong, and discovers he is neither as frightening cruel, or wanton as reputation would have her believe. As Ruth's fascination with the lawless area grows, she finds herself pulled deeper into its intrigue and dangers, particularly those surrounding Han-lin. But the two are from completely different worlds, and when both worlds are shattered by the Great Earthquake and Fire of 1906 that destroyed most of San Francisco, they face their ultimate test.

Seems Like Old Times

When Lee Reynolds, nationally known television news anchor, returns to the small town where she was born to sell her now-vacant childhood home, little does she expect to find that her first love has moved back to town. Nor does she expect that her feelings for him are still so strong.

Tony Santos had been a major league baseball player, but now finds his days of glory gone. He's gone back home to raise his young son as a single dad.

Both Tony and Lee have changed a lot. Yet, being with him, she finds that in her heart, it seems like old times...

The Ghost of Squire House

For decades, the home built by reclusive artist, Paul Squire, has stood empty on a windswept cliff overlooking the ocean. Those who attempted to live in the home soon fled in terror. Jennifer Barrett knows nothing of the history of the house she inherited. All she knows is she's glad for the chance to make a new life for herself.

It's Paul Squire's duty to rid his home of intruders, but something about this latest newcomer's vulnerable status ... and resemblance of someone from his past ... dulls his resolve. Jennifer would like to find a real flesh-and-blood man to liven her days and nights—someone to share her life with—but living in the artist's house, studying his paintings, she is surprised at how close she feels to him.

A compelling, prickly ghost with a tortured, guilt-ridden past, and a lonely heroine determined to start fresh, find themselves in a battle of wills and emotion in this ghostly fantasy of love, time, and chance.

Dangerous Journey

C.J. Perkins is trying to find her brother who went missing while on a Peace Corps assignment in Asia. All she knows is that the disappearance has something to do with a "White Dragon." Darius Kane, adventurer and bounty hunter, seems to be her only hope, and she practically shanghais him into helping her.

With a touch of the romantic adventure film Romancing the Stone, C.J. and Darius follow a trail that takes them through the narrow streets of Hong Kong, the backrooms of San Francisco's Chinatown, and the wild jungles of Borneo as they pursue both her brother and the White Dragon. The closer C.J. gets to them, the more danger she finds herself in —and it's not just danger of losing her life, but also of losing her heart.

Made in the USA
Las Vegas, NV
19 January 2021

16204028R00184